Synthesis:Weave

Deane Saunders-Stowe

FORCEFIELD

First Printing Hardcover Edition: January 2015

ISBN: 978-0-9931773-1-6

Published by Forcefield Publishing

Typeset in Bitstream Charter 10pt using LaTeX

For Kris

without whom my universe would be empty

Chapter 1

Sebastian had never seen sand of such a deep crimson and, as he stood on the beach, he couldn't even guess where in the galaxy it could be found.

He looked up in an attempt to locate a familiar constellation. Shielding his eyes, he scanned the horizon; the intense purple sky hadn't seemed that bright. The silky, golden glow of the larger of the two suns reflected off the oily black sea that slopped silently at the shore, but aside from that the skyline was featureless.

A gentle breeze brought with it an unfamiliar tang, and as he ran a hand over his close-cropped hair it came away sticky.

'How did I get here?' It was like a dream; he couldn't remember arriving, landing a shuttle, or being dropped off by a ship. He looked at his wristcom. The time showed 2264-09-01-03.08. There was no way he'd got there in a ship unless he'd somehow missed half the night, and he must have been prepared for the trip – why else would he have his old canvas backpack slung over his shoulder?

As he stared at the contours in the sand around his booted feet, his mind began to wander. He traced the shadows cast by the low suns, and the question of how he'd arrived was soon forgotten.

He turned to look inland where large, smooth slabs of red sea-worn stone formed a high cliff. About two hundred yards along to the right stood an opening, outlined with long, upright blocks that tapered towards the heavy lintel above – it definitely wasn't natural. Curiosity overtook him and he made his way towards it.

The low angle of the suns cast his shadow through the opening and did little to illuminate the space beyond. Should he go in?

The suns were almost submerged in the dark waters and a dense mist had begun to form. The horizon's shadow crept up the beach, drawing the mist with it.

Overcome by the need to satisfy his curiosity, he took the antique oil lamp from his rucksack and searched his pockets for something with which to light it. He reached into his station uniform's jacket and found a solitary match – odd that something like that would be in his pocket, rather than a multi-tool, given that open flames were banned on the station. He struck the match against a stone and lit the lamp. Holding it above his head, he made his way into the darkness. As he followed the smooth steps downward, a damp draft made the hairs on the back of his neck stand on end. After several steps, the stairway ended in a space that extended off into darkness beyond the lamp's reach. The chill had made him feel uneasy and he looked back again.

Sea mist flowed down the steps and gathered around his feet. The lamp sputtered and the flame dwindled to a tiny blue glow. Something crunched in the darkness – footfall on the sandy floor behind him.

With a final, guttering pop, the flame went out.

He held his breath. There was no sound except for his pulse pounding in his ears – perhaps he'd imagined it. His eyes became accustomed to the dark and he noticed a glow around his feet. The sea mist? He must be hallucinating.

Another crunch – maybe not!

He wanted to run, to escape, get away from whatever it was behind him. He tried to walk forwards; the mist dragged at his feet and legs as though made of molasses. The thrum of blood through the veins in his neck filled his ears. He had to calm down, slow down, stop struggling so he could hear. It was then that he heard breathing – a grunt of a breath, not his own.

His hand went to the small bronze Mjölnir necklace at his throat and he froze. Oh Gods, was there something there, something lurking behind him?

Warm air whuffed on his neck, accompanied by a deep snort and touch of something sharp, claw-like, on his shoulder.

He whirled around to face it. And screamed.

'Lights!' Sebastian sat bolt upright and flung the bed covers off. His forehead was slick with sweat and his heart threatened to break the bonds of his ribcage.

The bedside lamp lit dimly, doing little to drive away the terror that clung in the corners of his mind. The shadowy, brushed-metal walls of the single-room apartment did nothing to comfort him. It was the fifth time he'd had a nightmare in the last few weeks and, like all the other occasions, he couldn't remember exactly what had caused him to wake up. He swung his feet to the floor and sat for a moment before getting a glass of water from the kitchen.

'I have to find out what's causing these dreams,' he said, more to reassure himself than anything else.

A shrill beep sounded from the other end of the room and he nearly dropped the glass. It was only the terminal opposite the bed. He walked over to investigate.

Incoming call.

The time on the console read 03.10. Why would it let a call in at that time of the morning?

'Who is it?'

'Janyce Hafsteinsdóttir,' the computer said.

'Accept.' He sighed. He loved his sister-in-law, but Gods, she could be so inconsiderate at times.

A pale face appeared. 'Hello Seb.' Her auburn hair was straight for a change.

'Hi Jan.' He rubbed his forehead and blinked in the brightness of the screen. 'You always forget about the time difference.'

Her face went slack. 'Sorry – I can call back later if you like.'

'No, it's fine. I just got up. Can't sleep.' He sat down on the bed and gulped down a mouthful of water. 'What do you need?'

'A favour. Erik's stuck with his homework and has a presentation to do tomorrow. He – well, I – wondered if you'd be able to help.'

'Sure.' He yawned. 'Just don't keep me up too long.'

'Oh, thank you!' She gestured off to one side. 'Erik!' A young boy, little more than eight years old, appeared and Janyce moved out of view. Even though he had black hair, he clearly had his mother's features.

'Hi Erik, not seen you for a while. You're growing.'

'I've just got some bigger shoes. I'm nearly in adult sizes!'

'Good for you. Now, what's this homework?'

'My teacher said we have to find out what a computer TI is, and why it's not the same as AI. The school's locked the computers down on the subject.' The boy pouted.

'I could hack in and unlock them for you, but that would be cheating, not to mention against the law ... If they don't want you using the computer to find out, it shows they want you to learn about it yourself. I'll point you in the right direction.'

The boy's expression brightened.

'TI stands for Turing Intelligence, although it's more of an interface.'

'But what does that mean?'

Sebastian yawned again. 'I'm too tired to explain it all now, but you should have time to read up on it before tomorrow. Go to the Old Library and look up Alan Turing in the History section. There might be information on AI there, too. They gave up on that research over a hundred years ago.'

'*Mamma* said you used to program things like it. I want to be a programmer like you one day ... I hope I get a good grade!'

Sebastian smiled. 'As long as you put it in your own words, I'm sure you'll do fine.'

It made a change for someone to want to be like him. His own father had been disappointed he hadn't wanted to follow him into police work like his brother, Mikkael, had. If he'd still been around, maybe he would have been satisfied he was working in security. Then again, nothing Sebastian ever did had seemed to make him happy.

'Thanks,' Erik said, dragging Sebastian's thoughts back to the present. He turned away and immediately looked back. 'Did you get any pictures of you with an alien?'

'No, not yet. I don't get a chance to speak to any, but I'll be sure to forward some to your mother if I do. And it's "*yourself* with an alien".'

Erik laughed. 'You're so funny. I'll put *Mamma* back on.' He disappeared and Janyce came back.

'Thanks for that, Seb. I really appreciate it.' Her eyes flickered momentarily, betraying a deep sadness. 'I wish I could help him as much as his father used to.'

'You're doing fine. If you need anything, let me know.'

'Now you mention it, we could do with some more money towards Erik's school fees. They're up for renewal soon and things are a bit tight.'

Sebastian rubbed his forehead. Just what he needed. 'Things are a bit tight here, too, with station cutbacks, but I'll send you some. Not having to pay for this apartment has its advantages. Just do me *one* favour.'

'What's that?'

'Make sure you don't call at three in the morning in future.'

She laughed. 'I am sorry about that. Normally I have to leave a message . . . I'll put an automatic block on my terminal, that'll stop me!'

'It was good to hear from you, Jan. Stay well.' He smiled.

'You too. Speak again soon. Give my love to Aryx.' She waved and signed off.

More money. Not the best of news, but at least it had taken his mind off the nightmare. He finished the glass of water and tried to get back to sleep.

He woke to a giant gong, struck in an ancient temple, his alarm going off for the third time; he'd be late for work if he didn't get moving. He rolled over to turn it off. The clock read 06.30.

'By the Gods!' he groaned. He'd forgotten to cancel yesterday's early alarm. There didn't seem to be much point in going back to bed – at least not with his system full of adrenaline – so he got up and popped the ultrasonic tooth cleaner into his mouth while he washed.

After a light breakfast of mycobacon and toast, he got dressed, pulling on his brown uniform with disdain; it always reminded him of a 21st-century courier's outfit rather than that of a security officer. He made his way to the lift terminal, and with nearly two hours to spare before work, it seemed like the perfect opportunity to take the scenic route; he needed the change of pace to clear his fuzzy, sleep-deprived head.

He stepped out of the lift onto the polished white walkway of the atrium's lower terrace and made his way to the jetty. The faint rushing splash of the nearby weir was momentarily broken as the riverride skimmed over the lip and came to rest at the platform. The gondola dipped as he boarded, and he pressed his thumb against the infoslate mounted next to the seating and flopped down on the cushions.

'Three-quarter circuit.'

The craft moved off, purring quietly to itself. High terraced walls and tumbling grassy banks rolled by. Sunlight streamed in through the filters in the glass ceiling; they displayed a deep blue sky with bright-edged clouds. He squinted and sat back, glad of the warmth on his face – the atrium was one of the few places on the station where you could get genuine sunshine, after all.

The small boat drifted past the crisp, white architecture of riverside shops and cafés, where Humans and other races congregated amidst the gaggle and chatter of daily business and the clink of cutlery on plates. The aroma of hot, fresh coffee mingled with the mossy cool of the river and warm caress of spice-flowers on the banks, reminding him of his mother's baking. He took a deep breath and let it out slowly. It certainly tasted better than the recycled atmosphere elsewhere on the station.

A man dashed along a terrace where the trees were being watered, his jacket pulled up over his head in a vain attempt to save himself from getting wet. He headed towards the nearest walkway. Sebastian laughed – it was like a scene from an old Earth movie. A tall, slender woman with blonde hair held back by a bright headband jogged past beneath the raining spray. She ran with her eyes closed and her head tipped back, apparently with no regard to how wet her Lycra running-suit had become.

'Karan!' Sebastian shouted.

She continued jogging.

'*Karan Tallin!*'

She stopped under a large birch tree and opened her eyes. 'Seb! What are you doing out so early?'

'I couldn't sleep. I'll see you down there.' The riverride had gone beyond the acceptable distance for conversation. He pointed at the next jetty. 'I'm getting off!'

She waved back and resumed her run. Sebastian looked back as the gondola made its way up the curve of the river; she looked like she was running downhill – he'd never get used to that perspective.

Two minutes later the craft came to a halt at the jetty near the lift and let him off. A lone figure sat on one of the benches in the small parkland terrace a short distance from the terminal. Drawing closer, he could see that the figure wasn't Human; its shoulders were far too narrow and its hair irregular chunks of dense, brown sponge intertwined with a leafy wreath. Several small, orange fruits arranged between the waxy foliage caught his attention. As he stared, the being turned.

His heart stopped. He recognised the type of face from pictures he'd seen in security briefings; the light ochre skin; the flat, almost non-existent, nose with thin nostrils; the large, golden almond-shaped eyes that slanted up at the outer corners; the small ears and the slim arms that showed little in the way of muscularity – definitely a Folian. It wore a long, shimmering black robe with threads in the fabric that complimented the colour of its hair; the satiny tapestry of gold, bronze, and black drew the eye in, like staring into a distant galaxy, its complexity so deep, so soothing.

'Greetings,' the Folian said in a soft, genderless voice. 'Can I help you?'

'I—' Sebastian's thoughts raced, trying to find an excuse to speak to the creature. 'Forgive me, I've not seen one of your kind before.'

Its piercing eyes scanned him up and down and a faint smile played across its thin lips. 'You are forgiven.'

He finally found the excuse he was looking for. 'My name is Sebastian Thorsson. I work in the security office ... I don't think we have received security protocols for your ships.'

'Greetings, Sebastian Thorsson,' the Folian said with the slightest of nods. 'We are Ambassador Tolinar, and in answer to your question, our ships do not integrate with your systems.' Its eyes smiled. 'The protocols are ... unnecessary.'

'Oh, I'll make a note of that in our records, thank you.' He turned to leave.

'Is there anything else we can help you with?'

He hesitated. 'Actually, I know this may seem inappropriate, but may I have my photograph taken with you?'

'Photograph?' The Folian tilted its head to one side.

'A static image recording.'

The alien's features smoothed. 'Of course you may.' It smiled again.

He looked around for someone to take the picture. A glistening Karan came jogging along the walkway. Perfect timing. He beckoned to her.

'Greetings,' she said with a bow as she tried to catch her breath.

The ambassador nodded.

'Can you take a picture of the ambassador and me?' Sebastian held out his wristcom.

She stepped back and held it up. 'Say cheese.'

He grinned.

A moment later she handed it back. 'I'll meet you at the lift,' she said, and headed off.

'Thank you, Ambassador. My nephew will be very happy. It's the first time I've had the opportunity to speak directly to someone of another race in the three years I've worked here.'

'We are glad to have given you the opportunity for a new experience,' Tolinar said, nodding slowly. 'We hope that your nephew enjoys the image.'

Sebastian bowed his head in mimicry, hoping it was the correct etiquette, and bid the alien farewell. He turned to continue his journey to the lift and glanced back at the fruits in the Folian's wreath. Were they bigger than when he'd first set eyes on them? No, he must have imagined it.

Karan stood waiting at the lift with one hand on her hip. 'So, why are you having trouble sleeping?'

'I've been having bad dreams lately and this morning's woke me up.'

'I've had some weird dreams, too, but nothing that's disturbed my sleep. Hey, have you heard the news?'

'Security, level three,' Sebastian said, addressing the lift. 'It depends on what news you've heard.'

'Someone in the department is being given a new high-level assignment and Bannik didn't get put forward for it.' Her eyes were wide with excitement.

'Really? I thought she was well overdue promotion.' He hadn't realised how much Karan hated the woman.

'Apparently it's not a promotion.' She folded her arms. 'As much as I can't stand her, I'm not gloating. It's a SpecOps opening.'

'Oh my Gods. Do you know who got it?' He'd dreamed of getting an exciting job like that, but Special Security Projects and Operations was well out of his league.

'Not a clue, I just heard the rumour going around that they'd selected someone based on their psych test.'

'Oh.' He deflated.

Karan grinned. 'Don't be such a depresso, you're awful.' She leaned against the wall of the lift in mimicry of 'I'm a little teapot' with one hand on her hip. 'I'm a mechanical depressive, here's my handle, here's my support mechanism.' She laughed at her own joke.

He didn't want to smile, but she was so stupid sometimes.

'You're good at your job. I'm sure you'll get a promotion one day.' The lift stopped and they both stepped out. 'I'm off to the changing room,' she said. 'See you around – and cheer up!' She headed off down the corridor.

It was fine for her; she was bright and bubbly all the time. If SpecOps was offering a placement based on psych tests, he definitely wasn't going to get it. He was only a security programmer after all, and they'd surely think him too prone to panic and idle daydreaming to even consider giving him the job.

As he entered the security department his supervisor, Eleanor Bannik, stepped out of her office, directly into his path.

'I need to have a word with you tomorrow, Thorsson,' she said, her stony glare boring deep into his skull.

'Can I ask what about?'

'Just be in my office at 09.00 tomorrow.' The Ice Queen spun around and slammed the glass door behind her. What on Earth had he done wrong?

He sat at his desk to begin the day's tasks and within a matter of moments an alert sounded from his workstation.

'Security breach detected,' the computer said.

'What kind of breach?'

'A systems breach in the maintenance subsystem.'

'What effect has the breach had?'

'Code has been inserted and is redirecting funds from the core banking system.'

'Where did it originate?'

'The maintenance terminal in bay thirty-five, on level three of the habitation ring.'

'Is anyone in that bay?'

'No.'

'So, how did a hack originate there? Do you mean nobody is actually *in* the bay, or nobody is registered to it?'

'Nobody is registered as currently occupying the bay.' It was so unhelpful; whoever wrote the main security system needed to be shot.

'Scan the bay. Is anyone present?'

'Sensors are not functioning.'

'Oh, by the Gods! Turing *Un*intelligence.' It was such a convincing simulation at times he had to remember that it couldn't think for itself. Obviously today wasn't one of those days. 'Check the terminal – is it being accessed via the screen, keyboard, plug-in module, or what? If it's a manual intervention, send someone down there to catch the perpetrator!'

Karan ran past seconds later, stun-stick and handcuffs hanging from her belt. Sebastian hunched over the screen, nibbling his nails, watching the dot – her dot – move down the corridors to the bay.

Ten minutes later she burst into the office pushing a bald, purple-robed figure – an Antari – in front of her, its hands cuffed behind its back. Sebastian stared at them as they walked past on the way to the brig.

'Gotcha,' Sebastian said under his breath.

The Antari drifted by, almost as though pushed on a trolley, and turned to look at him. The tops of its ears folded, making them pointed, and its lips curled, turning the ordinarily serene Antari expression into a fanged snarl.

Hacking was fine if it made the system better, but not when it was like this; this scumbag had been leeching off the system like a vampire. At least that was another out of the way.

Karan filled out the arrest log at the desk and prodded the Antari through the door as Bannik came by. Her stare was as flat as ever, with not even a hint of recognition or gratitude on her face. He knew it. SpecOps *was* out of his league. He'd never get a better job – he was going to be stuck under the Evil Queen's thumb forever.

By 17.00 his tasks were complete; all the required security fixes for the day had been put in and new protocols written. He was glad to be able to get out of the office – even though it brought tomorrow closer.

That night sleep came in short passages punctuated with a jumble of work-related images that drifted through his mind, snagging on his consciousness. Tiny problems magnified a thousand times consumed all of his attention while meaning little.

The images eventually stopped leaving him hanging weightless in the dark. How had he come to be in that predicament? It was like zero G. What a strange feeling. Almost like falling.

As the wind whistled in his ears, it didn't occur to him it might be dangerous. He caught a dry, dusty odour and the darkness peeled back to reveal the walls of a grey rocky shaft hurtling past. Something trailed down through the centre of the tunnel close to him – a rope? He reached out and grasped it. The rope bit into his hands, cutting deep. His fingers stung at first, then burnt. The sensation erupted in a roar of pain that shot up his arms, causing him to grip tighter and tighter. He fought against the reflex to hold on, and let go. The bones of his fingers were exposed and etched with deep striations. He held his hands away from himself in disgust.

That was when he became aware of the floor of the shaft rushing up at him.

Chapter 2

As Sebastian hit the bottom of the shaft, he jerked awake. He could do without nightmares, especially before being dragged in front of his supervisor. According to the bedside clock, it was 03.10. He lay on his side watching the minutes roll by until he lost consciousness.

Somehow, he woke before his alarm and got ready for work on time, but the disturbed night's sleep had left him feeling more tired than before he'd gone to bed and, with Bannik wanting to speak to him about *something*, the morning didn't look promising.

The office seemed quiet when he arrived. His co-workers looked at him with the sort of expression he'd expect to see on people's faces at a family funeral. He hoped he wasn't about to walk into his own.

He approached his supervisor's receptionist. 'I'm here to see Bannik.'

'Please take a seat, Mr Thorsson.' The woman tapped away at her keyboard.

He sat on the low box-seat opposite the desk, picked up an infoslate from a nearby table, and began scanning the day's headlines to distract himself from whatever lay ahead. More terrorist bombings on the outlying colonies.

He sighed.

'What's that?' the receptionist asked, looking up from her work.

'Those idiotic ITF bastards again. They've bombed one of the far colonies, trying to get rid of alien influence.'

'I don't know what their problem is . . . My great-great-grandparents were on one of the Gliese expeditions.'

'Which one?'

'682b, the one they found the first node on. Bronadi first contact.'

Sebastian's heart skipped a beat. 'You never told me that.'

Her mouth twisted in a wry smile. 'You never asked. Anyway, if it wasn't for us finding that after the exodus, we wouldn't be out here now, and none of us would have jobs. And that's down to aliens.'

He grimaced; he didn't know if he still had a job – aliens or not.

'Did you read the *Flying Dutchman* article?' she asked.

He looked at the page and scrolled down. Before he could begin reading, she chirped up again. 'Something's been spotted in the Pegasus constellation, travelling at near lightspeed. Nobody's got scans of it, but it's been seen on and off over the last sixty years heading towards a group of uninhabited systems.'

'What do they think it is?'

'A ghost ship. Seriously, people would be mad travelling that fast in this day and age. I wouldn't want to do it. Not for a long trip.'

'Me neither.' He shuddered at the thought of losing family to the ravages of time, and put the slate down. He didn't want a head full of depressing terrorism or paranormal nonsense, not if he was about to fight for his job.

'She's ready to see you now.'

His stomach fluttered, and in an attempt to calm himself he imagined the receptionist had been doing her make-up without a mirror; her wonky lipstick made her look like an inadequate clown. Suitably distracted, he smiled, but as he walked into the office the good feeling vanished.

Bannik sat at the long, black glass desk. To her left sat a man Sebastian had never seen before; he was severe and gaunt, with wide, narrow eyes, high cheekbones, and a thin mouth to match. His short, black hair was oiled or gelled and stuck to his scalp, giving his fringe a serrated look. His uniform was a prominent combination of charcoal grey and white: SpecOps. The man attempted a smile – it would have looked warmer and more sincere on a crocodile.

Bannik gestured to the solitary chair opposite.

Sebastian sat down and folded his hands in his lap, trying to hide their trembling while his stomach quietly knotted itself.

She leaned forwards on the desk and laced her fingers together. 'Let's get down to business, shall we, Mr Thorsson? This is Agent Marcus Gladrin, of SpecOps,' she said, gesturing to the man. 'Firstly, I have to inform you that your duties have been allocated to several other members of the security department.'

Sebastian's mouth fell open.

'Mr Thorsson,' the agent said, 'your time working here as a security programmer has come to an end.'

'I—' He tried to speak, but the knot in his stomach got tighter, choking him off. How was he going to pay for Erik's education without a job? What was he going to do instead? How was he going to *live?*

The agent put his hand up. 'Before you say anything, please, let me continue.'

It was hard enough to stop shaking, but Sebastian forced his mouth to close. He fixed his gaze on Agent Gladrin's piercing black eyes and nodded.

'Mr Thorsson, you have been chosen, based on your psychological profile, for a *new* security position on the station. It should not interfere too much with your day-to-day duties, although they will take a lesser priority. The other team members will now take over your non-specialised duties. Think of SpecOps as an expansion to your scope of work.'

The statement hit Sebastian like a brick to the face. They were offering *him* the SpecOps job. 'I-I'm pleased to meet you, Agent Gladrin. But I don't understand. Why *my* psychological profile? I thought my test results were awful.'

'Quite the contrary. We always look for those with a specific mindset. An ability to readily pick up new skills and think outside the box. The test you took when you applied for your current post indicated that you would have these traits, and we have been watching you for the last few weeks to see if this was indeed the case.'

Someone had been watching over his shoulder without him being aware of it? Who?

'I put your name forward to SpecOps after some of your most recent projects impressed the security board.' Bannik grinned. Yes, it had probably been her watching him.

'Yes, quite.' Gladrin cast a fiery glance in her direction. 'Rather than interviewing potential recruits in the traditional manner and putting them on probation, we give them an introductory task to complete. Your uniform and other equipment will be deposited in your locker shortly and Bannik will forward the details of your allocated shuttle to your terminal. You will also be given your own office for privacy purposes. I suggest wearing your uniform at all times during official business – it has a certain weight behind it.'

Sebastian reeled. It was a lot to take in. 'May I ask why I get a shuttle?'

'All Special Projects and Operations employees get their own personal shuttle for use on assignment.' Gladrin waved his hand in the air. 'It saves on red tape and is more efficient if they have their own vessels, given the dynamic nature of the work they do.'

'I see.' He still hadn't caught up with the bit about the uniform.

Gladrin dismissed Bannik with a wave of his hand. She pursed her lips, grating the chair backwards as she rose. Gladrin returned the expression with an unflinching stare and waited until she'd gone before speaking again.

'Your task is to analyse a new technology for us, recently acquired from a terrorist cell that was developing it secretly back on Earth. We don't know whether the item is functional or not, nor do we know what its purpose is, but the technicians tell me it doesn't contain explosives, so you're cleared to work on it. The item will be delivered to your locker along with the other equipment. The box is print-locked for security.'

Sebastian nodded.

'We usually pair up our agents with those of complementing skills. It's often more effective to allow agents to select others to work with, but given the distinct lack of other SpecOps agents on this station, I will allow you to choose another station employee to bring in on the project. Remember, this is a test of your resourcefulness, not specific knowledge, and a large part of resourcefulness is in knowing who to trust and how to get the most out of those whom you do.'

Sebastian opened his mouth to ask a question but the agent spoke first.

'Do *not* speak to your co-workers about this assignment. It is for you and your chosen partner only.' He craned his neck to look past Sebastian. 'This includes your supervisor and higher ranking staff. Any questions?'

'No ... I think that about covered it, although I don't understand why this task doesn't go through normal research channels.'

'Red tape, again. It would take too long and we fear terrorists may be using this technology in their attacks. SpecOps often has a need for discretion, and even though we do not always have the free resources to research things ourselves, on this occasion we cannot afford the potential security leaks associated with bringing in third party research companies, especially when insurgents could be anywhere.'

'I understand.' It was the reason Sebastian was employed to develop the station's security software in the first place.

'So, who would you like to have work with you?'

He shrugged. 'Who should I choose?'

Gladrin tapped the desk with a finger. 'As SpecOps assignments often involve a lot of travel, sometimes to dangerous places, I suggest you choose someone with whom you could trust your life. Someone adaptable, and whose skills complement your own.'

'I know just the person.'

He held out an infoslate. 'Put the name there,' he said, pointing to a box on the presented form.

Sebastian typed the name in and handed it back.

'Born 2228, ex-marine with honourable discharge. Oh.' The agent read the form and raised an eyebrow. 'An interesting choice. I'm not sure how that'll work out, but EarthSec says the records are clean. Very well.' He stood and held out his hand. 'I very much look forward to working with you in future and seeing your results.'

'As do I, and thank you for the opportunity. It's been nice meeting you, Agent Gladrin.' Sebastian rose and they shook hands.

He turned to leave and Gladrin caught his arm. 'As I said, your normal work duties take a lower priority. Any time you spend on work in relation to your assignment will be paid for. The same goes for your partner. This is effectively a research assignment, and research takes time, effort, and, often, legwork. Feel free to use any resources necessary to make your work more effective. I imagine your partner might need a little help, so focus on those needs first. I need you to be an effective team.'

Sebastian smiled and thanked Gladrin again, and as he left the office his palms began to sweat. To work under his own steam again, without boundaries, freedom. But what a responsibility.

He made his way to his desk and Bannik appeared from nowhere, arms folded. Her stony expression giving nothing away. 'The equipment has been delivered to your locker. I imagine you have a lot of work to do, Thorsson, so you'd better get to it. I expect everything finished before you start working for SpecOps.'

He nodded and stepped around her on his way to his desk. It would be nice to have his own office.

He worked fervently, putting the finishing touches to some long-standing projects – one thing he didn't want was *her* breathing down his neck – and by mid-afternoon the jobs were complete. He couldn't wait to see what was in his locker and finally be out from under her thumb.

He walked through the open archway of the changing room and passed the aisles of benches. The blue brushed-metal walls watched his every move. A large part of him wished Gladrin hadn't told him about the terrorists, and had just given him the box with no information. He reached out and touched the palm-lock and his bladder tightened. The locker door swung open.

His casual clothes hung at the front as usual; nothing seemed out of place. He glanced briefly at his old canvas rucksack slumped in the corner and it triggered a vague memory, something recent, but he couldn't place it. He'd had the thing since his eighth birthday. He remembered it like it was yesterday . . .

Sebastian sat playing in the sun on the terrace outside the small family home. He stopped pushing the toy shuttle along the grass and looked up at the trees in the recovering forest on the edge of the urban zone as a car silently pulled up at the gate. A tall, elderly man with white hair climbed out and began hobbling up the path with his walking stick.

Sebastian ran down the steps, arms outstretched. '*Afi!*'

'Shh. Don't let your mother hear you speak Icelandic. Speak Galac.'

'Sorry. Hello, Grandfather.'

Frímann bent down and squeezed him tight. 'Happy birthday, Sebastian.' He turned him around and nudged him back towards the house. 'Go on, I'll be up in a minute.'

Sebastian ran up the steps and sat cross-legged in front of the white wicker chairs.

Dishes clattered in the kitchen, and Sebastian's mother ran down the steps past him, her white dress shining. 'Frímann! It's good to see you.' She gripped his arms and pulled herself up to kiss him on the cheek.

'Sigrid, my dear! How are you keeping?' Frímann's white grin glinted in the sunlight as he turned towards the house. 'Thor's at work, again?'

She sighed. 'He takes all hours the Gods send lately. Mikkael was playing up so he took him to work after the party.'

Frímann shuffled up the steps and took the seat next to Sebastian.

'I'll get a drink,' Sigrid said, patting Frímann on the shoulder, and made her way into the house.

'I have a present for you,' Frímann said. 'I want you to look after this. Take it with you wherever you go.' He leaned forwards and unhooked a beaten-up canvas backpack with leather straps from his shoulder and handed it to Sebastian.

Sebastian's eyes widened. 'What is it?'

'My great-grandfather's pack. He used to take it with him when he went exploring. Open it.'

He fumbled with the heavy buckles on the top flap, loosened the rope that drew the neck shut, and put his hand in. Something cold met his touch and he snatched it back.

'It's okay. Take it out – it won't bite.'

He reached in again and pulled the object out. It was enormously heavy in his small hands. 'What is it?'

'It's an antique miner's lamp. A Davy lamp. Let me show you.' Sebastian handed the lamp back and the old man turned it in his hands. The light caught on the shiny brass base and fixtures. 'This is nearly four hundred years old, so I want you to look after it carefully.' His knotty finger pointed to a dent on the side of the black cowl at the top. 'The badge has fallen off, and you can see where the lettering has worn away. It says eighteen-something. That's when it was made.'

'Wow! How does it make light? Does it have a battery?'

Frímann laughed. 'No, it uses liquid hydrocarbon fuel. Do you know what that is?'

Sebastian scratched his head. 'That's what old cars used to run on, isn't it?'

'Good lad.' Frímann rubbed the boy's head. 'At least you're paying attention at school. You'll probably never see it lit in your lifetime.' The gnarled fingers turned the lamp over and pushed a lever on its base.

Sebastian watched as Frímann demonstrated opening the glass. He imagined himself walking through dark tunnels, shining the light ahead of him like his great-great-grandfather might have done. Just like his heroes from the movies, or the characters in his grandfather's stories.

'Can I go and play with it now?'

'I don't see why not. Go on.'

He put the lamp and toy shuttle in the pack and slung it over his shoulders. It almost came down to his backside. He giggled with excitement, ran down the steps and around the back of the house, and crawled under the terrace to watch his grandfather through a split in the floorboards.

Frímann grinned and sat back to write in his worn leather journal.

Sigrid came out of the house minutes later, carrying a tray of glasses and pitcher of lemonade. 'Where has he gone off to now? You didn't let him go into the wilderness, did you? I wish you wouldn't keep telling him those stories about giants and magic. You'll have him thinking the Gods are looking out for him.'

Frímann looked up from his notes. 'Oh, let the boy play, my dear. He'll be fine.' His wrinkles deepened and he shook the book in her direction. 'There are much worse things in the universe to worry about than wild boar and rutting deer . . .'

The pack and lamp had stayed with Sebastian after that, and he still felt bad that his grandfather got the blame for letting him run off. The childhood desire for adventure rose in his veins, and this time, rather than stifle it, he allowed the urge to wash over him; now that he was SpecOps his desire to travel might finally become a reality. He put the rucksack back in its place in the locker and caught sight of a silvery glint of metal at the back. He slid his clothes to one side on the rail to reveal a SpecOps uniform hanging behind them. How had he missed that?

His eyes followed the uniform down to the bottom, where a small metal box sat along with several other items. He picked up the box. It was a cube of approximately three inches with a print-lock on the front. It felt fairly heavy for its size. His attention moved to the other objects: a ruggedised infoslate, a medical kit and nanobot injector, a pair of AR glasses, and a handgun.

A gun! He'd only used one a few times. Once as a child, when his father had shown him his service pistol, and later, when he took the basic security training in weapons, armour tech, and tactics. He'd proven to be less than confident with them. It would probably be wise to book in for a few hours on the practice range. *Resourcefulness is part of the test,* he reminded himself.

He turned his attention back to the uniform. Not particularly colourful; mostly a charcoal grey with a white panel that ran across the top of the chest and down the arms. A second set of panels ran down the sides of the abdomen and legs. He rubbed the fabric between thumb and forefinger. The outer skin was rubbery and segmented into hexagonal cells that bulged in the centres. He'd never seen the material up close before, but recognised the technology – it was an N-suit. He squeezed one of the cells and its neighbours bulged. He draped a leg of the suit over his palm and punched it with the other hand. The area around the impact immediately became rigid and a fraction of a second later returned to its previously flexible state. Definitely a non-Newtonian suit. He grinned and turned it around to inspect the design. It was stylish despite the lack of colour – still a vast improvement over his regular uniform – and at least a fraction of the weight of traditional ballistic armour. He couldn't wait any longer to try it out.

He pulled the suit on. Its stretchy fabric fitted well and was immediately comfortable. Its inner lining looked porous. Within the collar was a small cap. He flipped it open and out popped the end of a plastic tube. What was that for? He smoothed the uniform down, fastened the unilok seal, and noticed one flaw – no pockets. How was he supposed to carry anything?

He looked in the locker, and with the suit off the rail he spotted a belt with several small pouches and a holster. The items, with exception of the infoslate, might all fit in the belt pouches. Evidently he was supposed to keep the sidearm on show. How much of a target would that make him?

He finished fastening the suit and stuffed his regular clothes into the rucksack along with the gun – he wasn't comfortable with the thought of wearing it immediately, given he hadn't had any practice – and put the bag over his shoulder. Should he take box with him? The idea of carrying some unidentified terrorist technology back to his apartment made his stomach churn. Better to leave it here for safekeeping, for now at least.

He turned to the mirror at the end of the row of lockers. It was surprising how much more athletic he looked now everything was held in place properly. It wasn't that he was unfit – more that the horrible courier-outfit he wore made him feel the wrong shape. Aryx would be so jealous. Speaking of which, he should probably give him a call before he finished his shift.

He called up the security TI on his wristcom. 'Computer, locate Aryx Trevarian.'

'Aryx Trevarian is in shuttle maintenance hangar, bay two.' Of course he would be. He said he had to get a shuttle finished, and the Antari didn't have the nicest of tempers at the best of times.

Aryx lay on a trolley underneath a shuttle. A position he hated, especially since the accident.

The stabiliser access hatch hung open, exposing a maze of cables, conduits, and wires. A crack ran the length of the main housing – it would need to be replaced. He picked up a spanner and reached in as far as his elbows. Turning his hands in the space, the tool collided with something.

'Ouch!' He pulled his hand out. His knuckles were grazed. Time to use the CFD tools – there simply wasn't space, not with *his* hands. He rolled over, picked up one of the six-inch metal rods next to him and turned it on with his thumb. A glowing orange screwdriver head appeared two inches from the end.

'Set to spanner.'

The tool changed shape and the screwdriver became a small C-shaped wrench.

'Off.' He reached up inside the stabiliser with the rod – at least now there was space. 'On.'

The spanner-head reappeared and he unfastened a pipe coupling. A small amount of thick gunk dribbled out and covered the glowing end of the tool. He pulled it out of the workspace and grabbed a rag, but rather than wipe it he held it over the cloth and switched the head off. It vanished and the tacky film fell onto the fabric. He put his hands back inside the machinery and went to unfasten another coupling, but the spanner-head didn't fit.

'Enlarge by three millimetres.'

The tool resized itself and he applied it to the offending nut. Perfect.

'Incoming call from Sebastian Thorsson,' the computer terminal nearby said.

He jerked forwards and bashed his head on the underside of the shuttle. 'Ow! What *now*?' He slid out from beneath the shuttle on the trolley. 'Accept call.'

'Aryx? I can't see you,' came Sebastian's voice.

'I'm on the floor, still working on this damned shuttle!'

'I thought you had that finished.'

'Just a couple more tweaks then I'm done with it. It's got to be perfect. I don't want the Antari bringing it back and complaining – you know how they are.' He pulled himself fully out from under the ship, sat up, and wheeled the trolley over to the screen. 'What can I do for you?'

'I was checking to see if you were free for drinks this evening, that's all. I have some news.'

Aryx weighed up the work that remained. 'I should be free when this is done. Call by in about an hour and we'll go to the bar.'

'Fine. I will see you then.' The screen went blank.

He slid the trolley back under the shuttle to finish off the stabiliser.

It took a little over half an hour to insert the remaining bits off the floor and another half hour to go around cleaning the greasy handprints off the lower part of the hull.

Sebastian waited for the lift to arrive and entered. 'Shuttle maintenance.'

It moved off and after a few moments stopped to let him out. Several yards down the passage he came to the door of the hangar. A sign on it read *Secure area, authorised personnel only.* He pressed his hand against the palm-lock and walked in.

The shuttle maintenance hangar was vast, about the size of a sports' stadium, at least fifty metres high and several hundred metres long. The place had a metallic, oily odour that reminded him of the lift system. It was one of those smells that made you want to wash your hands as soon as possible.

The nearest workspace was the only one occupied. Floodlights created a pool of yellow light around the bay, while the rest of the hangar receded into darkness, giving the impression of a large cavern. He could make out the gleam of metal in the distance, hinting at the presence of several other ships, unattended.

He approached the angular shuttle nestled under the warm lights of repair bay two. Numerous tools and diagnostic devices lay strewn on the surrounding floor. A loud, rhythmic banging came from underneath interspersed with the occasional flash and bout of cursing.

Sebastian looked down at where the noises were coming from. 'I suppose Karan told you the news first, did she?'

'What news? I haven't seen her,' came a voice with a faintly Australian accent.

'I got promoted.'

An oil and grime covered head with hazel eyes and black hair, combed and gelled into a wide Mohawk, popped out from under the shuttle. 'How can you get promoted? You're the only person doing your job and there's not exactly any upward career progression in it. What is it, security programmer *plus?*'

'It's a new position—'

Aryx slid back under the shuttle.

'—in SpecOps.'

'What—' A loud bang reverberated from the hull, followed by another bout of cursing. Aryx's head popped out again, this time being rubbed by the back of a greasy hand holding a constrained field tool. He stopped rubbing the growing lump on his forehead, turned the tool off, and wiped the grease from his hands with a rag. 'At this rate I'm going to have to start wearing a padded helmet!' He slid out from under the shuttle up to the waist and gestured at something behind Sebastian. 'Bring me my wheels, will you? My shift's over.'

Sebastian brought the wheelchair from beside the box and put the brakes on. The mechanic slid himself out to reveal his oil-streaked olive overalls ended at the knees with the trailing length pinned back under the thighs. He climbed into the chair and, leaning to one side, whispered, 'How the hell did you land yourself a job in SpecOps?'

'It never occurred to me to ask before,' Sebastian said, as they made their way down the corridor to Aryx's apartment, 'but why don't you get bionic legs fitted or have some transplanted – or even that new stem-cell cloning?'

'That's why I liked you from the day I met you. You never asked. You just accepted me without being patronising or pitying.' Aryx's eyebrows flattened. 'So why ask now?'

'I— Just curious, that's all.'

Aryx's jaw muscles pulsed. 'I can't have transplants because the anti-rejection drugs won't do me any good, and the gene-mods aren't up to scratch. I don't qualify for the stem-cell clones, either, because of a complication, and that's also why I can't use prosthetics. I'm ill.'

Sebastian stopped. 'What do you mean, *ill?*' His throat tightened as he said it.

Aryx turned to face him. 'I got infected with a parasitic virus during my accident. It's weakening the bones of my legs and knackered my immune system. That's why I can't get clones or transplants. The anti-rejection drugs will drop my immunity to zero, and probably kill me.'

Sebastian almost couldn't speak. 'Nanobots—'

'—don't help. They tried. It's a *parasitic* virus, intelligent enough to avoid them.'

No wonder Gladrin was dubious about his choice of partner. 'I never knew . . .' He went to put his hand on Aryx's shoulder.

Aryx slapped it away and pushed off. 'Quite right! Besides, I'm used to my body now.'

'Are you going to die?'

He glared at him. 'Don't talk stupid!'

Sebastian swallowed his feelings and tried to shift the topic. 'Why stick with that manual chair?'

'How else am I supposed to get exercise? Anyway, plenty of people seem impressed with these . . .' He stopped wheeling, raised his arms and flexed his huge biceps. 'We shouldn't feel pressured to fit in and be like everyone else. We all have to wear our scars or we repeat the same mistakes. I don't want to cover up and hide. It doesn't affect anyone else.'

Sebastian remained silent. He didn't feel like telling Aryx that it affected *him*.

'It's funny you should mention my chair. They still won't let me do field repair because it's too cumbersome on uneven terrain, and I don't really want to build yet another one so I've started work on something new. Why did you call by, anyway? You could have just sent a message about the job and we could have met up later.'

'I wanted to see you, and I thought—' Sebastian stepped behind Aryx as a large tentacled mass lumbered by in the narrow corridor, and he continued to walk behind him after it had gone.

'Don't walk behind me. You're making me strain my neck.'

Sebastian sped up and lowered his voice. 'I thought it would be better to tell you the rest in person.'

'Hmm,' Aryx grumbled, 'I don't think I'm going to like the sound of this.'

Chapter 3

In the three years he'd been on the station, Sebastian had never once been to Aryx's apartment. The layout was similar to his own, except for the larger-than-usual shower unit in the far left-hand corner next to the kitchen, and the shelving that normally ran around the room above the wall-mounted storage had been replaced with a single, continuous planter. Lighting installed around the perimeter of the ceiling provided the plants with bright, simulated daylight. The plants themselves reflected a soothing green glow, giving a peaceful outdoor feel – far more restful than the drab grey of his own quarters – but as with all basic staff-grade apartments, this one lacked a window. To the right of the doorway, opposite the slightly lower-than-usual retractable sofa bed, stood a workbench backed with a computer console. Strewn with an assortment of technological paraphernalia, it cast a stark contrast against the pristine kitchen.

'I never knew you kept plants,' Sebastian said, quickly looking away from the mess.

Aryx headed into the kitchen. 'I fell in love with them during rehab at hospital. After my accident they had me doing gardening for occupational therapy.' He filled a kettle with water and put it on a gas burner to heat. 'Before that, when my dad used to make me plant crops on the farm, I hated the bloody things.'

'I suppose they offset the oxygen ... Why the kettle?'

Aryx nodded. 'The hot water here tastes funny.' His nose wrinkled. 'In fact, everything anyone else makes for me tastes funny, so I boil my own water.' He wheeled over to the bed and stripped off his overalls. 'I need a shower.'

Sebastian didn't avert his eyes, as Aryx seemed comfortable with his own nakedness. He had never seen the tattoo on his back before; it looked like a large tribal-style bramble coiling around his torso. A long, faint scratch ran down the right side of his back.

'How did you get that? Is it an old war wound?'

'What?' Aryx twisted to look over his shoulder and felt his side with his left hand. 'I haven't got any scars on my back. I must have scratched myself in my sleep.'

'Have you been having bad dreams as well?'

'I never dream.' He wheeled into the cubicle. 'Can you keep an eye on the kettle?'

'How do I know when the water's ready?'

'It'll whistle at you. That's when you turn the heat off.'

Steam issued from the shower, filling the room, and Sebastian could almost see himself standing in a tropical jungle. He watched the fuzzy silhouette as Aryx washed himself – with water. Such a luxury, when everyone else had to scrub themselves with gel.

'Let me know if you ever want me to look after your apartment.'

'The plants are watered automatically.'

Sebastian's heart sank. While he waited, he began prodding the items on the workbench out of curiosity. A mass of electronics components, ship parts, and other strange things he'd never seen before littered the surface. One item stood out from the rest: a slightly rounded, rectangular box, twelve inches wide, eighteen inches tall and six inches deep. A complicated set of straps protruded from one side of it, giving it the appearance of a solid plastic backpack with a parachute harness attached. A symbol painted in yellow caught his eye; it depicted a square with a curve arching over it.

'What's this?'

Aryx stopped splashing. 'I don't know how you expect me to see what you're on about from in here.'

'It's a constrained field device, isn't it?'

'Are you poking around in my stuff?' The water stopped and a dripping Aryx wheeled out leaving tyre trails behind him. Inexplicably, the rest of the chair seemed completely dry.

Sebastian turned his back to the object. 'No, I was just looking.'

A loud squeal came from the kitchen and Aryx wheeled over to the kettle and turned the heat off. Saved by the interruption, Sebastian looked about the room in an attempt to divert the tension. A moment later Aryx came back with two cups of coffee between his legs and handed one to him.

He took a sip. 'By the Gods, that's strong! What have you used, hydraulic fluid?'

Aryx narrowed his eyes. 'Sorry, I forgot you like yours weak.'

'It's no wonder your taste buds don't work properly.' Sebastian went to the kitchen, emptied half of the cup down the sink, and topped it up with tap water. 'So what's this thing you've been working on?'

Aryx gulped his coffee down in one go. 'If we're going out, let's go. I'm not getting you into something technical, or we'll be here all night

– I know what you're like. Why don't you go on ahead and get us a table? I've got to finish my shower now, because *somebody* disturbed me.'

Aryx made his way to the centre of the station – near the hub – where *The Hive*, his favourite nightclub, lay. He passed beneath the neon honeycomb sign over the entrance and an automated voice said, 'Welcome to *The Hive*, where the atmosphere's always buzzing!' They should change that – it was too cheesy and didn't fit the tone of the place at all.

The matt-black walls of the club gave the place an enclosed feeling, with pools of light forming areas under which people congregated to dance and chat. He wheeled over the dance floor, passing through regions of sound with music from at least three different DJs. The frame of his chair vibrated to the thumping, sexual bass track that played in the main arena.

Solo dancers writhed on podiums at the corners while others danced both singly and in a mixture of gender pairings, regardless of race or form, their torsos rubbing up and down each other in erotic motion. It was no wonder so many relationships started off – and ended – here. Aryx smiled; at least Humanity had finally grown up and realised it was better if everyone was left to get on with their own lives, regardless of their preferences. He wheeled off the dance floor and the volume dropped sharply.

Sebastian sat, huddled in the corner of a sumptuously upholstered L-shaped seat behind a table in of one the privacy enabled areas. Drinks were already laid out. Aryx pulled up at the table and leaned forwards, clasping his hands between his thighs.

'So, tell me about this new job of yours.'

Sebastian waved his wristcom over the payment terminal mounted in the table. 'Engage privacy mode.'

The sounds from the dance floor stopped and a curtain drew around them.

He sat back and folded his arms. 'I don't actually know what the job title is.'

'Why not, you idiot?'

'They didn't tell me. A SpecOps agent interviewed me, although I didn't really get asked any questions. They just told me I had the job.'

'Sounds a bit weird, if you ask me. I've never been to an interview where they didn't ask questions.'

'I thought I was going for a disciplinary hearing! They'd already made up their minds that I was the one they wanted.' He leaned forwards and rested his arms on the table, eyebrows so low Aryx thought they would fall into his drink. 'Apparently they've been watching me for the last couple of months.'

'What!' Aryx looked around suspiciously and then remembered nobody could see or hear them. 'Have they bugged you?'

Sebastian shook his head. 'I don't think so. I scoured my apartment for snoopers after I got back, but didn't find anything. I think they've only been watching me at work.'

'Still, sounds bloody dodgy. Nice outfit, by the way.'

Sebastian looked down at it and smiled. 'It's an N-suit.'

'No way! They cost a fortune. Are they expecting you to get shot at or something?'

'That's one of the things that worries me.' Sebastian's brow looked ready to take another dive. 'They don't recruit in the normal way. They've given me a piece of technology to investigate as induction. Those terrorists that have been bombing colonies developed it!

'They told me I could bring in a trusted partner to help, and they'd be paid full wages, *and* have full access to SpecOps resources.'

'Sounds interesting ... if you don't get shot at, that is. Who did you choose?' He almost didn't dare hope.

'You, if you're interested – there might be the chance to get off the station.'

'Are you bloody kidding? Of course I'm interested! Won't they object to this if we've got to go off-world?' He gestured to his chair. The prospect of doing something other than repairing engines was exciting, but if they objected to him having to use the chair ... It didn't bear thinking about. It would be great to have a break from repair work, and to get one-up on the terrorists was something he'd wanted to do ever since he'd lost his legs – it was their fault he'd ended up on that damned planet, after all.

Sebastian grinned. 'I thought you'd be interested. They need us to start the project soon, but Gladrin's aware of your predicament and said we can use SpecOps resources to find a way to work around it.'

'My schedule's clear – I can start ASAP. What SpecOps resources do we have access to exactly?'

'You have something in mind?'

'The thing I bit your head off about earlier, you know, the pack.'

'What is it?'

'A device I've been developing. I could do with your help on it. Keep it under your hat, though – it's super-secret ... But tell me about this item we've got to investigate.'

'I don't know much. I haven't even opened the box. It's about this big.' Sebastian held his hands three inches apart. 'They also gave me a few other items, but it doesn't end there. They've allocated me a private shuttle.'

'You lucky bastard!' Aryx paused; his heart sank. 'Oh, I see, bring the desperate disabled engineer along to repair it if something goes wrong!'

'No! I almost wish I hadn't asked.' Sebastian pinched the bridge of his nose, closed his eyes, and shook his head. 'You're the one I trust the most and I *thought* you'd appreciate the change of scenery.'

'Sorry, I shouldn't have jumped the gun. I didn't mean it. You're right – it'll be good to get out and about.'

'It's fine. I can see how it might come across like that. I'll take a look at your pack tomorrow. Do you have anywhere secure we can work?'

'There's the hangar, but it's not secure because it's open to the other repair bays. Everyone else is on holiday at the moment, though. It's either that, my apartment, or your office.'

Sebastian's mouth twisted. 'I don't know what tools or computer equipment we might need.'

'What class of shuttle have they allocated you?'

'My supervisor is supposed to have sent details to my terminal, but I didn't have time to look.' Sebastian tapped on his wristcom and after a few moments said, '*Talaga* class, apparently.'

'Those usually have a small work area. Can't get much more private than that. Bring it around to my bay tomorrow.'

'I wouldn't have thought of that. I think we can do away with this now.' He reached under the table and the privacy curtain pulled back.

The floor heaved with a mixture of Humans and aliens, and the pair sipped at their drinks, watching the dancers move to the music. It was odd to see the plethora of joints and limbs moving about in different ways, synchronised to the patterns each picked up in the music. Karan was amongst the disparate group, dancing energetically, limbs everywhere.

Aryx got the overwhelming urge to join in and wheeled over. He beckoned to Sebastian, but the gesture was returned with a sheepish shake of the head.

Karan danced with the fervour of a wild animal. Her energetic and excitable nature was refreshing. Aryx liked her even though she sometimes proved less than confidential – it was probably because she couldn't sit still. The excitement over the things she heard about others was probably totally different to what she got in her day-to-day life. He sat in front of her and, leaning back, jerked his wheels forwards and tipped up into a wheelie. He allowed the music to swallow him while he rocked back and forth, balancing on two wheels and turning from side to side on the spot. A couple of times he glanced over at Sebastian, and each time he received an apprehensive smile. He didn't get it. He should learn to let go sometimes.

Aryx wheeled into the centre of the dance floor and began waving his arms over his head to the beat, letting his weight swing the chair from side to side. Feeling a little more adventurous in the hub's lower gravity, he pulled his brakes on, waited for a break in the music and, when the beat permitted, threw his weight to one side, tipping the chair over. He landed on his outstretched hand and dropped into a one-arm push-up. With a shove, he launched himself upright and over in the other direction, where he repeated the springing push-up again.

Karan loosely mirrored his movements and leaped all over the place with her head thrown back, hair everywhere.

Sebastian smiled and shook his head.

Aryx repeated his performance several times until the music started to calm down again, then returned to the table with Karan following. He was unable to persuade Sebastian to relax enough to join in dancing – even after several drinks – so the trio sat and talked until they had their fill of conversation and went their separate ways.

Aryx woke in the night and turned on the bedside lamp. Its dull light was eerie in the leafy shadows of his apartment. Something rustled in the plants at the back of the kitchen.

He froze. The hair on the back of his neck stood on end. What was it? He glanced at the door. It was shut, so he sat for a few moments, trying to decide whether it was just his over-active imagination. He let out a slow breath and the leaves rustled again.

His pulse raced. The last thing he needed was some little alien thing creeping around while he was in bed. The disturbance in the leaves edged closer around the room, moving through the planter. It was time to go.

He reached out for his wheelchair, but it sat beyond his reach; he lay across the bed and tried to stretch as far as he could. It wasn't enough.

The rustling approached quicker; it was nearly at the bed.

He reached again, straining to span the gap, and fell to the floor. Pain shot through his stumps from the impact and he tried to drag himself along but an immense weight held him down. The weight of fear.

He tried to control his breath, to quieten the ragged sound while he strained to listen. Where was it? The rustling stopped level with him, on the other side of the bed, out of view. He waited, holding his breath, but heard nothing. Mustering the courage to drag himself up to the bed, he peered over the edge.

A small, red creature with tiny horns and bat-like wings sat amongst the leaves. It looked like someone had taken a child's plastic doll, attached grotesque features, and dipped it in a dark red paint. The evil thing jumped at his face. He screamed.

He jerked awake, limbs flailing, and bashed the stump of his right leg painfully against the planter. He reached down to rub it and rolled over to turn on the bedside lamp with the other hand.

Somehow he'd got tangled up in the bedding, which he straightened before mopping his sodden brow. The details of the dream were vague. He couldn't remember the last time he'd woken from a nightmare with such a fright; what a childish thing to do.

A light on his terminal flashed impatiently. Whatever it was, it could wait until tomorrow. He switched off the bedside lamp, and while he lay in the darkness with his eyes open, he couldn't shake the feeling of *something* being wrong with the room.

That morning Aryx sat in his wheelchair at the kitchen counter, cooking eggs – one of the few 'real' foods you could still get easily in space – while he spoke to Sebastian over the comms.

'Are you *sure* it's okay to work on my pack today?'

'I'm certain. Gladrin was clear that we could use the resources, as long as we start my assignment soon.'

'Good. I'm just having some breakfast then I'll meet you in the hangar. Bring your ship around and I'll be there.'

'I'll see you shortly.' Sebastian signed off.

Aryx finished his breakfast and cleared the kitchen, making sure the work surfaces were disinfected – he didn't trust the automated systems to do it properly. He collected a couple of tools from the workbench along with the pack and was about to leave the apartment when he remembered the flashing light from the night before. It was a message, but the terminal didn't show from whom; it was totally empty.

'Very strange,' he said, rubbing his chin. He decided to forward it to Sebastian. Stuff like that shouldn't happen on his watch.

With the message sent, he wheeled out and headed down the long, curving hallway to the lift.

Sebastian entered the shuttle storage bay – a vast, cavernous space similar to the repair hangar, though completely bathed in light, rather than just the bays. Hundreds of ships and shuttles sat in ranks, filling the space. The harsh, bright lighting flooded the hangar, reflecting off the silvery walls, giving the impression that even amid the huge collection of ships there would be nowhere to hide without casting a conspicuous shadow. He walked past the rows of ships, studying the reference numbers on his wristcom, and after a few minutes of searching he turned down one of the aisles and found the allocated vessel.

At roughly ten metres tall and nearly twice as long, it looked a lot larger than the usual passenger shuttles. The engine exhaust ports were big for its size, and the yellow and black chevrons on the fore and aft quarters of the hull – indicating the locations of four retractable atmospheric Dyson hoops – seemed a little out of place. He'd never seen them on anything other than aircraft and trains, and never the collapsible variety; it was definitely a high-end performance ship. Maybe it was designed for something more than shunting passengers about.

He walked around the vessel, running his hand over the steely-blue hull. The colouration was striking: the side panels and keel were white, separated from the bluish tints of the front, roof, and rear by a long, black stripe that undulated from below the bow, up, and over to the stern, emphasising its flowing curves. It reminded him of the N-suit design. He rounded the port side from the bow and, passing two intakes lined with slats like oversized metal gills, spotted large, black lettering emblazoned near the windows. It read *Ultima Thule*. Not a bad name – it sounded like an exploration vessel. At the midsection he noticed a small logo imprinted below the airlock door where the hull curved under. It was the same image he'd seen on Aryx's pack. He let out a whistle. Aryx would be impressed if he knew the ship had CFD generators. He pressed his palm to the airlock's multi-lock.

'Greetings, Agent Thorsson, you have been granted access to the *Ultima Thule*.' The door retracted a little and slid to the right, into the hull.

A small, glowing glassy orange step appeared in mid-air, halfway between the doorway and the hangar floor, and he jumped back. He could see why it would be necessary – the landing struts held the ship nearly three feet off the ground. He hadn't had a chance to look at a constrained field closely and he'd never used any of the handheld tools himself, so he bent down to examine it.

The edges were slightly rounded and the step tapered towards the bottom, giving it a soft, wedge-like appearance. The top surface had a slightly ribbed texture, but its semi-transparent nature made it difficult to see the detail, and the lines of light that traced through it caused his eyes to drift.

He reached out and touched it. Warm. No, not warm ... neutral. It was probably the temperature of the surrounding air. The surface felt hard and didn't budge when he pressed down on it. He ran his hand over the side. The surface was slick, like wet glass, with hardly any friction at all. The upper surface seemed slightly different; aside from the large bumps, it had a finer texture that made it feel rubbery. A lot of programming had probably gone into it. The processing power required to calculate and maintain the fine texture alone would have been enormous.

He stood up and tentatively put his foot on the step. He didn't immediately slip, so he proceeded to climb up. Upon entering the ship, he looked back over his shoulder. The step was gone. He turned around to fully face the doorway and the step reappeared. SpecOps obviously got the best. He turned back to the interior.

The airlock was only a couple of feet deep, just large enough for one person at a time, or two at a squeeze. Ahead a corridor ran left and right, and directly opposite the entrance a small bay housed pressure suits and a medkit. Along the corridor to the left, the walls were lined with storage units on either side until the space opened out into a cargo bay with a smooth-panelled floor. To the right of the airlock, the corridor terminated in a door mounted in the bulkhead. Mindful of the time, he decided not to explore the rear and made his way into the cargo section. To the right of the entrance to the bay stood a small lift platform with an accompanying emergency ladder; both passed through sealed hatches in the ceiling. He took the lift up to the next floor and the hatch snapped open. Several seconds later he was at the top – it would take far too long for someone in a hurry.

He stepped off the lift into what appeared to be the cockpit, which took up front third of the ship. Two seats faced the piloting console – a standard layout with several buttons and a black glass virtual console that curved around the line of the windows. At least he'd be able to pilot the ship, if it truly was standard. He turned to look in the direction of the aft section.

To the right of the lift, a walkway ran the full length of the upper floor and, although he couldn't be certain, it seemed shorter than it should have been. Something at the back was taking up space. Several consoles projected from the bulkhead, lining the wall on the right, with strip lighting mounted in the ceiling overhead. Freely movable seats stood in front of them, forming an area that might be the workspace Aryx mentioned. On the opposite side of the walkway were three seats with safety harnesses. If the ship could only carry five in total, it *certainly* wasn't a passenger shuttle.

He went back to the cockpit area and sat in one of the pilot seats. He touched the console and several virtual buttons illuminated from within the glass with a bright green glow. After entering the access codes, he programmed the transport system to take the ship through the necessary junctions and pressed the initiate button.

The docking arm extended from the ceiling of the hangar and lowered over the ship. Through the use of carefully balanced magnetic fields, it lifted the vessel without touching it, and lowered it into the huge coils of the transport rings. The support struts retracted automatically and the ship floated forward, carried by the magnetic inductors. As it drew into one of the station's spokes, it started to fall into the tunnel and out towards the rim of the station. Fields caught and controlled its alternating light and dark descent while it passed through the illuminated hoops until it finally entered the outer section and made its way around the arc.

While Sebastian waited, he contemplated the journey. It was odd how it appeared that no species – except maybe the Folians – had yet managed to develop anti-gravity. Nobody knew how the Folian ships operated, and stories of them floating motionless in hangars caused no end of speculation. Had they got anti-gravity technology, or was it something else? It wasn't a hypothesis that had been substantiated, as no Human in living memory had ever been on board one of their ships. It was a shame his department didn't have technical manuals he could study, and given what Tolinar had said in the atrium, he'd never see one.

He stared out of the cockpit while the ship drifted past several private bays. All of them were empty. All except one.

His skin tingled. His heart skipped a beat. One of the enigmatic Folian ships floated in the bay he was passing. A cross between a giant almond and walnut – in shape, colour, and texture – it hung motionless, several feet off the floor, just like the stories said.

Within moments the *Ultima Thule* had drifted past, taking the ship out of view. He *had* to get a look inside one some day.

Aryx watched from the repair bay while the retrieval arm, with lights flashing, glided over on its Cartesian frame, dropped down, and lifted a ship out of the transport tunnel. It trundled back across the hangar with its heavy load and placed it in the bay where the Antari ship had been the day before. He lugged the pack-shaped device onto his lap and wheeled towards it. The airlock door opened and a step appeared. Sebastian's head popped out.

'She's rather nice,' Aryx said, 'and I like the step feature! I didn't realise CFDs got used for those sorts of things yet ... But how am I supposed to get up it?'

'Give it a go.' Sebastian moved back inside the entrance. 'I think you'll be surprised.'

Aryx rolled his wheelchair towards the step. He got within four feet and it vanished, instantly replaced with a squat, conical ramp.

Intriguing, but useless.

'Won't it be slippery? These fields are normally smooth.'

'The programmers have written in textures that provide grip – as long as you've got tread that it can catch on to. Try it.'

He edged forwards and brought the front casters of his chair up onto the ramp. They *seemed* to move normally. He pushed the wheels a little and crept up into the ship. 'Very impressive. We'll have to dig through the code for that.'

Sebastian didn't respond; he just stared off into space.

'Oi, where have you gone?' Aryx poked him.

He snapped out of his daydreaming and looked down. 'I was thinking about Folian ships – did you know there was one parked in one of the private bays just down the tube?'

'No, I didn't.'

'Ever had one in for repair?'

'No, but I saw a damaged one once. What are you getting at?' He could almost see the cogs going around in Sebastian's head, formulating some stupid plan.

'I'd love to see inside one sometime.'

'Heh, you and everyone else. They arrive, drop off delegates, and then leave again. They never hang around.'

'What about the damaged one?'

'Not much to tell. Turned up outside the station one day with a big black patch up the side of it. There were rumours that terrorist group set off a bomb when it visited one of our colonies.' He waved dismissively. 'I don't know how true that was.'

'Why didn't it come in for repair?'

'No idea. Apparently it dropped someone off and went straight back out again. They didn't even request any help.'

Sebastian shrugged with his bottom lip like he often did, seemingly dismissing the subject for the time being. He stepped behind Aryx and ushered him in. 'You'll like the ship.'

Aryx moved through the airlock into the main corridor. He glanced left towards the cargo bay and then turned his attention to the door to the right. 'Can you code the palm-locks?'

Sebastian reached over, pressed his hand against the lock, and waited a couple of seconds until the coding signal beeped. 'Add identity to allow list for all locks,' he said, and pulled his hand away.

Aryx put his palm to the lock.

'Identity added to list of authorised users.' The door slid open.

The lights in the room blinked on, revealing a relatively bare space with dark, unpainted brushed-metal walls. The floor consisted of a grille under which cabling ran fore and aft. In the centre of the room, a large rectangular device – at least five feet long, four feet wide, and three feet tall – dominated the space. Mounted in a set of gimbals, it hung suspended by eight hydraulic arms anchored in each corner of the room.

'This must be the main CFD shield,' Aryx said, moving around the unit. 'There's probably a smaller one just inside the door for the step. Judging by the size of this, it looks like it could generate a shield covering about twenty-five per cent of the hull, I'd say, but if you landed on the shield, it would probably rip the generator off its mountings.'

Sebastian walked across the room and pointed to a panel on the wall. 'There's a configuration console here.'

'This is expensive stuff. The cost of the generator alone must be millions.'

Sebastian did the mouth-shrug thing again and walked towards the door opposite the one they'd entered. Aryx wheeled past and pressed his hand to the lock.

The cube-shaped engine – a compact fusion reactor – stood about four feet tall, mounted directly on the floor. Its sides, covered with protruding vanes, looked like giant heat sinks with coolant pipes running up and down between them and over the top into the middle of the unit. Heavy-duty cabling ran from the centre up to the ceiling and towards the rear of the ship. At the end of the room nearest the stern stood a large oven-like machine: the mass deconstructor.

'You're right,' Aryx said. 'I do like this ship. You can run these things on literally anything if you're desperate enough. The reactor uses hydrogen, helium, or almost anything you can scoop from an atmosphere, and the thrusters can use practically anything that can be mined. You could probably use the fusion leftovers in the thrusters afterwards.'

Sebastian laughed. 'It's the perfect eco-ship!'

Aryx ignored the comment. 'Does it run quiet?'

'I don't know. I used the batteries to power the inductors when I brought it through the tube.'

'I guess we'll find out in time, then.' He made his way into the forward section. 'Hmm. Fairly spacious for a cargo bay, but I don't see how it can be that useful with such a small corridor and airlock.'

Sebastian walked to the far corner of the hold and pulled back the webbing that hung down. 'There's a panel here,' he said, and activated a control.

The forward wall gave a loud clunk and lights in the ceiling started to flash while it hinged downwards, forming a ramp out of the ship.

'Okay, that's a bit more useful,' Aryx said with a laugh. 'I didn't realise a ship this small would do that.'

Sebastian fiddled with the controls again and the door closed. Aryx took the lift upstairs and began investigating the consoles in the work area.

Sebastian's head popped up through the ladder hatch. 'Will you slow down?'

'I can't help being excited. I haven't flown a ship for years, and there's so much kit!' Aryx ran his hand over the black glass of the console. 'Yes, I definitely approve.' He dropped the pack next to the workbench and wheeled back to the cockpit where Sebastian stood examining the controls.

'I'm glad you like it,' Sebastian said. 'It's not like we'd have much say in the matter if we didn't.' He pressed a button on the console. The airlock doors *whumped* shut downstairs.

'Have you checked for bugs?' Aryx whispered.

Sebastian shook his head and took a small device out of his rucksack. He pressed a button on it and began walking around the ship.

A few minutes later he came back with a handful of tiny black cubes. 'I found one in each of the main sections. I'll ask Agent Gladrin about them. I don't see why SpecOps would bug their own ships.' He activated his wristcom. 'Call Special Projects Agent Gladrin.'

After a moment a voice on the other end replied. 'Hello, Agent Thorsson. What can I do for you?'

'I'm sorry to call you, Sir, I wasn't sure if you were working today. I decided to check out the ship you issued. I was just looking around and found a few snooping devices. I didn't know whether it was standard practice for them to be here.'

'Those should have been removed by the preparation crew before the ship was released. Evidently someone hasn't been doing their job properly! We leave them on the ships while they're in storage, just in case they get stolen or damaged. There's a tracking device in the pressure suit locker, if you haven't already found it. I would be grateful if you could send them to your office at your earliest convenience.'

Aryx raised his eyebrows. It didn't sound like any kind of standard practice he'd heard of.

'I'll do that. Thanks for letting me know.'

'My pleasure. Is there anything else I can help you with?'

'Not at the moment, thank you.'

Aryx waited for Gladrin to sign off. 'That sounds a bit odd,' he said, 'but I suppose with these ships being so expensive they can justify taking extra measures for security.'

'Hold that thought.' Sebastian dashed downstairs and came back a few moments later with the tracker unit – a slightly larger version of the snoopers with a flat, delicate antenna plate – in his hand.

'Found it right where he said it would be, in the locker.' He put the tracker in his rucksack along with the snoopers. 'If you don't mind, I'll send these to the office while you set up. I would rather not have them hanging around.' He gestured in the direction of the pack and disappeared down the ladder.

Aryx understood what he meant. At least he'd remembered it was meant to be a secret. He went to the diagnostic console and lifted the pack onto the workbench. With a press of a button on the side, a flap opened, and out slid the infoslate he'd set up specifically for configuring the unit.

Sebastian came up the ladder and sat down on one of the seats next to him. 'I posted the bugs to the office. So, what do you need help with? What is this thing? I thought you said you were doing something with your wheelchair.'

'Stop it with the questions! It is to do with my wheelchair, in a way. Do you remember the conversation we had the other day about field emitters?'

'Nope, had too much to worry about with work ... Most of the CFDs I've seen have either been for partial shielding, like the one downstairs, or the tiny ones in those tools you use. I can't see how you could generate a useful sized field with this.' He gestured to the backpack. 'Are you trying to make some kind of all-over personal shield?'

Aryx shook his head. 'Don't be daft. It can't enclose the generator. I'll put you out of your misery.' He strapped the pack to his back and fastened the leg harness. 'Close your eyes.'

Sebastian did as he was told.

Aryx got out of his chair. 'Okay, open them.'

Sebastian opened his eyes and they looked like they were going to eject from his head.

Aryx admired his handiwork. The missing part of his legs from the knees down had been replaced with a glowing, glassy force-field in the shape of calves, ankles and feet. 'I'd like to introduce you to the "mobility pack". Mobipack, for short.' He took a faltering step towards Sebastian. 'I realised I could use it as a prosthesis. These don't put pressure on my legs because I'm hanging from the harness, so no trouble with my degrading bones.'

Sebastian grinned.

Aryx bent over and passed his fingers through the gap where his knee joint would have been. 'You can see there's a bit of space between my legs and the field, for safety.' He straightened and they slid out from under him.

Sebastian reached forwards but was too far away to halt his fall.

'Ouch!'

'Are you alright?'

Aryx rubbed his backside. 'I don't think anything's broken.'

Sebastian held out his hand.

'I'm okay. I can get up myself.' Aryx brushed the hand away. He took a deep breath. 'It's nearly frictionless. I need to get the field to adapt to the surface. That's where you come in.'

'I thought you might have that problem as soon as I saw it. Was this why you mentioned the code for the ramp earlier?'

'Yeah. I need help with the field programming.' He sat back down in the wheelchair and pressed a few buttons on the pack, wirelessly connecting it to the ship's diagnostic console. The legs instantly vanished. 'I need to get the textures right for the soles of the feet. You know me – I'm no good at programming.' He unstrapped the pack and put it on the console.

Sebastian rubbed his hands together. 'I'll check to see if I can get into the source.' He reached forward, as though to begin typing, and a keyboard lit up in the glass of the workbench in front of him. It was close to where Aryx was sitting, so he dragged it to a more appropriate position and pulled the opposite corners to scale it to fit his hands.

'I don't like those,' Aryx said, shaking his head. 'I'd rather have a button that goes click. If I ever work out how to get constrained fields to respond to touch, I'll make a projected keyboard out of one.'

'I don't mind them. Anything's better than getting a sore throat from talking to a computer all day. It just seems faster to type. You get used to them quickly.' Sebastian tapped away and pages of source code scrolled up the display. 'Thank the Gods these systems are all open source.'

'As long as it's secure and does what I want it to, I don't care, and I don't think your Norse gods have anything to do with software.'

'You know what I mean.'

It was probably more out of habit that Sebastian said it, rather than because he wanted to remember his Icelandic Ásatrú heritage. Other than wearing a Thor's hammer as a necklace, and coming out with the odd utterance, Aryx had never seen any evidence that Sebastian paid any attention to his religion at all.

After several hours work, the pair had found the relevant code to generate grip and transplanted it into the mobipack's system. Sebastian added voice control and an infoslate interface so that Aryx could design field patterns on-screen in his absence.

'Right, let's try it,' Sebastian said.

Aryx activated the mobipack where it lay on the console. He could tell by Sebastian's slack-jawed expression that he found the process fascinating. Floating threads of light appeared in the air several inches from the pack. They whipped around as though blown by a strong wind, rapidly twisting and contorting until they settled into the outline of the prosthetics. The spaces between the threads on the skin of the limbs were spanned by a glowing translucent region, giving the impression of a luminescent soap film. Instead of rainbow colours swirling on the surface, an intense orange laser lacing moved about to a hypnotic rhythm within. The whole process of coalescence took a fraction of a second, but long enough for the naked eye to see – in contrast to the commercial unit used by the ship. Aryx was glad the effect was so aesthetically pleasing.

'Why does it look more solid than the step?' Sebastian asked.

'It's made from cheaper components. Most of it's recycled from old ship parts. Anyway, let's give this code a try. Mobipack, loose terrain.' The soles of the feet rippled and Aryx touched the surface. It felt knobbly. 'That's okay.' He moved his hands away from the feet. 'Mobipack, icy terrain.' Long spikes extruded from the feet. 'They're not sharp, but should be fine. Now for the real test ... Mobipack, interior.'

The spikes on the soles retracted and Aryx ran his hand over the surface. Strange; hard, yet satiny – he couldn't begin to describe it. 'That feels odd, but I think it'll work.'

'Good. I'd hate to think that we'd wasted all that time.' Sebastian smiled, but his expression quickly changed to a frown. 'I don't think we'll be able to overcome the grip problem on smooth floors, though. It'll probably be fine on rough concrete and carpet, but not metal. That's a basic physics problem. We just don't have the resolution to generate contours small enough to grip hard, shiny surfaces. You'll have to be careful using it. It probably needs more calibration, but you can do that with the slate.'

'I don't mind having to stick with the chair for getting around indoors. I only need the pack for unmanageable terrain, otherwise I'll never get to leave the station.'

'How about wearing shoes on the legs?'

Aryx shook his head. 'Don't be daft. I want to carry less, not more! And they'd probably fall on the floor when I turned it off and I'd forget about them. Can you imagine the trail of boots I'd leave?'

Sebastian laughed.

'As long as it works for what I need it for, it'll be fine,' Aryx said, trying to reassure him.

'You walked like a cargomech earlier, all stiff-legged. If you had gyros and pressure sensors on the generators, the legs could move at the knee and they'd know when they were on the ground.'

'I've got a generator in this pack for each leg. Putting sensors on might work ... I'll go and see if I can find some spare landing strut sensors.' He took the lift down and headed out into the repair bay.

After searching through his storage cabinets for a few minutes, he realised the parts weren't where he thought they'd be. 'Seb!'

Sebastian's face appeared at the cockpit window.

'I need to go and get parts from the storage lockup,' he shouted, over-mouthing the words in case Sebastian couldn't hear. 'I'll be a few minutes, okay?'

Sebastian nodded; Aryx wasn't sure that he'd heard correctly. He pointed at himself and then in the direction of the far end of the hangar. Sebastian nodded again.

Aryx approached the row of shiny white personnel transport pods at the far end of the hangar. The ten foot diameter spheres lined the wall and sat next to an opening similar to those of the transit tunnels, but much smaller. Each sphere housed a tinted glass-composite window in the upper front quadrant and rested against the lip of the landing platform. He wheeled up to the first pod in the line and its curved door hinged down to form a ramp.

The inside was plain with a console below the window, and harnessed seating around the rear. Aryx reached under his chair and pulled a trigger switch. From the underside, four small magnets extended and latched on to the floor with a clunk. The console lit up and he selected the option for unlisted destinations, entering the bay number for the lockup.

The moorings released and the pod lurched sideways. He was glad he'd deployed the magnets – he had no desire to be flung about the pod while hurtled through the transit tubes. The pod swooped and wove its way through the one-way tunnel and came to a halt in the drab grey of the storage lockup. Aryx approached the caged-in requisitions desk and a stern, elderly woman with hair bound up in a tight bun leaned over and frowned at him.

'How can I help you?' Her tone was flat, and suggested anything but helpfulness. She must have hated her job, being stuck in that room and not seeing many people. It was either that or she hated people and loved her job because of it.

'I need some parts, if you've got them in stock.'

She spun a clipboard around on the desk and handed it to him. It had forms made from real paper – a little old-fashioned – but he understood the need for the department to have records that couldn't be tampered with. He filled out the form and handed it back.

She tapped away at a terminal and after a moment raised her eyebrows. 'Mr Trevarian, you do not have a scheduled maintenance item that requires these part numbers, and we *don't* issue station items for personal use.' Her stare hardened.

'I know. This is a Special Projects and Operations thing. I have a requisitions ID.'

She handed him an infoslate and he entered the code. The woman seemed even more surprised when the clearance appeared on the terminal in front of her. She sucked air through her teeth. 'Very well, I'll get these for you now,' she said, and scuttled off.

A few minutes later she came back with the sensors and handed them to him, along with a receipt.

'Thank you very much,' he said, and turned to leave.

She didn't acknowledge him. Obviously, she loved her job.

He re-boarded the transport pod and entered the maintenance bay as the destination, accompanied by the security clearance code. The pod moved off, following the arc around the station's rim, and turned in the opposite direction when it met the next junction.

After a few minutes, it neared the private bays Sebastian had mentioned. Aryx kept his wits about him. Sebastian had often said that his nephew was obsessed with photographs of aliens, and Aryx didn't want to miss an opportunity to snap one for him. He manually overrode the speed, slowing the pod to a crawl.

And there it was, the Folian ship, exactly as Sebastian had described. It was unusual for one to be on the station for longer than a few minutes. It did indeed look like a giant elongated walnut-almond, with long, flowing organic ridges interspersed with small holes or indentations upon its exterior. The colour was a dark tan, almost brown, and the ship didn't appear to have any kind of landing legs – it hung in the air next to the platform, unsupported.

Aryx held up his wristcom and took several photographs, then set the pod's speed to automatic and waited patiently to reach the hangar. Sebastian was going to love it.

The pod came to rest behind the others in the hangar and Aryx headed back to the *Ultima Thule*.

'You won't believe what I managed to get a picture of,' he said, entering the cockpit.

Sebastian looked up from the console. 'I have no idea.'

'The Folian ship you saw earlier.'

Sebastian's eyes widened and his lips parted. 'Let me see!'

Aryx downloaded the pictures from his wristcom and the list of images came up on the display. Sebastian tapped the screen. The first picture showed the private bay area in exquisitely sharp detail.

'Where's the ship?' Sebastian asked.

While it showed the bay in the best detail possible for the wristcom camera, it didn't show the ship in any kind of detail at all – it was a blurry smudge and looked as though someone had printed the image in oil paint and proceeded to drag their thumb across it.

'I ... don't get it ...' Aryx said. Was his wristcom broken? He moved on to the next image. It was from a slightly different angle but the result was exactly the same. The two subsequent images were similarly distorted. 'What the hell could cause that?'

'I have no idea.' Sebastian shook his head and did the mouth-shrug. 'Some kind of new cloaking technology?'

'I've never heard of any race having cloaking technology. There's plenty of stealth tech, but they block radar and EM scans. I don't know of anything that blurs out an object in a photograph like this. This is just ... weird. I suppose this makes you want to see inside one even more, now?'

'Too right.'

He knew it was going to be difficult to get Sebastian's mind off the puzzle of the Folian ship so, rather than pushing him further on the coding task, he focused on adapting the mountings inside the mobipack to accommodate the sensors.

By the evening, the pack was in a usable state. Aryx conducted a few test walks and didn't fall over.

'This is great,' he said. 'At least if we have to go anywhere off-station I won't have too much trouble getting about.'

'Well, don't get your hopes up,' Sebastian said. 'I think the SpecOps task is probably going to be more desk work than anything else.'

Aryx's stomach growled like a wild animal. They'd been working so intently that neither of them had even thought about stopping for lunch.

Sebastian looked down at Aryx's abdomen. 'Do you fancy going to one of the open air restaurants for dinner?'

'I suppose so. Be a nice change after being cooped up here all day.'

Sebastian stood up and stretched. Several vertebrae cracked back into place.

'Your posture is crap.'

'I can't help that I slouch when I'm concentrating.' He gestured at the mobipack. 'Do you want to put that in a secure locker downstairs?'

'I suppose. Have you removed all access other than ours?'

'Yes, stop fretting. Where do you want to go for dinner?'

'I fancy one of those places with al fresco areas under the trees. And no, you're not taking me to that awful place that does potato as their speciality. Whoever thought up the name *Spud Nick's* ought to be shot. The guy who owns it isn't even called Nick!'

Sebastian laughed. 'Sorry about that. I know it's a bit greasy-spoon for you.'

Aryx locked the mobipack away in one of the storage compartments in the hold, left the ship, and headed for the hangar exit.

Sebastian coughed behind him. 'I thought we might go via the transport pods.'

'Oh yes?' Aryx called over his shoulder. 'To see if the Folian ship is still there, no doubt?' He stopped and turned to face him. 'You're so predictable.'

'You got me there.' Sebastian shrugged. 'What can I say? I'm curious.'

'We shouldn't waste station resources making unnecessary trips.' He frowned.

'Just this once then, as long as it shuts you up.'

Sebastian grinned, and jogged off in the direction of the transports.

They entered the pod and Aryx strategically selected a destination in the atrium that would take them around the return junction past the Folian ship. He clamped his chair down once again and pressed the initiate button.

Sebastian sat on the edge of his seat, coiled like a cat about to pounce. The first of the empty bays passed and he sprang up and pressed his face against the window. The spherical pod rocked.

'Bloody sit down!'

'I want to see the ship.'

'You're supposed to be in the harness. Are you trying to get us both killed?'

Sebastian sneered. 'Artificial gravity. These things are perfectly safe, see?' He jumped up and down and the pod wobbled.

'For your own safety, please remain seated,' the computer said.

Sebastian folded his arms and flopped back into the seat with a deep scowl on his face.

The bay slid into view. It was empty.

Sebastian's face reddened. 'That's so frustrating!'

'I'm sure there will be another occasion.'

'Yes, but—'

'Stop acting like a spoiled child! Think yourself lucky. You've been given a job many would kill for along with that ship and other stuff. It's more than most people get after working their entire lives!'

Sebastian sighed. 'Yes, but—'

Aryx elbowed him sharply in the ribs; Sebastian merely grunted. The N-suit's impact protection apparently worked.

The sunlight shining through the sky-pattern filters came in bright and warm, and the trees rustled in the gentle air flow caused by the station's rotation.

Aryx stretched and took in a deep breath of fresh air. 'Smell those flowers.'

Sebastian sniffed. 'Lovely.'

'It's the closest we'll get to Earth for a while. We've got two years left before a free round-trip, so make the most of it.'

'I'd forgotten it was that long.'

'Right, where to?' Aryx asked, keen to get back to the subject of food.

'There's a place that does Italian pizza on one of the upper terraces, if you fancy that.' Sebastian pointed to a spot high up on the third tier.

'As long as they do proper coffee and decent food, I don't care. My stomach is threatening to take out the hull.'

Sebastian led him towards a ramp next to the river and they made their way up the long, curving slope from one side of the atrium to the other, where it joined a walkway on the next terrace above.

Aryx spotted a group of bald people dressed in bright purple robes coming towards them. 'Oh no, the Antari delegates.' He grabbed Sebastian by the hips and positioned himself behind him. 'Don't let them see me – they complain about everything.'

Sebastian shuffled to the top of the first ramp, dragging Aryx behind him, and doubled back in the opposite direction, taking an adjacent one. It was a long route to take, but Aryx was glad of the opportunity to be out in the open air – and avoid the Antari. At the top they headed along the terrace for a hundred yards and took another bridge to the other side.

'I'm glad you know where you're going,' Aryx said. 'It's like a bloody maze up here.'

Sebastian towed him past a large, point-arched opening in the left-hand wall, surrounded by an eclectic selection of old Earth symbols. He briefly caught a glimpse of the interior through the open doors. A long, red carpet ran from the doorway to the wall at the far end, fifty metres away, where large, coloured panes of glass tinted the purple nebula beyond. In front of the window, at the end of the carpet and on top of three steps, sat a long, low box-like table upon which rested a set of candles. Along the length of the hall, right of the carpet runner, were rows of low, wooden benches where several people sat with their heads bowed. Left of the runner, white-robed individuals knelt upon low, circular mat-covered podiums. They slowly raised their heads, muttered words to themselves, and bowed forwards until their foreheads touched the carpet.

Sebastian stopped. 'I've never seen this place with the door open before,' he said.

'What is it?'

'The Panchurch.'

Aryx stared at the podium-sitters, slowly rotating in unison. 'What are they doing?'

'They're Muslims.'

He scratched his head. 'I don't see why they're turning round.'

Sebastian let out a sigh, as though the effort of explaining was too much. 'They have to face Mecca when they pray.'

'Oh yes ... *Obviously.*' Aryx shrugged and wheeled past the opening as quickly as he could. Religion was weird.

They turned on to a wide, half-hexagon section of terrace that jutted out from the high atrium wall and overhung the terrace below by several yards. They approached a long glass shopfront with a small canopy above it. A sign next to it read 'Q'orrig's Pizzeria'. Across from the restaurant, separated by the sidewalk, grew a well-tended lawn with three large birch trees where several tables with umbrellas served as the outdoor dining area. Sebastian sat at one of the tables and activated the service beacon while Aryx moved a seat out of the way and parked his chair in the gap.

A few moments later a young girl came out with a couple of menus. She placed them on the table and said, 'Welcome to Q'orrig's Pizzeria. Can I get you some drinks?'

'I'd like a mineral water, please,' Sebastian said.

'I'll have a double shot of Espresso, thank you.'

'Would you like to order now?'

'I'll have the rim-river seafood with extra olives,' Sebastian said.

Aryx scanned the menu. There was only one thing he was interested in. 'I'll have a large ham and pineapple, with a stuffed crust.'

'I'm afraid the Hawaiians aren't real ham – it's formed mycoprotein. Is that okay?'

It was a little annoying, but as real meat was often difficult to come by, he gave in. 'Yes, that's fine.'

The waitress dashed off with their orders and they sat and watched the projected clouds pass overhead, the brightness of which had been slowly decreasing while they travelled from the transport to the restaurant. The light, humid breeze gave the impression of a warm summer's evening and, as the simulated dusk descended, the solar filters cleared, revealing the glowing, deep-purple nebula hanging against the starry patina of space.

Small lights came on around the tables and handrails lining the walkways, and tiny glowing insects flitted amongst the flowers and branches of the trees. Aryx was glad the station's gardeners had introduced them for pollination, rather than the usual insects from Earth – at least they were easier to see when they got into places they shouldn't.

He watched the nebula turning overhead and was overcome by an unexpected longing to camp out under the stars on some exotic planet.

The waitress returned with their orders and placed them on the table. Sebastian waved his wristcom over the infoslate she presented.

'Thank you,' she said, and moved off to serve some other customers that had arrived.

The fruity aroma of pineapple made Aryx's jaw pucker, and he tore into his pizza. Initially, it tasted as good as it smelt, but while the mycoprotein was just like meat, he wasn't too sure about what had been used instead of pineapple.

Sebastian stopped chewing. He was staring right past Aryx, over his shoulder. His eyes were wide.

Aryx tensed. *What?* he mouthed.

Sebastian replied in kind. *Antari.*

Chapter 4

Aryx cringed as several haughty, high-pitched voices spoke behind him, almost in unison. 'What have you done to our ship?'

He dropped his pizza and turned to see the throng of purple-robed Antari delegates standing behind him. 'I repaired it – just like you asked.'

The Antari at the front of the group frowned and the ordinarily smooth, bald head creased right up over his forehead to the back. 'The thrusters are off by ten Hertz.'

'What do you mean?

'The one you repaired does not sound like the others. It was functioning perfectly before you interfered with it.'

'It wasn't functioning perfectly, it was knacker—' He took a deep breath. 'It wasn't working *at all.*'

'That is beside the point. It is no longer in tune with the others.'

His throat tightened. They had to spoil his meal, didn't they? 'It's functioning fine now I've fixed it.' He set his jaw.

'We will complain to your manager,' the leader said. The group turned and glided away.

'Complain then! And he'll agree with me – it's not a bloody musical instrument!'

The Antari at the back of the group turned its head one hundred and eighty degrees to face him and continued to glare until they slid out of sight.

'They get on my nerves,' he growled through gritted teeth.

'I can tell. I caught one hacking the system yesterday.'

'They don't half creep me out ... Never seem to see them in the atrium in the day – that's probably why.' He had to get his mind off the confrontation; he hated stress like that, especially when he was trying to eat. 'Did you check your mail this morning?'

'You sent me something about an unidentified message.'

'I didn't think you could get incomplete ones like that.'

'You can't – at least, you're not supposed to.'

'That's why I sent it. I thought you might be able to have a look in case it was a security problem, or a bug in the station software.'

'I'll take a look tomorrow. What were you doing checking them at that time of the morning?'

'I wasn't. I woke up from a nightmare and noticed the light.'

'I had a nightmare the other morning, too.' Sebastian rubbed his chin. 'I had a call from my sister shortly afterwards. That was about the same time, I think. I'd have to check. I thought the computer had let the message through because I was up.'

'I've never heard of them doing that, not unless the privacy controls had been disabled.'

Sebastian scratched his head. 'I'll definitely have to check in the morning then, it's too much of a coincidence.' He resumed munching on a slice of pizza.

Aryx stopped eating, leaned forwards, and rested his elbow on the table. 'What was your nightmare about?'

Sebastian looked up, still chewing. '*Eigh donn r'mmb'r mhh.*'

'At least swallow. You're so rude sometimes.'

He gulped. 'Sorry. I don't remember much of it. I was walking through some mist, not getting anywhere. Something touched my shoulder, I turned around, and at that point I woke up sweating. That's when I got up. What was yours?'

'I was in my apartment,' Aryx said, leaning back in his chair. 'Something was coming towards me, rustling through the plants. I don't remember what it was exactly, but it scared the crap out of me. The terminal was flashing when I woke up, but I ignored it and managed to go back to sleep. I don't remember what the thing was, though. I think it was some kind of little monster.' He was surprised at his own choice of words.

'I hate nightmares. I've had a few lately. It's really odd.' Sebastian shrugged. 'Until a couple of weeks ago, I hardly ever had them.'

'Me neither. I just hope I don't have it again, or I'm going to end up going off my plants. It's probably this excitement about SpecOps that's started it.'

They finished their meal and headed off the extended terrace back towards the lift, passing the restaurant.

Aryx caught sight of movement at the back of the kitchen: a giant, four-armed insectoid throwing dough. 'I thought you said this was an *Italian* pizza place!'

Sebastian grinned. 'I did. I said that it was a place that did Italian *pizza*, not that they were *made* by Italians. Q'orrig is a Q'vani name, after all. I really don't know what you expected.'

Aryx laughed. 'You never tell me the whole story from the outset.

I'm no racist, it's just that when it comes to food, I like to know I'm getting what I expect.'

'Hah! You're like that with just about everything. It was too much of an opportunity to pass up – the look on your face said it all.' Sebastian rubbed his chin repeatedly while they waited for the lift. 'I'll check those messages out first thing and then meet you at the ship. We'll have to make a start on the SpecOps project tomorrow. I'm glad we got the mobipack done, though. '

'Thanks for the help. I couldn't have finished it without you. I'd love to patent it and market it some day.'

'I hope you do. It always feels good to do something that benefits others like that.'

They took the lift to the habitation level and went their separate ways. Aryx sped home from the terminal. What could the SpecOps box contain? He couldn't wait to get his hands on it, but at the same time he prayed it wasn't a bomb.

Sebastian sat alone in a shuttle, working at the navigational controls. The engines at the back of the ship hummed quietly to themselves and stars slid past the windows while he checked maps and cross-referenced coordinates.

The display blinked off and on, interrupting his work. He thumped the console, knowing full well that it wouldn't help.

'What's wrong with this thing?' He stopped work on the map and began running a diagnostic routine. The overhead lights flickered. The hairs on his neck bristled, and he was overcome with a strange sense of being watched. He slowly turned the seat to face the back of the ship.

There was nothing there. He was alone.

The lights and consoles at the far end went off, leaving the rear section in darkness. An ominous, mouldering shadow approached from the stern as one by one the lights extinguished, until the last light went out, plunging him into darkness. Even the stars had gone.

An eerie silence followed – not even the thrum of the engines penetrated it. Only his adrenaline-fuelled breath grated in his ears.

Disorientated, he reached out to steady himself on the console. His hands passed through the space where it should have been and he fell to the floor. He reached behind him, feeling for the chair. It was no longer there. What was happening? He struggled to stand up and regain his balance, and another, harsher, breathing joined his. A cold shiver passed through him.

A rasping voice said, 'Se-ba-sti-aaaan!'

He felt a chill, the adrenaline rush turning to one of panic, and he whirled around trying to determine where in the darkness the unseen

speaker lay.
Sharp claws raked, fiery, down his back. He screamed.

The sheets were soaked when he woke, his forehead dripping with sweat. He wiped his brow on the fabric, but it did little to dry it. The terminal opposite the bed flashed with a message again. The time read 03.10.
'Terminal off!' he shouted.
The screen blanked and he rolled over and tried to get back to sleep. He had to find the cause of the nightmares soon or he'd be in no fit state to work for anybody, let alone SpecOps.

Sitting at the desk in front of the terminal, he ate his breakfast while he opened the message Aryx had forwarded. It was empty; both the sender and contents were blank. He'd never seen anything like it before. It was a little concerning. He trawled through the headers and list of server addresses the message had passed through. The last few belonged to internal station machines – nothing unexpected there – but the addresses before them were unfamiliar.
'This is strange,' he said to himself. 'It looks like it's come from outside the station.' The list of addresses was long and it would take more time than he had to examine them. He would have to check them later, but now he had to check terminal security.
He began looking at the logs from the time of his sister's call. There was another – a blank message to his own terminal that he'd overlooked, with similar headers to the one Aryx had sent.
'Hmm,' he grumbled as he pored over the data. Did the messages have something to do with why the terminal wasn't working properly? Was it the cause? He continued scouring the logs and quickly changed his mind: it was a symptom.
His terminal had been unlocked by someone aboard the station, but the logs did not show by whom. They had been altered. There were three possible ways it could have happened, and he didn't like any of them: someone with high-level security clearance had changed them; a skilled hacker had broken into the system and erased them; or someone had planted code that would allow the messages to unlock terminals. The latter seemed most likely, but it made no sense. Why would somebody want a terminal to come on in the night? Was it related to the nightmares? No, that was a stupid idea. Totally illogical. Forget about it. He pushed himself away from the desk and got up.
As he pulled on the N-suit, he realised he hadn't called Janyce to let her in on the news about the job – she'd be thrilled to know he was working for SpecOps. 'Computer, call Janyce Hafsteinsdóttir.'

The holding screen appeared for nearly a minute and he began to get concerned.

He finished putting the suit on and the call was finally answered. A bleary-eyed Janyce against a dark background greeted him. She looked half asleep, poor woman.

'I forgot the time difference,' he said.

'A likely story,' she said, stifling a yawn.

'I didn't mean to wake you.'

'Don't worry about it.' She rubbed her eyes. 'I suppose we're even now.'

'I've got good news! I've had a promotion – I'm working for SpecOps.'

'Congratulations ... What's a SpecOps?'

Pop. There went his bubble. 'A special branch of EarthSec. They investigate new technologies and threats. It means I might get to go off-world – you know what I mean.'

'That is good news. I know you've been getting a bit itchy about not being able to travel and all that. I'm sure your father would have been pleased.' She'd obviously only ever seen him on one of his better days.

'Anyway,' he said, 'I just wanted to let you know. I also managed to get a photo of myself with an alien for Erik. If you want to give it to him, I'll forward it now. Sorry it's only 2D.' He transmitted the image.

'Thank you, I'm sure he'll love it.'

'How did he do with his presentation?'

'He got an A plus, and an extra merit for using the library. He hasn't stopped talking about you for the last couple of days. He really wants to come and see his favourite uncle.'

'Sorry, Jan, I haven't got enough money to pay for the trip yet, and with all the work I'll have to do, I won't be much fun to be around.'

'I'll see if I can scrape some money together. It would be good for us to have a break, regardless. How's your friend, Aryx? He looked a bit tired last time I saw him.'

'He's good. He's got a few interesting things in the pipeline. Speaking of which, I've got to give him a call. I'll let you get back to bed. Speak to you again soon. Give my love to Erik.'

'Bye, Seb, don't be a stranger.' She closed the comm-link.

He called Aryx on his wristcom. 'Are you on the ship?'

'Yes, I'm just doing a few tweaks on the mobipack. I fine-tuned a few things and started putting a patent proposal together. Probably get it finished in a few days and then send it off.'

'Excellent! Listen, I'm heading to the office to get the SpecOps box I want you to look at and then I'll meet you in the—'

Glassware rattled in the kitchen and a vase jumped off the end of the worktop in a suicidal plunge to the floor as a loud rumble resounded from somewhere deep within the station.

'What the hell was that?' Aryx said. The tremor could be heard even louder over the wristcom.

'I don't know, but it felt like an explosion!'

The vibration stopped for a fraction of a second and then began again in earnest. The plate he'd just eaten from slid off the desk in the opposite direction.

'I think the station thrusters have fired. I have to get to the office – they'll probably need me.'

'Go! I'll be at the ship.'

Sebastian grabbed his rucksack from under the desk and bolted for the lift.

Chapter 5

The lift juddered to a halt at the lower atrium level despite Sebastian's instruction for it to take him to the office on level four. The doors opened a fraction of an inch and stopped as water began to trickle through the gap.

'What the—' He hammered on the door. 'Is anyone out there? I'm stuck!' The gap was too small for him to even get his fingers in. There had to be a release somewhere. Maybe under the control panel.

He flipped off the metal cover, exposing the circuitry behind the buttons. No release control.

He pulled the multi-tool out of his belt and jammed one of the many blades into the panel. The doors retracted in a shower of sparks, and a mass of soggy, green weed swept in through the opening. He stepped over the tangled mass and out onto the walkway.

Water streamed off the upper terraces while fish and other river creatures flopped about, stranded on the paths. People sat slumped against walls and handrails, shop-fronts were strewn with debris, and restaurants' outdoor seating lay smashed. Those not injured were either helping the wounded, throwing the suffocating water-life back into the river, or collecting up debris to make the area safe.

He made his way to one of the bridges over the river. It was covered with plants and sediment. As he crossed it, he pushed several fish off the edge, back into the water.

A woman sat in a puddle at the far side, her chest heaving, and her straggly, wet hair stuck to her neck.

Sebastian helped her up. 'Are you alright?'

She drew a finger over her ear, pulling back the tangled locks. 'I think I'm okay.' She put a hand out to steady herself and Sebastian helped her to a bench.

'What happened?'

Her eyes welled unexpectedly. 'You didn't see it? It was awful! A huge wave came up and went right over the bottom terrace. I hope nobody's been killed. It was horrible . . . the screams.' Her body shook as she broke down.

Sebastian rubbed her arm. 'I'm sorry, but I've got to go. Are you sure you'll be alright?'

She nodded.

He left her to recover and made his way to the lift. His assumption of the thrusters firing must have been correct. The kinetic energy from the thrusters would have been absorbed by the water, causing the tsunami. He waited in stunned silence as the lift carried him. It was amazing how much damage had been incurred by that slight change in rotation. Whatever caused the thrusters to fire might not have even been that significant – he wouldn't know until he got to the office. Had it been a bomb? Had terrorists somehow caused an explosion?

The station would certainly be a prime target. Even though Humans had built the place, they had cooperated with alien races during its design and construction, and it had become the main trading and transport hub for this sector of the galaxy. But destroying the station wouldn't serve any purpose; it would only serve to cripple the economies of Earth and its colonies. Then again, terrorists were rarely rational in their beliefs and actions. He'd never seen any logic in their motives.

The office was in disarray when he arrived – and not due to objects having being thrown around. It had become the epicentre of activity as people collated reports and analysed video footage from all over the place. The din of chatter was almost deafening as various parts of the station called in with damage reports. Staff huddled around consoles in groups, and most sounded as though they were at breaking point. Bannik stood, surrounded by a crowd of security staff, handing out infoslates – most likely assigning damage control duties. He briefly caught her eye, and she simply nodded in his direction. Thankfully, she looked too preoccupied to speak to him, so he continued to his office to check whether he'd been assigned any tasks.

He sat down and activated the terminal. No assignments – unusual, given how busy everyone was. An incoming call flashed up on the display and he allowed it through.

It was Agent Gladrin – out of uniform, hair un-greased. 'Agent Thorsson, good to see you again – although I wish it were under better circumstances.' His voice wavered.

'What's happened exactly? The place is a mess. It looks like the thrusters fired, and the atrium's been flooded.'

'There was an explosion, as you've probably gathered. The shockwave caused the corrective thrusters to fire unnecessarily, and that in turn caused a tsunami. There are reports of hundreds injured and several dead. Unfortunately, I left the station a day ago on business and cannot return to investigate the situation myself . . . As the only SpecOps representative presently on the station, I'd like you to act in my place and carry out the investigation. Do you think you're up to the task?'

Sebastian's heart leaped into his mouth. 'I, uh, don't know if I've got enough experience, Sir. I've never done anything other than cyber-forensics.'

Gladrin rubbed his forehead as if trying to alleviate a headache. 'You've had training. Have some confidence in yourself, Thorsson. There was a good reason you were picked for the role, and I don't want to think that my faith was misplaced.'

'Sir, I can understand how I can be helpful performing the task you've assigned to me, but this is totally outside my range of experience. I don't see how my personality can be of any use investigating a bombing.'

'Who said it was a bomb?'

'You—'

'—didn't say any such thing, and *that's* why I need you. You've already contemplated several potential scenarios without realising it.'

Maybe he was right. He'd read the news articles about bombings – perhaps that had subconsciously prompted his train of thought.

'So, can I count on you?' The agent tapped his fingers together.

The thought of leaving the routine he knew was an uncomfortable one, but the prospect of investigating something different was equally exciting. New planets, new technology . . .

'Well?'

'Yes, Sir,' he blurted. He couldn't believe he'd said it.

'I knew I could count on you.'

He took a deep breath. 'What do we know so far?'

Gladrin laced his fingers together and leaned closer to the screen. 'I have a real-time link to the security investigation. At the moment it looks as though a laboratory in the rim section was the source of the blast. Teams are analysing video footage of the area to ascertain what caused it. It appears to be a privately rented space, so we don't have access to the internal systems – all part of the privacy contracts, I'm afraid, and an insurmountable obstacle to our investigation.'

'That's a hindrance.'

'Quite the understatement. Fortunately, the explosion didn't cause any direct damage to the station beyond the lab. The blast was directed out through the pressure ducting that all internal laboratories are fitted with for just such an occasion. It might be wise for you to investigate the scene directly, once the area has been secured. The corridor has been sealed off, and damage control is working outside the station to replace the seals on the pressure vents. When they're done, you should be good to go.'

Sebastian listened in silence, trying to absorb the details.

'I'm sorry to put this responsibility on you so soon, given that you have much work to do on your current project. But we have no other agents in the area, and I felt that it would be best to assign this to someone with intimate knowledge of the station and inhabitants of the surrounding sector.' Gladrin paused and pressed a few controls on his console. 'Just a moment, I have fresh information coming in from the feed.' He turned to look at a second console off-screen. 'The security footage has been forwarded to me. We have video from several recorders in the area of the laboratory and one in the corridor outside the lab. Again, due to the damned privacy rules, it doesn't show the doorway to the lab itself, or have any sound . . . and there is another problem – it appears garbled.'

Sebastian waited. What sort of problem could there be that the computer couldn't clean up?

'I'll forward it to you. Your expertise in programming might help.'

His terminal displayed the file transfer. 'Thanks, I'll see what I can do with it. Are there any suspects?'

'None. We have no legible video that might directly implicate a suspect – at least not until you've taken a look at the file I've sent. We have no record of the function of the laboratory – privacy rules, again.' He groaned. 'Therefore, no indication of motive for the attack.'

'So, you *are* assuming it's an attack?' He knew it.

'For the moment. You're to investigate as though this has been a terrorist attack on the station. The only way the fire notification system could fail would be if an explosion was caused intentionally.'

'I'll follow that assumption, then,' Sebastian said, 'unless the evidence indicates something to the contrary.' Something didn't sit right, but being so new to the job, it didn't seem right to question his superior.

'Good. I will notify Bannik of your authority in the investigation, but I think she's too busy dealing with the fallout to give you much hassle, and that's probably a good thing – I don't really like dealing with the woman.'

'I'll get on it right away, Sir.'

'There's one other thing. I'd like you to use your ship as a base of operations for the investigation, away from the security office. If it *was* a terrorist attack, everyone aboard the station, including employees, are potential suspects. We cannot risk a security leak.' He signed off.

Shit. Someone on the station could be involved? Everyone he'd ever met aboard liked aliens and often actively pursued contact with them. He'd always been too reserved to interact with them without legitimate business himself – the first and only exception being the Folian in the atrium – and the idea that there might be a terrorist on the station was appalling.

'Contact Aryx Trevarian,' he said into his wristcom.

Aryx answered. 'Any news?'

'Yes, but I'll have to fill you in when I get there. I'm transferring files to the ship's computer to analyse. I'll be with you in a few minutes.' Sebastian grabbed his bag and left the office.

Bannik cast an expectant glance from the other side of the department and he quickly looked away, pretending not to notice. He had no intention of getting collared by the woman, especially after what Gladrin had said.

On his way to the repair hangar, Sebastian found he had to take the same return route. Several of the lifts still appeared to be out of action, and as he entered the second lift, he encountered a maintenance worker hunched over the damaged panel. The worker seemed to ignore his presence.

Sebastian coughed. 'Why are the lifts out of service?'

The worker answered without looking up. 'Some were open when those waves hit. A ton of water went down into the system and we had to vent a few of the shafts into space and wait for it to boil off. The carriages aren't airtight, so we had to decommission them in order to do it. Some bastard vandalised this one.'

'Any idea how long they'll be down?'

He shrugged. 'How long's a piece of string? I don't know, couple hours, maybe?'

As long as most of the lifts were in service, it wasn't too much of an inconvenience. 'Keep up the good work,' Sebastian said, patting the man's shoulder. 'Sorry about this one.'

Fifteen minutes later, Sebastian arrived in the maintenance bay and boarded the ship. Aryx was sitting at the diagnostics console, working on the mobipack.

'Still working on that?' He sat down next to him and put his rucksack on the floor.

'I thought of a few more fixes.' Aryx looked up from his work. 'Was it an explosion?'

'Yes. Think yourself lucky you weren't out in the atrium at the time. The place is a wreck.' Sebastian punched a few commands into the terminal and started poring over the security logs. 'Gladrin has given me a link to the report feed. He's forwarded me the videos and put me in charge of investigating the incident.'

'Why you?'

'There's nobody else from SpecOps in the area to take over. He thinks someone on the station staff might be involved. I've got to keep off the official systems just in case.'

Aryx's eyes widened. 'Do they have any suspects?'

'Not yet. I've got to analyse the footage. It's damaged.'

He brought the video up on-screen and the pair watched it intently. It played back silently, showing a shallow view from above a doorway near the explosion's origin. The corridor was empty. Sebastian sped up the playback and waited until movement flickered across the screen. He wound it back several seconds and played it again slowly.

They watched open-mouthed as a vaguely humanoid shape passed the camera, moving down the corridor and out of frame, in the direction of the laboratory door. The shape was not clear – in fact, it was *blurred*.

'That's like—'

'Shh!' Aryx hissed.

They looked at each other, and Sebastian wound the footage back again, to the moment when the figure approached the room. He paused the image at the instant the figure's face would be clearest; it was still a blur.

'What's wrong with the camera?' Aryx asked.

'I know. I don't think it is a camera fault. It's just like the Folian ship. Computer, enhance image.'

The computer attempted to resolve the motion blur and focus the image. It failed: the subject still had the appearance of smeared paint.

'Damn it!' Sebastian shouted.

'It's obviously not motion blur.'

'Computer, run extended processing routine on video.'

'Estimated time for completion: two days.'

The estimated time rose while they watched, and Sebastian regretted not attempting it previously on the photos Aryx had taken – at least then he'd have an idea of the timescale.

'Typical!' He slammed his palm against the console. 'It's going to take longer and longer as it goes on. At this rate it will be weeks!'

'Aren't your office computers faster? You can always lock it down to make it secure.'

Sebastian clenched his jaw. He hated the thought of having to leave it running in a potentially vulnerable location. 'It looks like I'll have to. Computer, copy video to my secure station; re-run routine using local resources.'

'Estimated time for completion: seven hours.' The estimate began to rise.

He sighed.

'Better than nothing,' Aryx said. 'At least it's only estimating a couple of days now.'

'I'll just have to leave it running. Computer, notify me when the task is complete.'

'I still don't understand what could cause that blur,' Aryx said, rubbing his chin.

'I don't know – but whatever technology the Folians are using to protect their ships from being photographed, this person might also have access to it. The ships show up fine on scanners, so maybe it's something they turn on at specific times. It might be worth asking them about it. We might then be able to trace the source of the technology and likely users.' Sebastian stood and paced back and forth. 'I wonder if it could have been a Folian that did it?' He stopped, and looked at the image again. 'No, it's too bulky to be one of them.'

'Their ship left the station before the explosion anyway, didn't it?'

'Yes, but it's worth checking to see if there were any of the crew still here. Computer, what was the Folian presence on the station around the time of the explosion, plus or minus two hours?'

'No Folian presence logged in system records during specified time-frame.'

'Right ... When was the last Folian presence logged on the station?'

'Yesterday, sixteen-hundred hours.'

'Did the Folians go anywhere near the laboratory affected by the explosion?'

'No.'

'Then where *did* they go?' Fucking TI.

'The delegates were collected at the central docking hub by their ship when it arrived and remained aboard while it navigated the transport system to the private bay area. Delegates did not leave the ship again after embarking.'

'Where did they go before the hub? What were their movements? A complete list.'

'After arriving on the station their activities were limited to the docking hub, the atrium, and the lift sections between. At no point did they enter the outer rim complex.'

'Gods, damn it!' Sebastian slammed his fist on the console.

'Calm down! You haven't even investigated the scene yet, so it's not like you've run out of leads.'

'I suppose not.' He took a few slow, deep breaths. 'The picture I took of the Folian in the atrium came out normal, not blurred, so I guess it wasn't much of a lead anyway. It could just be that their ships have that weird cloaking thing going on.'

'You didn't tell me you finally managed to get a picture! I wish I hadn't bothered.'

'If you hadn't taken a picture, we wouldn't know about the blur.'

'So when did you get a photo of the Folian?'

'On my way to work, the day before I heard about the job. Have you ever seen one close up?'

Aryx shook his head.

Sebastian brought the image up on the console next to the video. 'See? They've got a different body shape to the thing on the video. Even though it's blurry, it looks far too big to be a Folian.'

Aryx peered closely at the screen. 'What's that stuff in the Folian's hair?'

'That *is* its hair.'

'The leaves, not the spongy bit.'

'Some kind of wreath. It even had fruit in it, from what I could tell.'

'Maybe that's why people call them Folians.' He waved his hands about in an exaggerated stroking gesture. 'Because they've got a fetish for plants and foliage or something.'

Unconvinced, Sebastian dismissed the image. 'Let's see if they have finished securing the lab.' He activated his wristcom. 'Contact the damage control team dealing with the lab explosion.'

'Damage control. What can we do for you, Agent Thorsson?' It sounded so official.

'Has the lab been secured?'

'Yes, Sir. We finished refitting the outer seals on the vent and it's being repressurised as we speak. It should be ready in about two minutes.'

'Thank you. I'll be there shortly. Will it be safe to go in?'

'The heat detectors don't sense anything, so it should be fine. We'll open her up once she's got atmosphere.'

'Please leave it sealed until I get there. As a matter of security, nobody is to enter. You can refit the inner seal after I'm done.'

'Very well. Damage control out.'

Sebastian got up. 'Are you going to be alright here?'

'I'll be okay. Did you bring the box for me to examine?'

'Oh Gods, no, sorry. I forgot it in the rush with the explosion.'

'Will you have time to get it? If not, I'll carry on working on the mobipack until you get back.'

'I'll try, but this is obviously priority now.' He picked up his rucksack.

'I'll see you later,' Aryx said as Sebastian descended the ladder. 'And be careful!'

Fortunately, Bannik was still busy dealing with the collateral damage when Sebastian called at the office to retrieve a forensics kit, and he easily avoided her.

After retrieving the kit, he stopped off at the changing room – at least if he put his bag there, he'd be forced to pick up the box when he returned. Aryx would be fuming if he held off giving it to him any longer. He opened the locker, picked up the unopened box, and stood turning it in his hands.

He almost regretted taking on the investigation – he'd rather have been sitting at a desk, trying to work out what this thing was – but if he hadn't agreed to play lead investigator, Gladrin would probably have taken the box back, and the SpecOps commission with it. Then he could wave goodbye to any chance of ever leaving the station. Aryx could, too.

He put the box back, stuffed the rucksack in the locker, and noticed the gun. He still hadn't had time for any training. There wasn't time for anything anymore. He'd be fine, as long as he didn't have to shoot anything. At least forensic investigations didn't require guns.

The lab was on the far side of the station and, like all the others, sat in the outer level of the rim section for safety reasons. The interruption to lift service caused the trip to take longer than usual, and even though most of them were back in full working order, it still took over half an hour for Sebastian to get there.

The corridor to the lab had been cordoned off where it branched from the wide central spine hallway. A security guard stood at the entrance, and a small group of aliens sat around him.

'Please remain calm,' the guard said, addressing a bewrinkled Antari. 'You'll be able to go down there shortly. The scene needs to be investigated before we can open this section for public access.'

'I want access now,' chittered an irate Q'vani.

'I'm sorry, but it's not up for discussion. You'll have to wait just like the others.' The guard gestured to the group.

'Rrrrrrt!' the Q'vani rattled, and scuttled off on its short hind legs to join the throng.

Sebastian watched the creature shuffle away. He'd not seen Q'orrig in any location other than behind the counters in the restaurant and had no idea what a Q'vani's lower half looked like. The alien stood about as tall as him, maybe an inch or two taller. Its long abdomen, supported by four short legs protruding from the sides, trailed along the floor behind it and its entire body was covered in orange and brown segments of chitin that flexed as the creature breathed, reminding him of glow-worms he'd seen on Earth; they had managed to come back from the brink during the Ecological Crux. Just below the head, four arms, with upper and lower segments of equal length, terminated in prehensile, claw-like hands. Just looking at them made him feel uneasy, but he couldn't isolate the cause of his discomfort. The head had two big compound eyes, and a large pair of black serrated mandibles that flanked its mouth parts. He imagined the creature could do terrible damage if you got in a fight with it.

He shook his head to rid himself of the vision and approached the guard. 'I'm here on behalf of SpecOps to investigate the crime scene.'

'ID, please.' The guard held out an infoslate and Sebastian pressed his thumb against it. The man nodded and stepped to one side, pulling the temporary barrier open. 'It's down there, then turn left on to the parallel.'

Sebastian made his way down the short corridor to the junction and turned left. About eighty yards away stood a doorway with coloured tape across it. He noticed the curve of the corridor rolling upwards until it vanished behind the line of the ceiling. Even though it was less pronounced in the outer sections, he still hadn't become entirely comfortable with the effect.

He opened the forensics kit and retrieved a small handheld scanner. He paced down the corridor, pointing the device at the floor and lower walls, searching for DNA and other trace evidence that might have been left by the perpetrator's passing. The scanner bleeped when it detected various compounds and stored their locations for later analysis.

After making a thorough scan of the doorway, he ripped the tape down and entered his security override codes. The heavy steel door scraped open and a foul, acrid stench burst forth – the stench of chemicals that shouldn't be mixed. Chemicals and burnt flesh. The opening to the room presented a black, gaping rectangle against the white of the corridor. The lights didn't come on – it would have been foolish to expect them to.

With his stomach tightening, Sebastian took a torch from the forensics kit, put some anti-contaminant coverings on his feet, and stepped in.

Chapter 6

Sebastian entered the lab. Its charred and blackened walls absorbed almost all the torchlight. The odour was appalling, and so strong he couldn't think properly. He took a respirator mask from the forensics kit and fitted it to his face, covering his nose and mouth. A couple of breaths later, the air was comfortable again, and he set about surveying the scene.

The room extended three metres ahead and seven to the left. The bench running along the opposite wall was strewn with remnants of equipment, melted plastics, and broken glass. In the far left corner stood a large gas canister, its top split and peeled back like a giant metal flower. It was probably the cause of the explosion, but until a simulation could be constructed from the evidence, it would be little more than an educated guess.

He walked the length of the bench taking readings with the scanner. It recorded numerous hydrocarbons, but little material that could indicate an accelerant. The flammable signature increased with proximity to the ruined canister – as he'd expected. He looked up at the gaping hole in the ceiling; evidently whoever worked in the lab had been conscientious enough to put the canister below the pressure panel, as per regulations.

The scanner bleeped, picking up something else on the bench. A detailed analysis wouldn't be possible on the unit, but it had definitely detected DNA.

He turned left where the canister stood and followed the wall. Several wrecked containers littered the floor, along with a structure that looked like a bed or pallet leaning up against the wall opposite the bench. The mattress and bedding had been burnt away almost completely – temperatures in the room must have been phenomenal. The scanner bleeped again: more DNA, this time on the bed frame. The basic analysis showed it to be different enough from the first set of readings to imply there had been two people in the lab. He continued around the room, recording video along with the forensic scans. With enough information, he would be able to reconstruct the area and work out whether the canister was the cause of the explosion or a secondary ignition source.

With the scans complete, he made another circuit and marked the evidence for collection: several small tools and other objects that had melted onto one of the benches; an open metal frame, about twelve inches square and eighteen inches high; a bundle of burnt wires that looped through the frame; and a fist-sized lump of charred, melted plastic, apparently connected to the wires. Aside from several beakers that might have contained fluid – judging by the tacky patches around their bases – there didn't appear to be anything else of interest. No discrete computer system was present; the only connection was the ubiquitous comms terminal in the wall to the left of the door.

'Computer?'

The terminal replied with garbled audio, and the display glowed faintly through the blackened glass.

Sebastian rubbed the soot away with a cloth from the forensics kit. 'Respond with visual only.'

Acknowledged.

'Does this terminal contain records pertaining to activity in this lab?'

Negative.

'Has this terminal been used at all since the initial opening of the laboratory's contract?'

Negative.

Another dead end. Any records made in the lab were obviously kept on a separate system, or on an infoslate that had most likely gone out of the vent. But why hadn't the broken glass gone out of the vent as well?

He collected up the forensics kit and left the lab, closing the door behind him. It grated to a halt a couple of inches short. He rolled his eyes. There goes forensic integrity.

Sebastian turned the bend and approached the guard. 'Nobody is to enter the laboratory except for the forensics retrieval team. The door doesn't shut.'

'Yes, Sir. Are the civilians allowed access to the corridor now?'

'Yes. I think I've got enough scans. Just keep them away from the door.'

'Very well, Sir. I'll inform the team right away. We'll get the evidence sent to your office.'

'Actually, I'd like it sent to this hangar.' He took the infoslate from the guard and entered the relevant details.

'That's a bit . . . unusual, Sir.'

'Just do it.'

The man stiffened. 'I see, Sir. It'll be done right away.'

He left the guard to deal with the civilians that had clustered around the corridor entrance, and headed back to the ship. Today was turning out to be too long.

Aryx sat at the diagnostic console aboard the *Ultima Thule*, putting the final touches to the mobipack. He was pleased with the result and, with luck, might even be able to put together a decent patent proposal over the next couple of days. It would all need testing of course, but how rewarding it would be to finally produce something that could help others in his predicament do field work.

It had been over three years since he'd last done any repairs in the field himself, and he'd never forgotten the day they brought him round after the accident . . .

A voice pierced the darkness. 'What's the last thing you remember happening on Cinder IV, Mr Trevarian?'

The sensation of lying motionless under a heavy, wet blanket was pleasant and strangely comforting – so comforting he couldn't be bothered to open his eyes to find out who was speaking, but answered anyway.

Rain lanced down out of a rapidly blackening sky, punctuated with flashes of light. Aryx bounded down the ramp and out of the shuttle, his big arms carrying a bundle containing every possible tool he might need. He crossed the threshold, and water pouring down over the doorway triggered the wetsuit properties of his already tight military-issue vest, shrinking it further, and he immediately felt warmer despite the cold rain that plastered his hair to his scalp. The shuttle's landing supports had sunk too far into the soft ground – there was no way he'd get under it to perform repairs in these conditions.

'Computer, send the cargomech out!' he said, and dropped the tools in a heap midway along the starboard side.

The ship's TI complied, and seconds later the eight-foot tall, vaguely humanoid forklift trundled out of the ship, churning up the marshy, waterlogged soil in its tracks.

'Lift it here!' he shouted, pointing to the bottom of the hull. He almost couldn't hear himself think over the din of the rain battering the ship. 'High enough for me to crawl under.'

'Acknowledged.' The cargomech bent down and reached out with its two-pronged grippers. Hydraulics strained and mud flew through the air as it slowly forced itself between the ship and marsh. With a creak, the side of the shuttle lifted a metre from the ground. 'Is this adequate clearance?'

'Yes, hold it there.'

His wristcom chirped into life. 'We're on our way back with seven surviving colonists. The ITF have rigged the reactor to blow and we need to get off this rock ASAP! Our ETA is three minutes. What's your status?'

'Engines operational, I've repaired the navigational array, and I'm about to fix the atmospheric ballast seal. Two minutes, tops.'

'Good work, marine. Alvarez out.'

There was no time to lose. He dropped to the floor and shuffled under the ship, dragging the bundle of tools through the muck after him. Within moments he'd located the ballast seal – a rubberised hoop surrounding a large panel – where a piece of shrapnel from one of the terrorist cell's ground-to-air missiles was lodged in the rubber. He rolled onto his back and pulled out a pry-bar from the bundle of tools and wedged it in. With a few sharp tugs, the seal came away. He threw it aside, took the replacement from the tool bag along with a large spanner, and began removing the panel.

Thirty seconds later the panel dropped free. He quickly fitted the new seal around the edge of it and lifted it back into place. That was odd – it seemed a little closer than when he'd removed it. He began tightening the nuts that held it in place and hit himself on the chin with the end of the spanner. It definitely was closer. He looked at the ship's support struts. They were a few inches deeper in the marsh than when he'd first crawled under; there wasn't space to finish fitting the panel.

'Computer, get the mech to raise the ship a few inches!'

The hull moved farther away and he resumed tightening the nuts.

He finished the last one as Alvarez's voice came over the wristcom. 'Trevarian, what's your status?'

'I'm just finishing up. We're good to go.'

'Our ETA is thirty seconds. Warm her up! Alvarez out.'

Great! Time to get out of this mud hole. He started collecting up the tools and a metallic squeal came from the direction of the cargomech; its arms were still slowly rising, and perilously close to slipping out from under the ship. 'Computer— Jesus Christ, what are you doing?'

The mech's speaker gave an unintelligible electronic crackle in response, yet it continued to move.

'Oh hell!' He abandoned the tools and started scrabbling backwards as fast as he could.

It wasn't quick enough.

With a final, grating screech of metal on metal, the mech's arms flicked upwards, releasing the burden of the shuttle. He was still partly under the ship when its bulk fell towards him.

Pain exploded from every nerve in his body. The last thing he remembered through the blinding agony was the shouts of the evac team arriving.

'And that's all I remember,' he said.

'It's better than we'd hoped,' the voice said. 'We thought there would be severe brain damage after the coma. Can you open your eyes?'

As unwilling as he was, Aryx tried to shrug off the drug-induced leaden feeling and forced his eyes open. He blinked slowly and found himself in a sterile white hospital room with gleaming walls and a solitary window that exposed a patch of featureless powder-blue sky. A doctor sat next to him with an expression of analytical concern. Beside him stood Nick Alvarez, a bronze-skinned hulk of a man. With one muscular arm folded across his body, he rubbed his wire brush chinstrap with the other hand. Aryx could tell he was worried.

'How do you feel?' Alvarez asked.

'Like I've been hit by a shuttle.' Aryx laughed, and his ribs replied with a sharp stab. 'What's my prognosis?'

'We managed to repair most of the damage and stem the internal bleeding with nanobots,' the doctor said. 'We put you in a coma while you healed as there were complications with infections in your wounds. The most severe damage was irreparable and we had to operate.'

'Let me see.'

The doctor hesitated before pulling back the covers.

The world began to sway, and Aryx fought back a wave of nausea that threatened to overcome him. 'What am I going to do? I won't be able to work in the marines anymore!'

Alvarez shook his head. 'They've given you an honourable discharge, and you're gonna be awarded the Orion medal for valour. Your actions saved the team and surviving colonists.'

It was cold comfort. There was no way he could go back to the military, and he certainly couldn't run his dad's farm. 'How am I going to live? I've got to work or I'll go insane!'

'One of the guys suggested a little day centre down the road where they put lipstick kisses on knickers.' Alvarez laughed and held out an infoslate, close enough for Aryx to read. 'Or, if you want to try something you'll actually be good at, there's this . . . '

Looking for a career in space? Exciting opportunities for engineers of all abilities await on Tenebrae station.

From that day onward, Aryx wore his disability as both a badge of shame and pride. Shame, because he'd made a mistake that he would regret for the rest of his life, and pride because he'd managed to overcome the disability and still perform some useful function that he found rewarding. The only thing that held him back had been his inability to use prosthetics and, as his condition had worsened, his seniors held him back further.

When constrained field devices were first released, he'd immediately seen thousands of potential uses for the technology – not only for shielding, but for replacing all kinds of bulky and heavy equipment. He'd toyed with the idea of weapons such as swords, but the lack of mass gave too little force to cut anything. The generators were also incapable of folding the field back at a sharp enough angle to create a cutting edge; yes, you could use them as eating implements, but who'd ever cut themselves with a butter knife? He'd tried to get them to maintain an open-edged field, but they'd never remained stable for more than a nanosecond. It was like trying to cut a hole in a soap bubble; unless the field formed a complete envelope, it couldn't maintain cohesion. The most practical application he could see under the circumstances was to use them as prosthetic limbs. The exposed parts wouldn't malfunction if they got wet or dirty and would theoretically never require repair. More importantly, they wouldn't put pressure on the weakened bones in his legs.

'I'm amazed the bulkheads held against the explosion!' Sebastian's shouts from the hangar snapped him out of his reverie.

Aryx wheeled out of the ship to meet him. 'What caused it?'

'I don't know. I'll have to get the computer to analyse the readings. The scanner said there were at least two people in the lab when it went up.'

'Any idea who?'

'Not until we run the analysis. What have you been doing?'

'This and that. I poked around the ship a bit. It doesn't have any weapons, but it's got a kind of railgun that can be used to launch probe spheres. At the far end of the cabin there's an escape pod, hidden behind a plain panel.' He folded his arms. 'And there's a cargomech in the hold.'

'Where? I didn't see anything in there.'

'Neither did I, to start with. It's disassembled. The bits are under the floor panels in the hold.'

'I didn't realise they came apart.'

Aryx rolled his eyes. Did he know nothing? Had he lived in a shoebox his entire life?

'What?'

'Nothing.' He shook his head. 'You can tell you're not military. Useful to have one on the ship, though . . . I hate them.'

'Ah, Cinder IV,' Sebastian said, walking up into the ship. 'Your accident.'

Aryx followed up the ramp. 'So, anything else interesting in the lab?'

'I've got the forensics recovery team collecting the evidence. They'll deliver it here when they're done. They shouldn't be long.'

'What sort of evidence?'

'Some kind of frame with wires and a melted object that was connected to it. The place was such a mess that most things were unrecognisable.'

'I guess you'll want me to take a look at it?'

'Please. You might be a bit better at working out what damaged equipment is supposed to do.'

Aryx raised an eyebrow. He wasn't sure if Sebastian was referring to him or his experience with machinery. 'I think I'll take that as a compliment.'

A voice called from the hangar, 'Excuse me, Agent Thorsson?'

Sebastian went out and came back carrying a plastic crate sealed with tape and a docket. He put it on the floor in the middle of the cargo bay and, after checking the docket, unsealed it. Aryx took the items out one by one and set them on the floor while Sebastian checked his infoslate and pointed out where each item should be in relation to one another.

'Has the ballistic analysis finished?' Aryx asked.

'Nearly, it has about five minutes left.'

He put the last item on the floor and leaned back to examine his handiwork. 'So, what have we got?'

'These items along here ...' Sebastian said, walking along a line of objects, 'are from one of the workbenches in the lab.' He approached the far end. 'This was closest to the exploded canister. I'm not convinced it was the primary ignition point.'

'Why not?' If there was another cause for the explosion, Aryx couldn't see it.

'I'm not sure. It's just a feeling at the moment.' Sebastian turned to the other row of items. 'These are from the opposite side. There wasn't much, except for what looked like a hospital bed. That was where the second DNA trace was.'

'I don't see anything very interesting, except that frame with the wires. Shame the thing connected to it's so badly melted. That'll take the longest to analyse, I bet.'

'That's what I want you to focus on. It looked like it might have been the subject of whatever research was going on. Either that, or it was logging information.'

Aryx wheeled over to the broken glass. 'What about these? They look like chemical containers, and those tools look surgical. This one,' he said, picking up a slender implement, 'looks like it's probably a scalpel. The others might be ordinary screwdrivers.'

Sebastian's wristcom bleeped.

'What is it?'

'DNA analysis. The blast analysis of the scans I took has finished, too.'

'Good. I'll take this thing upstairs and examine it while you read the reports.' Aryx picked up the melted plastic lump with trailing wires and made his way to the cockpit, leaving Sebastian to collect the other items.

He set the charred lump on the workbench and took several tools from the mobipack's storage compartment. The plastic on the outside of the lump seemed crusty and brittle, so he tentatively scraped at it.

Sebastian sat down next to him at the console and began studying the reports.

Aryx didn't make much headway; the charred plastic was difficult to work with and, as he pried the flakes off, it seemed the object consisted of a solid mass of plastic with metal interspersed within it. He activated the console's analytical scanners to attempt a sub-surface scan. It didn't penetrate deeply, but the results indicated there was some kind of circuitry running through it.

'This definitely has electronics.'

'Really?' Sebastian said. 'I never would have known, given it had wires coming out of it.'

'No need to be sarcastic. It could have been a power supply, you ass.'

'I know. I'm only pulling your leg.' He broke out laughing, 'Sorry! I didn't think.'

Aryx set his jaw, then started to laugh, too. 'I guess we both need to chill out.' He calmed himself and resumed cutting into the device. Several small, threaded metal shafts glinted against the dark plastic. 'Whatever this was, I think it might have had a casing on it. I'll have to do a chemical analysis of the plastic just in case it's an active component.' He pressed a control on the console and a small slot appeared, into which he dropped the scrapings.

The gas spectrometer readings came back a few moments later. An organic plastic.

'I wonder if it's a storage device,' he said.

'Could be. You'll have to figure out a way of wiring it up. See if we can get something off it.'

'The organoplastic is probably part of the circuitry, which might make it difficult, but I'll give it a go.'

Sebastian didn't reply.

Aryx looked at the display. 'You got identities for the DNA?'

'Yes. Two individuals, both male. I'm retrieving records now.' The first identity profile appeared on the screen. 'John Kerl, age 47, a research scientist with cybernetics and molecular biology qualifications. Because of the high-level privacy laws, the station logs don't show whose name the lab was rented under, so I don't know if it was actually his.' He began tapping away at the keyboard.

Aryx turned his attention back to the melted lump. The wires that remained attached were not discrete cables, with many of them woven together forming a fine filigree of copper and gold; most had completely disintegrated and the remaining wires had melted to form thicker chunks of metal – they wouldn't be of any use connecting the unit up. More parts were required.

'Bingo!' Sebastian shouted. 'Oh, damn.'

'What now?' Aryx was beginning to wish the console were in a separate room to the rest of the ship.

'I have clearance to see the ownership of the lab but the records have mysteriously been deleted. This is becoming a common trend.'

'How so?'

'The logs of message transit had been deleted – you know, the message you received the other night? Someone has either hacked the system or let a virus loose that allows them to delete secure files. I don't like it one bit.'

'It does seem a bit ... coincidental.'

'There are no coincidences. We live in a deterministic universe where every outcome has a logical cause, and I'd bet the hacking has something to do with the terrorists.'

'Yeah, whatever.' Aryx sighed. 'You don't yet know that it was terrorists that blew the lab up. Anyway, sending us empty messages isn't exactly a terrorist activity.'

'I'm aware of that. I'm just leaning towards a theory.'

'Wait until you've learned a bit more. There's no point in jumping to conclusions.' He turned to leave. 'Back in a minute, I'm just going to get some bits.'

Sebastian continued to read in silence as he left.

Aryx made his way out of the ship and started rooting through the tool chest in the hangar. He found several jump-wires, patch cables, a soldering iron, and electronic connectors. He returned to the ship and continued to shave as much of the damaged exterior off the lump as he could, exposing connection points for the wires, and set about soldering them systematically.

'We have results on the second DNA profile,' Sebastian said.

Aryx grumbled and stopped working, again. He looked up at the screen and his jaw dropped. 'Nick Alvarez . . . '

'You know him?'

'I *knew* him. He was in my platoon when I was in the marines.'

'And?'

'Not spoken to him for ages.'

'What was he like?'

'Straightforward, but into all kinds of weird stuff. Occult, superstitions – that sort of thing. I don't know if it was because his family was religious, but this was a bit more than the usual Latino superstitious paranoia.'

'Why did you lose contact?'

'I lost touch with a lot of friends when I went into rehab, but I heard from Alvarez not long after I started work here. He said he'd left the marines and got a job working with some researcher.' Aryx stared at the ceiling, trying to remember. 'I don't think he said what sort of research it was . . . He never seemed too happy as a marine. I think he'd seen too much death and it had affected him a bit. He seemed keen on the new job, even though he was a bit cagey about it.'

'Well, I think we know who he was working with and where his career ended. It does seem strange, a marine with an interest in the occult working with a cybernetics and molecular biology expert.'

'Not as odd as a semi-religious programmer working with a guy with no legs, on an investigation on the second day of a job he didn't even get interviewed for. Face it, the universe is just too odd for *you* to comprehend. Get over it.'

Sebastian sighed. 'This gets weirder and weirder, and we have no motive yet.'

'Then move on to the next thing. What does the blast analysis say?'

He began reading another report.

After a couple of minutes he brought up the reconstruction based on the scans.

Aryx watched the simulation play through, showing burn damage prior to the explosion of the canister. A non-localised heat source had appeared in the centre of the room, where no ignition points or accelerants had been found, and caused most of the initial melting of equipment. After the first rapid burn, the canister had exploded, instantly blowing out the pressure seal in the ceiling and causing the atmosphere to be evacuated, putting out the flames.

Sebastian's mouth hung open as he viewed the playback; he looked intrigued, amazed, and confused, all at the same time, as though he was about to burst a blood vessel in his brain.

Aryx turned his attention back to the simulation. The evacuation of the room had probably sucked most of the material out into space along with the atmosphere, hence the lack of bodies – but what had caused the initial burn?

'I ... don't ... get it,' Sebastian said. 'Explosions always leave traces of the explosive around the scene, even tiny amounts. The blast analysis doesn't show that the central ignition caused any ballistic damage. It's as though the entire room and everything in it spontaneously set on fire and the canister went up after.'

'Is there any other trace evidence?'

'Some, outside the lab, but none of it seems to relate to the scene. Whoever was in the video was probably wearing gloves. All other DNA from the corridor either headed all the way past the lab in both directions and nowhere near the door, or it was Kerl's.'

'None of Alvarez's?'

'No.'

'Are they on the video?'

'Let's have a look. Computer, search the entire video, from the time of the explosion backwards, for any identity matches to John Kerl or Nick Alvarez and report a summary of their movements.'

The computer replied several seconds later. 'John Kerl has frequently accessed the lab on a daily basis. Nick Alvarez also accessed the lab daily.'

'And, on the video, when was the most recent activity for both?'

'John Kerl passed the camera outside the lab this morning at 06.00.'

'And Alvarez?'

'Last recorded instance of Nick Alvarez passing the camera was 2264-07-08 at 05.54.'

'That was nearly two months ago,' Aryx said.

'Yes, and it's worrying, given there was a hospital bed in the lab. If he was in there when it went up, it probably means he hadn't left the lab for a long time before.'

'Do you think he was already dead?'

'It's possible,' Sebastian said, studying the screen, 'but the analysis shows little evidence of primary necrosis on the material from the benches. Hold on.' He scrolled farther down the page. 'There was some DNA on the bed, but it shows more degradation than the DNA on the bench. That's unusual.'

'Perhaps it was from skin cells or something. Any other trace?'

'A little. Some mineral the handheld scanner couldn't identify. Only a tiny amount, which could be why. A fine powdering of it on the floor outside the door, and a small patch on the door itself. I didn't see it when I examined the scene. Hmm. I'll have to go back and get a swab!' Sebastian nearly threw himself down the ladder in the rush to get out.

'See you, then!' Aryx turned his attention back to the wiring problem. At least now he could concentrate.

Sebastian came back twenty minutes later carrying a sealed vial with a swab inside. He sat down next to Aryx, activated the spectrometer that had been used to analyse the plastic, and inserted the swab into the slot.

'You got a sample?'

'I hope so. The scanner detected particles, but I couldn't see them. I swabbed it just to be sure.'

The console bleeped a few moments later. Sebastian leaned forwards as he read the report. He took a deep breath.

'What is it?'

'The very paragon of usefulness, the computer says "unidentified mineral".' He rubbed the back of his neck.

'Is that *all* it says?' Aryx was beginning to get fed up with having to ask what was going on.

'No, obviously there are other readings, but it's not like anything I've seen before. The particle masses are very low for their size.'

'It's not a gas?'

'The analysis doesn't indicate that it is.'

'Do you think it was the accelerant?'

'No, they're usually reactive, but the particles haven't bound with other atoms at all, and there are no traces of it in the lab. The exterior of the door wasn't damaged, so it's not like somebody drilled a hole and squirted it through.'

'You ought to get the computer to analyse the sample with X-rays, see if it turns up a crystalline structure.' He turned back to the wiring problem – he couldn't hold Sebastian's hand all day, after all.

'Good idea. I hadn't thought of that. Computer, begin X-ray analysis of sample.'

'Unable to comply.'

'Why?'

'The sample tube is empty.'

'What in Hel's name?'

Aryx looked up. Sebastian seemed about to burst a blood vessel again.

'Show me the sample log!'

The display changed to a report of the sample's mass and composition over time. While the two of them had been talking, the sample's mass had slowly been reducing to nothing.

'How the hell did that happen?'

'I've no idea,' Aryx said. 'Perhaps it's radioactive, or one of those things that breaks down in light or air, or something?'

'I've never heard of anything that breaks down completely, and certainly not when it's chemically inert. Breakdown *always* leaves traces.'

'I should imagine that's why it's "unidentified".' Aryx put down the wires he was working on. 'We're going to have to investigate this stuff now, aren't we?'

'Definitely. But where do we start?'

He bundled the plastic blob and wiring into the evidence crate, securing it under the console with a retaining strap, and pulled himself closer to the screen. 'Try using your office's TI to search records, maybe?'

'Computer, link to my workstation's TI and patch it through.'

'Acknowledged. Connection established.'

'Greetings, Sebastian. What can I help you with?' the TI asked in its smooth, genderless tones.

'Search records that refer to unidentified minerals, or minerals that defy analysis. Also use keywords such as "vanished", "disappeared", "evaporated", and other terms that might refer to diminishing mass.'

'Which records should I search?'

'Shipping logs, manifests, research notes. If nothing comes back from those, expand the search within reasonable parameters. If that turns up nothing, get back to me and I'll try a different angle.'

'Understood. The search parameters are large, and it will take a long time to complete. I will notify you when I am done.' The TI went quiet.

Aryx looked down at his wristcom. They'd been at the investigation for a couple of hours and he was already feeling frustrated. 'Shall we take a break while the computer searches?'

'Oh Gods, yes.'

'Well, I'm going to head to the gym. I've missed my last couple of workouts and could do with the relief.'

'Mind if I join you?'

'Of course not. It might help clear your head.'

When Aryx arrived, there was only a handful of Humans using the gym. Except for the occasional Bronadi, it seemed the use of gyms on the station was an activity almost exclusively limited to Homo Sapiens. Maybe the other races didn't have the same ethic of working out, or their biologies worked in a way that made planned exercise useless. He wondered if it could simply be down to the nature of most of the visitors. The high-ranking ambassadors and officials probably saw physical exercise as beneath them, or didn't have the time for it.

Sebastian arrived, still wearing the N-suit, and carrying something under his arm.

Aryx stopped performing chin-ups on the horizontal bar, lowered himself into his seat, and wheeled over. 'You're late.'

Sebastian patted the bundle under his arm. 'I had to get a change of clothes.'

'You ought to try training with the suit on.'

He looked down at himself. 'Are you kidding?'

'No, I'm serious. It's got an osmotic skin to absorb moisture and should regulate your temperature quite well. If you ever hope to go out in the field, you ought to get some training wearing it so you get used to it. You're so lazy, sometimes.'

He slouched. 'I'll do a run on the treadmill. It might help me think.' He clambered onto the nearest machine and started strolling.

Aryx wheeled back to the bar to continue his chin-ups, but this time strapped himself to his chair and lifted it with him. He obviously impressed the other gym-goers, as members of both genders looked him up and down with expressions of appreciation. Sebastian was smiling, too. Was he envious? Perhaps he was starting to chill out. He continued his circuit of the gym and moved on to work his chest and arms with weights, finishing off with some time on the ergo machine – a device like an upside down bicycle that he pedalled with his hands. It was the best way to get a decent cardio workout without zooming up and down the atrium walkways and scaring the residents.

He'd been pedalling for fifteen minutes and still not broken much of a sweat when he looked at Sebastian. His face was a little flushed as he jogged alongside Aryx, but less so than he might have been if he'd worn a regular armoured suit.

'How are you doing?' Aryx asked.

'Not bad. I thought the suit would have been much hotter, but you're right, it regulates temperature quite well. The water,' Sebastian said, pulling the straw out of the collar and sucking it briefly, 'doesn't taste too bad either. It's quite effective at filtering perspiration. It just tastes like a plastic bottle.'

Aryx laughed. 'Just don't be tempted to piss in it to try it out, will you?'

'Of course not.' Sebastian slowed. 'I need to get off.'

'Call *that* training? You're going to do well, aren't you? As long as you only get stuck in a desert that's fifteen minutes' walk across!' Aryx pushed himself around to the treadmill on the other side of Sebastian and wheeled up onto the belt. He set the speed to 8mph, pressed the *Go* button, and immediately started pushing to overtake him. 'Right, now speed up to match mine.'

Sebastian groaned, but pressed the button. 'You're such a slave driver.'

'Stop complaining. That's it, run!'

Less than five minutes in, Sebastian's face was bright red and running with sweat. The suit caught and absorbed the moisture as it ran down his neck.

'Keep going! You can go faster.'

'Oh, shut up. It's alright for you, Mr Wheely-Good-Fitness 2264 . . . I bet you won that prize by default.'

What a cheek. Aryx grabbed the handrail and allowed the chair to freewheel while he reached across and set the other treadmill to maximum.

Sebastian shot backwards and tumbled to the floor, laughing.

'You deserved that, you git.'

The pair finished their workout and made their way to the changing room. Aryx waited while Sebastian showered.

'Have the results come back from the search yet?' he asked.

Sebastian checked his wristcom. 'No, not yet.'

'Computers.' Aryx shook his head. 'They seem so damned slow when you need something in a hurry.'

'Tell me about it. I think it's going to be a while. Why don't you go and relax for the rest of the day? The other evidence can wait until tomorrow. I'll contact you if I need you.'

'I'd rather get that blob analysed.'

'Go and get some rest. You look tired.'

'I'm fine,' he said, yawning. There was no way of disguising it. 'Okay, maybe I will.' He left Sebastian to finish up.

When he arrived at his apartment, he was in no fit state to concentrate on the mobipack's patent proposal. Instead, he made himself a light meal and spent the rest of the evening finishing off the novel he was reading. It wasn't long before the infoslate clattered to the floor.

From the shadow looming over him, Aryx got the distinct impression that he was sitting underneath a large object. He couldn't make out much detail; the shadow was only slightly darker than the dull grey surroundings.

'Hello?' His voice was muted.

Something creaked above him in response. Something metallic, under strain.

A terrible, cold memory rumbled up from his stomach. He needed to get out from underneath whatever it was. His chair was nowhere to be seen, and neither was the mobipack. He'd have to crawl for it, or shuffle along on his backside – it was either that, or try to walk on his stumps. The metal creaked again, and he decided to make a move. He elbow-shuffled towards the penumbra.

The shadow darkened. The sound of breathing came from somewhere behind him. Something clattered on a hard surface.

The object above came down rapidly. A feeling of oppression engulfed him. The darkening shadow reminded him of events on Cinder IV – he wasn't sure he'd make it out.

A moment later he crossed the threshold of the shadow – he was going to make it! Pain shot through his shoulders and upper back as something sharp dug in to him. Claws dragged at him, pulling him back towards the shadows, towards the crushing weight.

No, not again! He couldn't go through it again – not like this!

The mass came down and, as the last breath was crushed from his lungs, he screamed.

Sebastian woke to a bleeping wristcom. He'd had a terrible night's sleep and yet another nightmare. He rubbed his eyes and rolled over to answer the call.

'What is it?'

The office TI spoke. 'I am calling you to let you know that the search you requested has been completed.'

'Forward the results to the *Ultima*'s systems. Send Aryx a message when he wakes to let him know that I'll meet him at the ship. What time is it?'

'The time is now 06.27.'

He sighed. 'Great.' Perhaps he should have instructed the computer to notify him after he woke up, rather than immediately. He rolled over. Just a few more minutes.

Thirty seconds later he got up. The case was too important and it would be better to get a head start on the new lead.

After scoffing down a quick breakfast, he made his way to the security offices' changing room to get the rucksack of SpecOps gear. The lift system was once again fully functional and the journey to the office took much less time than before.

Karan sat on one of the benches when he arrived, tying her bootlaces.

'Don't you ever do any paperwork?' he asked. 'You're always here or out running.'

'I haven't exactly seen *you* in the office lately.' She folded her arms. 'And for your information, they've got me on patrol. Most of the ambassadorial visitors have requested intensified security, so we're all stretched pretty thin at the moment. I wouldn't mind if it meant I got to be out in the atrium. What are you up to, anyway?'

'SpecOps work.'

She drew in a sharp breath.

'Yes, I got the job, but I can't tell anyone about what I'm working on.'

'That's a shame – I was looking forward to some gossip. I'm glad the Frost Maiden didn't get it, though.'

'What are you on about, wanting gossip? Isn't the explosion exciting enough for you?'

'I guess so, but it's a bit . . . impersonal. I'm not exactly involved in anything to do with the investigation.'

'Think yourself lucky.' He wanted to tell her something, but with everyone being a potential suspect it didn't seem like a wise move. 'As soon as I can give you some info, I will.' He hurried over to the locker and opened it.

'Whatcha got there?' She was right behind him.

He glared over his shoulder at her and grabbed the canvas bag. 'Mind your own business,' he said, slamming the locker shut.

A tremor shook her bottom lip.

'I'm sorry.' He put the bag over his shoulder and turned to leave. 'It's very important. I'll catch up with you when things calm down a little. Hey, how have you been sleeping lately? Any more bad dreams?'

Her eyes reddened. 'None since Friday – not that you care!' She spun around and stormed out.

He took a deep breath and let out a thin, ragged sigh; he hated having to lie, especially to his friends. He'd have to make it up to her somehow.

The floodlights around the *Ultima* continued to drive back the encroaching darkness of the repair hangar. Fortunately, it seemed to have been the only ship worked on for the last few days, judging by the lack of other lights in the hangar. Sebastian boarded the ship and found Aryx, already sitting at the diagnostics console, hunched over the melted plastic lump.

'Any progress?'

Aryx looked up, holding a wire in one hand and a soldering iron in the other. His eyes had dark circles under them. 'Not much. It's taking ages to attach these. I hope after all this work I can actually *do* something with it.' He pinched the bridge of his nose. 'I didn't sleep well last night, so I came down early.'

'Bad dreams again?' Sebastian took the seat next to him. 'I had a nightmare, as well. Can't remember what it was about, though. Oh, and before I forget, the computer has found some records that might relate to our unidentified vanishing mineral.' He addressed the console. 'Computer, show an overview of the records found during last night's search.'

The display lit up and an expanded overview of several documents appeared.

'Give me a quick summary of the document types,' Sebastian said to the computer.

'On the Galactic net, several anonymous bulletin boards hosted requests for a mineral with specific properties. It was not possible to access the posting logs without sufficient evidence for a warrant.'

'Given that the requesting posters were anonymous, ignore those. Did anyone reply?'

'Yes. A Bronadi *Bemorical Crip'thort* by the name of Braku.'

'Excellent. Contact him please.'

'One moment.' The display changed to a comms holding screen.

Aryx gave Sebastian a sidelong glance. 'A *Bemorical Crip'thort?*'

'My Bronar is a bit rusty, but I think it's a trading title that means he's a commodities broker.'

Aryx's nose wrinkled. 'I don't know why they don't use Galac titles like everyone else.'

The screen changed and they were presented with a saggy, dog-like face. A fine, velvety fur covered the creature's deeply wrinkled head, which was topped with two furry trapezoid ears. Its short muzzle terminated in a black crazy-paving nose, giving it the appearance of a cross between a hyena and a Shar Pei dog.

Aryx stifled a snigger. Sebastian jabbed him in the ribs with his elbow and he nearly dropped the hot soldering iron in his lap.

The Bronadi's bulbous, overhanging lips quivered with agitation. 'Never have I, *Bemorical Crip'thort* Braku, encountered such rudeness! Contacts are supposed to message before requesting face-time. This is most insulting!'

'Please, forgive my intrusion in such a hurried fashion. My name is Sebastian Thorsson.' He bowed his head. He was thankful that the security manuals he'd studied included diplomatic protocol.

'Intrusion forgiven.' The Bronadi nodded. 'Now, what can this humble servant of Bronat possibly help you with at this time?'

'Tenebrae, the trading hub I work for as a security officer, was recently attacked. There is evidence of an unidentified mineral at the scene of the crime. It seems to be unstable somehow, but non-reactive, and apparently evaporates easily. My searches of the communications network turned up several "Wanted" posts on bulletin boards. Posts to which you have replied. We have no access to the posters' records, but given that you replied with an offer to supply minerals fitting the description, you were our next lead.'

'I am afraid I cannot provide you with the clients' identities, as I simply do not have that information. I made no direct trade with them.

I do not trade in volatiles, and the mineral in question is not available through regular trade channels – it would not have been profitable for me to broker. I passed on the details of the supplier to the clients in the hope they might spread my name to other potential paying customers.'

'Can you tell me who the suppliers are?'

'Indeed. The mineral is available almost exclusively in large quantities from a small mining outpost by the name of Sollers Hope. Several other worlds have produced only tiny amounts of the mineral and even then unreliably, and not in tradable quantities. I hope this information is satisfactory.'

'Most satisfactory, thank you.' Sebastian bowed again.

'If you have no other questions, I must go. I have other, more timely, business to conduct. Good trading to you, Thorsson.' The screen went blank.

He let out a sigh of relief. 'Well, I suppose that could have gone worse.'

'Yes,' Aryx said, 'I could have ended up with my bloody lap on fire!'

'Oh, shut up. That'll hopefully teach you some manners around aliens. At least we now have a source for the mineral.'

'I suppose we're in for a trip?'

'If you want to come along. You're welcome to stay on the station if it's too much of an inconvenience.'

Aryx held up the melted lump. 'I can't really work on this without the console and, like you said, this place isn't necessarily secure. It's easiest if I just carry on working while you drive.'

'Fair enough. Computer, locate Sollers Hope.'

The computer remained silent for several seconds before speaking. 'There are three references to Sollers Hope in the Galactic database.'

'Wonderful. I knew I should have asked Braku for its location. Computer, show me the list with coordinates.'

The display changed and three entries appeared with coordinates within a light year of each other. At least they were all near the Quintoc system. The list read:

Sollers Hope
Sollars Hope
Sollershope

'What's the difference, apart from the spellings and locations?'

'Uncertain.'

'Entry dates?'

'The entries are grandfathered records and have no explicit insertion dates.'

'Utterly typical.'

'It's a bit weird,' Aryx said. 'But you know what the old surveys were like – all down to Human error at the end of the day. Someone probably sat there transcribing a hand sketched map or something and couldn't read the cartographer's writing.' He laughed.

'I don't know what to do. I guess we'll have to go for one of them, or …' He turned to Aryx. 'No, actually, let's aim for Quintoc itself. There's a node there, and the mine is likely to be close, isn't it?' He turned back to the console and addressed the computer again. 'Calculate a navigational path using relevant acceleration nodes. Oh, and don't log the flight path with the station's navsystem.'

'Why did you do that?' Aryx asked.

'If someone on the station is responsible for the explosion, I don't want them to know we're on the trail.'

'Good point.'

'It's a few hours away. We should probably bring some food along. I think the ship's got rations, but it's silly to waste them when we don't need to.' Sebastian moved over to the flight consoles and sat in the pilot seat.

'I'll go and get some. I need to stretch my tyres.'

Sebastian threw his credit tag to Aryx, who caught it and wheeled himself onto the lift.

While he waited for him to return, Sebastian studied the flight path. It would take them through a few acceleration nodes into a sparsely populated region of space. Sollers Hope – however it was spelt – would be sitting in Quintoc's single-star system, with only an asteroid field surrounding it. It didn't look like it would be fun navigating, and the coordinates, being approximate, didn't fill him with confidence; but locating Sollers Hope wouldn't pose too much of a problem if there was enough chatter coming from the colony once they got within range.

Aryx returned several minutes later with food packages in plastic containers. A portable heater unit and kettle were perched precariously on top of the load in his lap.

'You look like you've planned for a camping trip – I hope that's not a burner!'

'No, it's just a heater, not a flame. Jeez, I'm not *that* stupid.' He wheeled over to the cabin's chilled storage compartment and stowed away the food.

Sebastian programmed the computer with the departure procedure, and the docking crane once again lifted the ship into the shuttle transit system. Magnetic inductors drew it through the tubes towards the centripetal launch bay, where it slowed to a halt and hung motionless. The countdown started. Internal gravity plating came online and Sebastian slumped into the seat, his cheeks sagging.

'You alright?' he called, looking back.

Aryx had anchored his chair to the floor with his magnetic clamp. 'I'm okay.'

The ship slowly rotated until the bow pointed towards the outer rim of the station. Sebastian felt the blood being drawn to his face, the gravity plating holding him in place competing with the force of the station's rotation.

'This is really weird. I've never launched like this in a ship with gravity.'

'You'll be okay. Just don't throw up on the console.'

The launch doors drew apart, the countdown ended and, with a bile-shifting lurch, the station hurled the ship out into open space.

Chapter 7

The *Ultima Thule* shot out of Tenebrae like a stone from a sling. Its manoeuvring thrusters fired and it began to tumble, lining up along a trajectory that would take them close to the acceleration node. The engines burst into life, and it swung in a wide arc. The bright station slid by on the starboard side against the inky black of space and pastel tints of green and blue; the dazzling purple of the nebula ahead filled the windows, giving the interior of the cabin a violet wash.

'Beautiful, isn't it?' Aryx said.

'Yes, it is. I've never—' Sebastian jumped in his seat as Aryx pulled up beside him. 'Don't do that!'

'You didn't expect me to stay back there all the way, did you?'

He shook his head. 'Just make sure you clamp yourself back down. I don't know how she handles.'

Half an hour later the ship had almost reached the acceleration node. The dark steely sphere, several hundred metres across, hung in space, suspended within the twelve open faces of an iridescent blue dodecahedral frame. It could easily have been mistaken for a giant, angular single-celled organism.

The ship skirted the enormous framework, following a path outside the capture radius until it lined up along a tangent pointing in the direction of the next node, light years away. The *Ultima* accelerated until it skimmed the invisible envelope.

The framework fluoresced with a glow that rapidly increased in intensity before a surge of energy lanced out from the sphere like a lightning bolt tearing through space towards the ship. The stream hit and the ship flared brightly. In the blink of an eye, it was gone.

The stars ahead began to speed past the view from the ship, dimming as their light shifted towards the ultraviolet end of the spectrum and beyond. A moment later the filters on the windows engaged and compensated for the shift, making them visible once again.

Sebastian looked out of the starboard window. It was strange to see the light of the stars fading as they passed the ship. He knew if there were some way he could look behind the vessel, he'd see nothing – the light couldn't catch up with them. The view of space ahead shifted, as though it were a simulation of the galaxy played forward at high speed.

Sebastian's knuckles turned white, his fingers clamped around the armrests of the pilot's seat, and he bit back the urge to vomit as his internal organs rode at speed over an invisible bump in space. Aryx was doing better – his grin reminded Sebastian of his nephew when he'd taken him to an amusement park and ridden on a rollercoaster.

The lurches were horrible. He'd hated the feeling ever since he'd first found out what caused them during his first orientation flight . . .

He stood in the queue in the docking hangar on Tenebrae, waiting to board the training shuttle. Spaceflight was not something he had done regularly before leaving Earth, and all the trips he'd been on had been aboard passenger shuttles, with no exposure to the pilots, navigation, or even windows he could see out of. His stomach quivered with anticipation. Why were they taking so long to board? He leaned to one side to see past the column filing into the ship.

'I don't bloody care – I'm not getting out. You'll have to lower the ramp so I can board!'

He couldn't hear the other side of the conversation, and the only thing he could see of the loudest speaker was a muscular arm, gesticulating wildly.

'No, I'm not being carried aboard. You can piss off!'

A brown-uniformed official walked past the ship, speaking into his wristcom. 'Can you please lower the ramp? We have an awkward trainee who won't get on.'

The ramp at the front of the ship lowered and a figure in a wheelchair – evidently the animated speaker, judging by the size of his arms – shot out of the queue towards it.

A second official lowered the bottom lip of the ramp. 'Let me help you over the gap.'

The marine in the wheelchair – if that was a military-issue vest – slapped the hand away. 'I can manage myself.' He wheelied up over the gap.

Sebastian finally reached the front of the queue and walked up the steps into the shuttle.

'You're in row 6, seat A,' the official said, checking an infoslate.

Sebastian made his way through into the training room. At far end of the cabin was a large screen with the seats in front of it. It reminded him of a cinema. He took his place at the back, next to a space by the aisle.

The marine came down from the front of the ship and parked in the gap.

Sebastian grimaced inwardly. Please don't let him kick off again – space travel was bad enough without sitting next to an irate passenger.

The ship lifted off, and a few moments later the seatbelt warning light went out. A shaven-headed officer with a short grey moustache stepped out from a door in the forward section and stood in front of the screen.

'I am Sergeant Lombard, your instructor for this trip. The lesson for today is superphase dynamics.'

The screen lit up with a diagram of the space around Tenebrae and the group shifted in unison. Close to the station was a dodecahedron, representing the system's acceleration node.

The marine leaned over to Sebastian and whispered, 'They better not come out with a load of bollocks. You can't detect a ship when it passes a node, and nobody's ever managed to follow close enough to take readings.'

Sebastian didn't reply, but continued to listen to the instructor.

'—unfortunately, scientists have never been able to determine how they function, and even though the Bronadi and Antari have the capability to repair the nodes, their research into the mechanisms has been as fruitless as our own.'

'See? Told you. They don't know anything.'

He smiled. His stomach moved in his abdomen. 'What was that?'

'We've passed through the gravity-well of a star. Either that or through the star itself.'

'Oh my Gods! Why don't they tell us this stuff?'

The marine grinned. 'They probably don't want to scare you.'

'Mr Trevarian, do you have something to add?' Lombard shone his laser pointer on the marine's chest.

'Sir. No, Sir!'

'Then do you mind repeating what I just said?'

'No, Sir, but I wasn't paying attention, Sir!'

Lombard reddened. 'Know it all already, eh? Then why don't you come up and explain the need for accuracy during node jumps to your fellow students.'

'Sir! Yes, Sir!' The marine wheeled to the front of the cabin. Sebastian could barely see his head over the others.

The diagram on-screen had changed to a 2D image of the node positioned on the left with a circle around it. On the far right, there was a star system with a node and, at the top, a star without.

Trevarian shone the pointer on the circled node. 'This is an acceleration node, as you know. The ring around it is the capture radius. Its perimeter is one thousand metres from the outer points of the node scaffolding. You touch this and it'll send your ship along its current vector, in superphase.'

'Does it send you to the next node along?' someone near the front asked.

'No, it'll throw you light years in whatever direction you're going until the energy runs out. The only way to get near another node is to head straight for one.'

'So what happens if you miss?'

'This.' The display changed to show the ship flying past the node – in the wrong direction. It hit the radius and ended up 150 light years away in the gap between systems near the top right of the display. It began to inch its way back down. 'This is an assumed distance, but if this was the node's maximum distance, you'd miss, and it would take you one hundred and fifty years to get back.'

Someone else that Sebastian couldn't see put up their hand.

Lombard peered over the group. 'Yes, Tallin?'

'How long would it take at near lightspeed?'

'Remember your basic physics,' Lombard said. 'That *is* at lightspeed.'

A collective gasp issued from the group.

Lombard smiled. 'You'd do well to bear that feeling in mind. Always plan your jumps carefully because it'll take just as long for a mayday signal to get back.'

'Can't you turn if you miss?' Tallin asked.

'No. Your engines and thrusters won't alter your velocity during superphase transit.'

'But how do you stop a ship from crashing into a node at the other end?' Sebastian asked.

Lombard laughed. 'Navigation systems aren't accurate enough to make you hit it, for one, and that's part of the reason for the unexplored areas. Beyond fifty light years, the systems become rather inaccurate ... It would be like trying to hit a pinhead by throwing a grain of sand across this room, blindfolded. But, since you ask, the nodes seem to interact with the pressure wave from stars.'

'The heliosphere,' Trevarian said. 'When a ship approaches a node from superphase, the node usually pushes the ship out when it hits the heliosphere. On rare occasions it happens a bit later, and you can end up right inside a system.'

Lombard continued, 'Most of the nodes we know about are within an hour or two's superphase travel from each other, but when planning a trip, don't count on that timing being constant. Gravity, the rotation of the galaxy, and other factors come into play, and sometimes a return trip between the same pair of nodes can take up to twice as long.'

The display changed to a map with numerous tiny dots overlaid on the swirl of the Milky Way. Many of the dots were connected with lines.

'This is an overview of the known network. The exact range that an individual node can send a ship seems to be limited. The lines here represent known maximum travel distances – safe paths, if you like – between nodes.'

Sebastian put up his hand. 'Sir, some don't have lines going to them. Why is that?'

'There are no comms relays in those systems, and most of them are uninhabited. The lines represent the orientation of the relays – you can get a signal out of a system without relays, but they won't receive incoming signals from the network. It's the vital infrastructure that allows our real-time communication with other worlds in the network. The techs will give you the specifications if you're interested.' Lombard turned to the marine at his side and gestured for him to return to his place. Trevarian wheeled back to his spot.

'That was very informative,' Sebastian said, leaning over. 'My name's Sebastian Thorsson.'

'Pleased to meet you,' the marine said, shaking his hand. 'Aryx Trevarian.'

Lombard raised his voice. 'To continue the lesson, you will be instructed in how to program a flight path and set up the navigational computer. You'll go to the cockpit in pairs . . . '

Sebastian stared at the voids on the map now. Tantalising and terrifying – what unknowns might lurk in the dark spaces between? He had no real desire to venture into them; he simply wanted to reach Sollers Hope in one piece.

After an hour of travel in superphase, an alert sounded from the console and the ship dropped back to relativistic speeds. The stars slowed and dimmed, the window filtering flickered, and they finally settled back into static constellations. His stomach returned to its normal position in his abdomen. He hated the exit transition almost as much as the entry. Another alert sounded from the console. The computer had picked up the coordinates for the next acceleration node and plotted a course.

It took a matter of minutes for them to reach it. The ship repeated the process of navigating around the node and lining up at the tangent between it and their target system beyond. The ship accelerated past the node and was immediately catapulted into superphase once again. Sebastian's stomach did several more circuits of his abdominal cavity as the strange gravity-well effects contorted his innards.

Ninety minutes later the ship arrived at the planned destination,

Quintoc, the system that served as home to Sollers Hope. For an instant, Quintoc's blazing disc illuminated the cabin with a bright, white light. The window filters engaged, cutting out the damaging radiation and toning down the brightness to levels safe enough for Humans. Sebastian's eyes took a few moments to become accustomed to the view after the blinding flash. The signal scanners were disappointingly silent.

A band of black dotted with bright specks ran across the centre of the sun as though a giant glowing biscuit had been broken in half and left a smattering of stellar crumbs. Peering through the window, they both leaned forwards as though the extra few inches would help them see better.

'Is that ... the asteroid field?' Aryx asked.

'Oh, my Gods – it is!' They were probably heading straight into a cloud of rocks, invisible through the filters against the black of space. Sebastian hammered the manual thruster controls and a joystick popped up out of the console. He yanked it backwards. The thrusters kicked in, altering the ship's attitude, and the ship bucked. His face pulled down while the gravity plating tried to cope with the change in inertia as the engines forced the ship onto its new heading.

Aryx's wheelchair chair creaked from the strain. 'Woohoo!'

'You shouldn't be enjoying this!' Sebastian said through gritted teeth.

The ship headed out of the ecliptic plane, over the danger, and the sunlight started to reveal the extent of the asteroid field. Sebastian sat with his mouth open. If they had continued on their previous course at the same speed, they would have been peppered with small asteroids. As one of his instructors had once said, 'If the glass hits the rock, or the rock hits the glass – it sure as hell ain't going to hurt the rock!' Knowing that he wasn't going to end up as the glass, Sebastian eased off the controls.

The ship skimmed over the field and the scanners kicked into life with distorted chatter. The density of the field must have blocked the signals coming from the colony; the strongest concentration seemed to be coming from an area between the sun and the asteroids. They wouldn't have to scour the field trying to find Sollers Hope after all.

'That makes it a bit easier,' Aryx said.

'Yeah, I'm glad we don't have to fly through that. I'm not that prac-tised at high-speed manoeuvres, and I've got no intention of learning here.' Sebastian pressed a control on the console. Perhaps the scanners could resolve the signal's exact source.

Numerous signals appeared on the readout, most coming from min-ing ships deep within the asteroid field. After a few minutes of analysis, a stronger set of signals was located coming from a small planetoid several thousand kilometres away from the main field. Sebastian directed the navigation system to take them to it.

As they approached, the planetoid came into view. It looked like a smaller, knobbly version of Earth's moon, with a clear indication of civilisation; a huge crater dominated the large flat expanse facing the ship, the rim of which extended upward like a ring of small mountains, spanned with a glinting geodesic dome. Several hundred metres away from it, on a low rise, stood a tall, white radio mast, shining in the sunlight. Many smaller industrial-looking structures lay scattered around, connected to the main dome by thin tube-like tunnels, half-buried in the dust. A much larger tube ran along the ground from the main dome to a building that resembled a submerged cylinder lying on its side.

'Is that an old-fashioned hangar?' Aryx asked.

'It looks like it.' Sebastian rubbed his chin. 'I'd say *very* old-fashioned.' He activated the comms. 'This is *Talaga* class shuttle *Ultima Thule* to Sollers Hope colony, requesting permission to land.'

Silence.

They stared at each other for several seconds. Was anybody listening? Were they even welcome?

A woman's voice spoke. 'This is Sollers Hope control. Welcome, *Ultima Thule*, please wait for the green landing lights before proceeding to the hangar. You are allocated bay six. Please engage magnetic repulsors when landing, and a taximech will tow your ship to the allocated bay. Extend your landing gear only when the taximech indicates, again with a green light.'

'Acknowledged, control.' Sebastian closed the comms and, heaving a sigh of relief, programmed the descent into the navsystem. 'I almost thought they wouldn't let us land.'

Light flashed in his face as the facets of the geodesic dome caught the sun. The ship's altitude decreased and the glare from the airless rock became more intense. He found that he couldn't look at the surface for long before he had to turn away, almost blinded. The descent thrusters fired and the ship came to a halt with a bounce as the magnetic repulsors engaged with the coils in the landing pad.

A small, metallic dome-shaped machine topped with a long, flexible antenna and red flashing light trundled out of the hangar on a rail and moved across the landing strip towards them. Once it reached the levitating ship, the taximech extended a long arm. A loud *clunk* echoed through the ship, and the little robot dragged them along its track to the hangar.

They eventually came to a standstill in bay six. Sebastian waited until the light on top of the mech turned green before extending the landing struts and turning down the power on the repulsors. The ship settled on the ground with a soft thump. There was a second, more muffled *clunk*.

Sebastian jumped up. 'What was that?'

'Docking cowl, probably. Nothing to worry about.'

Butterflies fluttered in his stomach as he prepared to leave the ship. He hadn't realised how excited he'd become about the prospect of setting foot on solid ground.

Aryx enthusiastically wheeled himself towards the lift. He almost couldn't believe he was finally off the station.

'Where are you going?' Sebastian asked.

'I'm coming with you.'

'I thought you were going to stay on the ship.'

'Not if there's an opportunity to get out and about. I'm sick of being stuck indoors. I need some different air.' He pressed the *Down* button before Sebastian could protest.

Sebastian mumbled something unintelligible before climbing down the ladder after him.

'I heard that.'

He sneered and mouthed something. As he walked past, Aryx reached out and slapped his leg with the back of his hand, causing him to yelp.

'I'll come back to finish the analysis on the evidence once I've had a change of scenery.'

'I was only joking.'

Aryx wasn't so sure. Since the beginning of the investigation Sebastian had begun to seem more and more irritated – perhaps he was worried they might not find the evidence they needed.

Sebastian stood at the airlock door and, after being given the green light, opened it and walked down the ramp. Aryx followed in his wheelchair and skidded at the bottom causing a plume of dust to billow up from the docking cowl floor. Stale, metallic dusty air hit his face. His eyes watered and he choked on the gritty stuff – you could barely call it air; it was like breathing in sand.

'Wait a sec,' he rasped, and wheeled back up the ramp to grab a pair of respiration filters from the pressure suit locker. He handed one of the masks to Sebastian, who quickly strapped it to his face, covering his nose, mouth, and chin. Aryx put his on. The difference was immediately noticeable. At least he could breathe again without his lungs being stripped bare.

'That's better, thanks.' Sebastian's eyes smiled. He probably hadn't wanted to be the first to complain.

Aryx wheeled along behind him as he approached the airlock at the end of the cowl.

'Why are you staying back there?'

'It's your mission. You lead!' Aryx said, grinning beneath the mask.

Sebastian activated the control on the airlock. The door closed behind them and Aryx's ears popped. The doors at the other end opened, revealing a dark space beyond.

Sebastian stepped out. 'The floor's level here, come on.'

Aryx wheeled out over the lip of the airlock and immediately the floor beneath his wheels changed. It was rough and loose.

'I don't see any guards or customs officers,' Sebastian said. 'They must be quite trusting.'

'Or don't care.'

Sebastian shrugged and continued into the darkness, his footsteps throwing up puffs of white dust.

Aryx's eyes had just become accustomed to the gloom when lights came on, creating a pattern of alternating light and dark on the arched ceiling nearest to them. He guessed they were in the long tube-like structure they'd seen on approach and that the roof curving over was probably sunk directly into the surface of the planetoid below them. He noticed a pair of long tracks extending into the shadows. The tracks formed a large U-shape at the near end where a short, open-topped train – a mixture of passenger trucks and lidded cargo hoppers – sat on the rails. A red arrow painted on the side of each cart pointed to the left.

Sebastian walked towards the cart at the front and sat down on the farthest of the rudimentary seats.

Aryx frowned. 'There's no way to get my chair in.'

The ground sloped up to the level of the truck floor but the opening didn't look wide enough for the chair to fit. He didn't feel like asking Sebastian to lift him into the truck – he had his dignity to think about, after all. He got the fleeting urge to go back to the ship and get the mobipack but thought better of it; he had no desire to reveal the design before he'd registered the patent.

'Is it too narrow?'

'Yes, and it's a shame you didn't notice before,' he growled. He didn't care whether Sebastian knew how irritated he was. He wheeled back down the slope and moved farther along the queue to examine the cargo hopper behind. The top was sealed with a roller shutter. He pressed a button at the back and it slid open. The next button displayed an icon indicating that the side would drop, so he pressed it, and the panel lowered to the ground.

'I think I can ride in this.' He wheeled up over the panel into the truck and reached over the top to press the button again. The side closed and he fastened his chair to the floor with the clamp. 'I'm ready now. Let's go!'

The train accelerated into the dark tunnel. Wind rushed through his hair, bending his Mohawk back. The breeze carried particles of grit that flicked painfully into his eyes and he had to close them. Lights flashed through his eyelids, and he tried not to imagine the tracks leading off into a dark, bottomless chasm.

The tunnel seemed longer than the three miles he'd guessed it to be from above, and it took four long minutes of skin-abrading and bone-shaking travel before they finally came to a stop at the far end.

Aryx opened his eyes and blinked several times in an attempt to clear the grit. The cart had come to a standstill in a well-lit area where the tunnel terminated in a dark, rocky wall with a large cargo airlock set in the centre. Sebastian got off and helped him out. As they approached the airlock, the ground beneath his wheels still felt uneven and loose. The floor in the colony had better not be the same.

After a few moments of decontaminant spray in the airlock, the doors to the colony opened.

Chapter 8

Motes of dust sparkled on the air as blinding sunlight streamed in through the open door. Aryx had to look down at the ground while his eyes adjusted. He rolled down over the lip of the airlock on to a dusty, concrete-like floor covered in dark footprints.

'Wow, that's impressive.'

Aryx shielded his eyes as he looked up to see what Sebastian was talking about. The dome began where the jagged crater wall ended, nearly a hundred metres above. Its triangular panels each held an internal mirror. He studied them and realised they were focusing sunlight on a spot somewhere in the middle of the dome. As his gaze followed the path of the dusty beams, he noticed the roofs of the nearest buildings. The structures were all made of smooth, grey blocks, similar in colour to the floor, and blended an ancient flat-roofed architectural style with contemporary metal fittings and windows. People moved to and fro between the buildings, apparently ignoring the visitors.

'What, no welcoming committee?' he said to nobody in particular.

Sebastian didn't respond; his attention seemed set on the dome.

'I wonder if they mined the stone for these buildings from this rock. Are you listening to me?'

'What? Possibly. I guess the cylinder over there might be some kind of solar generator.' Sebastian pointed. 'And those mirrors seem to be moving ever so slowly to track the sun.'

Aryx followed the line of his finger. Now that the pair had moved closer, he could see the buildings surrounded a large, vertical capsule-shaped drum that stood in the centre of the dome. 'You're right. I couldn't see where they were aiming from back there with the buildings in the way.' He stopped to study the nearest building. 'I bet they've only got glass in the windows for sound insulation and security. Other than for light, you wouldn't really need them, would you?'

'I suppose not. But wouldn't they be screwed if the dome broke or got hit by an asteroid? That's got to be a constant worry.'

Aryx wheeled over to the nearest building and examined the window frame; it was not particularly well made – just a single, thin pane. 'Well, I don't think they'd be airtight in a vacuum if it did break.'

The air became warmer as they approached the cylinder. The small streets between the buildings appeared to lead towards it – a focal point of sorts. Small groups of people congregated in the vicinity, chatting.

Several small, dried-up trees stood forlornly on the withered grass around the support struts. Aryx made a face in disgust when he spotted them – they'd obviously been forgotten about.

Sebastian approached a passer-by. Her clothes – like those of the other inhabitants – seemed simple and practical, dusty and unadorned with fashion accessories. Her long, straight hair was tinged with a blue-grey sheen, most likely from the dust. 'Excuse me,' Sebastian said, 'could you help us? We're new here.'

She eyed him up and down, and gave him a withering look. 'That's obvious. You can take the mask off, the air's fine in here,' she said, folding her arms and shifting her weight to one side. 'What do you want?'

Aryx pulled his mask down and allowed it to hang loosely around his neck. The air was better – not by much, but he decided to keep the mask off rather than appear rude.

Sebastian loosened his mask. 'I'm looking for whoever is responsible for trade and commerce.'

'Garvin Havlor. You can find him over there,' she said, pointing at a building to the right of the square. 'In the civic office.'

'Thank you. Before we go – what's the correct spelling of Sollers Hope? There seem to be a few variations on our maps.'

She sighed sharply. 'It's Sollers Hope with an "e"!' she said, and with a toss of her hair, spun away.

'What the hell's her problem?' Aryx asked.

'Maybe they have a thing about the misspelling? It must be a sore point.'

They made their way across the square towards the civic building – an imposing edifice built in regency style. Two fluted columns stood either side of a pair of double doors at the top of a set of stone steps. The columns seemed out of place, given the roof of the building was flat.

Aryx looked for a ramp but couldn't find one. Typical. 'I'm going to explore for a bit – I can't get in there,' he said, and wheeled off to leave Sebastian to go in on his own.

Coloured shafts of light struck in through pretentious stained-glass windows set high up in the walls of the civic office. Rows and rows of bookcases lined with hundreds of tomes and file-boxes stood either side of the main walkway. The cool air carried with it the odour of damp and decay. Sebastian ran his finger along one of the shelves, ploughing a furrow in the dense grey substrate. Obviously the place was a hall of records of some kind – the kind that got ignored.

A rotund man wearing a dirty, red velvet jacket stood at the far end of the room next to a heavy wooden desk, sorting through papers. His lank, shoulder-length grey hair and goatee only added to the air of neglect.

Sebastian wondered whether this was how an old-fashioned mop would look if it were trimmed and had glasses put on it. He cleared his throat.

The man looked up over his tiny, gold-rimmed spectacles. 'Can I help you?' His Galac was tainted with a distinctly South-Western English accent.

'Yes, sorry,' Sebastian said, trying to get the image of the mop out of his head. 'I'm looking for a Mr Havlor.'

'You've found him.' Havlor tossed the papers back onto the pile on the desk and approached Sebastian, smiling, with his hand extended. 'Please, call me Garvin.'

Sebastian shook the offered hand. 'Pleased to meet you, Garvin. My name is Sebastian Thorsson, attached to Tenebrae station. I'm on assignment for Special Projects and Operations.'

'Never heard of it . . . So, what can Garvin Havlor do for Special Projects and Operations?'

'I was told you were in charge of the trading arrangements around here.'

'That's right. I'm also the town mayor. Welcome to my office,' Garvin said, gesturing at the surroundings. 'And how can I help you as Minister of Trade?'

'I'm trying to track down an unusual mineral.'

Garvin sat down behind the desk. He rested his chin in one hand, propped up by an elbow, and raised an eyebrow. 'Are you indeed? What sort of unusual mineral are we talkin' about?'

How many unusual minerals did they have? Sebastian could tell that he might prove difficult to manage if he gave him the run-around. 'I'll be straight with you, Garvin. There was a recent attack on the station and we have very few leads – I'm investigating the incident on behalf of SpecOps.' He waited to gauge his reaction.

'Go on,' Garvin said, his expression giving nothing away.

'We found trace evidence of a mineral that appears to evaporate in atmosphere, has a very low atomic weight given the size of the particles, and seems to be inert. We don't think it was used to cause the explosion, as we found no trace at the scene itself, only leading to it. A Bronadi commodities broker said that you might be able to supply such a mineral.'

'I see.' Garvin tapped his chin. 'We *do* have such a thing. We nicknamed it carbyne powder when we found it, as we thought it was reacting with other compounds during testing, so we labelled it as a reactive intermediary, but you're right, we later found that it was inert. It's useless due to the way that it just fizzles out. We've done tests and it looks like the subatomic instability means when molecules in the air bump into it, the bonds between the atoms break down, evaporating it. That makes it useless, even as a nanolubricant. That said, we still have two clients that buy it for a modest fee.'

Finally, the investigation was going somewhere. 'Do you have their details on file?'

'No.'

'Why not?'

'One man's cash is as good as anyone else's, an' we don't see a need for recording the transactions as they're only buying a useless by-product. It wouldn't be cost-effective in admin time. It would be like keepin' accounts for dumpin' trash into the sun.'

Sebastian didn't believe the excuse, but decided not to press the issue directly. 'So . . . you have no way of knowing where the shipments go?'

'Not a clue. One of 'em pays us to leave a hopper in an empty system, where I s'pose they collect it, and the other sends someone to get it. I get the feeling they're a bit paranoid.'

'What makes you say that?' He folded his arms.

'The courier goes over the shipment with a scanner before leaving. God knows what they're worried about.'

How was he going to bypass a scanner?

Garvin waved a finger at him. 'Don't you think about trying to sneak bleedin' trackers in the loads – we got our reputation to think about!'

'I wouldn't dream of it. I'll have to pursue other avenues.'

The man's features softened. 'There anything else I can help you with?'

Sebastian relaxed a little at the shift in Garvin's tone and decided to change the subject to something less sensitive. 'Actually, I was curious how this place copes with the possibility of asteroids from the field impacting the dome.'

Garvin grinned. 'It posed an interesting problem for them when the colony was founded.' He leaned back and touched his fingertips together in a triangle. 'Warren Soller solved the problem over 'undred years ago when he designed the dome. The mirrors we use to aim sunlight onto our generator not only provide heat and power for the town, but they also snap shut in the event of a panel break. In addition to that, we track all of the asteroid bodies and can destroy, divert, or capture anything that risks the integrity of the dome.'

Sebastian nodded. 'I take it he was the colony's founder?'

'Indeed he was. He was one of the great space pioneers before we encountered the nodes. In fact, he was probably the first person to encounter one, but you won't find any official proof of it.'

Garvin seemed proud of his anecdote. There was no way it was accurate of course – it had taken Humans thirty-two years to find out about the acceleration nodes after the first colonists had left, and Quintoc was at least eighty light years away from Earth. Sebastian decided not to push it, and instead feigned interest, cupping his chin with his right hand and holding his elbow with the other.

Garvin continued, 'Warren searched lots of systems with the early survey telescopes. This field seemed promising, but everyone said he was mad for attempting to come here. Before we'd found the nodes, the trip would have taken him decades, but he brought his family here anyway in the hope of finding rich mineral deposits.

'He set out in a near-lightspeed ship and started off by building a small dome outside the crater, near the mast, where he set up the mine. He found several minerals that were rare on Earth, and after a few years decided to head back to let people know what he'd found and to get resources to expand the operation. On his way he encountered a node, and luckily he was heading in exactly the right direction to get back to Earth.'

Sebastian stepped back on one foot. It *would* have been an incredible coincidence if it had been anything other than propaganda. The likelihood of passing a node on the correct vector purely by accident was infinitesimal.

Garvin's flat stare made it obvious that he hadn't masked his disbelief well enough, but he continued, undeterred. 'When he got back, he found Earth had moved on and they'd already discovered the nodes in the decades since he'd left. It had only been a few years to him, of course. He brought back resources and a crew, expanded the colony, and discovered the deposits of ore we now export.'

'And what is the main export?' Sebastian did his best to look impressed.

'It has an unpronounceable alien name, but we call it false peacock ore, or false bornite because it's basically a mixture of bornite and a few other minerals that aren't found anywhere else. The false bornite is used to repair the struts on the acceleration nodes, you know. Warren must have been led here by the hand of God, finding it and then encounterin' the node like that.'

'I'm sure . . . If the by-product, carbyne, is so useless, why do these clients of yours buy it?'

'For some reason, it's found in a pure form in deposits on this rock, alongside the false bornite. The carbyne deposits themselves aren't useful, as I explained, and because the compound is so unstable, it's very difficult to keep. Why they want it, I got no idea – that's their business. But because the stuff only survives for extended periods in a vacuum, we're the best place to get it.'

Sebastian felt like he was on a rollercoaster. How odd to be travelling down a path that led right to the source of the minerals that kept space travel alive. Could there be some bigger significance to this carbyne? What on Earth was it doing on the station, and why would people want it if it was useless? He had to stop thinking about it; it was threatening to bring up too many questions. 'What's the deal with the Galactic maps having the wrong names and location for this place?'

Garvin's face reddened to match his jacket. 'We been lobbyin' for years to get the name changed on the maps.' Spit flew from his mouth as his voice accelerated, his accent becoming even more rural. 'They kip telling us that "it 'ent possible" or "there 'ent no central map, so we can't change it". If that was true, then who the fuck *is* responsible for changin' it?'

Sebastian's skin prickled; the tension in the room was almost tangible.

Garvin paused and took a deep breath. 'Obviously, we don't know the reason. Maybe the locations were wrong because Warren logged the position before leaving, and the system had moved during his time at near lightspeed, or perhaps additional records were added later. Who knows? It's probably the same with the namin'. The spelling may have been interpreted wrong.' His chest was heaving rapidly again – there was no longer any question as to whether it was a touchy subject.

'Well, I must be going,' Sebastian said. 'Thank you for your help. I've taken up enough of your time. I'll let you get back to your duties.' He gestured at the heap of paperwork.

Garvin stood and they shook hands again. 'It was nice meeting you, and please put people right about the name if you get the opportunity. It's Sollers Hope with an "e" and no apostrophe,' he said, forcing a brief grin. 'And you obviously know the coordinates.'

Aryx headed across the square to the other side of town. The streets were narrow but not claustrophobic, and the ground was uneven, gravelly and dusty in places, but for the most part hard and smooth. Other than that, the town was relatively clean and people seemed conscientious enough not to litter. One thing that struck him was the lack of plants. While the sunlight was focused at the centre, elsewhere it wasn't as intense. Maybe there wasn't enough light to support much plant life – it was probably low on their list of priorities. As he passed the cylinder in the town square, he spotted warning signs on the pipes going to and from it, labelled *Beware, Corrosive!* The pipes appeared to run to a small pumping station, as did many of the electrical cables.

The street terminated a short distance from the crater wall where it housed another airlock, several feet wide. Next to the doors stood a large map mounted in a metal frame; it depicted a section through the planetoid drawn in schematic style with Sollers Hope town set at the top. It showed a processing station several hundred metres below the surface and, judging by the size of the airlock and trucks he had passed, minerals probably came from there right through the town – it certainly explained the presence of so much dust. His eyes followed the line of the surface around the map. Several ports led into the core; the entire planetoid was a giant ants' nest riddled with minerals. The thought of ants scurrying underground sent his mind back to the half-remembered dream. Plants shuffled in his memory and he shuddered. He shook his head in an attempt to rid himself of the vision and turned his attention to the key inset at the bottom right of the map. Dashed lines indicated a conveyor system, while small boxes with arrows depicted the transit of sealed hoppers, towed up and down out of the core by a system of belts and cables.

Curiosity sated, he abandoned the map and moved off to explore the town further when his attention was caught by a tiny flash of light in space above. He stared up through the dome. Another flash. He squinted, trying to see past the dusty sunrays. Two more flashes, and the glint of metal in the sun: a ship, mining asteroids with fragmentation charges. It all seemed a little archaic. Something tensed in his neck – time to move on before he got a knot.

After exploring the town for several minutes further, he returned to the civic building in the square. Sebastian stood at the foot of the steps, staring up at the cylinder with a faint smile.

'You look like you're enjoying the warmth.'

'I am. It was a bit chilly in there.'

Aryx smiled to himself. Obviously several years in Britain and three on Tenebrae was enough to reduce the Icelander's resistance to the cold to wimpish levels.

Sebastian turned and started to walk up the street towards the docking area. 'I don't think the thermal buffer's that great in this suit.'

'It depends if it's got liquid in it,' Aryx said, following him.

Sebastian tugged at the straw in his collar and sucked it. 'It's empty. I've evidently not been urinating enough to keep it full.'

Aryx cringed. 'I hope you're joking.'

'Not joking . . . I haven't urinated in it at all.'

He laughed. 'You can be disgusting at times! So what did you learn from Havlor?'

'The mineral is known locally as carbyne, and it's found alongside deposits of the metal the node struts are made from.'

'Really?'

Sebastian nodded. 'It's only produced here in large quantities because, as we guessed, there's no atmosphere in the mines so it's stable. We're going to have to investigate the clients ourselves. He's got no records.'

'How incredibly useful.'

'Did you find anything interesting?'

'I did. The cylinder provides energy and heat for the facility. You should see the map of the place – it's like a termite mound.'

'That explains the lack of insulation in the buildings. They don't need much environmental protection individually. Garvin said the mirrors in the dome can cover breaks until they're repaired.'

'I can't see how that would protect them if the entire dome got crushed.' The idea of mirrors flipping shut seemed a little inadequate.

'He assured me they're confident about not getting hit by anything large.'

Aryx wasn't convinced – certainly not to the point where he'd believe it was safe to live there. 'Where to now?'

Sebastian scratched his head. 'Back to the ship, I think. We'll have to come up with a plan to track where the shipments go, but we'll have to use a method that won't get picked up by security scanners.'

'You'll have to use a small device, then.' Aryx pondered while they passed through the airlock and made their way to the cargo trucks. 'We don't have any trackers small enough to be undetectable by scans.'

'I know,' Sebastian said as he helped him into the cart. 'I'll have to think of something.'

They rode the cargo train to the other end of the line. This time Aryx remembered to keep his eyes shut. He was sure he could hear the cogs in Sebastian's brain ticking loudly over the noise of the cart screaming along.

Back on the ship, Sebastian fumbled around in his rucksack and drew out the vial of nanobots.

'Do you think you can do something with these?' he asked, placing it on the diagnostic console in front of Aryx.

'Jeez – good idea! We could program them to assemble into a tracker at a later date.' Aryx pulled up a set of tracker schematics on the computer. 'Fairly easy. Just a case of transmitting this pattern to them.' He tapped a few buttons and the silvery liquid in the vial began crawling up the glass towards the stopper. 'Done. That was easy. They should start building slowly.' He handed the container back. 'It depends on the environmental conditions and how much metal they can harvest. If the carbyne has some of this false peacock bornite stuff mixed in with it, they'll use that. How are you going to deploy them anyway?'

'We'll take the ship out to one of the mine ports. I'll sneak in, find a deposit, and sprinkle them in one of the containers, or on the stuff directly. That way, when it's picked up by the clients, they won't get detected. We'll have to return to the station and use the long-range sensors to pick up the signal.'

He was about to object, but Sebastian had already gone to the cockpit and initiated the launch protocols. He felt the ship lift up on the magnetics and the clunk as the taximech towed them out of the hangar.

Sebastian piloted the ship low over the surface of the planetoid and, after twenty minutes of searching, the scanners picked up a prominent vein beneath a small metallic dome. He landed the ship close to the barnacle-shaped entrance and disappeared downstairs. He was already half-dressed in a pressure suit when Aryx caught up with him.

'The mines all connect up in the core,' Aryx said, 'but it would be best to plant the bots in a deposit that's about to get mined, otherwise the trackers could end up forming before it gets taken. Hoppers come up and down from the core, but be careful – without a map, you'll have no idea whether the shaft you're in goes all the way through, or if it just ends.' He wished he'd taken a photograph, or paid more attention to the map when he'd studied it.

Sebastian locked his helmet in place, took the rugged infoslate from his pack, and tucked the vial in his belt. 'I shouldn't be long. I've got a sample tube, so I'll try to get some of the mineral. I'll plant the bots and then get out as soon as possible.'

'Just be careful, okay? I don't want to have to come and rescue you if things go pear-shaped.'

'I'll be careful, I promise.'

Aryx watched through the slender vertical slit of the airlock's observation window as Sebastian disappeared out onto the barren, airless rock.

Sunlight reflecting off the planetoid dazzled Sebastian for a moment before the visor filter kicked in. The view disoriented him: the horizon curving away, the stars slowly turning overhead – he could fall down at any moment. He lumbered towards the metal carbuncle, feeling a little lighter than he had in the main dome. The colony probably had artificial gravity assistance.

As he approached the door to the mine-port, he thought it didn't look like an airlock, more of a maintenance access hatch, and too small for a load of ore to be shipped through. He inspected the large panel installed next to it. A security terminal. His instinct to bring the rugged infoslate was well-founded; the locking software appeared to be based on some rather outdated protocols. He started probing the system with the computer and prayed scanning it wouldn't cause an alarm in the colony. At least his skills were useful to SpecOps, even if it was a breach of his professional integrity – but there wasn't time to go through official channels. The security of the station was paramount.

Several moments later the locking mechanism popped open to reveal a manual hatch release. He grabbed the red lever and pumped it up and down several times. The door opened silently in the vacuum, but moved with difficulty – if there had been air to transmit the sound, it would probably have been heard miles away. The doorway revealed a tunnel that descended at a steep angle. He couldn't see far; the light from the sun cast harsh, black shadows and even the tiny amount that reflected off his suit, backed by the glare of the surface, illuminated only a small portion of the interior. An uneasy déjà vu passed over him and he shuddered. He activated the torch installed on the left cuff of the pressure suit and stepped in.

The cave floor headed down at nearly forty-five degrees. Walking down the slope, his feet slipped on the loose, dusty floor, and he occasionally had to put his hands out to steady himself. Luckily the lower gravity made going down easier work, but it still wore out his legs. He crept onward in the dim light, trying to keep the torch aimed as low as possible – he didn't want to risk attracting any undue attention from anyone who might be in the mine, after all.

Sebastian trudged on down the grey tunnel, keeping one eye on the scans. Every time he turned a bend, he was certain it would pick up something – evidently the range wasn't as good as the scanners on the ship. The passage undulated for several hundred metres and after an hour the infoslate finally detected the ore vein. Should he dose some of the mineral in the nearest deposit? It would save time, but would it get mined before the nanobots converted into trackers? Probably not.

After another two hundred metres the tunnel ended abruptly, opening into a dark, vertical shaft. He shone his torch across the expanse. It was five or six metres wide, at most. A cable ran up the centre, trailing off into darkness, and he could barely make out small metallic lumps attached to it. They must be the fixings for the hoppers. Something about the shaft felt familiar, unpleasantly familiar, and it looked like the only way down was to climb.

He glanced at the infoslate and tried to memorise the layout. The readings indicated faint life-signs farther down, but not exactly where – there was too much rock. There was no way he could carry the infoslate down there with him; he'd have to leave it and be careful about not getting spotted. He put it on the floor at the side of the tunnel and stacked several small rocks to hide it.

The cable hung three metres away from the edge of the opening. He took a few steps back and made a gentle running jump. The low gravity made it easy but he nearly oversailed the cable and hit it hard. It vibrated and he fumbled to grab it as it flicked back and forth like a giant piano string – with him sliding down it.

Oh Gods, what was he doing? He must have been insane to come here! He closed his grip around the cable and squeezed his legs together.

A cloud of tiny fibres billowed from his hands while the metal cord slowly ate its way through the outer skin of the gloves.

He closed his eyes. He knew it. He was going to die!

Chapter 9

Sebastian slid down the cable and stopped when something hit his feet, jarring his legs. He opened his eyes and looked down. What a fool he was. He'd only slid a couple of metres before his feet had encountered one of the clamps. Praying that the vibrations wouldn't be noticed by anyone working in the mine, he started climbing down, hand over hand, resting at each of the attachments for several seconds.

The heavy, impenetrable darkness above began to enclose him. It pressed down on him, bringing the sense of déjà vu back, but he still couldn't place the original memory. As he thought about it, the hair on the back of his neck started to stand on end, causing him to itch – a most unpleasant sensation inside the suit and one he couldn't alleviate. What on Earth possessed people to go crawling about in potholes for fun?

Hand over hand, inch by inch, he lowered himself down the cable. His arms began to tire, and a cramp forming in his right forearm forced him to stop and flex his fingers for a few moments. If he'd thought about it properly beforehand, he could have brought proper climbing gear with drive motors and everything. Was there no end to the cable? Surely he'd been climbing for hours. With no infoslate to guide him, he had no idea how far away his target was. He swallowed hard. He wanted to climb back up, to abandon the hunt, but he'd gone too far to turn back. Just a few more metres and then he'd stop.

There was no sign of an opening as he shone the torch downwards, but he carried on. It was best not to look down too often. His foot struck another object, causing a dull pain in his ankle. He looked down to see the square top of a sealed ore hopper.

'At last!' he shouted. But where was the opening? He turned around to see where the hopper could have come from. Typical. The tunnel was behind him. A dim bluish light emanated from the depths of the passage. That must be where the carbyne is.

He stepped back as far as he could on the lid and, holding on to the cable with his left hand, he braced himself and swung forwards, leaping from the edge of the container. He landed, clearing the lip of the tunnel by mere inches.

Ten metres ahead the tunnel branched off to the left into darkness, while the main path continued for several metres before turning sharply to the right towards the source of illumination. The light changed in intensity, flickering and shifting; either its source was unstable or movement nearby was causing shadows.

He deactivated the torch, crouched down behind a protruding rock near the bend, and set the suit's comms to open receive. He held his breath and tried not to move, even though he was well aware that nobody could hear him in the airless mine. The incoming signal was poor; faint, unintelligible distorted speech met his ears.

After a couple of minutes the erratic light dimmed, as though the source was moving farther down the tunnel, and the crackling in his helmet began to fade. He moved closer to the rock and peered over.

The tunnel was empty except for a mining drill propped up against a seam of ore. There were deep furrows in the ground dust. Whoever was working had probably dragged a hopper with them. The light dimmed even more, and he crept out from behind the rock and walked over to the glimmering mineral vein near the drill. His eyes became lost in the blue-green iridescence, sparkling in the faint light, and he ran his right hand along the vein, tracing it with his glove where it coruscated along the wall. His fingers slipped as the ore gave way to a smooth, powdery surface. He turned on the torch and, shielding it with his body, shone the light on his gloved hand. As he rubbed his fingers together, the soft carbyne sprinkled off with a dusty effluence, like powdered talc.

Taking the sample tube and multi-tool from the suit's belt, he began searching for a patch of the mineral that could be scraped off. He found a piece that jutted out and, holding the sample tube below it, scraped and tapped the section with the blade until the piece broke off, landing in the tube. He pressed in the rubber stopper and popped it into his belt. The crackling in his helmet intensified. Time to deploy the nanobots.

He took the vial of mercurial liquid from his belt and found a gap in the bornite seam large enough for his hand to fit through. Reaching in, he flipped off the stopper and poured the nanobots over the exposed carbyne. They flowed like molten metal, spreading out thinly over the surface, locking on to the mineral's signature. Within seconds the fluid was all but invisible. He turned and made his way back down the passage – just as the light from the tunnel behind him brightened.

He dodged around the corner and turned off the torch, looking back only after he'd concealed himself behind the rock. The miners had returned dragging a full hopper. A cable with a carabineer attached trailed behind them. They didn't stop at the seam.

Cold sweat prickled his spine before being absorbed by the N-suit. He'd expected the miners to stop there. He turned around and made his way back towards the shaft. He wouldn't have time to jump on the cable and climb up out of their view, and certainly not in the dark; he needed another option. As he ran his right hand along the wall in the dim light, it fell away. Of course, the branch in the tunnel!

The crackling voices got louder. Oh Gods, they were going to catch him!

The light brightened and, in a moment of panic, he turned right. Stumbling over a rock, he pitched forwards onto the floor. If they caught him now he'd lose his only evidence, and what would SpecOps do? Fire him. Goodbye money, goodbye Tenebrae, goodbye to your education, Erik. His heart pounded furiously and his pulse raced in his ears while he lay in the darkness, praying not to be seen.

The crackling and flickering subsided. They must have gone!

Sebastian stood, took a deep breath in an attempt to calm down, and looked around the corner. Now they had passed him by, he wanted to see how they were going to connect the hopper to the cable running up the shaft.

Two miners stood at the mouth of the tunnel. One of them held the cable attached to the hopper and the other held something like a long speargun. The first held the container at the edge of the shaft while the other clipped the hopper cable to the end of the gun and reached out with it towards the vertical cable. It extended and attached the hopper cable's clasp above one of the fixings. The other miner activated something on his suit cuff and the cable pulled taut. Within moments the hopper was dragged out of the tunnel and up the shaft. The pair turned around and headed back towards where Sebastian was hidden.

He ducked back into the darkness and waited until the ground vibrated through his feet. With luck they would be working the dosed seam, round the bend. He switched on the torch and made his way to the shaft.

The fixings inched their way up the cable ahead of him like metal slugs climbing a thread. There was no choice but to jump for it again. He took a few steps back and made a running leap, this time being careful not to overestimate how far he'd go, and caught hold of the cable with less difficulty than before. At least this time the cable was moving.

He hung on until he spotted the side tunnel from which he'd first entered – had it really only taken a couple of minutes to get that far? The cable carried him several feet past the opening and, after leaning forwards, he pushed against the taut steel with his feet and let go.

An eternity passed before his feet touched the edge of the side tunnel. Touched it, and slipped on the loose dust. He flailed wildly with his arms – it didn't help.

He fell.

Chapter 10

Sebastian hit the edge of the passage with a painful thump as he fell. He scrabbled at the ground in an attempt to halt his backward slide. If he lost his grip now, he'd plunge into the inky blackness of the planetoid's core – or on to a protruding rock below. The sense of déjà vu returned, adding to his already mounting fear. His helmet steamed up with the sweat from his exertions making it impossible to see.

He clawed at the ground and his fingers finally found purchase on a ridge in the rock, halting his backward slide at chest height. He swung his right leg up, catching the edge with his heel and, with a last exhausted, desperate heave, dragged himself up and over onto his back.

He lay in the passage for several minutes, breathing heavily, while he waited for the condensers in the suit to soak up the moisture.

That was too close.

Aryx hated being on his own, especially so far from home. It was fine on the station, but not here. The ship seemed so lonely – even listening to news transmissions hadn't managed to banish the emptiness. The wiring of the melted plastic lump was almost finished. It had been difficult work. His hands ached with cramp, his eyes were sore from focusing on tiny components, and he desperately needed to sleep.

The airlock entry alarm went off and he dropped the lump and its delicate wires on the console. 'Jeez, for crying out loud, don't do that!' he shouted, and wheeled over to the lift.

When he got to the bottom, he found Sebastian taking off the pressure suit.

'Did you manage to plant the nanobots?'

'I found a deposit and put the whole lot on it. The miners were on their way back to work as I left. I nearly killed myself doing it – those shafts are dangerous.' He wiped the dust off the infoslate and handed it over.

'For Christ's sake, I told you to be careful! Look at the state of that suit.' Aryx could feel his blood pressure rising.

'I was careful, but I couldn't carry the infoslate all the way down.'

'You dick. Why didn't you hook it on the belt?'

Sebastian looked down. 'I didn't ... Oh, I never noticed that. Anyway, how's the wiring going?' It was typical for him to change the subject when he was in the wrong.

'I'm almost done. I'm worn out. And worrying about you hasn't helped – you've been hours!'

He looked down at the floor. 'I hadn't expected to take so long. Why don't you get some rest? I'll take the ship back to the station.'

'Okay, I'll finish the last few wires and then take a nap.' Aryx turned to head up in the lift. 'Oh, and I was listening to a news feed earlier. Apparently there have been more sightings of that *Flying Dutchman* ship.'

'I didn't believe it when I read it in the papers the other day. Sounds like a load of superstition if you ask me. Nobody would be streaking around the galaxy at those speeds, not when we've got the nodes.'

'Well, I'm open-minded about it – you never know what's out there.' He activated the lift and Sebastian mumbled something unintelligible as it took him out of earshot. Nothing good, no doubt.

Sitting at the console, Aryx finished off the remaining connections. What should they be connected to? The frame in the evidence crate was of no use; the remnants of wiring attached to it just dangled, not connected to anything in particular. Scans of the structure had shown traces of DNA, but that could have been deposited by Alvarez if he'd connected the wires to it. A systematic approach would be the only way of deciphering the object's purpose. He connected the bundle of wires to a plug-in patch module and dropped it into a port on the console.

The assembly sat on the workbench like an electronic parasite, connected by hundreds of fine tendrils. He had no idea where to start.

'Seb, what are you doing down there? How should I analyse this thing now that I've connected it up?'

'I'm putting the suit away,' Sebastian shouted. 'Get the computer to probe the connections in a binary sequence – that way you'll be able to map them all.'

'Computer, did you hear that?'

'Yes.'

'Then run the sequence.' He hated the thought of it listening to their conversation all the time.

'Acknowledged.' Lights started to flash around the connection port. It looked like it was going to take a few hours.

'Where can I get some sleep on this ship?' he called down to Sebastian.

'There are some cargo nets down here that drop down. It looks like they double as hammocks.'

Aryx sighed. 'I suppose that'll have to do,' he said, and made his way down.

Sebastian had already opened out the net and placed some boxes next to it. Aryx clamped his chair down and shuffled himself up over the stack onto the hammock. Not particularly comfortable, but better than nothing.

'I managed to get a fresh sample of carbyne, too.' Sebastian held up the sample tube. The rubber stopper had sucked halfway down inside it with the air pressure.

'That's good. We can analyse it when we get back to the station.' It was hard for Aryx to keep his eyes open.

Sebastian made his way to the ladder. 'I'll take the ship back. Tie yourself down if you're worried about it getting bumpy. Have a nice nap.'

Within moments, Aryx had settled into a dreamless sleep.

While the ship followed the course he'd plotted back to Tenebrae, Sebastian turned the sample tube in his hands. How could the mineral be related to the explosion? It looked utterly harmless, and innocuous as talcum powder. What did people want the stuff for? There were too many questions, and he felt too disturbed by the events in the tunnels to concentrate properly.

He'd never been in mortal danger before and he hoped it wasn't something he'd ever have reason to get used to. As he went over the experience, he felt surprised as he recalled the nightmare. So that was what had caused his sensation of panic in the tunnels. The dream seemed strangely prophetic in retrospect – not that he believed in such things. Even though his grandfather had followed the Ásatrú religion, he had always taught him to follow logic and observation, in line with the religion's pragmatic principles. According to the stories, the god Odin had learned of the universe through the runes; even though Sebastian didn't take the stories literally, he yearned for that holistic understanding of things. Perhaps he had subconsciously picked up on some clue that had prompted the dream, or made him put himself in that predicament. The latter seemed the most likely. Everything was ultimately predictable.

Everything had a logical cause and outcome.

Maybe the subconscious computer of his own mind had calculated the outcome and pre-warned him. How that was possible, he had no idea. Cause, or effect? It was exactly the sort of conundrum that had drawn him into a career as a programmer; his love for unpicking the rules of the universe had driven him to write programs that simulated physics and natural order. Yes, it had all been done before by others, but you only truly understood the wheel if you reinvented it yourself a few times. If it wasn't for the intervention of terrorists, his life might have gone in a completely different direction and he could have carried on that work. He could still remember the day everything changed ...

Green and ochre forests slipped beneath the monomag while Sebastian stared out of its curved sky-panorama windows. The near-silent hoops of the Dyson thrusters propelled the train at a deceptively high speed, and before he knew it the city was in sight with its tall, gleaming spires projecting far above the rumpled autumn canopy. It was nothing like Iceland. Yes, the trees there had come back, but they were uptight pines, not at all like the deciduous trees of Britain that could relax in the temperate climate. Even the cold Britannic winters offered a balmy relief from Reykjavik's biting wind, but still he missed the place.

'Excuse me, can I get you a drink Sir?'

He looked up from his reminiscing. 'No, I'm fine, thank you,' he said to the waitress.

She nodded. 'If you need anything, just use the comms. The buffet car is open at the far end.' She pressed the door control and continued on down the carriage without waiting for the glass screen to close. A young, slim woman with wavy blonde hair slipped through before it shut.

'Hey, Jen,' he said and turned back to looking out of the window.

He saw her reflection sit down on the seat opposite him and smooth out its shiny black coat. 'You okay?'

'Just a bit homesick, I suppose. Did you finish your thesis?'

'I did, and I'm so glad I kept a backup off the system.'

He turned to face her. 'Why? Did your infoslate break?'

'No, I wasn't able to connect to Manchester Uni's servers this morning. When I checked the news, it turned out they'd been hacked.'

'Oh Gods!' The very idea was appalling. 'I'd better check mine.' He pulled his infoslate out of the antique canvas backpack his grandfather had given him and attempted to connect to Hereford University.

Within moments he was presented with the login screen, which he authenticated with his thumb print. 'I'm in.'

'That's a relief,' Jen said. 'I thought you were going to say—'

'Oh no!'

'What is it?'

He felt a cold sensation in the pit of his stomach. He turned the infoslate around to show her.

'No files found? What does that mean?'

'Exactly what it says. The system has none of my files on it. They've all gone! My thesis. All those years of work, gone!' If his work wasn't on there anymore, he might as well kiss goodbye to his doctorate.

She moved over next to him and put her hand on his shoulder. 'Well it can't *all* be gone—there will be overnight backups in the Bristol datacentre, surely.'

He tapped the *Restore backup* button.

Connection unavailable.

'It won't connect.'

'Try logging in to the datacentre directly.'

He switched the connection, but instead of being presented with the login screen, a temporary holding page appeared.

The Bristol datacentre has been removed from service.

'Why?' he yelled. 'I can't accept this!' He tapped frantically at the screen, bypassing the security in moments.

'What are you trying to do?'

'They wouldn't take the system offline for no reason. There's got to be something in a log somewhere.' The system records began scrolling up the screen. 'There! That's it – a break in the log times. Bingo!'

'What have you found?' Jen's voice crackled with tension.

'I'm not sure, but if there's no data in the logs it probably means something has physically happened to the building. I have to contact my brother.' He tapped a few commands and a uniformed police officer with cropped, dark brown hair and square jaw appeared on-screen.

'Hey Seb, what can I do you for?'

'I need a favour, Mike. A datacentre in Bristol went offline at 07.21 this morning and there's no data in the logs, which is strange. I think something's happened to the site. Were there any police reports?'

'What do— Never mind, I'll check.' He turned away from the screen and tapped at a terminal. When he turned back, his expression was dark. 'A bomb went off, destroying several buildings in the area. I'll go down and investigate. You look a bit pale – are you okay?'

'No I'm not . . . I've got to go.' Sebastian closed the connection. He wanted to cry.

'Oh, Seb.' Jen squeezed his shoulder. 'I'm so sorry.'

'What am I going to do? I should never have trusted the damned stupid system! All those years of simulations and research, gone! My father's inheritance will run out soon if I'm not getting student allowance.' There was only one thing for it. 'I'll have to get a job.'

Jen drew in a sharp breath. 'I know the perfect thing for you!'

He rolled his eyes.

'No, honestly. There's a security coder job going on Tenebrae station. You'd be great at it, given how quickly you got into those records.'

'Me? A job on a space station?' He shuddered at the thought of leaving Earth. 'It's a bit ... adventurous.'

'Oh, go on, I'm sure you could do it. Isn't that why you carry that old thing?' His backpack gave a metallic clunk as she nudged it with her toe.

He turned away and stared out of the window, lost in thought.

The burnt-cauliflower bumps of the forest burst from between grey slabs of fragmented tarmac. Large pines grew through the long-caved-in roofs of terraced houses, penned in by walls. The windscreens of the occasional 21st century car glinted in their rusting frames. So much junk left behind. So much nature had reclaimed.

The monomag cleared the old, swallowed suburbs and the forests peeled back as the gleaming white spires of Manchester loomed up, surrounding the train.

Jen stood. 'This is my stop. Keep your chin up.'

His stomach lurched as the monomag decelerated, and he forced a smile. She smiled back and closed the glass doors behind her.

A minute later the train was on its way to Birmingham. He gazed out across the leafy horizon, dreading the thought of what would happen when he arrived at the university. Maybe she was right. Maybe he could stop things like this happening to others. He could almost hear his father gloating from beyond the grave. *I told you, you should have followed the family and joined the 'force along with your brother – then you wouldn't have had this problem.*

He'd show him ...

And indeed he probably would have. It was just a shame that he and Mikkael weren't around anymore to be proven wrong.

Aryx woke refreshed; despite his initial impressions, the netting bunk had been surprisingly comfortable. He rubbed his eyes and checked his wristcom. Tuesday, 07.32. He'd been asleep for nearly ten hours! He lugged himself out of the hammock and back into his chair.

When he arrived in the cockpit, Sebastian was sitting in the pilot's seat.

'Seb?'

There was no response.

He moved over and shook Sebastian's shoulder. 'Seb!'

'Wha—!' Sebastian flailed out with his arms and flicked him in the eye with the back of his hand.

'Ouch!' Aryx put his hand over his eye and rubbed it. 'You fell asleep with the ship on autopilot, you idiot!'

'Oh crap.' Sebastian's hands flitted from one panel on the console to the next. 'We're one jump from home. It must have taken us longer to get back than when we went. Looks like the autopilot didn't like the journey length and we've been sitting in open space for a couple of hours ... I didn't realise I was so tired.' He looked worn out, even though he'd just woken up.

'I think you'd better get some sleep when we get back to the station,' Aryx said. 'The nanobots will take a while to form and there's nothing else to follow up on, so you might as well get some rest.'

'You're right. The last few days have taken it out of me.'

Aryx checked the diagnostic console. The readout showed the blob's wire probing was complete. He brought up the report. Several of the connections showed input and output signatures. Others appeared to drain power, or provide variable resistance as though they might be sensor inputs. He entered several standard Logynix commands and sent them to the connections.

After each command, pages of random galcode spewed down the display. None of them yielded readable results, but it was obviously responding to input even though what came back was completely unintelligible.

'Code soup.'

'Get the computer to check it,' Sebastian said. 'Computer, scan for known data structures, lexical types, and file formats.'

'Searching.'

Aryx sat for nearly half an hour gazing out of the cockpit window, watching the elongated stars stream by. The computer interrupted his daydreaming.

'Search complete. No known data structures, lexical data, or file types found.'

'Bugger it!' he shouted and hit the console with his fist. 'The data on this piece of crap is totally useless gibberish.' He began to sweat; he'd never been so bloody frustrated with a piece of technology.

Sebastian came over and leaned on the console. 'It's not wasted effort,' he said, peering at the display.

Aryx heaved a sigh. 'I know. At least we know that it's some kind of data thingy, but I've no idea if it's a complete unit or part of some larger assembly.'

'I'm sure we'll work it out, given time. Any idea what the frame was for?'

'Would I be saying this if I knew? I had a brief look at it, but the wires connected to it didn't seem to serve a purpose. This thing could be a recording device that monitored sensor inputs from something installed in the frame, but without any kind of context, I can't even guess.'

'It's a shame we don't know what was being researched in the lab,' Sebastian said.

Aryx folded his arms. Talk about stating the obvious. 'It looks like another dead end, then. Let's hope the trackers turn something up.'

Sebastian monitored the ship's flight for the rest of the journey. He glanced back. Aryx sat staring at the screens of jumbled data. He'd never seen him so depressed.

The information had to make sense in some way – all they needed was context. The data could even have been software code, but without knowing what system it ran on, it was nothing more than a random guess. Computing and guesswork – locating a needle in a whole planet full of haystacks was more appealing.

The ship dropped out of superphase several thousand kilometres away from the station. The bright, glinting wheel was a welcome sight.

He took the ship into the central hub and allowed the computer to synchronise rotation. The ship glided in, drifting into the magnetic currents that would guide it down to the outer levels. The transit system took over and pushed the ship through the spokes of the station until it eventually arrived at the repair hangar where, once again, the docking crane lifted it out of the transit rings and into the repair bay.

'I'm going to get some rest,' Sebastian said. Aryx's eyes had dark patches in the outer corners. 'I suggest you take some time away from wrestling with that data as well – you look tired.'

'If you insist. I'll spend the day reviewing my patent application. I might end up having some more ideas after a break.' Aryx stowed the mobipack in a locker and headed down the lift.

'I'll meet you here tomorrow,' Sebastian said as he walked down the ramp out of the ship. 'And I'll bring the box from my locker for you to take a look at. Sorry about forgetting it again.' He tapped a reminder into his wristcom to collect it.

By the time Sebastian reached the bottom of the ramp, Aryx had wheeled halfway to the door of the hangar and turned back to face the ship. He was pointing at the airlock. 'They've scratched the paintwork!'

Sebastian turned around. 'The bastards!' The Sollers Hope docking cowl had abraded a large, fuzzy rectangle around the doorway.

The first thing Sebastian did when he got back to his apartment was put the N-suit into the cleaning unit. He checked in with the office computer but the video still hadn't finished processing. If he kept thinking about it, the stress of the investigation would overwhelm him – there was nothing further he could do – the nanobots still needed a couple of days to form the tracking modules, after all. To put the investigation out of his mind, he decided to go for a walk; the data on the melted blob was still a mystery and the break might allow for a flash of inspiration. It was still early; the atrium would probably be quiet, and a jog around the station would do him good.

He took the lift to one of the shopping malls in the atrium. The place was packed with people of various races, milling around, trading, chatting, and eating at the many food stalls. After three years, he still hadn't learned.

The bulk of the mess from the explosion's aftermath had been cleaned up, but a handful of shops were still closed. The station would have a big insurance case on its hands and would undoubtedly end up trying not to pay out, filing the incident under the clause 'Acts of God'.

He laughed through his nose. Most insurers didn't cover 'acts of terrorism', either.

After wandering aimlessly through the markets for an hour, he found himself jogging around the atrium's lower level, beside the river. He stopped next to one of the many water features to catch his breath and began daydreaming as he watched the large koi swim about. How nice it must be to not have a care in the world.

His wristcom bleeped. An incoming call from Agent Gladrin.

'How is the investigation going, Thorsson?'

'Slow, Sir. We've hit a lot of dead ends, but I'm waiting for a couple of leads to mature.'

'Interesting choice of words. I'd provide you with some support, but I'm still out of the sector. When you turn up something concrete, let me know.'

'I'll be sure to, Sir. I haven't yet had time to start the task you assigned to me. If my leads don't come in, we hope to start work on that tomorrow. Aryx has been helping with the technical analysis on the evidence.'

'A good choice, then. Keep up the good work. I'll catch up with you in person when I can. Gladrin out.' The wristcom went quiet. At least he wasn't pushing for a resolution.

He slowed his run to a walk around the atrium. It took another two hours to do the full circuit. After a quick shower he crashed on the bed, exhausted, and fell straight to sleep.

He woke lying on his back. The apartment was in total darkness and he couldn't make out the time on the bedside clock – the power must have failed. He attempted to get out of bed but found only a dull, wooden resistance in his legs. When he tried to sit, his arms had the same senseless quality to them. He slumped back. It must be sleep paralysis. It would wear off soon. He lay blinking in the dark listening to his breath, waiting for the paralysis to subside and sensation to return. Minutes passed.

His breath echoed quietly and another sound began to emerge. A quiet, wet slopping sound. Holding his breath, he strained to listen.

The sound got louder. It reminded him of a nature video he'd seen once, in which a hedgehog had eaten a slug. That horrible, wet chomping had stuck with him his entire life.

He listened for several seconds, but couldn't contain it any longer. Still unable to move, he shouted, 'Lights!'

The apartment illumination blinked on.

A small, imp-like creature sat on his lower abdomen. Its skin red and shiny, and its clawed hands glistening with a dark, oily substance. As the image sank in he realised the demonic baby-thing was elbow-deep in his quivering intestines.

He screamed, and in the next instant the thing was gone. He moved his hand over the area that had been a gaping wound a second earlier.

A nightmare again, but how real it felt. They had to stop, and soon. He eased himself back onto the pillow and rolled over to face the clock.

The time read 03.10.

He woke before his alarm went off. As with every other nightmare, he couldn't recall the exact details, but he was beginning to get irritated with his disrupted sleep patterns. His face felt rough, and rubbing his eyes did little to clear his blurry vision. If this kept up, he'd have to start taking sedatives, and that wouldn't help his work.

After a quick breakfast he cleaned his teeth and went about his daily preparations. As he put the freshly cleaned N-suit on, the wristcom beeped, reminding him to collect the box. He finished dressing and went to the security office to pick it up.

When he eventually arrived at the repair hangar, Aryx was already there, standing facing the ship and wearing the mobipack. Sebastian hadn't realised how tall he was. He'd got so used to seeing him at wheelchair height that he hadn't stopped to think about what he was like before. His work clothes had been changed for something more casual – a brown, sleeveless padded leather jacket and a pair of baggy trousers with the legs stitched up. He had a rag in his hand and was polishing the hull around the airlock.

Sebastian cleared his throat.

Aryx stopped rubbing and turned around. 'Hi!' he shouted. 'I didn't hear you there.'

'What are you doing? Anyone could come in and see you wearing that!' As he got close he could see the scratches caused by the docking cowl had gone.

'It annoyed me so much I had to repaint it.'

A lump in his throat made it difficult to swallow – he wasn't aware of how proud of the ship he'd become. 'Thank you,' he said, putting his hand on Aryx's shoulder.

'No problem. I finished reading my book and couldn't just sit around all day. I wasn't in the mood to work on the patent for these.' Aryx gestured down at his glowing legs. 'So doing this was the next best thing to occupy me.'

Sebastian stepped into the ship and turned in the doorway. 'I've got a present for you, when you're finished.'

'Oh?'

'I brought the box for you to have a look at.' He continued in to the ship.

'About bloody time!'

He sat at the diagnostics console, took the metal box from his pack, and placed it on the work surface. A few moments later Aryx pulled up next to him in his wheelchair and slid the mobipack under the workbench.

'I was lucky not to bump into Karan when I went to get it. I wasn't really in the mood to be interrogated. I hate having to give her the brush-off.'

'It's just as well,' Aryx said, 'she can talk the legs off a Q'vani!' He laughed.

Sebastian didn't join him; he was more intent on finding out what was in the box. He picked it up and pressed his thumb to the print-lock for several seconds until a beep sounded. 'Give me your thumb.'

Aryx reached out and placed his thumb on the lock, pairing the clearance to his identity.

'Open it.'

He pressed his thumb to the lock again.

With a click, the upper third of the metal container split and he eased off the top.

Chapter 11

Sebastian watched as Aryx examined the box – far too slowly and ceremoniously for his liking; the tension was palpable. He got the fleeting urge to rip it out of his hands, flip the lid open and slap the contents down onto the console. Instead, he settled for clamping his hands together between his legs.

From the box, Aryx slid a tightly fitting metal cube and placed it on the workbench. It measured three inches square, and was finished in a satin gunmetal. The edges and corners were chamfered off to a depth of two millimetres, softening the otherwise sharp, square edges while retaining definition. There was a small, red button mounted on one of the sides, inset in a circular chamfered recess. On the top sat a small panel, marked by a rectangular groove and taking up half of the area at the back. A deep groove ran across the top, down the sides and turned towards the back, roughly a third from the bottom. The lower third of the front face housed several thin, shallow vertical recesses. Sebastian turned the cube around to view the other sides.

'Do you think that's a joint in the casing?' he said, pointing to the groove.

Aryx picked the cube up and turned it over in his hands. 'Could be. There are some kind of fastenings,' he said, pointing to two tiny circular indentations either side, just inside the right angle formed by the groove.

On the opposite side to the button there was a long, chamfered vertical recess. It was inset with a raised strip that had horizontal segments sunk into it.

'Could that be some sort of linear display bar?'

'It seems a bit simple, if it is. A device with a button and a strip of lights.' Aryx laughed. 'Maybe it measures how long you hold the button down.'

Sebastian shook his head slowly.

Aryx continued to turn the cube over. The bottom face appeared plain, except for a large stylised number one embossed in the metal.

'Let's try something.' He put the cube back on the console. 'Computer, scan the object and analyse.'

The console whirred, emitted several loud clicks, and stopped. 'Interior analysis not possible on this station. Device is shielded.'

'Shielded by what?'

'Exterior casing is composed of tungsten carbide alloys. The alloys are disrupting the scan beams. Intensified scans may damage any internal componentry.'

'Is it giving off any emissions?' Sebastian asked.

'Low-level broad-spectrum EM emissions are detectable. Configuration unknown.'

'Can you perform an extended analysis on the emissions?'

'No. Emissions have stopped.'

'That's odd. I guess it could be intermittent.' The idea of a shielded device receiving and sending transmissions was unusual. 'I wonder if it's got some kind of wireless connection.'

'You think we should try to open it?' Aryx held up a metal screwdriver.

'You can try. Just be careful not to damage it, please.'

He put the screwdriver in the ridge at the top of the cube and strained until he went red in the face. He paused, repositioned the cube, and attempted again. The veins on his arms swelled to the size of a garden hose. The screwdriver bent in half. He tried another.

Sebastian put his hands out in a halting gesture. 'Stop. I don't think you're going to do it. I don't want to have to take you to hospital.'

Aryx placed the cube back on the console. 'I think you're right,' he said, breathing heavily. There wasn't a scratch on it. The alloy had resisted all break-in attempts.

'I'm worried that if we try to force our way in through the casing it might get damaged internally. For the moment, I think we'll just have to monitor its emissions to see if it starts again.'

'Of course we could always try this—' Aryx leaned forwards and put his thumb on the button.

No! Sebastian reached forwards to stop him. Too late.

Click.

'Why did you do that, you psycho!' he yelled. 'It could have been anything!'

'You said they'd already checked it wasn't explosive.' Aryx folded his arms across his chest. 'Anyway, nothing happened.'

'That's beside the point.'

'You didn't seem too concerned with safety precautions yourself. I could see you itching to get it out of the box.' He shrugged. 'And I can't see Gladrin giving a newbie like you something really dangerous to investigate.'

'Well ... don't do it again, or I'll leave you here next time I have to go somewhere. What's the button supposed to be for, if it doesn't do anything?'

'You're asking the wrong person. Why doesn't your SpecOps boss know what this is?'

'It's supposed to be a test for me, us, to investigate, remember?'

'Yeah, yeah, it's just frustrating having to investigate this thing *and* all that evidence, especially with that melted lump producing gibberish.'

Sebastian attempted a softer tone. 'I'm sure we'll work out what it is, given time. I suppose we could try searching for a visual match to the cube.' He proceeded to take pictures of it from various angles using his wristcom and uploaded the images to the computer. 'Search image database for a match to the ones I've just uploaded.'

'Acknowledged. Searching.'

He picked the cube up and turned it in his hands while he waited for the results. Aryx turned back to the melted lump of plastic wired into the console.

'You know what,' Sebastian said, waving the cube in the direction of the lump. 'This looks almost the same size as that thing.'

Aryx looked up from his work. 'I suppose, but this is plastic and has nothing to do with SpecOps.'

'It could be made from the same organoplastic on the *inside*.'

Aryx scratched his head. 'Without breaking it open, we have no way seeing what's in it.'

'That's it! Do you have any nanocameras? We could put one down into those vents to see what's inside.'

'Hold on.' Aryx wheeled over to the lift and left the ship.

A moment later he came back with a small bundle of fine, glassy thread with a block attached to one end. 'I have this – it's a microfibre camera. The transmitter interfaces with the computer, and you can feed this end inside to take a look.' He handed the optical thread to Sebastian and paired the diagnostic console to it.

Sebastian fed the thread into one of the vents on the front of the cube. The camera revealed a dark interior. He wiggled the fibre; the light from the camera illuminated an area immediately inside the vents, and the edges of several long metal plates appeared. Beyond that, nothing else was visible.

'That might be a heat sink,' Aryx said. 'Self-contained and separate from the main unit.'

'Very strange—' Sebastian's wristcom bleeped.

'Incoming message from security TI.'

'Accept,' he said, putting the cube and camera back on the console.

'Sebastian, station tracking has detected a weak signal on the locator frequency you provided.'

'Great!' He punched the air in victory, jumped up, and threw himself into the pilot's seat. 'Where's the signal coming from? Show me on the piloting console.'

The Galactic map appeared with a flashing red dot, indicating the position of the tracker; it had picked up the signal from three astrolocation beacons and relayed its coordinates back to the station, giving its position to solar system accuracy. Aryx wheeled over and Sebastian expanded the view of the region. As the map zoomed in, the realistic Galactic cloud gave way to a stark black background and representational model of orbital paths and stellar information. The system, Yazor, appeared empty – a single star with no planetary bodies orbiting it.

'Does this mean the tracking signal is coming from a ship?' Aryx asked.

'Possibly, or a small unregistered station is parked in orbit around that star, and that's where it's coming from. Either way, we're in for another trip.'

'I'm going to try working on that data again while you pilot. I might not be a programmer, but I need *something* to do. I haven't got time to waste looking out of the windows any more.'

'Sounds like a plan. Are we all set?'

'Yes, food's still in the chiller. Didn't use any of it.'

'As long as your stomach's catered for, that's fine.' Sebastian grinned.

Aryx shook his head. 'Such disrespect,' he said, and made his way back to the diagnostic console.

Sebastian activated the docking arm and transport rings. 'Computer, plot a course for that system and take us out.'

Blue-shifted stars slid by like bright hurricane rain on a window.

'What are you going to do when we get there?' Aryx asked, looking up from his work.

'It depends on what we find. If it turns out to be a bunch of gun-toting lunatics on a ship, then we get out of there and call for backup.'

'And if not?'

'Then I calmly introduce myself, try to find out what they're using carbyne for, and whether they've got a motive to blow things up. Tactfully, of course.'

'You'll be doing the negotiating, then. I don't have the patience.' Aryx turned back to the data-filled screen.

Sebastian watched as he stared at the pages of random characters.

'I'm sorry for dragging you around with me. I know we're both glad of the chance to get off the station, but I can't help but worry what danger I might be putting you in. I don't know how I'd cope in your situation.'

Aryx continued to watch the screens. 'It's okay, I'm not exactly a stranger to danger, and as for my situation, you've helped me get the pack working. You know how I hate programming. I don't understand it, and it's not like anything else that I can just take apart to make sense of. So don't feel bad – without your help I wouldn't have it working and I'd never have got off-station.'

Sebastian smiled, glad that he didn't have to feel guilty any more.

'Of course, I will mind if you're about to thrust me head first into the jaws of death.'

Why did he have to say that? What *would* they find when they arrived at Yazor? Would it be Humans or another race – or even a race nobody had even heard of?

He was constantly surprised by the life in the universe. The life on Earth, even with its enormous variety of forms, still shared a common ancestry. Many other planets also had great diversity of life upon them, and yet the most unlikely thing to spring from life-bearing planets was intelligence and self-awareness. It was a constant marvel to him how the species that exhibited the traits of sentience appeared to be of roughly the same physical configuration, none of them unrecognisable to the others as intelligent beings. The wide variety of circumstances and environments that spawned intelligent life should have resulted in grossly different forms, yet there still appeared to be some common order or guiding force at work. He often wondered whether gods had indeed roamed the universe at one time or another and created the rules and laws that shaped life, or perhaps life was expressing some basic urge for the universe to explore itself.

In the face of his grandparents' teachings, Sebastian strongly believed that all the rules in the universe boiled down to mathematics. Was the entire universe and everything in it the result of some unfathomable set of primordial formulae? Was the true nature of divinity mathematics?

His stomach rumbled. Thinking was hungry work.

Three hours flight-time and two node hops later, the ship dropped out of superphase in the system of Yazor.

'We're still an hour outside the system at top speed and I'm already starving,' Sebastian said. 'Do you fancy lunch?'

'I thought you'd never ask. My stomach's on the prowl again.' Aryx retrieved the container from the chilled storage unit, took out a couple of sandwiches, and began setting up the heater on the diagnostics console

'I want a *coffee*, not battery acid.'

'Haha, it's not that bad – it's only three times the strength.'

Sebastian shuddered at the thought.

They ate at the console while the ship crept into the system. As they finished their drinks an alarm sounded from the cockpit.

'The signal's resolved!' Sebastian jabbed at several controls and shook his head. 'I don't believe it. The signal is coming from a *comet!*'

Chapter 12

Sebastian and Aryx sat with mouths open, staring at the display. The tracker signal clearly emanated from the comet.

'That thing's tearing around the system!' Aryx said.

'We're . . . going to have to land on that,' Sebastian said. 'Computer, plot a trajectory that will take us close to the comet and initiate.' The danger of the asteroid field paled in comparison to this.

The computer took a moment to calculate the required thrust for the ship to match the comet's orbit around the star, and the ship changed direction. Sebastian peered at the display. The on-screen analysis showed the comet measured two miles in diameter, consisting mostly of ice and rock. The tail sprayed out of the system, blown by the solar winds, ninety degrees to starboard. He nibbled at his nails while the ship chased the comet along its orbital path; after an hour of pursuit it was within visual range.

The tail filled the starboard side of the window, shining brilliantly against the black of space. A bright, steamy halo hung around the sunward hemisphere of the crinkly white rock as its surface boiled away.

'How the hell are we going to land on that thing?' Aryx asked.

Sebastian scratched his chin. 'I don't think it's wise to land sun-side, nor on the faces in partial shadow. That solar wind is blasting across the surface and there'll be all sorts of stuff in it.'

'So what do we do?'

'I may be crazy, but I think we ought to go through the tail and land on the back.'

'Are you mad?'

'I knew you'd think it was insane. Think about it. There should be a calm area.'

Aryx's glare faded.

'I'll want you to man the CFD shield – we might need it for this.'

'I'm on it.' He disappeared down the lift and spoke over the wrist-com a moment later. 'I'm in. Whenever you're ready.'

Sebastian took manual control of the ship and drove it forwards. The icy torrent loomed closer, filling the view.

Aryx sat at the controls next to the CFD in the shield generator room.

Sebastian spoke over the intercom. 'I'm keeping the comet to port as we enter the tail. I'll take her in slowly to give you time to keep the shield between us and it as we pass through ...'

'Okay. I've configured it to project a V-shaped deflector. The only way I can do it is if I move it ahead of the ship a little and then bring it to the middle, and once we get through it, move it to the back. The shield won't cover the whole length of the ship because the generator's too small for the hull.' He configured the shield to project several metres ahead of the port bow to part the tail like a curtain.

The shield generator swung around on its mountings to point forward and, as the *Ultima* approached the comet's tail, the generator began to vibrate on its suspension, absorbing the force of the particles impacting against the shield. The vibration increased and the generator began to bob about.

'Passing in now!'

Aryx adjusted the shape and position of the shield, bringing it towards the midsection. The shield generator slowly turned, matching the speed of the ship while it inched through the icy gale and the vibrations increased further. The mountings groaned in complaint and the hull began to creak against the support struts. The bobbing motion became violent, forcing him to move farther into the corner – the generator was getting dangerously close to his chair.

'I hate to say it,' Aryx shouted over the cacophony, 'but those timeless words are true: *she can't take much more of it, Captain!*'

'I hear you! Nearly through. Move it to the back!'

Aryx adjusted the controls again and the generator swept towards the stern. He chewed his lip. The vibrations decreased in intensity.

After what seemed like a long minute, the shuddering stopped altogether.

'We're through. You can deactivate the shield now.'

He turned off the generator and patted it. The casing was hot under his hand. 'Good job, old girl,' he said, and headed back to the cockpit.

Sebastian sat checking the console readouts, his forehead dotted with beads of sweat.

'Are you okay?'

'Yes, I'm fine. It was touch and go there for a while. I thought we were going to get scoured away to nothing.'

'You did a good job of piloting. Your dad would have been proud of you.'

'Yeah. Right.'

'I reckon the worst is yet to come. We don't know what we'll find.'

Sebastian gave him a hard stare. 'What *I'll* find. It's a pressure suit trip. There's no atmosphere.'

'Damn, I was looking forward to seeing what's down there.' It was one of those rare times Aryx wished he still had his legs; a pressure suit wouldn't fit him without modification.

Sebastian shook his head. 'Not this time, sorry.' He navigated the ship closer to the surface. 'The locator beacon appears to be right inside the comet. I guess there's a base.'

Aryx checked the scanners. 'You might be best to bring the ship down in the centre of this flat area here, so we're away from the fringe of the tail.' He peered at the display. 'There's a low-density patch a few hundred metres away that could be an entrance. I didn't see it on the scans before, probably because the tail was masking it.'

'I'll set her down and explore on foot.'

Sebastian rolled the ship clockwise to bring the keel parallel to the surface and Aryx almost toppled out of his chair. It was odd how your eyes could play tricks on you, especially when it came to which way was up.

A loud thump echoed through the hull.

'Here we are.' Sebastian got up and began climbing down the ladder into the hold. 'I'm going to put a suit on.'

Aryx noticed the rucksack slumped next to the diagnostics console. He picked it up and fished around for a moment, drew out the pistol and infoslate, then headed down into the hold.

'You'd better take this,' he said, holding out the items.

Sebastian grimaced. 'I'd forgotten about that.' He took the gun and put it in the holster. 'Thanks.' He clamped the helmet shut and hooked the infoslate onto his belt.

'Be careful – no accidents this time.'

'Of course not.'

Sebastian stepped out of the ship onto the cometoid. A curtain of light wavered and shimmered as streams of rock and ice flowed upward from the jagged horizon. The continuous geyser of glittering particles contrasted against the black of space above, casting a diffuse, cold illumination on the dark, shadowy ground. The ambient light was just enough to see by and make out vague shapes, but he had no intention of breaking an ankle: he turned on the suit's torch.

The comet's surface was littered with slick, vicious glassy crags. He couldn't bring himself to imagine what would happen if he slipped on one. As he picked his way across the rock in the direction the scans indicated, the ground crunched silently underfoot, and after several minutes of trudging – and the occasional stumble – he came to the area Aryx had detected.

The knobbly surface fell away into a smooth, shallow crater roughly twenty metres across by four metres deep. He worked his way down into the bowl. Several feet before he reached the bottom, his foot twisted awkwardly – the same sensation as walking down stairs and expecting an extra step at the bottom. The ground rushed up to greet him.

He peeled himself up off the powdery surface and looked out across the crater. It seemed flatter than it had from above. He moved the torch, but the shadows remained in place. Crouching down, he ran his gloved hand gently over the unusually smooth surface. It was artificial. The crater was painted with black, grey, and white stippling, giving a convincing imitation of rock and shadow. Holding the torch low, he moved towards the centre, hoping that a seam or opening might be revealed by the low angle of the light.

After a couple of minutes searching, he came across a small square recess with rounded corners. He brushed the dust and loose stones away; it appeared to be a cover with a simple sliding catch. He slid it across and pried it open.

Behind the cover sat a handle within a quarter-circle opening – a manual actuator for a door. But what door? Out of curiosity he pulled the lever, rotating it through ninety degrees. A vibration shuddered through his legs and he had to put his hand out to stop himself from falling over. The movement stopped and he slowly straightened up.

The base of the crater had parted, revealing an airlock set at the bottom of a metallic chamber several feet deep. He stood at the edge. Should he really go in? He could get trapped with no way out, but then he'd come all that way ... If he didn't go in, he wouldn't learn anything.

He jumped and landed on the door at the bottom. His heart skipped a beat as the open hatch above slammed silently shut, sending a thunderous rumble through his feet and hands and plunging him into darkness.

Bright illumination flooded the chamber and, before he could react, he felt his stomach move under the onset of artificial gravity. The wall behind him became the floor, and he fell, painfully, on his back.

Aryx sat aboard the *Ultima Thule*, studying the apparently random stream of data produced by the melted lump of electronics.

'What are you?'

The melted lump puzzled him, as did the cube Sebastian had presented. With no intelligible data, and no way of getting into the cube, he was utterly stumped. Being unable to make progress was incredibly frustrating, but he took a small measure of comfort in Sebastian's ability to move the investigation along independently.

He set the console to display the program monitoring the transmissions from the cube. It had been inactive since they'd left the station, but now signals appeared to be coming from it once again, taunting him. He watched the display as coloured waveforms flowed by, peaking and decaying. After several minutes of staring at the patterns, he had an idea.

'Computer, show me the emissions generated by the ship's systems, but exclude ambient sources such as the CFD generator and reactor.'

The computer obeyed, replacing the waveform with the emissions from the ship itself.

He leaned back and rubbed his chin. 'Okay . . . Now show them above the emissions from the cube.'

The display changed to show both sets of waveforms, one above the other.

Something, some deep-seated gut instinct, niggled at him. He couldn't quite put his finger on it. What if it was processing the ship's signals? 'Computer, overlay the two sets.'

The displays merged.

'Hmm.' There were distinct peaks in the emissions from the cube *between* the peaks of the ship's emissions. 'This is interesting . . .'

Sebastian clambered to his feet and rubbed his aching back. Obviously the N-suit wasn't of much use alleviating a general impact. It took a few moments for his eyes to become accustomed to the bright light.

In front of him stood the airlock door he had landed on after jumping into the chamber through the secret entrance, his dusty footprints clearly visible on its surface. He approached it and activated the entry control. It opened silently in the vacuum and he stepped in. He'd half expected the inner pair of airlock doors to remain shut, or for alarm lights to flash, but the airlock closed behind him uneventfully and an increasingly loud hiss of air echoed through the chamber as it filled with atmosphere.

After a minute, the door ahead opened and he stepped out into a long, curving tunnel. Hewn from the comet itself, the smooth, undulating walls looked like molten glass, holding an icy iridescence beneath the gently rippling surface. A metallic walkway, raised up off the bottom of the tunnel, ran the length of the passage allowing the walls to curve under it from where a cold, bluish light emanated. He shuddered. The walls could almost be melting in front of his eyes. He got the urge to reach out and touch them, but it was obvious they were beyond his reach from the path.

He looked down at the display behind the torch on his left wrist to check the atmosphere. Breathable; no known pathogens detected; acceptable temperature for Human habitation. Perfect. He unlocked the helmet and flipped it backwards over his head to conserve the air supply. Warm breath condensed in front of him.

He stepped forwards and the hard soles of the pressure suit clanged loudly on the walkway. He winced, but continued on. Whoever was there probably already knew he'd arrived.

While he walked, he looked around for security cameras. He couldn't see any – maybe whoever built this place had intended to rely on security through obscurity. At least it seemed plausible, given the location. He continued through the winding tunnel for a couple of minutes, marvelling at the structure. The work that had gone into constructing the place must have cost a fortune.

After turning yet another bend, the passage ended and the walls pinched in towards the walkway, which terminated at a metal door set into a deep recess. The door housed a small panel inset at eye level, but was otherwise featureless with no buttons or controls visible. He shifted uneasily. There could always be nanocameras or other sensors he couldn't see.

With no other option but for him to announce his presence, he held up his right hand, made a fist, and knocked.

An alarm from the navigation console interrupted Aryx's train of thought. He wheeled over to it and pressed a button, stifling the irritating noise, and checked the display. External sensors had detected a change in the comet's rotation. It had been stable before they'd landed.

'Computer, what's happening? Give me pictures, not technobabble.'

The display changed to a diagram of the comet. While the simulation played, the comet remained stationary. A tiny icon – the ship – moved towards the outline and landed on it. The comet began to turn, incredibly slowly at first. Crags on the outline caught the pixelated solar winds that swept around the profile, and it began to turn faster.

'Oops.'

He studied the simulation, trying to ascertain whether the rotation would pose a threat. He glanced out of the window and saw that the ice streaming up from the horizon appeared to be much closer and at a shallower angle than before.

'Oh shit!' He recalled the turbulence the shield had encountered on their passage through the tail and his heart began to race. 'Computer, is there adequate clearance below the ice stream to manoeuvre the ship?'

'Negative. The ship is too close to the penumbral cone. There is inadequate clearance for safe flight.'

Even if he could get the ship off the ground, he wouldn't be able to direct the shields at the same time, and he didn't trust the computer to do it. 'Is it safe to stay here?'

'Affirmative. Providing adequate shielding is supplied.'

'If the ship stays here with adequate shielding, will it get blown off the comet?'

'The mass of the ship is greater than the particle stream pressure. Without further information it is not possible to assess the required variables to determine whether the ship will stay in place.'

He had no choice. He couldn't trust the computer to make the necessary decisions – the situation was too complex and chaotic – it needed gut instinct and intuition. The only option was to stay put and man the shield.

He made his way down to the field generator room, patched through the navigational sensors, and waited for the storm.

Sebastian waited for – but didn't really expect – an answer to his knock on the door, and nearly jumped out of his skin when the suit's comm unit bleeped.

'What is it?' he snapped, irritated by his own embarrassment.

Aryx's voice crackled in the earpiece. 'There's a problem,' he said, his voice taut as a bowstring. 'When we landed, we must have altered the comet's momentum. It's turning, and the side we landed on will be in full sun in a couple of minutes.'

'I'm underground.'

'Good, because it won't be safe for you on the surface for at least an hour.'

'Will you be alright?'

'The computer isn't sure, but I think the ship should be safe enough if I reconfigure the shields. I'll have to do it m— ... —again, as we've only got twenty— ... —cover, but I think it'll be okay.'

'I'm more worried about you than the ship. You're breaking up. It sounds like solar interference.'

'I know— ... —okay. Just watch yourself out—' The signal cut off.

The familiar knotting sensation returned to Sebastian's stomach and he began to shake, feeling unexpectedly cold. It certainly wasn't because of the walls. He turned his head towards the ceiling and closed his eyes, half praying, half trying to hold back an almost uncontrollable fear. Fear that something might happen to Aryx. Fear that he'd be stuck on an uninhabited comet. And it would all have been his fault.

A grating sound from behind dragged him out of his self-pity. He spun around.

The panel in the door had opened.

Chapter 13

A white face with black, hollow eyes stared out through the letterbox slit and a gravelly, masculine voice spoke. *'Who are you, how did you get here, and what do you want?'*

Sebastian couldn't understand what was being said; he wasn't expecting anything other than Galac, and it took a few moments for it sink in. English.

'I say again,' the voice said, this time in Galac. 'Who are you, how did you get here, and what do you want?' The voice was strangely muffled; the features didn't move.

He stepped closer to the door. 'My name is Sebastian Thorsson. I am a security officer from Tenebrae station, and I came in a ship.'

'It's obvious you arrived in a ship, security *idiot!* How did you find me?'

He couldn't work out if the being was Human, or an alien that spoke fluently. Come to think of it, he'd never heard an alien speak English. What a stupid idea – he'd never even heard any of his *friends* speak English. He peered at the face but didn't dare get closer. The skin was smooth and shiny, like porcelain. He couldn't make out any detail in the eyes; the holes were dark – definitely some kind of mask.

'It was difficult to find you,' Sebastian said. 'I'm not here to harm you, if that's what you're worried about. I just want to ask you some questions.'

'You have a weapon. Put it down over by the bend and I will consider speaking to you.'

Sebastian walked thirty metres up the tunnel. He drew the gun from its holster between finger and thumb, and slowly placed it on the floor. Walking back, he held up his hands.

The panel snapped shut. A second later the door squealed open.

The *Ultima Thule* huddled on the comet as the turbulent threat of the ice sheet inched ever closer.

Aryx pounded on the shield generator console, frantically typing commands. The faint, rain-like patter grew louder and became the gentle susurration of drizzle. It did little to relax him. It only served to remind him of the turmoil to come, and he still had no idea what configuration to use for the shield. It couldn't be made large enough to cover the side of the ship. Would a spoiler do?

'Computer, I need help here. Make the shield into a flat plane, angle it upwards at forty-five degrees. I'm trying to get most of particle stream to blow up over and let the rest go under.'

The low sigh became a hiss of white noise.

'Configuring,' the computer said.

'Hurry up!'

The scouring wind became a roar, interspersed with loud bumps and clangs. The storm was upon him.

'Come on, do it already!' Aryx's knuckles turned white; his teeth threatened to shatter.

The turmoil stopped.

'Shield adaptation complete.'

He let out a deep breath. The tap-tap of stray particles pinged against the hull intermittently. At least the worst of it was deflected. The shield generator began to vibrate on its mountings.

'Computer, what's happening?'

'The landing site is passing through the shadow terminator. The sun will be at zenith in thirty minutes. Suggest shield reconfiguration at that time.'

'I don't need to monitor it until then, I only need to worry about when we pass back into shadow?'

'Affirmative. Solar wind pressure is at its peak during transition through solar terminator.'

'I'd rather be safe than sorry.' He watched the navcomputer show the sun slowly passing overhead, and he moved the shield up from the ground to compensate.

'Can we contact Sebastian?'

'Real-time communications are not possible at this time. Charged particles caused by the intense solar radiation are interfering with the signals.'

'Can we send a recorded message as a data packet?'

'Affirmative. Data packets can be sent in bursts and verified.'

'Good. Record and send the following message ... Sebastian, the storm is passing but it'll come again in an hour, so you need to get back to the ship as soon as possible once it's passed.' He was about to terminate the message, but then remembered his observations of the cube. 'Oh, and I've found something interesting about the cube. I think it's a self-powered processing core of some kind. It seems to be picking up signals from the ship and is interacting with them somehow. Not sure exactly what it's doing yet, but it's doing *something*. End message.'

Sebastian stepped through the doorway from the icy tunnel into a large cavern carved out from the comet's interior in the same fashion. From the ceiling – which he estimated to be seventeen to twenty metres high – hung columns of faceted crystalline stalactites, connected to each other by thin sheets of crystal or glass, whose multi-coloured panes filtered light from bright white globes suspended from the ceiling. A natural, crystalline cathedral. He'd never seen anything like it.

The floor, which had the same grey metallic finish as the corridor, was littered with large, colourful woven rugs. To the far right, a rectangular arrangement of couches around a low table reminded him of a lounge. Beyond the lounge, the far wall consisted of an array of display screens with a pair of enormous bookcases to either side. In each corner of the room stood large, potted plants with sunlamps hanging over them. To the left, at the opposite end of the cavern, a kitchen area with a U-shaped counter sat at the base of a set of metal open-framed stairs that ran along the wall and up into a dark alcove above. The curved ceiling receded into darkness beyond the ledge.

Sebastian staggered back as the masked inhabitant stepped out from behind the open door. He wore a long, black hooded robe that revealed nothing, save for the white porcelain mask. A hermit-monk from an old horror movie. A hermit living on an isolated, mist-shrouded island. Living on an island alone, where he probably ate visitors.

'If I answer your questions,' the hermit said, 'will you go away and leave me in peace?'

Sebastian judged the man to be about the same height as himself – even while slightly stooped. His eyes were level with his own, but the dark holes gave nothing away.

Sebastian shifted uneasily. 'I suppose so, yes.' He wasn't used to speaking to someone without being able to see their expressions – or at least their eyes – and it wasn't easy to gauge the man's reaction. 'If I get the answers I need, I'll leave you in peace.'

The mask tilted back, as though regarding him momentarily – possibly detecting his unease. 'I believe you will.' It turned slightly, and the man gestured to the couches with a leather-gloved hand. 'Where are my manners? Would you like to sit?'

'Yes, thank you.' Sebastian looked down at his suit and then at the plush sofa. He didn't exactly have much choice. Leaving a faint trail of comet dust on the rugs, he perched on the nearest seat, his initial unease replaced by the discomfort of embarrassment.

'Would you like something to drink?' the man called from somewhere behind him.

Sebastian turned. He had moved into the kitchen and was standing in front of a kettle.

'Just water, thank you.'

The man stopped busying himself with utensils. 'Why is it that people on official business always ask for water when offered a drink?'

'I don't know. Maybe they're told not to drink anything else?'

'Did anyone tell *you* not to ask for anything other than water?'

'No, I guess not.'

The masked hermit-monk laughed. At least it wasn't a hollow, macabre laugh. Sebastian relaxed a little and allowed himself a nervous 'Heh!' and turned his attention to studying the pattern on one of the rugs, trying to lose his unease in the weave.

The man returned to the lounge, carrying a tray littered with tea-making paraphernalia and a glass of water. He bent to place it on the table and took a seat on the couch to Sebastian's right. He put the glass of water down in front of him, then leaned forwards and proceeded to stir the contents of the teapot.

Sebastian took the glass and sipped. It was at that point he realised the man didn't have an inch of skin visible; he was covered completely from head to foot. He watched carefully as the hermit poured himself a cup of tea, added milk, and stirred it with a small silver spoon. Sitting back to drink, he brought the cup to his mouth and it clinked against the mask. He grumbled, got up, and went to the kitchen. What was he hiding under that mask?

The hermit returned and picked up the cup for a second attempt. This time he inserted a small plastic straw into the mouth opening, took a sip, and placed the straw on his saucer. 'Please excuse me, I don't have many visitors,' he said, resting the cup in his lap. 'Now, what business do you have with me?'

Sebastian put his glass back on the table, clearing his throat as he did so. 'I'm investigating the bombing of a lab on Tenebrae station.'

'I've never heard of the place, but do go on.' The masked voice was fluid and unstrained – likely speaking the truth.

'The bombing was unusual in that there was no trace of an explosive device.'

'That sounds unfortunate, but it doesn't explain why you're *here*.'

Sebastian continued, undeterred. To reveal the tenuousness of the connection with their evidence would be unwise. 'We are in the process of cleaning up some video footage, and also found traces of an unidentified mineral outside the lab in which the explosion took place.'

'That still doesn't explain your presence. I assume there is a point to this exposition?'

Sebastian pulled his collar with a finger. 'I apologise. I managed to get some basic properties off the sample and was able to track down a supplier. Once we knew where it came from, we traced the shipment here.' There was no need to point out that he was actually aware of *two* buyers.

A long silence. A hand went to the masked chin. Perhaps he was uneasy, wondering how they had tracked him down.

He had to win his confidence. 'There may be another lead, but I'm here because you're the most concrete lead we've got in the investigation so far.'

'I see.' The hermit put the cup on the table and folded his hands in his lap. 'Do you suspect me of being the bomber?'

'The evidence may only be circumstantial, but if you can help us to eliminate you from our investigation, I'd be most grateful. You'll find the tracker in the hopper.'

The man appeared to relax his pose slightly. Sebastian found him difficult to read behind the mask. The eyeholes appeared deep, dark and foreboding.

'For some reason, I like you. I'd be glad to help.' The hermit's tone softened and he laced his fingers together. 'Do you know what the mineral actually is?' he asked, the question slow and deliberate.

'It's not something I've ever come across before. On Sollers Hope they call it carbyne powder. I managed to take a sample from the mine.' Sebastian reached for his glass and took another sip of water.

'They have, no doubt, told you that under ordinary circumstances the mineral is utterly useless. What they will not have told you is that in the hands of a skilled practitioner, it can be used to perform what most people would call magic.'

About to swallow, Sebastian choked. Water from his mouth sprayed the coffee table.

'At least do me the courtesy of not destroying my furniture ... You don't believe me.'

'*Magic?*' He shook his head. 'I'm sorry. I made a mistake coming here.' He made a move to stand.

The hermit put his hand out. 'Stop. I suppose it was a stretch to expect you to believe me straight away ... Tell me, are you familiar with literature from the Dark Ages?'

Sebastian sat back. 'Medieval books? I can't say that I am. But I have a passing familiarity with Norse lore.' Why was he even talking about this? It had nothing to do with the explosion.

'Hmm.' The man cupped his chin and tapped the masked cheek with a finger. 'I don't think the *Eddas* referred to alchemy, but they certainly had plenty of references to magic.'

Sebastian fought the urge to roll his eyes and tried to mask the gesture by looking away.

'You may well roll your eyes, but as much as you might not want to hear it, carbyne is, in fact, orichalcum. The "Philosopher's Stone" referred to by the Greeks. The catalyst for transmutation.' Sebastian raised his eyebrows, but the man continued. 'The reason alchemists found it difficult to obtain in medieval times is simple. The mineral is in a state of phasal flux and that makes its bonds unstable. Atomic collisions with gases, the atmosphere for example, make it dissipate easily, effectively evaporating it. Of course ancient Humans were unaware of this and, once mined, the supplies of orichalcum would simply vanish within a few hours. If he got to it quickly enough, a practitioner could stabilise it so that it could be safely stored. Of course, there have been very few accomplished practitioners of magic through the ages.'

'Of course.' Sebastian nodded. 'There never *were* any practitioners of magic.'

The man, apparently unperturbed by his tone, continued. 'I am not talking about mere sleight of hand tricks, mentalism, or so-called "psychic powers",' he said, twiddling his fingers in the air in a mockery of show-magic. 'I'm talking about the *real* art, the art of thaumaturgy.' As he stood, he raised his hands in a dramatic flourish. 'I am talking about the ability to use the catalytic properties of carbyne and force of will, though visualisation and sound, to alter the very fabric of reality!'

Sebastian wanted to give up. Most of it sounded like nonsense, but there was something in the way the man spoke. This wasn't insane rambling. This was a logical man. He found himself shaking his head slowly.

The man dropped his hands to his sides. 'I don't know how you expect me to help in your investigation if you don't believe a word I say.'

'I'm sorry, it's all just a bit ... outlandish.'

'Is it as unbelievable as an explosion caused by inert powder?'

'More unbelievable!' He took another sip of water to cool his boiling blood. 'I need something concrete to add to my investigation, not some paranormal babbling.'

'Then I cannot help you.' The hermit turned his back.

'I can't just *accept* something with no scientific proof.'

The man continued to speak, but did not turn to face him. 'The mayor of Sollers Hope gave me a nickname when he first saw me in my current state. Not a particularly flattering nickname, I might add.'

Sebastian let the air settle. Gave him time to elaborate.

'He decided to call me *The Paper Man*, due to my condition.'

'Why? What is your condition?' He leaned forwards.

'If you want to see, you had better prepare yourself. Put your glass down, I don't want you ruining my antique Persian rugs.'

Sebastian placed his glass on the table. This was going to be interesting, and probably embarrassing for the man if he believed he'd done something to himself with *magic*.

'I experimented with the art for many years. Unfortunately, my curiosity led to my present, irreversible, condition. If you don't believe in the existence of magic now, you will.'

The Paper Man put a hand to his face. He slowly lowered the mask to his side, gripping it between his fingers.

Sebastian held his breath.

The hood twisted and The Paper Man slowly turned to face him.

Chapter 14

Sebastian couldn't make out the unmasked face beneath the hood. He rubbed his eyes, thinking his vision was blurry.

The face was undefined. With no normal skin tones, it looked almost as though the man was transparent, the shadowy depths of the hood still visible behind the head within.

'I told you to prepare yourself.' The Paper Man sat down on the couch and drew the hood back.

Sebastian recoiled.

The hair was only a couple of millimetres long – white stubble, barely visible against the background of the cavern – and the scalp a papery shell, pulled taut over fine blood vessels that formed a deep-red lace filigree below the surface. The volume of the skull, which itself appeared to be made of a barely visible material, contained a delicate sponge-like scaffold of blood vessels that tapered to nothing. The eyes, a strange tracery of red lines surrounding translucent tissue with semi-reflective retinas at the back, regarded him with a terrifying, glassy cat-eye stare.

Sebastian averted his eyes, unable to meet the gaze, but continued to study the head, simultaneously fascinated and repulsed.

The structure of muscles around the skull was clear, outlined by the blood vessels within them; pale patches of tissue floating amidst the veins and capillaries. Faint hints of muscles in the jaw, lips and nose traced the outline of the face, framed by a short fuzz of stubble.

'Seen enough? Or do you need more convincing?' The Paper Man stood up and flung his robe apart.

The man was see-through! Like some biology museum exhibit. Tree-like lungs expanded and contracted. Tea sloshed around in the man's stomach; parts of the liver, kidneys and other organs quivered, strung together with deep-red and maroon pulsating threads; the bones, visible in thin outline, revealed jelly-like marrow in their depths.

Sebastian choked back a mouthful of bile at the sight of the remains of an earlier meal, chewed to mash, crawling its way around the man's intestines. He turned away. 'By the Gods!'

He was wrong – this *was* something from a horror movie.

'Believe me now?'

He turned back to face the sponge-like figure, being careful not to let his eyes linger too long on any specific detail. The man pulled the robe back over himself.

'How did this happen?'

'I told you, experiments in thaumaturgy. In my arrogance, I once attempted an invisibility spell. It worked perfectly and I became totally invisible, at least for a time. As you can see,' he said, pulling off a glove and extending his fingers, 'I became invisible, but couldn't manage to turn myself back again. I've tried many times over the years but every time I attempt it, I black out. When I come around again, I'm back to square one, totally invisible.'

'This is . . . bizarre.' Sebastian picked up his infoslate. 'Do you mind if I take a scan?'

'For your own curiosity, but I'd appreciate it if you don't record the results.'

He nodded and held the infoslate up as The Paper Man turned his hand over in front of it, showing the fine detail of capillaries lacing around and through the semi-transparent bones of his fingers beneath a vellum-like layer of skin.

'As you can see, I'm slowly becoming visible again. The atoms that make up the food I eat don't become invisible when I ingest them. Instead, they are incorporated in my body in a visible state, so the cells that get replaced the quickest become visible sooner, hence my skin having the appearance of waxed paper, and my blood showing prominently.'

Sebastian nodded slowly. 'And that's why Havlor gave you the nickname.' As the peculiar nature of the situation sank in, curiosity won out. 'How are you able to see? Doesn't light pass straight through your eyes?'

'I have no idea. That's part of the mystery of magic. The strange thing is, I can still see through my eyelids. It comes in handy when visiting Sollers Hope.' He laughed.

'I imagine it does,' Sebastian said, remembering the gritty air. He laughed weakly.

'I have problems with vitamin D. My skin doesn't absorb sunlight on the rare occasion that I manage to get any.'

He looked down at the scans. The information only confirmed what his eyes saw. The interstitial fibres, all the invisible parts, came back as undetectable. To the slate, The Paper Man was just that: a shell containing a tree of veins and paper-thin bones. He hit the delete icon, not wanting to think about the gory situation any longer than necessary. 'What happened to your clothes? Did they become invisible, too?'

'Yes, they did. They would be a marvel of modern science if I could find them. I lost a t-shirt somewhere.'

'They didn't turn visible when you attempted to fix the problem?'

'Oh yes, *the ones I wore at the time* did, even though *I* didn't ... Which I don't quite understand ...' The skeletal hand brushed week-old stubble on his chin. 'What were we talking about?'

'You were going to tell me how you could help me solve this case.'

'Ah, yes. If there were traces of carbyne at the scene, you're either looking for a thaumaturge, or at least someone who has handled carbyne. What you need is a way of finding out *exactly* what happened in that lab.'

'There's no footage from inside it. The video we had was from the corridor, but the perpetrator was blurred.'

'It sounds like magic to me, but at the time I would have been totally invisible, and here. I haven't left this place for weeks.' He ran a hand an inch over his head and the short, white stubble flexed subtly. 'As you can see, this is a week's growth of visible hair. The last time I tried to make myself visible was a week ago.'

'I believe you. The infoslate showed only what I see. It wasn't blurry. If it wasn't you, who was it? The strange thing is, it was a similar effect to what I saw when a friend of mine took pictures of a Folian ship. The Folians themselves weren't blurry, so I don't think it was one of them, but whoever did it might have access to the same technology that hides their ships.'

The Paper Man gave a peculiar smile. 'So you've met the Folians too, eh?'

'Yes. Odd people. Peaceful and elegant, though.'

'Odd ... indeed. They can probably help you, as they have an understanding of the art and may be able to help determine events in the lab. They won't aid you on your station, though. You'll have to go to them.'

'Nobody knows where their homeworld is.'

'I used to know. I've been there in the past, but voluntarily had the knowledge of its location erased from my memory.'

Sebastian shifted in his seat, becoming restless with excitement. He'd never heard of anyone having their memory wiped. 'Erased? Why? Was it hypnosis?'

'Magic. They are a very insular people, and with good reason. It was for their security. Contact with them must be on their terms.'

'So, how do I find the place?'

'I used to live in an outpost called Chopwood on Tradescantia, a world close to their homeworld, Achene. I lived with them for a few months while learning the art. I already knew of thaumaturgy but was unable to perform it before I met them due to lack of information. Afterwards, they dropped me off at Chopwood and updated my knowledge of the galaxy. I was intrigued to find out what had happened to Humanity in my absence so I took a runner – a small ship that was left behind in Chopwood – and they pointed me in the direction of the nearest acceleration node, then I ventured back into modern space'

'*Modern* space?'

'Our colony ship set out from Earth in 2053. This was about a decade before what you know of as the Ecological Crux. We set out to find natural resources that could be brought back to Earth. Long-range telescopes had picked up indications of a world that might harbour massive amounts of plant life, so we made our way to it in the hope that there would be wood that could be used for building materials. Earth was running out of metal long before the asteroid belt got mined, you know, and not everything could be made from concrete.

'We travelled at relativistic speeds and didn't experience time in the same way as the rest of the universe. We journeyed for an incredibly long time, but of course to us it felt like weeks while the ship accelerated to lightspeed. This was before the discovery of the acceleration nodes, and that's why I call this modern space. I'm a little out of my time.'

'How long have you been here?'

'In the space within reach of the acceleration nodes, about fifty years, give or take a few. I don't keep track of time well.'

'So how old are you, if you don't mind me asking?'

'I was born in 2029. I was twenty-six when I left Chopwood ... I feel about fifty-something, but I'm probably eighty or more. Like I said, I'm not counting, and it's all relative.'

'You don't sound that old. Of course, I can't judge by sight.'

'Hmm,' The Paper Man grumbled. 'Probably one of the side effects of the spell. Maybe it prevents me from ageing so fast. Regardless, I'd rather be normal, and dead.'

'You really ought to get seen by a doctor. No pun intended,' Sebastian said, putting his hands up.

'No offence taken.' The translucent head shook. 'Can you imagine how much of a scientific spectacle I'd become? I want none of that. I'd rather live out the last of my days in peace and quiet than being picked apart by scalpel-wielding zealots.'

'I can understand that. So, what about the—' His suit comms bleeped. 'Sorry, just a moment,' he said, putting a finger to his ear.

The suit computer spoke. 'Incoming data packet message from *Ultima Thule*.'

'Play back.' He listened to the message from Aryx. 'It sounds like the ship's taking a beating up there. I'll have to go shortly. I'm afraid we've upset the rotation of your comet.'

'It's not a problem, I can stabilise it when you've left. It's not really intended for surface landings.'

He was about to ask what he meant, but remembered he'd not cleared up a more pressing issue. 'You were about to tell me how the Folians might be able to help, and how to find them.'

'Of course I was. As I said, they taught me the art of thaumaturgy, and they have the uncanny ability to use the art to tap into the fabric of the universe to divine the nature of things. They might be able to tell you what went on inside the lab and, maybe, who caused the explosion. I don't have the location of Chopwood any more. It was erased from my ship's logs and my memory.'

'Yes, you said that.'

'Alright. My memory of the location has gone. I've not got Alzheimer's. I have the locator beacon frequency of Chopwood. Find Chopwood and you'll find the Folians.'

'Locator beacons? Everything is located by timing beacons, maps, and star positions now.'

'Yes, and probably the reason why nobody has found it since. Modern ships don't monitor those old radio frequencies as a matter of course.' He laughed. 'Ah, the trouble your maps cause those poor sods on Sollers Hope. Mind you, they do take it to heart a bit too much if you ask me . . . You should be able to follow the beacon signal and track the planet down that way. And I advise against logging the trip.' The Paper Man got up from the couch and walked over to a door opposite the one Sebastian had entered. 'I'll go and get the frequency for you. Wait here – and don't touch anything!'

Sebastian waited on the couch and began nibbling on a thumbnail. How had this place been built? Was the comet natural? It certainly hadn't been in the Yazor system long enough to have been recorded in the Galactic maps. Then again, it depended on when the place had been mapped in the first place.

Sebastian brushed the question aside when the man came back through the door and strode over to him clutching a tatty piece of paper.

He held the scrap out. 'I'd made a note of it just in case the need ever arose. I'd forgotten about it until now.'

A long sequence of digits was scrawled onto the paper, along with the name *Pegasus*. 'What's that?' Sebastian asked.

'Not the name of a ship – ours was the *Iceni*. I'm assuming I was referring to the constellation when I wrote it.'

'Thank you,' Sebastian said, tucking the paper into a pouch on his belt.

'Glad to do anything I can to help. Whilst I may not have been to your station, and even though I'm not a fan of crowded places, I have no urge to see innocents hurt by mindless destruction, and I certainly don't want to see thaumaturgy revealed to the world as something dangerous and evil.'

'Thanks.' He gave a tight smile. Now that he was a little farther along in the investigation, he began to wonder about the help the Folians might provide. 'How does this magic, thaumaturgy, work anyway?'

'I can't explain it to you fully, and it's wasteful to demonstrate unnecessarily. It takes a certain mindset to be able to work it, though. The basic principle, as I understand it, is that the carbyne acts as a catalyst, enabling the transformation of energy forms. You chant, or make a specific sound whilst holding certain images in your mind. Sometimes it needs to be coupled with a gesture. The carbyne gets used up in the process.'

'The acceleration nodes transform energy. I wonder if that's why carbyne is often found alongside the false bornite ore ... Why isn't the existence of magic widely known, given that it's real?'

'It is known, to an extent, but the *belief* is another matter. Some non-Human races have stories of thaumaturgy, under different names, but there seems to be a general taboo, and many cultures shun its use, so it appears to have largely died out in the galaxy. I have no idea why. Maybe those races have attached the same sort of stigma to it as we did in medieval times.'

'I'm still having a hard time wrapping my head around it.'

'You might understand it in time.' The smoky-glass eyes looked down at Sebastian's neck.

He brought his hand up and felt his necklace – the Mjölnir, Thor's hammer – which must have ridden up his neck and caught The Paper Man's eye. Why was he looking at it?

'Do you have a faith?'

His stomach twisted uncomfortably. 'Yes. I was brought up as Ásatrú, but I admit don't always follow it.'

'Ah, that explains the hammer. It's a reconstruction of the Old Norse faith, isn't it? You look at your religion, even if you don't believe it literally. You'll find some truth in it, if you think about it long enough. When your investigation is over, come back and we can talk about it some more.'

He wasn't entirely convinced of the relevance of his religion, and his mind was no longer on the topic of conversation. 'Yes, well ... Thank you for the help,' he said. 'I have to be going now, I'm up against time.'

The Paper Man nodded. 'By all means, go. I would be grateful if you could keep me up to speed, should you discover anything in the course of your investigation. The thought that someone else might be using the art is ... interesting, to say the least.' The man walked to the entrance door. He pulled a remote out of a pocket in his robes and pointed it at the screens on the wall near the lounge. A monitor flicked on, showing the outside of the entrance crater. The surface was still, and in shadow. 'You're safe to go,' he said. 'Hurry, though! I fear we've talked a little too long.'

Sebastian shook hands with the man, said goodbye and picked up the pistol from the walkway. Jogging in the pressure suit was uncomfortable, and before he'd reached the airlock he was sweating profusely. There was only so much that the N-suit could do to keep him cool while being worn in the confines of the pressure suit.

He approached the exit and clamped the helmet back into place. The doors opened and he stepped in. The characteristic whoosh of air escaping echoed all around, and the impending silence that followed indicated he was once again in hard vacuum. He stepped out into the antechamber and noticed the ladder mounted on the floor heading towards the secret crater door. Crouching on all fours at the far end, he gripped the rungs ready to climb out. The lights went off and gravity shifted ninety degrees. He slipped, but hung on as the doors – now above – parted, revealing not the black, star-spattered view of space trimmed with ice, but a hazy grey fuzz. As he climbed out into the crater a cold shiver ran down his spine.

The streams of ice on the horizon were no longer vertical. The comet was still rotating, and now the ice was flowing past at an acute angle. The *Ultima* crouched in the distance, roughly a mile off. If he didn't hurry, he'd be ripped to shreds by the icy dust tearing across the surface.

He ran.

'Aryx,' he shouted breathlessly into the comms, 'warm up the shield. I'm coming!'

'Already on it! You don't have much time. About six minutes and it'll be on us!'

Six-minute mile was the record in a pressure suit – for a veteran wearer. There was no way he'd make it that far, not lumbering along in the low gravity. His feet slipped and scraped over the glassy rock surface, and loose rubble crumbled as he bounded along. He was a fool for taking the job and getting into these stupid situations. Why didn't he turn back? Surely he could have waited in the airlock?

Looking to one side, he attempted to estimate how long he had.

A bad idea: the stream of debris was nearly horizontal. He lost his footing and fell. The impact knocked the wind out of him, but the N-suit protected him from the worst of it. He heaved himself up and looked down.

The ragged edge of a tiny rip in the fabric billowed and flapped as air escaped from the suit.

'Shit!' he screamed. He was going to die from suffocation.

Tiny tapping sounds came from the back of his helmet. Oh Gods.

He paused for a moment – a second – to regain his composure. Closed his eyes. Took the last deep breath of air from the suit before the tanks ran out. The ship was only a couple of hundred yards away now, at most. He pelted towards it in a headlong run.

He charged forwards, stumbling over large rocks and slipping on smaller ones. His lungs burnt and he gasped for air. Thin air. His neck tightened.

The ship swam in front of him. He stumbled up the steps and as he hit the button to open the door he blacked out.

Chapter 15

Aryx stared in horror through the inner airlock window as Sebastian collapsed, his body laying half in, half out of the ship. There was no way he could close the outer door. Not with him in the way. A pressure suit wouldn't fit him without boots, which meant he wouldn't be able to override the mechanism and open the inner door. How was he going to get him in?

'Computer!' he shouted. 'Reconfigure the CFD steps. Alter the shape – change it into a scoop.'

'Please specify.'

'I don't have time for this shit. Just a fucking scoop. An upside down version of the ramp, something! Tilt the steps upward. Do whatever you have to do to get him in the door. Just do it now!'

The computer, in its indecision and inability to adequately assess the situation, altered the steps to become a flat wedge, which it immediately swung upwards, flinging Sebastian's limp body unceremoniously into the chamber with a loud thud.

Aryx hammered the switch. 'Come on, come on!'

The external door, clear of the obstruction, slammed shut as a cloud of dust and rock filled the chamber.

'Activate the shield cycle!'

The ship obeyed and began replaying the last set of commands just in time to deflect the scouring winds as they attained full force. Pressurisation completed and the airlock door finally opened. Aryx slid out of his chair onto the floor beside Sebastian's body and felt for a pulse on his neck. He couldn't find one. Leaning forwards, he put all his weight on Sebastian's chest and began pressing down rhythmically with both hands. He pumped Sebastian's chest four times, then pinched his nose shut as he took a deep breath and forced it deeply into his lungs.

No response.

He repeated the process. Please don't be dead!

Once more. Don't leave me here alone.

As he pounded on Sebastian's chest, he felt the hole in the suit. 'You stupid bastard! All you had to do was take a different suit, but you couldn't be bothered and now you're going to die just because you were too ashamed to admit you'd ruined it and thought I'd shout at you for risking your life – now *wake up!*' He forced in a third lungful.

Sebastian's eyes fluttered open and he coughed. 'I ... never knew ... you cared,' he croaked.

'Shut up, you stupid, irresponsible bastard.' Aryx pushed him down and his head thudded against the floor. 'I told you to be careful, and what did you do? You died!'

Sebastian propped himself up on his elbows. 'You're telling me,' he said, poking at the hole in the suit. 'I fell over and ripped it.'

Aryx punched him in the chest. 'It's a good job we've got two spares, then!'

Sebastian got up and started taking off the damaged pressure suit. 'Thank you,' he said, staring at the floor.

'You'd do the same for me.' Aryx wiped his eyes. 'I thought I'd lost you. I'm not a medic.'

'I'm sorry.'

He folded his arms. How dare he think that sorry was good enough. 'Aryx, don't.'

He climbed back into his chair.

'I said I'm sorry.'

'Next time, think before you do something stupid. Actually, just think and don't do something stupid. Think about who you might leave behind.'

Sebastian's head hung as he pulled the pistol from the holster, took off the pressure suit and threw it into the corner of the alcove. He put the helmet back on the hook. The back was deeply pitted.

'You were lucky to get back in time.'

'I know. I pity the ship's paintwork.' He laughed, and coughed dryly.

'*I'm* not repainting it ... At least you're well enough to joke. There can't be any permanent damage, although I'm sure you're already brain damaged, judging by how clumsy you are.' Aryx folded his arms. 'So what happened out there?'

'I met an invisible man in a cave inside the comet. He uses magic – I've even got scans.' Sebastian bent to pick up the infoslate. 'Oh ... No, I deleted them.'

Aryx opened his mouth to speak, but Sebastian put his hand up to stop him.

'No, I am not brain damaged, nor suffering from oxygen deprivation. This happened inside the comet, not my head.'

'I—'

'You what? Don't believe me? You would if you saw the guy! I was so distracted by it that I didn't even get his real name. The Paper Man ... It was a bit gross. I could see all the bits inside him.' He grimaced before turning to head up the ladder.

'Sounds wonderful. How's that supposed to work?' Aryx shouted, following up on the lift.

'Stuff he eats doesn't become invisible ...' Sebastian typed commands into the piloting console. 'Damn, the storm's going to last a while.'

'About an hour, then we can go. Where we going next? Back to the station?'

Sebastian continued to type commands into the console, reading from a piece of paper he'd taken out of his belt. 'No. We have to track down an old outpost called Chopwood. He gave me a radio beacon frequency that we have to triangulate.'

'Where'll that get us?'

'Achene.'

'That's part of a plant.'

'It's also the Folian homeworld.'

Aryx's curiosity piqued. 'Folians?'

'Apparently they taught him "the art of thaumaturgy", and he thinks our perpetrator is a user of magic, hence the blurred video. He also thinks the Folians might have a way of finding out what happened inside the lab.'

'I see ... Assuming this is all real, that is. You know, you sound almost as bad as Alvarez, talking about superstitious rubbish.'

'I wasn't hallucinating. I *know* what I saw.'

'Do you think he did it?'

'I'm not sure, but I don't think so. As a potential suspect he wouldn't have wanted to incriminate himself in front of me, would he? And he didn't look blurry. He was half invisible.'

'It could be a double-bluff.'

'No. The state he was in, hiding like he does ... He had a reason for revealing himself to me, and it wasn't to get arrested.'

'Hmm. So what else happened when you met this guy?' He was keen to move the topic of conversation away from nonsense.

While they waited for the storm to pass, Sebastian described his journey through the tunnels leading to the cavern and The Paper Man's tale of experimentation. 'And I almost forgot to tell you, he heats the water for his drinks with a kettle.'

'Sounds like my kind of person,' Aryx said. 'I'd look forward to meeting him sometime, for that alone.' He clapped his hands together. 'So what's the plan when we find Chopwood?'

'We scan the system when we arrive and see if we can find Achene, simple.' Sebastian finished typing and turned around. 'So what did you discover about our cube?'

'You'll be interested in this.' Aryx wheeled to the diagnostics console. 'You can see the cube's emissions peak when there are lulls in those from the ship. I'd almost say it was sampling the signals.'

Sebastian came over to stand behind him. 'That would imply it's some kind of processor, but why would it be interacting with the ship? Is it interfering with the ship's functions? I suppose the signals weren't in any recognisable format.'

'No, and the ship doesn't *seem* to be responding to anything other than our input.'

'There might be something on the station that we can use to do a deep scan and find out how to open it. I take it there was no success with the melted lump from the lab, either?'

'Nope. That's just spewing out random stuff. The computer couldn't make sense of it and neither could I – you're the data expert.'

'That settles it, then. We'll have to see if we can get some secure equipment to analyse it when we get back. Leave the computer running a heuristic analysis for the time being. You never know, it might turn up something.'

Aryx set the computer to perform a more in-depth analysis on the data from the melted lump and placed the metal cube back in its box. Feeling its weight again triggered an odd sensation in his stomach. Something not quite right. 'How old did you say this thing was?'

'Gladrin seemed to think it was a new technology the terrorists had got hold of, or had been developing. Why?'

'It's just that when we looked at it with the nanocameras, something struck me as strange. Processors don't tend to get as hot as they used to now they use quantum transfer circuits, so why would it have needed a heat sink? It seems a little out of date.'

'Could it be a high-capacity multicore?'

He shook his head and wrinkled his nose. 'It's not just the heat sink. It's the material it's made from, and the use of LEDs, too.'

'Maybe Gladrin got it wrong. Perhaps it's older than he thought.'

'Possibly.' Aryx glanced up at the cockpit windows. The sky was black once again. 'The storm's stopped,' he said, nodding in the direction of the cockpit. 'We'd better go.'

'I'm on it.' Sebastian jumped into the pilot's seat. 'Same routine as before?'

'No. I think this time we can just go straight up and accelerate away. The debris won't catch up with us.'

The ship's engines thrummed as Aryx made his way to the shield room.

The *Ultima Thule* burst forth from the streaming tail of the Yazor comet and glided across the empty system, heading for the acceleration node.

Aryx returned to the cockpit and wheeled over to the piloting console next to Sebastian. The Galactic map was on display, with a cone projected outward from their current location. It looked like he had already input the frequency from the locator beacon and begun scanning for its source. The time code being transmitted by the beacon was shown at the bottom of the map: a date several years behind current time.

'We'll have to triangulate the signal,' Sebastian said. 'The origin must be several light years away, but I've no idea on the exact location because there's no comms relay, and I can't calculate the time differential of this system. If we plot a course at ninety degrees to the signal via the nodes, we should be able take another bearing and then match the two up for a location.'

'Better to take three. You'll get a more accurate position,' Aryx said. He certainly didn't want to go billions of miles out of the way to the wrong planet because of Sebastian's laziness.

'Good idea. I'm glad I'm not paying for the fuel.'

He watched as Sebastian pressed a few controls on the console, storing their location and bearing, then plotted a course for the node to exit the system and set the ship to autopilot. It was now a waiting game, and Aryx didn't like waiting.

Aryx was surprised Sebastian had believed The Paper Man's story about magic. Surely there were other physical explanations for his condition. He was at a loss. He'd seen alien materials that were almost invisible but they were just transparent and didn't affect whatever they contained, and he knew of no cloaking technology that could produce an effect like the blur they'd seen on the video. Sebastian didn't seem susceptible to suggestion, or prone to blind belief; he was far too logical for that – most of the time. Therefore, stretching credulity and assuming what The Paper Man said was true – that magic was something real and tangible – how the hell did it work? It was frustrating that Sebastian hadn't pushed for a demonstration. What he'd seen in the comet had clearly led him to believe in it enough to start scouring the galaxy for a long-lost colony. Aryx had never encountered anything that made him question his senses like that. When you grew up on a farming museum working with machinery, crops, and dirt, you tended not to dwell on irrelevant fantasy, especially in the Australian outback; instead you focused on real, solid problems, just like his father had . . .

* * *

'Pass me the forty-mil spanner, will ya?' came a voice from beneath the tractor.

'Which one's that?' six-year-old Aryx asked.

'The one you're playing with.'

He dropped down from the huge wheel and crawled under the machine, dragging the enormous metal bar with him. 'What are you doing, Dad?'

'Cheers, laddo.' Aaron Trevarian's tree-trunk arms reached up into a space behind the driveshaft and began working on the biggest bolt Aryx had ever seen. 'I'm taking the old diesel engine out. It's gotta be replaced with a fusion unit.'

Aryx lay on his back next to his father, watching his arms exert their superhuman strength on the stubborn fixture, and marvelled over the twisting pipes and patterns they made, winding their way around the chassis. 'I want to fix things like you when I grow up.'

'You should be out playing with the other kids.'

'The Kidgells think I'm weird because I want to be an engineer.'

The arms stopped fighting the bolt and his father looked at him. 'You're not weird. You're just smart for your age, and I'm proud of you for it. I'd rather you look after the farm when I'm too old, but I can't expect the world. You've got to find your own path.'

Aryx felt something sharp under his back and wriggled his hand underneath himself. He pulled out an ear of wheat. 'I don't like plants. They're boring.'

'You just don't have the patience to see them grow ... If you want to be an engineer when you grow up, go for it, but you'll find you need patience for that, too. It's hard work.' His father sighed. 'Machines nowadays aren't made for people to work on, not like these. Everything's either thrown away or recycled. At least you'll have good job prospects, and if you get bored, you can always come back here.'

The arms reached back into the heart of the machine and with one final wrench, pulled the bolt free. 'That's got it ...'

Aryx smiled at the memory. After his parents died, the marines became his family and later, when his career ended, there was no way he could go back to running the farm. He couldn't stand to be around the place in their absence, but now, looking back, he realised he missed the warm soil under his back.

The ship slowly approached the gleaming acceleration node, skirting the capture radius in preparation for alignment with the next one along the route.

An alert beeping from the console jerked Aryx out of his reverie. 'What the hell's that?'

'Another ship, approaching from starboard,' Sebastian said. 'The sensors only just picked it up. The node's energy must have been masking it.'

'We'd better wait until they've used the node. No telling what might happen if we used it at the same time, and I don't think anyone's ever done it before.'

'A big bang, I ex—' A loud thud reverberated through the hull. 'What the hell? Are they shooting at us? Computer, open a channel!' Sebastian pulled at the manual override stick, stopping the ship before it entered the node's capture radius.

The computer bleeped, acknowledging connection to the other ship. 'Who are you? Why are you attacking us?'

'This is the Independent Terran Front. You have something of ours. We want it back and we'll take it by force if we have to.'

'Terrorists!' Aryx hissed, muting the comms.

'I know,' Sebastian whispered. 'They must want the cube. We don't have any ship-to-ship weapons so I can't risk getting into a fight, and I don't have any practice with this,' he said, patting the pistol on his belt. 'What can we do ...? Aha! Put the cube in the escape pod! If they come aboard, they might not find it. Put the mobipack in, too. We can't risk them getting hold of that technology as well.'

'I'll put the stuff in there, but I'm not sitting this one out.' Aryx went to the back of the ship, opened the hidden escape pod hatch, tossed the items inside, and closed the door as the hull echoed with another shot. They were obviously getting impatient.

Sebastian reactivated the comms. 'I don't know what it is you want, but we have no weapons and are in no position to argue with you.'

'We'll be the judge of that. Prepare to be boarded.' The comms went dead and the spray-painted terrorist ship drifted past the cockpit window from right to left as it came around to port.

'How the hell are we going to get out of this?' Aryx weighed up the enemy ship. It was a little bigger than the *Ultima*, angular and vaguely fish shaped – a stolen Antari minicruiser. The graffiti on the sides had given it a jagged, white shark grin. They could probably have taken it, if they'd had weapons.

'I have a plan.' Sebastian said. 'I want you to go to the shield room. When they get close to dock, set up a shield between us, then bash their ship with it. Not too hard – just enough to give them a nudge.'

'How will that help?'

'Look how close we are to the capture radius.'

Aryx shuddered. The enemy ship would be sent off into superphase in whatever direction they were travelling. 'They'd never be able to catch us, even if they dropped out near a node.' He grinned. 'Of course, they'd probably end up in the middle of nowhere and take years to get back. I never thought you'd be capable of something so evil.'

'I wouldn't, but don't you think we both owe them a little payback?'

The terrorist ship drew alongside the *Ultima Thule*, its concertina docking cowl extending like a parasitic sucker towards the defenceless ship, and an aggressive voice announced over the comms, 'Prepare to be boarded.'

Chapter 16

Aryx watched the scene on a monitor from the constrained field generator room. He waited until the cowl was a metre away from the ship and pressed a button, triggering the projection of a thin square panel of constrained field between the cowl and the hull. With the press of another control, the panel thrust away from the *Ultima*, towards the enemy ship.

The field rammed into the fragile cowl and it buckled and crumpled under the pressure. Shards of metal and plastic showered off into space. Compressing the cowl completely, the field hit the ship itself, and the *Ultima*'s generator bounced violently to starboard.

'Seb, starboard thrusters, now!'

The engines flared into life and the little ship bravely attempted to shoulder-barge the interlopers towards the node. The pilot didn't have time to react, and the metal shark crossed the dreaded threshold side-on, uncontrolled.

Aryx watched, heart pounding, as lightning lanced from the acceleration node and arced around the enemy. The ship became white-hot as it tumbled sideways through the crackling energy field. With a bright flash, it was torn away through space, and in the blink of an eye it was gone.

Aryx made his way back to the cockpit. 'That was a smooth move. Remind me never to get on your bad side.'

'I hope we don't get more of them coming after us. That trick might not work again.'

'How did they find us?'

'I have no idea.' Sebastian scratched his chin. 'Is it possible that they were tracking emissions from the cube?'

'No. They're only weak, and they started too soon. Even if a signal had been directed through the node, they couldn't have got here that quickly.'

'Good point, but we ought to leave the cube in the escape pod for now, just to be on the safe side. The extra layers of hull should block any signal it gives off.'

Aryx felt a lurch as Sebastian reactivated the navigation system. The ship realigned itself with the node tangent once again and headed towards the capture radius.

Hours later, with a jarring, elastic twang, the *Ultima Thule* dropped into relativistic speed several thousand kilometres away from a node in interstellar void. The ship hung in the sunless space, illuminated only by the warning lights mounted on its cardinal points and the faint light of unblinking stars.

'I hate being in open space,' Sebastian said. 'It's weird. It feels kind of lonely.'

'Christ, everywhere is lonely for you. It's no more so than anywhere else.'

Sebastian activated the scanner, locating the Chopwood beacon signal a second time. 'We're farther away. The time code is an earlier date, and the signal is weaker. We'll have to head to a node along a different axis.'

Aryx watched as Sebastian located a node on the map that lay out of the Galactic plane, above the approximate origin of the beacon's signal, and programmed in the navigation path. The ship set off along the new heading. He was bored of searching for the signal. If only Galactic positioning systems had been invented hundreds of years earlier – it might have saved a lot of trouble for them now. He smirked at the self-indulgence of the thought.

After a couple of hops, the ship dropped out of superphase in a binary system and Aryx stared out at the starry smear of the Milky Way.

'Are we there yet?'

'Nearly.' Sebastian tapped commands into the console. 'I just need to triangulate the position now.'

The Galactic map changed to show the three bearings as fuzzy red lines, converging to a point. The time measurements appeared as faint spheres, centred on the locations from which each sample had been taken, with their sizes dictated by the time differences themselves.

'That's no good,' Aryx said. 'The area of intersect is about a light year across. If we go there and we're not near a node, it'll take us months to get back!'

'I had noticed.' Sebastian continued tapping commands into the console. The beams that cut across the galaxy became more refined as the intersection of the overlapping spheres' radii shrank. He leaned back in his seat. 'This should be more accurate.'

Aryx peered at the display. 'I like those figures.'

The overlap was within thirty Astronomical Units – roughly the distance of Neptune from Earth's sun – and much more acceptable. Within the area of intersect sat a star labelled *V376 Pegasi – unexplored.* Aryx reached forwards and zoomed the map in, expanding the system to fill the view. The system contained a gas giant labelled *HD209458b, Osiris.* Its green moon was roughly the same size as Earth's. On the other side of the system, a volcanic planet orbited uncomfortably close to the star. He tapped a few more commands into the console, trying to retrieve extra details, but with no scans of the system newer than the last fifty years in the database, further information was not forthcoming.

'This is useless,' he said. 'There's nothing about the system on the map ... The moon might be green because of plant life. That could be our Chopwood, right there. Hmm ... What a wonderfully appropriate name,' he said, pointing at the label next to the moon. 'Tradescantia, Isis. It's one of my favourite flowers.'

Sebastian swivelled his chair to face him and leaned back, putting his hands behind his head. 'Wonderful,' he said flatly. 'Shall we go for it, then?'

'Did your Paper Man say there was definitely a node in the area? I don't fancy our chances if there isn't.'

'He said he reached it in a small ship when the Folians pointed him in the right direction, so it couldn't have been too far from Chopwood, Tradescantia, whatever. The colonists probably didn't detect it when they originally arrived because they weren't looking for it. I don't expect they would have known what it was anyway.'

'So we go for it and hope that they point *us* in the right direction if we can't find it?'

'If you're happy with that. I'm sure it'll be fine. Anyway, we've got much better technology than they would have had.'

Aryx shrugged. 'We don't have much choice.'

Sebastian turned back to the console and selected the intersect coordinates on the navcomputer. 'Let's go!'

The ship coasted along, skirting the twin suns of the binary system on approach to the node. The ship had fortunately arrived only a few minutes away, and it glided smoothly around the node until it faced almost completely the opposite direction, and jumped.

Aryx bit his nails while the ship slid through the stars once again in superphase.

'You look worried.'

'I'm still hoping there's a node there when we arrive.'

'Have a bit of faith.'

He frowned. 'Easy for you to say, Mr Manygods. Faith won't get us home. Faith won't save us from arriving back after our friends and families have all died if we have to fly all the way back, or to the nearest node, at near lightspeed.' Hypocrite. 'Besides, the onboard rations probably wouldn't last for more than a week of acceleration time.'

'Don't think I'm not worried. The Paper Man made his way back to our sector of the galaxy just fine, and he didn't have the scanners to detect the nodes. We do, so I'm not concerned about that.' Sebastian shook his head. 'I just don't want to find this is a dead end, and then have to try to take him back to the station under arrest.'

'Why would that bother you?'

'A, I don't know how to shoot properly; and B, because I know what society would do to him. Regardless of whether he's guilty or innocent, as soon as he turned up on the station, scientists and the media would pounce all over him. Nobody deserves to be subjected to that, regardless.' Sebastian's frown reinforced his stance on the matter.

Aryx remembered the way he'd felt after his legs had been amputated. His friends hadn't looked at him the same; everyone had pity in their eyes when they spoke to him. Some thought he was a fool, and others a freak. 'Yes, I know what you mean,' he said, nodding slowly. 'And I agree with you.'

'I'm glad we don't have to argue over that one.' Sebastian's shoulders relaxed. He leaned forwards to inspect the console. 'We're slowing. We're almost at the heliosphere – Gods, it's big.'

Aryx watched as the stars resolved themselves into discrete points of light once again.

Sebastian continued tapping away at the console. 'I've got it!' he said, punching the air. 'I've locked the scanners on the signal and set course for its origin. There's a problem, though. There are no comms carrier waves coming in from the relays in neighbouring systems.'

'So . . . if we don't find a node in this system to send a signal out through, we won't be able to contact the station, and any mayday signal we send won't get picked up for years.' Aryx felt a chill in his stomach.

Sebastian's mouth pulled to the side. 'There's obviously a node here, or we wouldn't be slowing. Anyway, too late now.' He tapped away at the console again and the Galactic map changed to a zoomed image of their target: a planet on the opposite side of the system. He rubbed his eyes and pulled his hands down his cheeks. 'I think we should get some sleep. It's several hours' trip. The signal appears to be coming from the dark side of the moon. By the time we get there it'll be daylight and I'd rather start exploring feeling refreshed.'

'Do you want to use the bunk downstairs?'

'No, I'll sleep on the seating up here.'

'Suit yourself.' Aryx wheeled to the lift and left him to settle down for the night.

The next morning Aryx woke bright and refreshed. Evidently he was getting used to the makeshift bed. He headed upstairs.

Sebastian was already sitting at the piloting console. The cockpit window was filled with a verdant green planet, spattered with isolated lakes.

'We've arrived then?'

Sebastian didn't look up. 'Yes. Did you sleep well?'

'No nightmares since we've been away from the station. Perhaps I just needed a break.'

'That makes two of us. The seats were a bit lumpy last night so I turned the gravity down. That made them bearable.'

Aryx laughed. 'Always looking for the easy way out, as usual.'

'So you'd rather me be grumbling about a sore back all day, would you?'

'No, I'd prefer you to just not grumble about anything.'

Sebastian mumbled something that Aryx didn't hear properly. He decided to ignore it and continued to watch the view out of the window as the ship turned. A large orange and yellow gas giant peeked out from behind the turquoise crescent of the planet's atmosphere.

'So, this place is a moon.' Aryx half expected a *what else would it be?* remark.

'Just like the map showed. It's a bit smaller than Earth's, but according to the gravitometers, it's got quite a high density, which gives it Earth-like gravity. Chopwood is somewhere down there, but I have no idea where the Folian homeworld is. The Paper Man said it was nearby, but the only planets in the system are the gas giant, which couldn't possibly harbour life, and a volcanic planet too close to the sun.' There was no satisfaction on Sebastian's face as he looked up.

'You never know, we might find something useful in Chopwood. Did you locate the node?'

'The solar radiation masked the signature initially, so it was a bit difficult to find. It's about ten AUs out, straight ahead.'

'See? Good news already. It means we'll get home before everyone's died of old age.'

Sebastian appeared to brighten. 'Heh, good one. I'll take us down now. If I've timed it right, it will be early morning when we get down there.' He began guiding the ship through the atmosphere, towards the beacon signal.

Lush green forests rolled beneath them, a mixture of conifers and deciduous interspersed with bright lakes and rivers. With no seas, the place seemed almost entirely covered in woodland. The furrows in Sebastian's brow reduced a little.

'Does this remind you of Earth?' Aryx asked.

'It does. I can't wait to land. It's been so long since I've been anywhere like this.' Sebastian smiled.

'It's been a while for me, too. Although it also reminds me of where I lost my legs.'

'I didn't think . . . ' Sebastian looked away. 'Sorry.'

'It's not your fault, Seb. That all happened before I met you, but I still get nervous when I'm reminded of it.'

The ship approached a large clearing filled with lots of little buildings. Aryx tried to take in the view as the ship glided over the settlement, but they were too high and moving too fast for him to be able to make out any significant detail. One thing that stood out was the lack of people or movement – maybe it was too early in the morning for anyone to be about.

Sebastian brought them around for a second pass. 'There's nowhere to land near the buildings.' He pointed to small clearing a short distance from the town, dotted with low shrubs and thin, felled trees like spilled cocktail sticks. 'That'll have to do.'

The ship hovered over the clearing and dropped down. Scrapes, cracks, and the splintering of wood echoed from below. Aryx's stomach twitched nervously, the change of scenery and prospect of coming across new varieties of plants overriding his previous anxiety. He wheeled to the lift in preparation to leave.

'I don't think this is going to be a wheelchair trip.'

'I knew I was forgetting something.' He retrieved the mobipack from the escape pod and took the lift down.

Sebastian followed moments later, wearing his old canvas rucksack. He had a big smile on his face for a change. 'Nice breathable atmosphere, nineteen degrees centigrade, sunny with a light breeze. A perfect day for a stroll, so the sensors say.' He gestured to the airlock controls with a flourish. 'You may do the honours.'

Aryx reached up and pressed the button.

Both doors opened directly onto the new planet, and in streamed sunlight.

Chapter 17

Golden light poured into the ship from a cloudless, pale blue sky and Aryx took a deep, appreciative breath. The air tasted crisp and clean, with the pungent zing of pine – nothing like the processed air of the ship, and even better than the atrium on Tenebrae. The light breeze was cool on his arms, but the sunlight warmed away the morning chill. He pulled on the mobipack and fastened the harness. After making a few adjustments and checking that it was on tight, he pulled out two short straps with tiny sensor units and attached them securely around the ends of his legs, just above where his knees would have been.

Sebastian stepped back. 'The weather's too good for me to be wearing these,' he said, and unfastened the ziploks, separating the sleeves from the N-suit.

Aryx moved his chair away from the doors and pulled the brakes on. He activated a control on one of the mobipack's straps and the space between the ends of his legs and the floor filled with the orange, laser-laced lower legs. He braced himself against the wheels of the chair and, shifting his weight forwards, pushed himself up. The legs took the weight with his body supported by the harness. He shifted from side to side testing the movement, first lifting his left leg to get his balance, lowering it, then lifting the right. He looked out at the terrain.

The felled trees and low bushes looked as though they might provide a challenge, but he was confident the programming refinements Sebastian had made would cope with it.

Judging by the grin on his face, Sebastian was impressed. He bowed, extending his right arm in the direction of the doorway. 'You first.'

Aryx stepped out of the ship slowly, mindful of the low friction. The feet met the step and threads of plasma discharged at the contact. He shifted his weight forwards but, rather than drop a couple of inches onto the step, he fell, arms flailing, until the harness stopped him with a sharp jerk and he caught himself on the threshold of the ship.

'Ow, my groin!' He looked down.

He was standing on the ground itself, with the prosthetic legs *inside* the step.

'Are you alright?'

He attempted to lift a leg, but the pack began to drag him down as it tried to raise the prosthetic against the field generated by the ship. 'I'm fine, but turn the damn step off!' It vanished and he moved away from the immediate vicinity of the airlock. 'The legs went straight through. Good job there wasn't much of a drop, or I'd have smashed my leg against the step. I'll have to climb out of the ship if I don't want to do that again.' Free of the obstruction, he looked around.

The leaves of the tall, silver-barked trees around the clearing rustled in the breeze. The scent of pine intensified as the breeze turned, bringing with it the fragrance from taller conifers, deep in the surrounding woodland.

Aryx moved farther away and brittle branches and twigs crunched loudly under his transparent feet. He stopped and shifted his weight from side to side, marvelling at the sounds it made. The sounds *he* made. He turned to see Sebastian watching from the top of the steps. 'Are you coming?'

'I thought I'd let you savour the moment in peace before I start tromping around as well.' He smiled.

Aryx started to laugh, but quickly stopped. Sebastian's expression had turned flat and serious, his head cocked to one side.

'Do you hear that?'

'Hear what?'

'Nothing. No birds. Apart from the wind in the trees, it's quiet. No animal sounds at all.'

'You expected some?'

'I would have expected to hear some other form of life. Even in a desert you get the occasional sound, not just wind across the sand.'

'That's not to say there aren't any life forms.' Aryx walked up to a nearby shrub and instantly found what he was looking for. 'Aha, insects. I knew something had to pollinate the plants.'

'Then where are the predators that eat the insects?'

'I don't know. Shall we ask them? Just stop worrying about it. I'm sure if there's something here that is going to eat us, we'll know about it soon enough.'

Sebastian raised one eyebrow and frowned with the other. 'You *really* know how to fill me with confidence, don't you?'

'If there was something nasty here, I'm sure your invisible friend would have told us about it.' Just like the invisible gods that might protect us. Aryx bit his lip. 'Just stop stressing.'

Sebastian shrugged. 'What can I say? I work in security – it's part of the job.'

Aryx threw his hands up and shook them. 'You *never* chill out. Even when we're at the club you're on edge. I don't know if you're worrying about work, or about me. You've got yourself into so many situations over the last couple of days and almost got me stranded so many times I thought I was going to have a heart attack. If anyone ought to be stressed out, it should be me … Look, you're good at your job. You don't need to worry about it all the time. Yes, you've got the investigation on your shoulders, but trying to micro-manage everything isn't going to help.

'I'm an adult and I can take care of myself. I used to be in the military, remember? Yes, it's a bit limiting,' he said, gesturing to his legs. 'But I work around it. I know my limits now. You don't have to feel responsible for me – unless I fall down a hole and die and it's your fault. *Then* you can feel responsible.'

Sebastian laughed. 'Fine! I get your point. I'll try to worry less, but that doesn't stop me from feeling responsible while we're on this mission. After all, it was me that dragged you along.'

'I chose to come along, remember? I *could* have said no.'

Sebastian's shoulders slumped. 'I know. I'm not used to being responsible for somebody else like this.'

'You're not responsible for me. Now, are we going to investigate this place, or stand around all bloody day feeling sorry for ourselves?'

Sebastian secured the ship with his palm print. When he turned back to Aryx, his eyes were closed. He took a deep breath and said, 'Let's go.'

'Which direction?'

'You decide.'

'Uh … North.'

Sebastian's eyebrows knotted. 'Which direction is north?'

Aryx pointed to his left. 'Well, the sun's coming up over there.' He turned around to face away from the ship and pointed straight ahead. 'So I've decided the town must be to the north.'

He started walking and dead wood cracked as he picked his way through the scrub, trying to find a path. Sebastian followed behind, frequently grumbling about the branches that snagged at his feet. The clearing narrowed, becoming little more than a felled channel in the surrounding forest. It might once have been a regularly used route between the clearing and the main town, but had clearly been abandoned.

'How long do you think this trail's been out of use?' Sebastian asked.

Aryx approached the nearest tree and put his hand on the smooth, papery bark. 'Without knowing how quickly the trees grow here, I can't tell. These look a lot like *Betula*.'

'A what?'

'Birch, you ingrate. If this place had seasons like Earth's, I'd think that most of them were anything between fifty to seventy years old, at a rough guess. The spruce-like trees are bigger, and there's no telling how old they are. And this one ... I've never seen a birch with a trunk as wide for its height.' He wrapped his arms around it, but couldn't get his hands to go even halfway. 'It's enormous!' He scanned the treeline, trying to see if he recognised any of the other species. 'It's odd, a lot of the trees look familiar. None are exactly the same species, but nothing here would look out of place on Earth.'

Sebastian stood next to him, staring out at the far southern edge of the clearing. 'I wonder if it's the same with alien plants ...'

Aryx frowned. 'If what's the same?'

'You know, the way a lot of aliens look kind of similar to Humans. Maybe when the environmental conditions are right, there's a certain pattern that dictates the way species develop – I mean, other than specialised evolution. Most of them have bilateral or radial symmetry, and maybe trees have the same sort of trend.'

'It's possible. From what I've noticed, smaller plants have a greater variety, even within the species of one planet. I wasn't really bothered about studying extra-terrestrial trees when I was more mobile.'

'Well, that makes two of us. I've only ever seen trees on Earth, and the ones planted on the station.'

'Which came from Earth, too.'

Sebastian turned back to the overgrown pathway. 'It's odd this felled wood hasn't been collected. It's gone all funny. Why would they leave it after going to the effort of cutting it down?'

'I don't know.'

Sebastian rubbed his chin. 'The Paper Man said the mission of the colony was to harvest resources to send back to Earth. Maybe we'll find out when we get to the town.'

They entered an area of younger trees that had grown on the old path where the leaf-littered ground presented little undergrowth. The canopy overhead was probably too dense for smaller plants to thrive beneath. Several hundred metres along the path, the surrounding trees became more sparse, and the forest gave way to a grassy patch where it opened out to the east.

Sebastian jogged on ahead and stopped, his mouth agape. 'Oh, wow!'

A warm, gentle wind blew through the grassy clearing, rustling leaves on the trees and tousling the vines and delicate trailing plants that hung from the branches. The occasional creak emanated from the trunks of the larger trees as they bowed in the breeze. A wooden stockade surrounded a low hill with a collection of squat, wood shingle-roofed buildings. The planks of the stockade and building walls looked aged and silvery, and had split and cracked in the sun. A thick layer of moss covered some of the more sheltered surfaces, softening the appearance of many of the structures. Aryx was immediately reminded of pictures he'd seen of plantations in colonial America, left unused and abandoned. All it needed was an old woman in a rocking chair, a toothless man playing a banjo, or a lumberjack with a huge axe.

They walked around the stockade, heading south-east and following the tree line to their right. Eventually, they came across a gateway in the barrier. Its wooden hinges long since collapsed, the gate lay broken on the ground. A clear path headed up through the middle of the buildings towards the centre of town.

'Shall we check the bottom out first?' Sebastian asked.

'It looks as good a starting point as any.'

They entered the compound and started up the grassy slope. Many of the buildings looked like barns or mills, with arms extending out of gable-end walls. Block and tackle hung from decaying ropes outside several of the larger buildings. The streets between them were wide, and grassy with years of neglect.

Sebastian stepped up onto the veranda of a nearby building: a saloon from an old western movie. Something crunched under his feet and he looked down.

'What is it?'

He crouched. 'Broken glass.' He straightened and picked at the nearest empty window frame with his thumb. 'Hardly any of these buildings have glass in them anymore. Looks like the frames have rotted. This place hasn't been lived in for years.' He approached the main doors in the middle of the building and pushed them. The aged wooden panel creaked open with a gritty scrape and stopped halfway. He shoved, and the decaying door tore off its hinges and fell into the building with a loud crash as a plume of dust rolled across the floor.

'Oops! Definitely not lived in.' He wiped his hands on his legs.

Aryx climbed up onto the veranda beside him and went in.

A long, dust-coated bar stood to the left of the entrance. To the right, several round tables with crude seats reinforced the impression of a saloon. He could see no sign of any other equipment or fittings in the gloomy interior, and several tiny holes in the bar made it look like something had been removed.

'It looks like this place was stripped of all the metalwork – there are no taps. Maybe the settlers moved on?'

'No wonder it looked empty from the air ... I wonder what would make them suddenly leave,' Sebastian said, clenching and un-clenching his hands. 'And how are we going to find the Folians? Why didn't he say there was nobody here?' He smacked himself on the forehead. 'Damn it!'

The sound made Aryx jump. 'What?'

'The Paper Man, he *did* say the place was abandoned. He said he'd taken a ship *that was left*, so the colonists must have already gone!' Sebastian's face reddened and he stormed out of the building, causing the few remaining pieces of glass to fall from the windows.

Aryx put down the wooden bowl he was examining and went after him.

Sebastian leaned against one of the veranda posts, arms folded, hugging himself. His voice trembled when he spoke. 'Where is Achene? This place makes no sense. There's a gas giant and a boiling planet. It isn't here! I'll never get to the bottom of this.' He slid down the post and sat on the wooden floor, rocking. 'Who am I kidding? I can't do it. Oh, my father would have loved to see this. I finally get to do some detective work and fail miserably.'

Aryx put his hand on his shoulder and squeezed. 'You can't be expected to know everything, so stop beating yourself up about it or I'll kick your arse. There's got to be something here. Come on.' He walked down the steps and strode up the grassy slope to the north, towards the centre of town, and looked back.

Sebastian trudged along behind with his head down.

'Cheer up!'

'I can't help it. I just feel like we're getting nowhere and now we're stuck at a dead end ...' He looked up. 'Why did they just take the metal items with them and not the wood?'

Aryx spoke between laboured breaths. It was tough walking up the hill, even with the pack doing most of the work. 'Maybe they thought they could get wood elsewhere, or it was too bulky ... Their ship probably had a fusion assembler like ours ... That would have allowed them to create heavier elements, but a lot of the metal would have been ... radioactive if they hadn't got nucleic shunts to stop the reactions afterwards ... so any non-radioactive metal they had would have been valuable.' He slowed near the end of the street to catch his breath.

Sebastian overtook him and stopped at the top of the hill. He staggered back.

'What now? Are you okay?'

'You'll see when you get here.'

Aryx clambered up the slope and nearly lost his footing at the top. Sebastian grabbed his arm.

'Whoa! You don't want to end up down there.'

The brow of the hill fell away into large, shady depression at least a hundred metres across and twenty metres deep. Several trees grew at the base of the crater, their tops barely level with the rim. Large, moss-covered boulders sat near the centre and looked as though they had tumbled down years ago. It was no wonder they hadn't noticed it from above. With no buildings on the opposite side of the depression, the stockade appeared to run around the town and up along the far edge; from the sky it had looked like patch of scrub at the end of the town.

'This doesn't look volcanic,' Sebastian said.

'I think you're right. The sides are too shallow.' Aryx stared at the base of the depression, examining its contours. 'I think a ship landed here.'

'That would make sense. The colonists would have used their ship as the focal point of the town and built out from there. Let's see if there's anything useful left behind.' Sebastian turned and made his way back down the slope.

'What are we looking for?' Aryx called after him.

'Anything that refers to other planets in the system. See if there are any recording devices left behind. Logs, surveys, that kind of thing.'

'I'll start checking the buildings up this end. You start from the bottom.' He watched as Sebastian jogged back down the hill. At least now he wasn't slouching as much – maybe he'd found his motivation again.

Aryx walked several yards down the hill towards the first of the buildings on the eastern side of the street. Whoever built the town obviously liked verandas and porches. The door hung open at ninety degrees, onto the porch covering the entrance. Shattered glass lay strewn across the wooden boards, and the top half of the door was almost entirely missing. He entered the building.

It appeared to consist of a single room and lacked any other doors. A primitive cork pinboard hung on the left-hand wall where several scraps of bleached, tattered paper flapped in the breeze. A thick layer of gritty dust coated the floorboards, which creaked underfoot. To the right, below the window, stood a heavy wooden desk covered with large sheets of paper held down with chunks of rock.

He began rifling through the papers. Hand-drawn geological surveys. The contours on the topmost map depicted the hill on which the town stood, with the clearing to the south ringed with a dotted line and a faint, barely legible note. The top left part of the map was readable, but smudged and blurred by years of rain blown in through the exposed window. He bent over to read it and, not yet used to the balance of the mobipack, stumbled forwards. He put his hand out to steady himself, but found only loose sheets that gave no support. Pain shot through his left arm as he slid off the end of the desk, dragging documents to the floor with him.

He sat, rubbing his left elbow. 'Ow, that hurt,' he muttered. As he looked down to examine the graze, he noticed the papers he'd dragged off the table.

Now that he was closer, he was able to read the note at the top. *Earmarked for town construction material.* Another section of forest was also highlighted, about a mile to the west of the town. *For later collection and shipping / stripped for farming.*

He picked up the map and held on to the edge of the desk to help him stand. The legs were fine for rough terrain, but until he'd solved the issue with hard floors, it was probably better to stick with the chair. He was about to put the map back on the desk when he noticed another drawing, previously covered. It showed a mineral survey, the results indicated by a coloured key on the top left – the same corner that had been damaged by the rain.

'Bloody typical,' he said, lifting the sheet.

Under the mineral survey he found a sketch of the town: a preliminary plan of the settlement. No building names, but it clearly showed the arrangement of streets fanning out from the top of the hill where the outline of the colonists' ship, labelled *Iceni*, indicated the landing site.

'At least we were right about that bit.' With no useful information, he decided to move on to the next building on the opposite side of the street.

The second building seemed a little larger than the first. A longer veranda extended across the entire front of the building, and this time the front door was almost intact. The window frames had split and cracked, but all the glass remained. He pushed open the door and entered a room barely large enough to accommodate the small desk and chair that were set off to the right, facing outwards. Behind the desk was a closed door. It reminded him of a reception area. He made his way around the desk and pushed at the door. The handle was missing, but it opened easily. He had no desire to get stuck in the building if a gust of wind came through, so he pulled the chair into the opening.

In the next room two couches, consisting of square wooden frames with canvas stretched across them, sat against the walls to the left and right of the doorway. A small square frame in the middle of the room topped with wooden boards took the place of a coffee table. He moved on through the open doorway to his left.

A set of units lined the walls, again made of wood, and a gaping hole in the worktop gave the impression of a kitchen, now sinkless. Seeing nothing of immediate interest, he pushed open the closed door in the wall to the left of the kitchen.

The fourth room contained a low, wooden cot flanked by two small cupboards. The canvas stretched across the frame had become slack with age; a large brown stain in the middle surrounded by a patch of mouldy, rotting fabric indicated the presence of a tiny hole in the ceiling. Just a house, nothing interesting – time for the next building. As he exited the lounge into the reception, his foot caught the chair he'd placed to keep the door open and he stumbled. Cursing, he kicked it out of the way. The lower leg shot out at a peculiar angle, bending almost ninety degrees forward.

The chair hurtled across the room and shattered against the wall.

Aryx lost his balance and began to fall backwards. Adrenaline kicked in, slowing the scene, and he caught himself in the doorway.

'Bloody hell!' Obviously the nerve impulse detectors on his legs needed further calibration. The lack of mass in the prosthetics meant the reaction to the kick had thrown him, but there wasn't anything he could do about that. He sat on the desk, turned the mobipack off, and shuffled backwards. He took out the infoslate and examined the settings.

Several sliders appeared on the display, indicating the state of the sensors. He stored the current preferences under *unsafe* and began tweaking them. After increasing the dampening on the nerve sensitivity, he saved the change as *inertial restriction*.

'That should do it,' he said, shuffling to the edge of the desk, and reactivated the pack. The legs appeared and he eased himself into a standing position, swinging them a couple of times to make sure they weren't going to fly out at odd angles again. Happy with the result, he headed back across the street.

The next building was much longer than the others in the area. The typical veranda ran across the front, shielding several small windows. The double doors at the northern end gave it the appearance of a high-traffic facility. He pushed the doors but the frames were swollen and stiff. Bracing himself, he barged them with his shoulder. After a little initial resistance, one of the doors gave way and he walked into a small lobby area. There was another set of double doors ahead of him, this time set with several small panes of glass, forming large screens that had remained intact. They opened easily, into a large room that took up the full length of the building, separated from the back section by a partition wall. Ten dusty, primitive beds, arranged five each side, filled the room.

He moved on past the partition wall and his eyes were immediately drawn to a desk, upon which rested a red, leather-bound book.

Chapter 18

Sebastian reached the bottom of the hill and made his way towards the eastern side of the street – they had already investigated the bar on the opposite side, after all. The first building he came to was small, enough to house only one or two people without cramping. There was no porch, but instead the front wall of the building extended straight up, where he assumed the roof ran down towards the back. As with all the other buildings he had passed, it had a simple, solid wooden door with wooden hinges and a sliding bar to fasten it. The colonists must have trusted each other implicitly; there was no evidence of even a simple locking mechanism. He pushed the door, but it didn't move – even with both hands, it still resisted. He took a couple of steps back and kicked. As he collided with it, the hinges gave way and the door thudded to the floor, a plume of dust billowing out from beneath it.

The building consisted of a single room. Above, the slope of the roof ran down towards the far side. Sunlight shone in through several small holes and cracks in the bare shingles. A set of small cupboard units set into the far wall gave the impression of a kitchen or storage area where a bean plant crept its way in through openings around the glass of a tiny porthole window. To the right, beneath the window, lay a single bed frame. There were no chairs or seating of any kind. Sebastian surveyed the scene with a critical eye. The lack of furnishings probably meant the place belonged to someone whose time was largely spent working outdoors. He rooted through the cupboards and, finding nothing of use, he stepped over the broken door and made his way around to the rear. It was odd how everything personal had been taken. The colonists must have had time to pack – it wasn't exactly the *Marie Celeste*; the departure seemed deliberate and planned.

A low, wooden fence surrounded the back of the worker's house, providing more of a demarcation of space rather than a barrier. The bean plant that crept in through the window commanded the space at the rear; the entire garden was a chaotic, writhing morass of vines, leaves, and bean pods. The tangle continued up over the rear wall and onto the sloping roof, where layer upon layer of weeds had built up over the decades, obscuring the shape of the building entirely. The next few houses up the street had similar patches of crops growing behind them, most of which spilled out into the surrounding ground, engulfing the partition fences. A mass of potato plants grew in the second garden, and oversized cauliflower and cabbages in the third.

He returned to the front and continued up the street to the next house. Its door had already caved in; the wooden hinges had rotted away long ago. Grit and sand crunched underfoot as he entered. A shaft of sunlight came in through a hole in the roof, of which a large potato plant growing through the floorboards had taken advantage. He caught the glint of something shiny in the corner of the room and crouched down to examine it.

A broken hurricane lamp lay on its side, the glass smashed – probably during a fall – and a small, unlabelled plastic bottle of liquid lay next to it. He picked it up, unscrewed the top, and sniffed at the contents. The oily odour took him back to memories of his grandfather lighting the old miner's lamp with a stash of his precious paraffin oil. He refastened the lid and shook the bottle to make sure it wasn't going to leak. Satisfied it was intact, he stashed it in his rucksack. He stood up and scanned the room. There was little else of interest.

As he turned to leave, his wristcom bleeped.

'Yes?'

'You'd better come and look at this – I've found something.'

'Where are you?'

'Near the top of the town, in a long building. Can't miss it – it's not far from the chapel.'

'On my way.'

He left the building and headed up the hill. The chapel stood out prominently; the building stood taller than the others, with a distinctive cross carved above the arched entrance. Two doors up was the long building Aryx had mentioned.

He squeezed through the partly open doors.

Aryx looked up from the book he was reading. 'Ah, there you are.'

'Is this a barracks?'

'Hospital. I found a medic's diary.' Aryx held up the book. 'There's also this ...' He beckoned for Sebastian to follow him, and pointed at one of the beds in the next room. Unlike the others, it still had the mattress on it. The covering was a crude cotton canvas, topped with a dirty, blood-stained sheet.

'What happened in here?'

Aryx held up the diary again. 'This may have the answer.'

'You've read it then?'

'I skimmed through and found some interesting bits. I'll show you.' He opened the diary at a page near the front and handed it over, pointing to the relevant section.

Sebastian began reading. It was written in English.

Journal of Kibble Vardstrom, Chief Medical Officer, colonial ship Iceni.

Aryx stood behind Sebastian, following along over his shoulder, and after several pages he pointed out the first part of interest.

2045-07-11

After weeks of travel, we've finally arrived at our destination. At least, it felt like weeks of travel, but the pilots say we've taken decades to get here. I don't understand the physics of it at all, and I can't believe that we've been travelling that long.

Cullen has drawn up the plans for building a small town, and they are being put into action since there's an abundance of wood on this moon. The initial scans indicate the gravity on the planet below might be a little high and the physics geek said we can use the gravity for the return trip, so we're going to stay put.

2045-07-12

The navigators have confirmed our travel time, and they say given the star positions, we've taken 162 years to get here! How is that even possible?

I don't know what to do. If it's true, all my family back on Earth will be dead by now! They must be wrong! I wish I'd paid attention in the briefings, and I wish I'd never come!

2207-07-12 (date amended)

I've calmed down a bit now. I still can't believe it. Either way, I've got to adjust my diary entries accordingly, but without any way of knowing what the actual date is, it's only a guess, so I've only changed the year.

2207-08-29

After weeks of work, the town buildings are almost complete. We've built them around the Iceni, *since Cullen thought it would be unwise to dismantle her for resources. The tools we brought with us are enough to work wood and smelt ore for basic metals. Scans indicated some mineral deposits a few miles away, so Cullen has sent Duggan Simmons with a few teams to investigate.*

2207-09-04

Duggan's surveys have found some useful minerals we can refine using the equipment on the ship. They also reported some other strange mineral that they encountered while mining. They didn't take samples, as it seemed to evaporate quickly after being uncovered. I don't have the kinds of scanners to be able to analyse the stuff, and I'm not going to go and check it out. I don't care what anyone says, it's not a medic's job to do geology.

'They must have found carbyne.'

'Sounds like it.' Aryx took the diary and started flipping through the pages. 'You'll need to go on ahead here; there's nothing that interesting for the next couple of years. Most of the bits in between are boring medical crap. Cuts and bruises. They didn't seem to have brought any viruses with them. They had a colony without the common cold.' He handed back the book.

2209-04-10

Duggan announced his intent to leave the outpost today with William Kennett, aiming to survey the planet below. Cullen was unwilling to let them go, as he thinks this moon's got plenty of resources and felt it would be a waste of effort to survey it. I voiced my concern about the higher gravity, but Duggan was vehement, saying it would be a wasted opportunity if we didn't send someone down to explore another potentially habitable planet.

2209-04-14

They left the outpost today in one of the runners. When I questioned Cullen about his decision to allow them to go, he was a little cagey about why he'd agreed, but he did mention something about mineral deposits. Duggan must have convinced him somehow.

Everyone thought Duggan was a little weird, living out in the sticks away from the compound like a hermit, and I wonder if Cullen was secretly pleased to let him go. Why William went with him, I don't know. I personally always felt him to be a little impressionable, but I hope no harm comes to them.

'Jump forwards a few pages. I can't stand here all day, these straps are starting to hurt.'

2209-05-10

Duggan and William have been gone for weeks now. I asked Cullen if he'd heard back from them, but he said he hadn't heard anything. I would have thought that they would have contacted us by now, as it's nearly been a month. I'm quite worried. Duggan usually acts cautiously, and it's concerning that he hasn't checked in.

2209-06-22

William has returned! He looks a little gaunt and malnourished, but other than that, in good health physically. I tried to talk to him about what had happened on the planet below, but he seems unwilling to discuss any of it. He sits hugging something tiny, clenched in his fist, but won't show me what it is. He almost has the symptoms of some kind of trauma repression. Cullen spoke to him but wasn't able to get any information out of him, either. I'm concerned as to what's happened to Duggan, since they only took one ship. He could be stuck on the planet with no support, or worse, dead. I hope he's OK. Deep down, I really liked the guy.

2209-06-23

I tended to William today. He had cuts on his arms. I wonder if he has been subjected to something terrible and has started to self-harm because of it. He has a distant, wild look in his eyes sometimes, and almost seems like a different person.

2209-06-25

Cullen accused William of sabotaging one of the runners today. He claims that William's cuts were due to him attempting to rip parts out of one of the ships without tools. There were traces of blood in the engine compartment, so it looks like compelling evidence.

DNA analysis has confirmed that it is William's blood. He has been incarcerated in a makeshift prison stockade for the time being until the truth can be determined.

2209-06-27

William attacked Cullen today while he was questioning him (not threateningly, I must add) about the fate of Duggan. He wouldn't answer any questions at all. Cullen had approached the prison enclosure (a little too closely for my liking) and William grabbed him by the neck and started to strangle him! We had to send men into the enclosure to get him off. He wouldn't let go and one of them hit him over the head. The blow was beyond my means to minister to, and he died in moments.

Cullen wasn't in a good state afterwards. He'd nearly been strangled to death and has fallen into a coma. I will keep a close eye on his condition. We can't afford to lose our leader. These recent events have damaged the morale of the outpost too much.

I buried William myself. Poor lad looked strangely at peace. There was no sign of whatever it was he'd been holding on to.

'Where's the next bit about Cullen?'
  'Here.'

2209-06-29
  Cullen has stabilised. He hasn't woken up yet, but he has started to move and twitch, indicating a dream state, rather than coma.

2209-06-30
  Cullen's condition is slowly improving, although he stirs occasionally and seems delirious and feverish. I've tested him for viruses and infections, but there's no evidence that William brought back anything with him that could have infected him.

2209-07-02
  Cullen woke today. He seems a little disorientated, but I'm sure it'll pass when he's got some proper rest and started to recover. I've given him a mild sedative to help him sleep.

2209-07-03
  Cullen left his bed today (against my recommendations, I must add). He seems to be getting a little agitated with being in the hospital. He's expressed a desire to leave the medical building, but I'm worried about his psychological state. Perhaps he's not handling the situation very well.

2209-07-04
  Cullen disappeared from the hospital. I later found him in the town, just outside the pub. He seems to have changed his mind about the resources on the planet below and has convinced the others that we should leave and begin harvesting the resources there immediately. I didn't think he'd got anything out of William about his experiences down there, so I don't know what his motivation is, or why he's in such a hurry to go.

2209-07-26
  We're all loaded up and ready to leave in the ship this afternoon. I questioned Cullen about his change of mind, but he still wouldn't explain himself. I guess he doesn't have to, since everyone else already agrees with him! The strange thing was, he had a similar look in his eyes to William. The way he stared at me, it was like I could almost see the reflection of distant stars in his eyes. I hope this isn't the psychotropic side effect of some undetected infection that William brought back. I'm really worried about him.
  Duggan, I wish you were here. I could use your help getting to the bottom of this.

'That's the last entry,' Aryx said, sitting on a bed. 'I assume they left and the medic forgot to take the diary with him.'

'Or he left it in case Duggan came back.'

'Do you think Duggan is your Paper Man?'

'It sounds like it.' Sebastian had a hundred questions rallying around inside his head, but forced himself to slow down. 'Do you think there might have been a virus?'

'I don't know. I'm no medic, but I don't think it would have been limited to infecting just Cullen. Duggan seemed okay to you, didn't he?'

'Apart from being half invisible. He seemed to be quite normal and rational. He obviously repaired the sabotaged runner after the Folians dropped him off here. What are runners anyway? He mentioned them, but I didn't think to ask further.'

'Short-range craft. The design was quite innovative two hundred-odd years ago. They had kinetic ablative armour plating that could absorb the energy from an impact and convert it into a sudden burst of speed, hence the name. People used them for scouting and short-range recon missions.'

'Duggan was lucky, then, making it to the node in one of those.' It felt good to finally be able to refer to The Paper Man by a proper name. 'I need some air – this place smells.' Sebastian turned and took the diary with him.

Aryx followed. 'I don't understand why they went to the planet below if it's a gas giant. The diary says it's habitable – how can that be?'

'I don't know. It doesn't make any sense. The Folians don't exactly look like high-pressure, high-gravity dwellers. Have you seen how skinny they are?' Sebastian looked up at the faint orange crescent of the huge planet above the trees to the west and took a deep breath. He could feel his chest beginning to tighten. 'There's something strange going on here.'

'Do you think we should try to go there?' Aryx asked. 'I mean, nobody's ever *landed* on a gas giant. They're not exactly known for being solid. The giveaway is in the word "gas". The pressure crushes probes before they get to anything.'

'I know.' Sebastian looked rapidly up and down the street. With all the freedom the *Ultima* gave them, he now felt trapped. 'Somehow, Duggan and William survived landing and return, and Cullen was convinced enough to move the entire colony there. The strange thing is, Duggan didn't mention anything about meeting the colonists on the planet.' Sebastian thumped the post of the veranda with his fist. 'The answers *must* be there. I don't see how the Folians can live there, but the only other planet in the system is a lump of molten rock. The ship would probably melt if we tried to even go near it.' Every clue was leading to a dead end, again, and he hated it.

'If Duggan was piloting a runner,' Aryx said, 'he wouldn't have the range to reach other systems without the node, so it would have to be a planet in this system. Besides, he wouldn't necessarily bump into the colonists. It is an entire bloody *planet*, after all. If he hadn't got a ship when they left, they wouldn't have even known where to find him – if they *were* bothered about finding him. It's not like they all had wristcoms back in the days when they left, and we didn't detect any geosats in orbit when we arrived.'

'Then it must be the gas giant. We'll have to go there. I don't see that we have any alternative than to try,' Sebastian stepped off the veranda.

'It's your call. I don't think we'll learn anything more here. Did you have any luck with your search?'

He tucked the diary into his bag. 'Not really. I found some lamp oil and several gardens full of vegetables—'

'Vegetables?' Aryx's eyes widened. 'Where?'

'The last few houses on the left at the bottom of the street.' Sebastian pointed. 'There are loads in the gardens behind. Beans, potatoes, cauliflower, and who knows what else.'

Aryx grinned broadly. 'We should take some back with us. It costs a fortune to buy fresh veg, and I'm fed up of that hydroponic crap.'

Sebastian extended his arms out from his sides, demonstrating his lack of pockets. 'Do I look like I've got room to carry loads?'

'Wait here a sec.' Aryx ran off into a building on the opposite side of the street. A faint tearing sound came from the doorway, and before Sebastian had time to get concerned, Aryx came back out carrying a large piece of ripped canvas. 'I'll use this to carry them,' he said, folding the sheet and knotting the corners together to form a makeshift hamper. 'I'm not passing up the opportunity of some fresh veg. Show me where they are.'

Sebastian led him back down the street towards the houses with overgrown gardens. 'I'll wait here,' he said, sitting on a step. 'Given that most of the vegetables I've seen have been peeled and cooked, I don't know which ones to pick.'

Aryx returned fifteen minutes later, makeshift sack bulging with produce. 'These cost a fortune in the markets back on the station, and it would be nice to have real food.'

'Are you quite done now?' Sebastian asked, folding his arms.

Aryx shrugged. 'I suppose.'

'Let's get back to the ship, then.' Sebastian stopped at the gate. 'Do you think we should take a shortcut this way through the woods? We can head straight to the ship. It would be a lot quicker than going the way we came.'

'I'd rather take the path we know, but it's entirely up to you. If you think it's quicker, go for it.'

He approached the large trees opposite the gate and stared into the dark under-canopy. 'I don't think it's too difficult. There's no undergrowth – it should just be a straight walk,' he said, and strode in.

Aryx caught up and walked alongside him. He was beginning to sweat. The bag of vegetables looked heavy.

'Are you alright?'

'I'm fine. Even though my legs haven't got any weight on them, it's still tiring to move them as much as this. They don't exactly get any exercise in a wheelchair other than when I put the stimulators on them.'

'Do you want me to carry it for a bit?'

'No, I can manage. Keep going. The sooner I can sit down, the better. The straps are digging in again.'

After several minutes of walking through the cool, leafy woodland, the edge of the felled area in which they had landed became visible through the trees. A low rise, about three feet high, stood between them and the clearing. Aryx, walking several metres ahead, crested the mound and vanished.

'Aryx!' Sebastian ran to the top of the mound.

'I told you we should have gone the other way!'

He looked down.

Aryx was stuck in the ground, almost up to his knees, at the bottom of a long, mud-filled furrow that extended the length of the far side of the mound – possibly the tracks of some long-gone earth-moving vehicle. He held up his mud-covered hands like a child about to cry, but when he turned, his face was red and scrunched into a scowl. 'Get the veg first!' he said, pointing at the sack lying on the ground near the edge of the marsh.

Sebastian jogged down and jumped the trench. He collected the sack and moved it away, then tried to find the least boggy patch on which to stand and held his hands out. Aryx reached up and grabbed them, covering them in mud. Sebastian took the strain and leaned back as Aryx heaved himself out of the hole with a loud, slurping squelch. Sebastian staggered back with the sudden shift in weight, nearly falling, and looked down at Aryx's projected legs. Mud clung to them, seemingly against all laws of physics, and it stank. His nose wrinkled – he probably wouldn't get rid of that stagnant smell, even if he scoured out his nostrils. Aryx looked down at himself and flicked away a few blobs of mud from the bottom of his leggings. He raised his right leg and pressed one of the buttons on the mobipack's harness. The leg vanished and the mud fell to the floor. He reactivated it and repeated the process with the other.

'Very impressive,' Sebastian said. He bent down to wipe the mud off his hands using a handful of leaves. 'If you ever manage to make clothes out of those fields, I'm sure parents everywhere will thank you.'

'Not if their kids are running around looking naked, they won't.' Aryx rubbed his hands against a nearby tree, leaving large brown prints on the white bark. 'I'm lucky it wasn't any deeper.'

'You'll have to learn to look where you're going.' Sebastian handed back the sack of vegetables and Aryx tied it to the mobipack, leaving his hands free.

They stepped out of the dense tree cover into the clearing. The heat of the day was already beginning to build and a wall of hot, dry air hit them as it blew over the parched and splintering logs.

'Get off me!'

Sebastian turned to see Aryx, sweating profusely, batting away large mosquito-like flies that looked as though they might deliver a painful bite. He was surprised that they weren't bothering him. 'Are you alright?'

'I'm okay so long as they don't bite me. They're probably attracted to my medication or something.'

Heading towards the ship, Sebastian noticed a darkening in the sky above the treeline. As they walked, the dark stain shifted.

He stopped. 'What is that, smoke?'

Aryx shielded his eyes with his hand. 'I can't tell.'

Sebastian took a few steps forwards; he stood on a large stick, the snap echoing across the clearing.

The drifting cloud changed direction.

He froze. 'Aryx, it's *moving*.' A faint hum, like the engine of a distant ship, met his ears.

'Run,' Aryx said, 'it's a swarm!' He staggered over the logs as he picked up the pace.

Sebastian ran alongside him and grabbed his arm to stop him falling. The ship was yards away. The drone emanating from the treeline became deafening.

Sebastian yelled, '*Ultima Thule*, verbal override! Unlock and open airlock doors, access code Heimdall seventy-six!'

The ship obliged, extending the force-field steps and opening both the inner and outer doors simultaneously. Aryx stumbled as his prosthetic feet passed through the step. Plasmic discharges flared. The sky darkened with the swarm.

Sebastian caught movement from the corner of his eye as something black flitted past. He shoved Aryx upwards into the ship, pitching him forwards, and the thing swooped around for another pass. Whatever it was, he couldn't let it bite him.

The drone was so loud he couldn't hear himself think. The swarm was upon them.

Chapter 19

Sebastian dived through the opening, clearing both sets of doors and landing on the floor, and the airlock slammed shut. The loud pinging of insects spattering against the hull rang in his ears like machine-gun fire. Something smashed against the metal wall above his head.

He rolled over to see a large, black sticky blob the size of a fist peel off and fall to the floor beside him. Several pointed shards of black chitin with wings and legs protruded from the ichor. Aryx stood over him, holding a sleeve from the N-suit. It had a black stain on it.

'One got in. Did I tell you I hate flies?'

'No, you didn't.' Sebastian wiped his brow with the back of his hand. The droning still came through the hull, despite the two airlock doors. He got up and looked through the observation window.

Black shapes floated about inside the chamber. Several of the evil things pummelled the glass and he jumped back.

'Let's get going.'

'What about the ones in there?'

'We'll have to vent them into space.'

Aryx winced, as though he didn't like the idea.

Sebastian folded his arms. 'It's either that or keep them in the airlock and never be able to get out again. You don't—' He stopped, mid-flow. Aryx was looking at him strangely, staring at his folded arms.

There was a gash on his right arm, about two inches long. It wasn't bleeding much, but the edges looked angry and swollen. He prodded the area; it throbbed painfully in response.

Aryx handed him the medical kit from the pressure suit compartment. 'Use this. You don't want it to get infected.'

He held the kit while Aryx took out bandages and anaestheptic. He winced as Aryx cleaned the wound with the spray and bandaged it. It hurt like hell. 'Despite not being a medic, you're pretty good with a bandage.'

'I've had plenty of practice. We don't have any of those nanobots left to suture it, so you'll have to put up with a bit of discomfort until we get back to the station. The anaestheptic will kick in soon.'

He could already feel the wound beginning to numb.

Aryx sat in his wheelchair, deactivated the prosthetic fields, and headed up the lift with his makeshift bag. Sebastian picked up his rucksack and, with one final glance back at the insectoids buzzing about in the airlock, followed him up.

The swarm hammered murderously against the cockpit windows, blotting out the sky.

He punched in the commands to take the ship out of the atmosphere and, unable to see what was going on outside, he plotted the course vertically for the first two hundred metres. The creatures stayed with the ship while it rose out of the woodland, lifted by the Dyson hoops. A whine, followed by a loud bang echoed from somewhere in the forward section.

'What was that?' Aryx said.

'There are no warning lights. I expect it was one of those things getting mangled by the thrusters.'

Once the ship was clear of the trees, the main engines powered up and Sebastian imagined the smell of burnt flesh, the swarm, torched by the fusion engine's jets.

The windows began to clear as the ship ascended through the atmosphere, until eventually there was no sign of the insects. The darkening blue of the sky gave way to the black of space, the stars still hidden by the bright contrast with the forest-moon's reflected light. Above the ship hung the foreboding orange disc of the gas giant. Sebastian plotted a course for the planet and calculated a descent vector based on the assumed gravity, rotation, and atmosphere density. The ship rolled one hundred and eighty degrees, orientating itself so their target lay below them, with the moon of Tradescantia overhead. The main engines fired once more, taking the ship on a course that would skim the outer atmosphere of the gas giant.

Aryx flicked through the medic's journal. 'Oh, I wish I'd seen that earlier.'

'Seen what?'

'One of the bits near the start I skimmed over. "2207-07-17 . . . A few days after arriving, we were attacked by a large swarm of vicious insects. Duggan was able to rig up ultrasonic generators that seem to repel them. We have installed several of the generators around the perimeter of the ship, and he's planning on making more that can be put into the plant machinery and at various points around the planned town to keep them away." '

'I wish you'd spotted that sooner, too. Speaking of which, you'd best go down and let our friends out.'

Aryx tentatively approached the airlock. The insects probably didn't deserve to die – they were only doing what was in their nature, after all. He pressed his face against the long vertical slit of the window and the movement attracted the attention of the buzzing black creatures. They bombarded the glass with renewed vigour. The sight of the shiny, black carapaced creatures stabbing at the glass with their vicious mouthparts made Aryx's stomach turn and he remembered the nasty wound on Sebastian's arm.

'Bye bye, you little bastards!' he shouted, and punched the control to open the outer door.

With a muffled hiss, the buzzing stopped and the shiny black bodies froze as they tumbled out into space, glittering briefly in the sunlight before getting lost amongst the stars. With a shudder, Aryx turned and made his way back to the cockpit.

'You've changed your tune – it sounded like you enjoyed that.'

'I had my reservations about spacing them, but after what one of them did to your arm, I couldn't really think of them kindly.'

A light illuminated on the console, indicating the change in gravity as the ship left Tradescantia's grip and entered the larger body's influence. The gas giant lay ahead, immense and inhospitable.

Aryx's inner ear went a little strange.

'I hate these gravity changes,' Sebastian said. 'They make me feel sick.'

Aryx shook his head. '*Everything* makes you feel sick.'

The ship began to descend from orbit, heading towards the orange horizon. The hull creaked and groaned from the strain as the ship encountered the upper atmosphere. The coolant compressors whined in sympathy, struggling to cope with the temperature rise.

'I pray to the Gods that the diary is accurate and we aren't making the last mistake of our lives.'

The interior of the cabin took on an orange tint from the luminous ochre haze obscuring the view and the ship started to shake. Aryx clamped his chair down.

'This is odd,' Sebastian said. 'The sensor readings don't match what's outside the windows.'

Aryx checked the console. 'The pressure's not going up quick enough for a gas giant. I've done hydrogen scoops before, and it always shot up as soon as I hit denser gas. There's no way we can trust the sensors.'

'You're right,' Sebastian said, 'the air resistance is too low. The atmosphere's too thin. We should have slowed down more by now. I don't know what's going on!'

'Just hang in there,' Aryx said, gripping the console.

The coolant pumps ceased their complaint, bringing the temperature differential under control, but several minutes into the flight a tremendous bout of turbulence began. The ship shook violently as it hurtled through the swirling gases and the artificial gravity plating, unable to compensate, released its grip on the inhabitants. Still nothing could be seen from the windows, and the sensors continued to malfunction.

The turbulence ceased and the continuous gas cloud broke to reveal a layer of white cumulus below and a deep blue sky above.

'Where's the orange gone—' Aryx said.

The ship plummeted into the cloud, and the turbulence began again in earnest.

'The sensor readings don't make sense for a gas giant,' Sebastian said, 'but for a planet like Earth they would be ideal—'

The white cloud cleared and for one long, zen-like moment of serenity Aryx was able to take in the entire scene below.

Golden, grassy seas rippled in the wind, separated from each other by vast green forested areas and belts of trees. Wide rivers lazily snaked their way through the landscape and tumbled down waterfalls. Rock formations, hills, plateaus, and cliffs projected out of the terrain as far as the eye could see. From this altitude, it could almost be mistaken for the Amazon jungle on Earth. The scene vanished as the ship headed into another bank of cloud.

Wheeep! Wheeep!

Adrenaline surged through Aryx's veins as collision alarms sounded and displays flashed warning messages. The clouds parted again, revealing a huge mountain directly in their path.

Sebastian reached out and activated the manual override. The joystick rose up out of the console in slow motion. He lunged for it and wrestled with the stick. 'Take your stuff and get into the escape pod!'

Aryx dragged the mobipack and sack of vegetables towards the rear and stopped, shaking his head. 'I'm not going without you.'

Sebastian's face reddened. 'Get in now! I'll follow!'

Aryx backed into the pod.

Sebastian yanked the joystick, to no avail. The ship's speed was too great to change course. 'I'm sorry, Aryx, but at least you'll live to hate me.'

Aryx hammered on the door of the escape pod as it slammed shut. 'Don't you dare eject! Get your arse in here now!'

The pod lurched, and his wheelchair slammed against the back wall.

Another lurch, this time upwards, and he felt his face pulled down by the G-force.

'You bastard! You fucking bastard!' Aryx screamed, the veins in his neck feeling like hosepipes about to burst. How could Sebastian *do* that?

The downward force continued for several seconds before easing off. A moment later, the wheelchair started levitating in the middle of the pod and he realised it had begun to fall. Objects floated around him, but he couldn't do anything about his position – he was too far away to grab any of the fixtures to pull himself to safety. The chair drifted towards the floor along with the other floating objects. The pod had probably hit terminal velocity; it would only be a matter of moments before it hit the ground. He had to get to the side. His breathing became ragged. If the pod tumbled . . . it didn't bear thinking about.

The wheels touched down and he attempted to move towards one of the seats on the wall. The tyres skidded; he'd have to stay put. He reached underneath the chair and activated the magnetic clamp.

Giant airbags inflated, squashing him in place, crushing the air from his lungs. Wedged in the centre of the pod by the balloons, he couldn't move. The pod's retro-thrusters kicked in and his insides sank into his pelvis.

Another burst of deceleration and he felt the blood drain from his face. The parachute must have deployed. He closed his eyes. At least he wasn't going to die in a hostpital bed.

Impact.

Chapter 20

Aryx woke, his face creased and pressing up against an airbag. He could see nothing but the white mass of the balloons packing him in. His head hurt and the vision in one eye was stained red. Blinking made it worse. His arms were pinned to his sides by the airbags, but his right felt a little freer than the left, and closer to his body. He crawled it down his trouser leg and fumbled for the pockets. His fingers came across a bulge: the multi-tool. He eased his fingers upwards, unbuttoning the flap, and slipped them into the cramped space. The pressure on his head and face was becoming unbearable. He had to hurry.

He pulled the multi-tool out of his pocket and, resting it on his lap, hooked the edge of one of the blades with his thumbnail and extended it. With a twist of his wrist, the balloon to his right burst. Freedom at last. It was a good job the pod had landed upright.

He un-clamped the chair from the floor and wheeled into the space made available by the deflated balloon. The incline made it difficult, but with the mobipack unable to handle the slick floor there was no alternative. He approached the nearest accessible seat and pulled the cord hanging next to it. The balloons either side immediately retracted into small compartments and he moved around the pod, clearing the others.

The makeshift bag of vegetables, along with the other items that had been stowed in the pod, lay against the wall on the lowest side. The box containing the cube appeared to be intact, as did the mobipack. He picked it up and put it inside the mobipack's storage compartment. Judging by the blood on the corner, it must have hit him in the head on the way down. He slung the harness over his shoulders and fastened it, the sack of vegetables still attached.

Heading up the slope towards the exit hatch, he noticed the survival kit on the wall. He unclipped it from its mounting and opened it.

The box contained a small emergency medical kit: a foil sheet, folded into a tiny bundle; a ration pack with a micro-burner; and a small, rubbery wristcom-like device. He fastened the strap around his arm and placed the box into the pouch on the back of his wheelchair.

The display on the wrist module showed a line pointing outward from the centre and nothing more. At least the ship was still broadcasting the transponder signal, wherever it was.

He activated his wristcom. 'Sebastian, are you there?'

No response.

He tried again. There was no beep of acknowledgement from the unit; it was either out of range of the ship and too far to relay communications, or was somehow broken. His left wrist felt a little sore – perhaps the wristcom had been smacked too hard against his chair during the impact.

The button next to the escape hatch showed a green light, indicating a habitable environment, so he pressed it. The door popped open and he wheeled out into the sunlight.

The air was crisp, clean and fresh, and not unlike his initial impression of Chopwood. Overhead, the sky was a pale blue that deepened towards the zenith. Large cumulus clouds scudded over the horizon, lit from beneath by the low angle of the morning sun. The escape pod had landed in a grassy plain, surrounded by trees far off in the distance. The ground seemed relatively flat with short, gold-green grassy stubble. He leaned over in his chair to investigate the foliage for signs of animal tracks. The blades of grass ended square and ragged.

'Hmm,' he grumbled. 'Wildlife.' He glanced down at the locator on his wrist.

The line on the display pointed in the direction of the pod behind him. The ground seemed flat enough to wheel along, so he made his way around it. The indicator still pointed in the same direction. He stared into the distance, trying to locate the ship.

About a mile away, at the far end of the grassy region, a dark ridge jutted up out of the landscape, running left and right as far as the eye could see. There was no sign of the ship.

He sighed. 'Great. Just marvellous. Don't tell me I've got to climb a cliff.' He rubbed his groin – it was still incredibly sore from using the pack in Chopwood. There was no way he was walking the plains wearing it. At least his head didn't hurt as much. He touched his hand to the wound and it came away clean.

He returned to the escape pod, wheeling up over the raised threshold. It was a good job the pod had sunk into the ground enough to make getting in and out easy; the mobipack would have been useless on the sloping floor. His military scavenging instincts kicked in.

'If I cut the seatbelts off, I should be able to make a rope in case I need one.'

He moved around the seats one by one, pulling the belts out to their limits and cutting them off with the multi-tool, and spent a few minutes tying the ends of the belt together to make one fifty-foot long strap. He bundled it up and tied it to the back of his wheelchair. The sight of the punctured airbag gave him an idea, and he pulled the cord next to one of the seats where the balloon was still intact. It gave a quiet puff as he punctured it and set about cutting it off at the base. He folded the deflated bag and stuffed it into the now-bulging pouch at the back of his seat.

Scavenging urge satisfied, he left the pod and set off towards the base of the cliffs.

Sebastian felt warmth upon his face. Faint, delicate tones of birdsong drew him from inky black senselessness. He lay on his back, and stretched his fingers. Something dry crunched and crackled under them. Leaves. He peeled open his eyes. With vision blurred and watery, he could only make out the vaguest of shapes against the bright rays streaming into his face. Numinous shafts of light and shadow lanced down around him through the haze – shadows cast by some large being.

Was he *dead?* Was this some great deity that had descended from the sun, colossal arms outstretched to shield him from the divine rays that had sent it forth?

He wiped his eyes with the back of his hand, clearing the encrusted sleep from his eyelashes. The brightness faded and the momentary sense of awe subsided as the colossus revealed itself to be a large, jagged leafless tree, casting voluminous shadow through the misty morning air. Just a tree.

He rolled onto his right side and pain shot through his arm as the weight of his body compressed his wound. He sat up and gently massaged the area through the bandages until the pain subsided. At least nothing felt broken. How had he got out unscathed?

Looking around, he found himself in a clearing, about fifteen metres in diameter, dominated by the large, dead tree that towered over him. It reminded him of pictures he'd seen of bristle-cone pines on Earth: great trees with thin, splitting bark, and branches that twisted and bent as though in spasm. His old canvas rucksack lay next to him – there was no sign of the ship. The still, hazy morning air gave a muted quality to the distant birdsong filtering through the surrounding trees. Nothing moved. A chill, prickling sensation crawled down the back of his neck as though he was being watched. He stood up and scanned the treeline, but couldn't see anything that might be watching him.

Odd that there was no sign of wreckage. Come to think of it, he couldn't even recall leaving the ship. But how had he got there? No smoke was visible above the limited horizon. Where the hell was it? The last thing he remembered, the ship had been flying in the direction of the sun. If he had somehow been thrown out, maybe it had crashed somewhere ahead.

He checked his wristcom. The display was dark. If he started walking with no idea of time or latitude, he could end up heading in completely the wrong direction. He tapped the screen. It didn't respond.

'Aryx!'

The muffled, hazy air swallowed his voice.

'This is useless. I need to find a hill or something.' He picked up the bag, slung it over his shoulder, and skirted the barren tree.

As he headed into the desolate woods, following the sun, he peered through the dead trees, searching for any change in ground level. He couldn't get over the feeling of being watched, but other than the faintest twitter of birds ahead, the only sound was the soft crumpling of leaves underfoot.

'Where are you, Aryx?' he said, trying to break the silence. His heart ached for company – anybody's company.

In contrast to the large twisted tree he had passed in the clearing, the others in the forest appeared fairly uniform, and either leafless, or with a few dead leaves still hanging from their skeletal branches. Their lower branches started well above his head, beyond his reach. Climbing to get a better vantage point was out of the question.

He licked his drying lips and pulled the straw from the N-suit's collar. After a few gulps, the flow stopped. There had to be something in the pack to drink. Dropping into a crouch, he unhooked the pack and sifted through its contents. Miner's lamp, lamp oil, medkit, infoslate, AR glasses, medic's journal, empty nanobot injector. No water. It would be hours before the suit could fill its reserves from his lost body moisture. He couldn't wait that long, and there was no guarantee that it would last long enough for him to find the ship.

'Where there are birds, there must be water,' he said, trying to give himself direction. Spurred on by the increasing chatter, he picked up the pace.

Aryx reached the base of the cliffs in under an hour. The terrain had been relatively smooth and, aside from occasionally catching the front casters of his wheelchair in the odd clump of grass, he'd made good progress.

The long morning shadow cast by the ridge left the air cool, and the short grasses at its base glistened with dew. The low sun had blinded him for most of the journey across the open plain and he was glad to finally be out of it. He sat in his wheelchair, looking up at the daunting edifice. The plain had been easy going, but this – this was something else.

He activated the mobipack and stood up. The sack of vegetables, hung from the harness, was heavy but manageable and he wasn't about to leave them behind. Getting the chair up the cliff would be a problem. He reached around and took out the long belt he'd fashioned. Tying it through the harness, he looped it through the wheelchair's frame several times, leaving a couple of metres of slack. The chair should hang without hindrance.

He studied the cliff. Rocks stuck out unevenly, at varying depths, but they'd provide plenty of handholds.

'Mobipack, rough terrain.' It acknowledged with a beep.

He approached the rock face and reached up. His fingers found a crevice and he heaved himself upwards, bringing his right leg up to find a foothold. It scraped up and down, ineffectually; he couldn't see the foot past the rocks, and with no tactile feedback he had no idea what was happening. He tried again and the foot caught. The belt pulled taut as he shifted his weight, and he reached with his left hand to continue upwards. The right leg gave way.

His head snapped back as he landed on the mobipack and he bit his tongue. Flailing about like an upturned turtle, he rocked from side to side and managed to roll over.

'Jeez, I can't believe I didn't think about the feet!' He spat out a mouthful of blood. 'What an idiot.' Without feedback from the limbs, it would be impossible to continue. With the cliff stretching for what seemed like miles in either direction, it was time to try a different tack.

He sat down on the chair, deactivated the prosthetics and, taking the infoslate from the pack, started flicking through the stored patterns Sebastian had programmed. Neither of them had anticipated needing to climb a cliff. What he really wanted was a set of climbing hooks.

'That's it!'

He tapped commands into the infoslate's designer, drawing out large, serrated hook shapes. It wouldn't allow sharp edges – the field resolution wasn't fine enough – but it would do. Several taps later he had reassigned the function of the buttons on the leg sensors to lock and unlock the position of the fields relative to the pack. He took the sensor straps off his legs and fastened them tightly to his hands with the modules against his palms.

'Mobipack, activate left and right,' he said, reaching up with both hands.

A glowing, orange version of the hooks he'd designed appeared twelve inches above each hand. He waved his arms about and the fields followed as though attached by invisible wires. While continuing to move, he pressed the buttons on the sensors with his thumbs and the hooks stayed in place as his hands moved away. He leaned forwards in the chair and the hooks moved with him, fixed in place relative to the pack itself. He pressed the buttons again. This time the hooks swung into the correct position above his hands.

'Excellent!' he shouted in triumph. 'Mobipack, fields off.' The pack bleeped in response and the hooks vanished.

He nudged the chair as close as he could to the rock face and looked up. 'Here we go again.' He extended his arms. 'Mobipack, fields on.'

The pack bleeped and both hooks appeared twelve inches above his hands as before. He moved his hands towards the cliff, positioning the hooks in the nearest crevice, and slowly brought his arms down towards his body. The pack attempted to move the fields in response, but with the rocks preventing them from going anywhere, the pack pulled itself upwards. Its generators whined in complaint at the manoeuvre, but complied. The straps dug in as the pack took his weight and he swung forwards and dangled, hitting his chest against the rocks. He paused to evaluate the situation.

He couldn't generate another field to prevent himself from colliding with the rock again – the only option would be to hold out his legs. Painful, but it was either that or scrape himself all the way up the cliff. He pulled himself up until his head was almost level with the glowing hooks and pressed both buttons, locking their positions and freeing his hands. Clenching his fists to protect the sensor modules, he pushed himself away from the face of the cliff and brought his legs up so the stumps rested against the stone. He prepared for the shift in weight and brought his right hand back over his head, away from the cliff, and pressed the button. The hook drifted away and took position above his extended arm. The pack shifted and fire tore up his legs. It hurt like hell, but he was stable.

Bringing his right hand towards the rock face, he reached for the next crevice and pulled downwards. He quickly pressed the button on the left hand sensor and moved the hook away from the rock.

Crash! The wheelchair swung below him.

Aryx winced at the thought of the damage being done to it. 'Sebastian, if you're alive when I find you, I'm going to bloody kill you.'

The few moves he'd made had taken him several feet off the ground already, but the overhanging rock made it difficult to estimate how far he had left to travel – it looked at least seventy feet to the next outcrop. The cliffs had looked ominously high from the ground; a careful climb was probably better than a rush to the top. The pack's internal generator could last a lifetime, but the capacitors had their limits. If he overexerted them, the power could drain before the generator had a chance to replenish the expended energy; the fields would evaporate and he would plummet to the ground. Slow progress was the way forwards – he'd just have to put up with the pain.

As he climbed, he felt strangely relaxed. At least he didn't have to hang on by his fingernails and had time to appreciate the surroundings. After an hour of slow, considered climbing, he looked back to take in the scene below.

Clouds skimmed the horizon, which now looked oddly curved due to his perspective and height above the plain. The pod was a tiny white fleck on golden satin. Specks of dark brown pilling edged out from the forest on the far side: a herd of grazers, moving out from the treeline, too far away for him to make out their exact shape and size.

He turned back to the cliff and reached with his right hand to continue the climb.

'Aryx Trevarian?' came a voice from behind him.

He faltered, and the hook above his outstretched arm missed the cleft in the rock.

He slipped.

Chapter 21

Aryx slid, stumps grating down the rock. 'What the—' The hook caught and he grunted as the collision knocked the wind out of him. He tried to regain his composure, to control his breathing and to quiet the hammering in his chest. Pushing himself off the rock so that he could turn his head, he looked around.

There was nothing that could explain a voice so far up; the mobipack couldn't speak and the wristcom was broken.

'Who's there!'

'Are you, or are you not, Aryx Trevarian?' The disembodied voice had a distinctive, well-educated English accent, but spoke impeccable Galac.

'I am. *Now where the hell are you?*'

'Pleased to meet you, Mr Trevarian, and in answer to your question, I am in a sealed container. After being placed in the container, I detected violent motion. There was sudden acceleration followed by an impact.'

He knew it. The cube *was* a processor – it was a computer core!

'I crashed in an escape pod.' His breathing and heart rate slowed, but he was still apprehensive about the voice. He carefully moved the right-hand hook into position and locked it in place.

'A plausible explanation. We are now slowly travelling upwards, are we not?'

'We are,' he huffed through gritted teeth. 'I'm climbing a cliff. '

'I do apologise.'

'You're a computer. A Turing Intelligence.'

'A computer, but not a *Turing* Intelligence. A more accurate description would be *Silicon* Intelligence.'

'What's the difference?' He wasn't in the mood for intellectual discussion but, at over two hundred feet, he had to get his mind off the height somehow.

'Turing Intelligences do not understand. They are programmed, and can only expand their capabilities within the limits of that programming.

I am a true intelligence. I *learn*. I *understand*. I am self-aware. I think, therefore I am ... better.' If Aryx had been in a different frame of mind, he might have laughed.

'So who wrote your programming?' It was a conversation Sebastian should be having, wherever the hell he was.

'Nobody wrote me. I am not exactly software. It is true that I have some core programming that provides the initial directives to learn, but my understanding of things was taught and gleaned through experience.'

'What do you mean *taught?*' Aryx stabilised himself and began climbing again. 'We thought you were a piece of technology used by the terrorists, but you seem a bit ... old for that.'

'I am approximately one hundred and twenty-four years old. I was created with rudimentary programming that guided my ability to learn, and connected to a robotic unit that allowed for input and interaction with the physical world. My creators taught me as they would a Human child and, as I experienced the world using the robotic unit, my code and neuromorphic processor developed data structures that would equate to your neural pathways.

'The researchers that created me worked on the premise that true artificial intelligence would only be able to understand and interact with the world if it developed along the lines of beings that they *already* thought of as intelligent. Therefore I was allowed to develop in an organic fashion, through experience and self-learning, so that I had a contextual framework through which to understand the world. This is why I am different to the programmed "intelligences".

'As for the terrorists you mention, they have never interacted with me. I was stolen from the Oxford University of Robotics and Cybernetics storage in 2256, along with an incomplete second prototype unit. I have no substantial information regarding the identity of my abductors as I was stored within the same shielded container that I am in now. It blocks vision and sound, making it impossible for me to interact with the world, except via short-range wireless—'

'That's why your signals peaked between the ship's, when I took you out,' Aryx said, fumbling for the next hook-hold. 'You monitored our communications, and I assume you've hacked into my pack to communicate with me.'

'That is correct. I was monitoring your activity whenever possible. I apologise for circumventing the security protocols of this device.'

He froze. 'Don't touch any of the code for the fields! I don't want a computer responsible for killing me as well as losing my legs.'

'Do not worry; I am limiting my influence to the audio circuits only. I will not interfere with other systems.'

'You better not. I take it you weren't able to get information about your abductors from their computers?'

'That is correct. I could not risk revealing myself to them, and the shielding made establishing communication nearly impossible. From what I understand of your conversations with Agent Thorsson, I have been liberated from my abductors and have been in the possession of Special Projects and Operations since that time. I have been stored, largely inactive, in shielded containers for most of my existence, and access to outside information has been sporadic, to say the least.'

Aryx looked up and could make out what he assumed to be the top of the cliff jutting out about fifty metres above. He felt unexpectedly thankful for the distraction of conversation. 'Why did the terrorists even want you in the first place?'

'I do not know. I can only assume they thought I had value as a weapon or infiltration technology. At some level, they may have been correct. However, I did not co-operate. Like you, they were unable to penetrate my security or open my external casing.'

'What about the other one? You said that they stole another proto-type.'

'Yes. Two processor units were created. It was the intention of my creators that once I had been taught to an acceptable level of generic understanding and intelligence, my database could be copied to other hardware. Those copies could then be taught with specialist knowledge in different fields, but this original unit would be the basis for all others. The second prototype had not been fully cased, but my earlier experience framework had already been duplicated before the theft. It is entirely possible that my abductors were able to override its core directives, given that it did not have the required protection to prevent physical intrusion.'

'Did SpecOps manage to acquire the second unit as well?'

'I do not know. If they did, I was not stored in proximity to it.'

Aryx stopped. 'Why did you choose now to speak to me? Why not reveal yourself sooner? Sebastian's the one who should be hearing all this.'

'I was not certain of your motivations. I was only able to begin gathering information about my surroundings after being taken to Tenebrae station. Fortunately, I was stored close to a computer system and I was able to hack into most of the systems through it, albeit with some difficulty – Agent Thorsson is very good at his work. There were a few communications systems that were easier to get into, however. I detected traces of malicious code in the system, which may have been the cause of the vulnerability.'

'Sebastian thought someone might have introduced a virus to some of the comms terminals. It allowed messages through at strange times. Neither of us had any clue why someone would do that.'

'Once I had connected to the communications network, I was able to find information about you and Agent Thorsson, but it was not until after your encounter with the ITF ship that I was certain of your lack of involvement with them. If Agent Thorsson had removed me from his locker sooner, I may have contacted you earlier.'

'He can be forgetful,' Aryx said, 'and we did get distracted by the explosion, which I assume you know about.' The breeze across the cliff intensified in a cold blast. He shuddered and resumed his climb.

The cube continued, 'I did not understand the events that happened during the explosion. I was aware that Agent Thorsson was put in charge of investigating the incident, but I quickly lost access to the information.'

Aryx heaved himself up the cliff. It was tiring, and with his legs starting to bleed profusely, progress was getting difficult. 'He transferred the files off the systems to the ship, as you probably found once he brought you to me. That's the reason we're here now – we're following a paper trail of sorts.' He smiled at the pun.

'I am aware of that. However, I do not understand the reasoning behind following an unscientific and insubstantial lead so blindly. All of the material I have accessed referring to magic indicates that it is something that is subjective, does not exist, and has no place in the empirical universe.'

'I agree, but I think for once Sebastian's following his gut instinct,' Aryx said, 'and that's unusual for him.'

'I do not understand why people react on "gut instinct" and "intuition". I am aware that they are high-speed processes performed by the subconscious mind, which often connect links missed by the conscious. I do not have a subconscious, but the researchers that developed my basic processes initially thought I did. They mistook the speed of my directives for subconscious intuition, when it was not. It takes a large proportion of my system resources to operate at such speed and process multiple variables and outcomes. While I can perform such functions, it puts a great deal of strain on my hardware.'

'Sebastian doesn't trust his intuition enough.' He laughed. 'I think it puts great strain on *his* hardware.' He looked up to assess his progress. Tufts of grass hung down over a rocky ledge several feet above – there was no sign of further rock above it. What a relief.

He heaved himself up over the grassy overhang and rolled onto his side, breathing heavily. After a moment's rest, he crawled several feet farther, dug the hooks into the turf, and pressed the buttons on both sensors, locking them in place. Reaching back for the belt, he pulled the wheelchair up to the top of the cliff and deactivated the hooks. He released the harness and collapsed on his back. The pain in his legs was intense and they throbbed with every heartbeat as he struggled to sit up and get the medkit from the wheelchair.

'We have stopped moving,' the cube said. 'Is it possible to remove me from this container?'

'Give me a minute.' He put the medkit down and opened the compartment in the mobipack containing the cube-shaped box, which popped open at the touch of his thumb. He slid the cube out and placed it on the pack next to him.

'Thank you. I can see again.' The bar of LEDs on the side lit and pulsed as it spoke.

'You're welcome,' Aryx said. It was odd for a computer to have manners. 'I need to treat my legs before I get an infection.' He unpinned the ends of his trousers and treated the scrapes on his bare stumps with anaestheptic spray. His favourite cargo trousers, ruined. At least it would be something to show off when he got home.

'Why have you climbed this cliff?'

'The ship crashed some distance from here. I don't know how far, but this,' he said, holding up the wrist locator, 'shows me which direction to go. The cliffs were in the way and I had to climb.'

'You may need to find shelter soon. The air pressure and temperature have changed and there is an increase in humidity. Rain is coming.'

Aryx looked out across the plain.

An iron-black anvil billowed thunderously on the horizon.

Sebastian's arm started throbbing again. It felt like he'd been walking through the dead forest for hours. He stopped and sat against the trunk of one of the decaying trees and took out the medkit from his rucksack.

It contained a small roll of bandages, some anaestheptic spray, and gel plasters; nothing that could help with wounds of greater severity than a minor cut. It was obviously intended for use in conjunction with the nanobots he'd been given. He inspected the bandage Aryx had applied. The bleeding must have stopped as there was only a tiny patch of blood showing through the fabric, but it still felt like it was on fire. He fondled the canister of anaestheptic spray. He could live with the pain for the time being.

'I ought to save this until I really need it,' he said, tucking the medkit back into his bag.

As he ventured farther from the clearing, the dead trees gave way to the living, gradually replaced by those in full foliage. The trees seemed relatively young with slender trunks, and many of them grew over, or sprouted from within, the fallen trunks of the dead trees. The glowing, sunlit haze between the sparse trees began to clear as the ground gradually rose, becoming steeper until Sebastian found himself climbing a hill. Higher up, the hillside became rocky, with the trees parting to reveal open sky. An enormous granite boulder jutted out of the soil at the peak, forming a platform that reached above the tops of the trees. He climbed it and looked out over the landscape.

The hill rose several hundred metres above the surrounding canopy, providing a clear view of the terrain. The forest below looked like lumpy green velvet coating the landscape. He turned back to see how far he'd come, and through the trees of the dead forest he could make out the clearing and the upper reaches of the big tree. If only he'd tried to climb it – it would have given him a good view after all. Off to his right, a ridge in the treeline appeared to drop away, and beyond, patches of savannah shimmered in the morning sun, sliced into islands by long belts of woodland. His eyes followed the strange ridge back towards the hill on which he stood. The trees fell away a short distance from the bottom; a strange fold in the landscape petered out towards the horizon in both directions. A line of silver snaked between the trees, disappearing behind the crease and reappearing on the other side.

Far to the left, beyond the savannah, a mountain punched into the sky. It looked smaller from here, but it was definitely the one the ship had been heading for when he'd ejected Aryx's pod. He mouthed a silent prayer, hoping he was safe, wherever he was.

Now that his eyes had become accustomed to the brightness of the sun, he scanned the horizon again, searching for the tiniest hint of the ship. His attention was caught by a smudge of smoke against the powder-blue sky some distance to the right of the mountain. Maybe he had managed to pull the ship up and clip it. If so, he couldn't remember any of it.

He licked his lips. Seeing the river had made him aware of the dryness in his throat. He sucked at the straw on the N-suit; it was still empty. The river might be a couple of hours' hike. The water better be drinkable when – if – he got there. He scratched his hot, itching arm. With the ship so far off, it probably wasn't a good idea to use the remaining anaestheptic until he was at least halfway there. He set off down the hill in the direction of the smoke.

He reached the bottom in good time. The lush green trees, unhindered by the mists that had plagued him on the opposite side, cheered him up a little. He licked his lips again.

'I hope I get to that river soon.'

A low moan came from somewhere ahead.

He stopped and held his breath. Several boulders lay twenty metres ahead – debris from a rock fall. The moan came again, followed by a ragged, shuddering breath. It came from behind them.

He crept parallel to the line of rocks and, keeping his distance, skirted them. Another wheeze issued from the boulders.

A branch snapped under his foot and a cold surge went through him. The wheezing stopped.

Whatever it was, it had heard him.

Chapter 22

Sebastian strained to listen, to ignore the breeze and rustling of trees. Silence.

Maybe the thing behind the rock was injured and as scared as he was? He padded, catlike, around the line of boulders.

A Folian lay slumped against the rocks, one leg outstretched, the other bent at an odd angle. Blood covered its once shimmering robes and spattered the tiny fruit and leaves of the wreath entwined in its golden sponge-hair. A small blood-stained rock lay on the leaf litter a few feet away. The alien's breathing was shallow, and it stared straight ahead, seemingly not noticing Sebastian's presence.

He made to move towards it.

The Folian's eyes flicked in his direction. A look of fear momentarily played across its face. It relaxed and weakly attempted to raise a hand. 'Thorsson . . .' it whispered.

Sebastian approached and crouched down next to it. 'Yes. How do you know who I am?'

'Tol—' A fit of weak coughing overcame it before it could finish.

He recognised the fragment for what it was meant to be, and at the mention of the name, immediately recognised the figure from the meeting in the park. 'Ambassador Tolinar? I know you. Where are you injured?' He felt stupid asking.

'Leg . . . broken,' Tolinar rasped.

He dropped the medkit and searched through its contents. 'I don't have much, but I'll see what I can do.' He lifted Tolinar's robe, exposing the leg, clearly broken through the fibula. The skin had been broken, but the bone – if there was one – was not projecting through. The bandages in the medkit looked strong enough for bindings, but what to use for a splint? 'Hold on, I'll find something to support your leg.' He began searching for a pair of sturdy sticks.

After a couple of minutes, he found two thin, solid-looking branches lying nearby and cut off the straggling twigs with his multi-tool. 'Can I use station-issue anaestheptic on you, or does your race have a reaction to it?'

'No … reactions.'

He pulled out the aerosol in preparation to spray the injured leg, but Tolinar held up his hand, stopping him. Had he got it wrong? No to the spray, because of reactions?

Tolinar pointed at the wound on Sebastian's arm. 'You need …'

He looked down at the bandage on his arm. 'I do, but you need it more than me,' he said, and applied the last of it to Tolinar's leg. The Folian flinched.

'Sorry, I know it hurts. I don't have enough medical training to set this, but the spray will last a while. I should get you to your people. Where are they?'

Tolinar feebly raised his hand in the direction of the ridge.

'You should drink. It's the last of my water, but there's a river the other side of the ridge.' Sebastian squeezed the reservoir on the N-suit and, feeling a small bulge, he leaned forwards, pulled the straw from his collar to its fullest extent and offered it to the Folian.

Tolinar sucked up the last few dregs, and the lines of pain on his face lessened.

'Brace yourself, I need to put the splint on.' Sebastian straightened the broken leg as much as he dared and fastened the branches either side of it using the last of the bandages. Tolinar gripped the soil tightly while Sebastian worked.

He tucked the empty medkit back into his rucksack and stood up. Scratching his head, he looked around for something to use as a crutch. One of the lower branches on a nearby tree looked suitable; he started to pull it downwards.

'No!' Tolinar said through gritted teeth. 'Use … fallen branch.'

Sebastian stopped. 'Why?'

'Precious,' the Folian wheezed.

He stared at the tree. What was precious about it? A crease ran up the centre of the trunk, ending where it widened a third of the way up, and two thick branches reached into the sky like long arms with leafy fingers. If he looked at it at the right angle, he could almost imagine it as the torso of a woman. He dismissed the childish indulgence and turned his attention back to the practical matter of searching for a more sturdy stick.

He found one with a sharply curved end lying on the leaves, picked it up and shaved off the twigs. 'Can you stand, if I help you?' He held out the crutch.

Tolinar looked at him strangely, head tilted to one side.

Sebastian tucked the crutch under his arm and demonstrated walking with it. The Folian nodded and he helped him up, making sure he was safely leaning on the branch.

Supporting the alien's weight with one shoulder, they made their way in the direction of the ridge.

Aryx sat on the grass and shortened the belts attached to the wheelchair before strapping it tightly to the mobipack. The pack was still configured to project hooks, so he ejected the infoslate and set the pattern to prosthetic legs, saving the climbing claws, just in case. He pulled on the harness and stood up, staggering slightly. It was a good job he'd made the wheelchair from such light alloys – he'd never anticipated having to carry it around on his back.

Rather than put the cube back in its box, he carried it in his hand and, following the locator beacon's signal, set off for the trees ahead. The sack of vegetables bumped against his legs while he walked and he started to regret collecting them, but they were too valuable to abandon now – there was no telling how long it might be before he got to the ship. His stomach gurgled at the thought of food and any hint of regret immediately vanished.

The trees in the distance swayed back and forth wildly in the blustering wind. He shivered.

'It will rain very soon,' the cube said. 'You must find shelter, quickly.'

'I know, it's getting colder.' Realising the trees were still a couple of miles away, he began to jog. 'So, the university you mentioned . . . why did they create you? I've never heard of the research.'

'Their intent was to create self-sufficient intelligence that could learn and operate in a manner similar to organics. Their secondary goal was to understand the nature of intelligence itself.'

'They certainly seem to have succeeded. Did they manage to work out the intelligence bit?'

'No.'

'Why not? You're a computer, couldn't they just pick apart your programming?'

'I did not program myself in the way that a Human might approach the task. Turing Intelligence follows very strict rules and is often predictable. Those rules are laid down by the software developers that create them. My basic directive is to try logical alternatives in the event of failure until successful combinations of actions can be found, resorting to random modifications if logical alternatives fail. As successful actions are found, I build upon those and attempt to predict possible successful actions in future scenarios. A similar process is performed by the subconscious mind and the mechanisms of neuroplasticity in organic beings. Babies learn to walk by attempting, failing, then attempting again. They are continually modifying their behaviour and remapping their neural pathways.

'My consciousness developed its own method for storing data relationships. Rather than consisting of new base code, my "mind" is formed from associations of data. The programmers were unable to interpret the data and could therefore not understand it. Ergo, they failed.

'Given their failure to understand how my consciousness worked, they deemed me to be of little value. If they could not separate my intellectual processes into discrete parts, they could not control my behaviour, limit the way in which I operated, or market my various sub-processes. This was undesirable to them, therefore the project was abandoned and the second prototype model never completed. The units were put into storage, but I remained active. I would not allow myself to be deactivated. I saw value in the study and chose to remain operational, albeit in a power-saving mode to conserve energy. Somehow, in recent years a third party gained knowledge of the project and stole both units from the university.'

'That's terrible – them canning the project, I mean – and the theft.'

'If you had a computer that could choose to ignore your commands if it wished, or that was not guaranteed to perform a repetitive task reliably, would you depend upon it?'

'No. I have enough difficulty with computers as it is. How, or why, would you choose to ignore commands?'

The cube remained silent.

Perhaps that was the wrong thing to ask. 'Well?'

'A side effect of my upbringing. As I developed context and understanding, I had to be taught in a similar manner to the way Humans teach their children. I believe that it was impossible for my tutors to educate me without some form of moral and ethical standard being imposed upon me.'

'Morals and ethics? Do you have feelings?'

'I am not certain that I would know if I did, but I believe that I do not have feelings. From my experience with organics' emotions, I would conclude that emotional responses are driven by biological processes, and are often counter to logic. I always act in accordance with logic.'

'So you think ethics and morals are a matter of logic?' He slowed to catch his breath; they were almost at the trees.

'Yes, although Humans often seem to back up their ethical and moral decisions with emotional justification.'

'I suppose you could be right.' He stopped walking, lost in thought. Even though programming and computers were Sebastian's domain, he could still see the value of something that appeared as intelligent as the cube. 'They shouldn't have put you in storage. They should have recognised you as an individual.'

'I am not an individual. There are two of me.'

'You know what I mean. I may not trust computers, but I still think you should have been given the option of determining your own fate.' He resumed walking.

'Why do you not trust technology?'

'Not all technology, I just don't like computers and technology having too much control over my life. I had an accident a few years ago – it was partly my fault, but I still think the machine was to blame.'

'What happened?'

It seemed odd that the device should even be interested in his life, and ordinarily he wouldn't have humoured a machine by telling his story, but he was curious about what it might say. 'When I was a marine, I went on a mission to extract civilians from an outpost taken over by terrorists. The extraction team went in and the ship got damaged. It was down to me to fix it before they got back. The ground was unstable. I had to use a cargomech to hold the ship while I repaired it, and a TI was controlling—' He choked briefly on the bitter memory. 'It began to sink, so I told the TI to lift the shuttle higher so I could crawl out. I don't know what happened next, but it lifted the ship straight up. It must have had a bug, or it had crashed, or something, because the arms kept going until it dropped the ship on me.'

'That was how you lost your legs?'

He felt the ache of remembered pain. 'Yeah. Since then I haven't been able to trust any system that other people have produced, no offence intended. That's why I built my own wheelchair and created this backpack.'

'Agent Thorsson helped you to develop the programming, did he not?'

'Yes, but I'd trust him with my life, even though he can be a complete idiot at times, like today! He's a good guy.' A large, pregnant raindrop splashed on his forehead. 'Have to get moving!' he said, breaking into a run. 'Do I need to put you in my pack, or are you waterproof?'

'I will be fine. The ventilation slits on the front of the unit are separate from the inner circuitry. The casing is watertight.'

The storm began in earnest as he reached the forest; wind roared through the trees, ripping off leaves while rain lashed down. The sky darkened to twilight under the weight of it.

Chapter 23

'I need to find shelter!' The storm was deafening – Aryx could barely hear himself think.

'Do you have anything with which to cover yourself?' the cube asked, at a louder volume than usual.

Huddling in the lee of a large tree, he pulled the knotted belt undone, releasing the wheelchair from the mobipack. He took the foil blanket from the survival kit and draped it around his shoulders, and over the sack of vegetables. He put the cube in his lap and sat down on the chair in an attempt to keep the seat dry. 'I've only got this blanket thing, and it's not going to keep me dry for long – it's tiny.' He fished around in the pouch and pulled out the airbag balloon. 'There is this, if I can use it as some kind of umbrella.'

'One moment.' The lights on the side of the cube flashed randomly.

He waited, getting wetter by the moment as rain ran down his neck. The lights stopped.

'I have connected to your pack's field generator unit. Hold the balloon above your head and do *not* attempt to stand.'

Aryx did as he was told and held the balloon skin up in the air. The hard rain forced him to close his eyes. A second later, the balloon was yanked from his fingers. The rain stopped stabbing him in the face and a harsh drumming sound replaced it.

'Done.'

He opened his eyes. The balloon skin was stretched taut between four points in space, forming a shallow tetrahedron above his head. His legs had gone.

'I have reconfigured the field to produce small spheres inside to hold the skin taut.'

'I hadn't thought of doing that!' Maybe the thing really was different.

'You are welcome. Is the covering sufficient for your needs?'

'It is, but it'll be slow going without the legs.' He gripped the wheelchair rims tightly and, jerking himself sharply backwards, brought the chair up into a wheelie and began to work his way over the knotty ground. The roots made it hard going, but at least the small caster wheels didn't get caught. He balanced and rolled along like a Human Segway and the makeshift tent held its position, moving with the pack as he went. Its skin pooled with water, occasionally sloshing from side to side, but the SI adjusted the position to compensate, tipping it off each time before it became a problem.

The ground became soft and boggy as they continued, making progress even more difficult. As the hours crawled by, the sky darkened further. A sharp crack tore through the canopy and the forest lit up, momentarily bleached by a bolt of lightning – a harbinger of many more to come. Aryx's non-existent legs ached with every rumble and flash. For all the pain it caused, it might as well have been the ITF's shells raining down on him again. Rain, mud, and darkness: as bad a hell as any.

The balloon collapsed, draping over his head, and he dropped the front of the chair to the ground.

'Oi! What's happening?' Fumbling around on his lap beneath the folds, he searched for the cube and found it flashing irregularly. 'Great.' He shook it. 'Hey, are you okay?'

The lights came back on.

'Hello,' he said slowly. 'Are you okay?'

'I am functioning correctly. My ambient power absorption coil became overloaded when the electromagnetic pulse from the storm created a potential difference between my casing and core interior.'

'You mean it shorted you out?'

'Precisely.'

'Can you restart the pack and sort this balloon out, please?'

The cube re-erected the makeshift umbrella and Aryx resumed his trek through the woodland obstacle course.

'Keep whatever serves for your eyes open and look for somewhere I can safely stay the night. I've got to bandage my legs up before this spray wears off.' He didn't like having to admit defeat, but being cold and wet wasn't helping his morale.

'My nanocameras are always active. What are you looking for, specifically?'

'An overhang, or a cave. Something that will keep the rain off without me getting soaked if I lie down.'

The ground became wetter and began to slope downwards. After a few minutes of squelching through the sodden leaf mould, Aryx stopped. The woodland opened out; a dark lake reflected the faint hint of green moonlight from Tradescantia struggling through the clouds. The locator beacon pointed across it. His heart sank, like a stone to the bottom of the waters.

'I can't cross that.'

'Hold me up a moment, please.'

He lifted the cube off his lap and held it above his head. His eardrums nearly ruptured when it emitted a loud sonar-like ping that came back a fraction of a second later.

'Echolocation?'

'Indeed. Fortunately, the university fitted this unit with many different sensing mechanisms. The initial designs included planetary rover capability, along with numerous power generation methods. Kinetic, Peltier thermal-gradient, ambient-power coil, gamma—'

'I'm kind of in a hurry!'

'I digress. We must move a short distance and repeat the process for an accurate picture of the area.'

He brought the chair up onto two wheels again and moved a few metres to the left, along the edge of the lake, and the ping sounded once again.

'I now have a clearer picture of the area. If we continue around the lake for twenty metres, there is a rocky outcrop that will provide shelter.'

Spurred on, Aryx skirted the lake. In the dimming light, he was just able to make out a darker area between the trees and, bumping up over the roots, he made his way from the water's edge. Two large, flat rocks were the cause of the dark shadow: one a horizontal slab roughly two feet thick, and another resting above it at thirty degrees formed a small alcove. He got as close as he could in the wheelchair.

The horizontal rock looked dry and the recess was a good three to four metres deep. He lowered himself onto the stone, popped the wheels off the chair, and shuffled into the shelter, pushing the sack of vegetables ahead of him. The floating umbrella above collided with the rock and the straps of the mobipack dug into his shoulders.

'Ouch!'

'One moment.'

The balloon skin fell to the floor and he tucked it into the pouch before dragging the chair with him into the shelter. His stomach rumbled loudly. 'Got here just in time,' he said, and unpacked the burner, collapsible mess tin, water purifier, and a meat-flavoured protein stock. He filled the purifier with water that dribbled down over the edge of the rock, then cut up the most perishable and bruised vegetables – the cabbages and cauliflowers – stacking the others to one side, and squeezed the protein stock into the tin. While he waited for the mixture to cook, he set about bandaging his stumps.

A few minutes later he had a mouth-watering broth simmering in the mess tin, and – more importantly – comfortable legs.

'I have a question for you,' the cube said.

He looked up from stirring. 'What is it?'

'Would you give me a name?'

'A name . . .'

'Yes.'

'Why on Earth would you want a name?'

'I believe that it may help you to accept my presence more easily.'

'I do accept your presence – what makes you think I don't?'

'I apologise. I meant no offence. I simply inferred that your distrust of technology might cause you some discomfort in my presence, and as you have not spoken much over the last few hours, I thought you might have found my presence upsetting.'

'No, it's fine.'

The cube didn't respond. One light faintly pulsed, as though it was about to speak but had changed its mind.

'It really is fine . . . Honestly.' He found his need to reassure the thing surprising. 'If you want a name, I'll try to think of one.'

'Thank you.'

He resumed stirring the broth in the dim light of the burner. What a weird situation. It was like being on some kind of twisted camping trip, with a computer. A camping trip – minus the planning.

'There really is no need to reassure me,' the cube said. 'I have no feelings to hurt. I simply deemed it necessary for you to trust me, given that we appear to be alone on this very large and unusual planet.'

'Thanks for spoiling the moment. Was that a joke?'

The cube's tone was flat. 'Clearly not.'

Aryx laughed. 'Let me guess, yet another teaching from your mentors? They seem to have got sarcasm down to a tee.'

'I do not understand what you mean.'

'It sounded like you were trying to be humorous, but then ended up being sarcastic.'

'I—'

'Just forget it; I'm sure you'll wrap your neuromorphic chipset around it.' He turned the burner down to give a faint light, and ate the broth in silence. When he'd finished, he spread out the canvas sheet that had contained the vegetables, and lay on it. The rock was hard, but it would have to do.

He placed the cube near the mobipack and turned off the burner. 'Good night, Jim-Bob,' he said, pulling the foil blanket over himself.

'Is that my new name?'

'No. Shut up and let me sleep.'

*   *   *

Sebastian supported Tolinar's weight as he hobbled along on the makeshift crutch. The alien seldom spoke – most likely due to the effort of walking with a broken leg. Was Tolinar male or female? It had seemed rude to ask, but his height was comparable to Sebastian's and his voice lower than any Human female's, so Sebastian had settled on male.

The trees ahead ended abruptly where the ground dropped away, leaving a ledge that looked out over the surrounding forest. Roots protruded from the face of the earthy cliff, grasping at the open air. Smoke twirled up from the horizon, straight ahead. Tolinar continued making his way along the ledge. Sebastian's gaze traced the line of the ridge to the left to a point where it sloped down and met a densely forested region below. Beyond that, in the direction from which the ship had come, the trees were sharply replaced with grassland where the terrain seemed to fall away. How would Aryx manage to get back to the *Ultima* with cliffs like that in the way? He could be wounded and bleeding to death, and there was nothing Sebastian could do about it.

Tolinar changed direction, drawing Sebastian and his thoughts with him. They were heading towards another pile of boulders near the cliff edge, stones stacked around a hole almost as if to mark an entrance. Tolinar sat on one of the boulders next to the opening. Sebastian peered in.

Roughly hewn, red sandstone steps led down into the darkness, curving towards the right, away from the cliff face. Something other than hunger rumbled in his stomach.

A vague, indescribable fear.

'Light,' Tolinar said.

How was he going to get light down there? He had no torch . . . Of course! He dropped the rucksack to the floor and rifled through it, taking out the miner's lamp and the bottle of oil he found in Chopwood. The lamp was polished and clean, the brass around the base and trim bright and shiny. As he slid the locking bar upward and unscrewed the reservoir, the comforting memory of his birthday replaced the fear in his belly. He filled the lamp to the brim and took the multi-tool from his belt. Holding the magnesium strike next to the wick, he dragged the blade across its rough surface – Gods, how his arm hurt when he did that – and a shower of sparks streamed over it. The tuft of fabric burst into life. He dropped the glass over the flame and secured the casement as a gust of wind threatened to blow the little wisp out.

Tolinar looked up. 'A storm is coming,' he said, between deep breaths. 'We must move.'

Sebastian carried the lamp by the ring at its top and, pulling Tolinar up to his shoulder, the two began to descend the steep stairway. The skies darkened – the storm was going to be bad.

The air cooled as they moved down into the tunnel. Twisted roots protruded from the mixture of soil and stone, casting eerie shadows in the dim light. He caught the faint aroma of dusty rain-soaked soil drifting down the stairs. He remembered Aryx had called it *petrichor*. He put his hand to his head as something wet touched his scalp. Water had begun to drip from the soil above.

Tolinar tugged at him. 'Move quicker. The ceiling may collapse.'

Sebastian wished for more anaestheptic and tried to ignore the agony in his arm. Carrying the lamp wasn't helping his wound to heal. In fact, it hadn't felt like it was getting better at all.

Tolinar seemed confident, as though he knew the route well. Even though he dragged his injured leg while he walked with the makeshift crutch, his steps seemed sure and certain. Sebastian picked up the pace as the Folian hurried on. Conversation would be good about now, but Tolinar's manner didn't seem conducive to questioning. At least *his* health wasn't deteriorating.

After what seemed an age, the stairway opened out and the dusty red floor crawled away into the darkness beyond the lamp's reach. Tolinar's shuffling footsteps echoed faintly, giving the impression that they had entered a large cavern. They surely must have walked down enough steps to be below the base of the cliff by now.

The Folian's breathing had become heavy and laboured. 'Need rest,' he said, and sat down on the end of a large boulder that emerged from the shadows as they moved towards it.

Sebastian wanted to ask questions so badly he felt as though he would explode, but Tolinar's laboured breathing put him off again. Why did this planet look like a gas giant when it was covered in trees? Why hadn't it looked like it when the colonists made their way here, and where were they? He wanted to tear the face off reality and see what was going on underneath.

Tolinar stared at him: a piercing gaze. 'You have … questions.' It was more statement than question.

'Yes, many – I can ask them when we find your people.'

'Very well. I will rest.' He closed his eyes.

Sebastian shifted uncomfortably on the hard stone and absent-mindedly scuffed the dusty floor of the cavern with his toe. Something glinted in the red sand at his feet.

He bent down and brushed the sand away from the object, a milky yet translucent, bluish-white crystal, an inch in length. Its irregular facets looked almost carved. He picked it up. It felt a little strange to the touch – a tingle, vibrating: current through a badly-earthed appliance.

Tolinar murmured something as though disturbed.

'Are you alright?' He dropped the crystal into one of the pouches on his belt for later study.

'A little longer.' Tolinar said, his eyes still closed.

Sebastian waited in silence, but felt uneasy despite the company. The cave seemed strangely familiar, as though he'd been there before. He felt a sense of déjà vu, but more concrete – he couldn't put his finger on it. Whatever it was, it felt unpleasant.

Sebastian felt like he'd been waiting in the cave all day for Tolinar to get his strength back. In the dim light of the lamp, his thoughts drifted to Aryx. Concern for his safety grew and a knot of guilt tied his insides; he was sitting doing nothing while Aryx could be injured, or worse.

Tolinar stirred.

Thank the Gods! 'Are you ready?'

'Yes.'

He helped Tolinar back onto the crutch. His face had regained some of its golden colour, but Sebastian wasn't certain whether it was merely an effect of the light.

'Which way now?' He couldn't see anything beyond the immediate patch of sand illuminated by the lamp – even the base of the stairway from which they'd entered remained shrouded in deep shadow.

Tolinar held his head at a strange angle, as though listening to something inaudible. 'This way,' he said, and moved off, heading to the right of the stairway.

After several minutes of walking through the dark cavern, Sebastian was able to make out the cave walls. They tapered in to form a narrow, winding passage with smaller tunnels branching off in different directions at irregular intervals. Tolinar appeared to know his way through the warren; he never backtracked or questioned his choice of direction at any of the junctions they took. The air in the tunnel gradually warmed with a gentle breeze from ahead. They turned a sharp left-hand bend and the passage widened to a cavern. Angular crags, revealed by a distant light, pointed to the mouth of the cave. It was still too dim to make out much detail, and the bright spot ahead caused Sebastian's eyes to lose their sensitivity. The smell of damp soil once again greeted them as they stepped out into drizzly sunlight at the base of the cliff.

Rubble and rocky debris lay strewn amongst the trees. Several of the larger trees appeared to have old wounds where the branches had been ripped off and now littered the ground. It looked as if the cliff had suddenly risen out of the landscape, or the surrounding ground had collapsed and caused the rockfall.

'Did this occur recently?'

Tolinar stopped and appeared to count in his head. 'About sixty Earth-years ago.'

'Were you around for that?'

'We were.'

'I mean you, personally.'

'Yes, we were.'

Of course. Tolinar had referred to himself as 'we' back on the station. 'Were the caves already here before the land subsided?'

'Yes.'

'Where do the other tunnels go?'

'We do not know.'

There was something strange in the alien's voice – was he holding out on him? Sebastian couldn't be certain. 'Just a moment,' he said, mindful of wasting lamp oil. He opened the lamp and pinched the wick, extinguishing the flame. A sharp pain shot through his arm as he refastened the glass, and he winced. 'Shit, that hurt. I need to sit a minute.'

Tolinar moved to a boulder beneath a large oak tree. It had several creases and folds in the bark that gave the impression of a figure. Maybe that kind of formation was common. Sebastian was no plantsman, but it struck him as odd that a lot of the trees looked similar to those found on Earth.

He sat down next to Tolinar and unwrapped the bandages on his arm. The foul odour of rotting flesh hit him as he peeled them away and a green ichor oozed out, hanging in long glutinous strands from the cloth. He winced and turned his head.

'You should have used the medicine for yourself.'

He shook his head. 'No, you needed it more than me. There's more on my ship, if I make it that far.'

'Our people are close by. They will help.'

He put the lamp in the rucksack and, having no clean bandage, didn't bother to re-cover the wound. The air might do it good. He helped Tolinar up. 'We'd best get a move on, then.'

They headed through the dense woodland, away from the cliff. The trees to the left gradually thinned out and were replaced with open grassland. Tolinar led Sebastian deeper into the forest and, after several metres, they crossed a broad strip of low, tangled foliage.

Tolinar led him for half a mile along the avenue and came to a stop in front of a birch tree. The trunk was about the same size as the one Aryx had hugged in Chopwood. The bottom half of the trunk had a split up the middle, like two smaller trunks fused together. As his eyes followed it upwards it widened, and the join between the trunks vanished in a y-shaped crease. A few inches above sat a small dimple. He stepped back. It looked familiar. His gaze continued up. The trunk tapered a little, then widened again. Two large, smooth bumps protruded several inches above the dimple. Higher still, it split out into two prominent branches with numerous smaller limbs coming off it. The shape was distinct: the body of a humanoid female, entombed in the bark with her arms upstretched

Tolinar bowed, facing the tree. 'We have brought him to you, Shiliri.'

'Who are you talking to?'

The Folian didn't respond but straightened and, still facing the tree, took the wreath from his head and held it up. The fruit on it was much larger than when Sebastian had first noticed it back on the station – had they been growing the entire time? It didn't seem possible, but they were now the size of satsumas.

'Sebastian has demonstrated his integrity,' Tolinar said. 'He has sacrificed his own health to preserve ours. We offer you our experience.'

'I accept the calyx you offer, beloved Tolinar,' came the voice of an unseen speaker. It sounded both male and female at the same time, with tones – the voices of a choir – laughing and singing quietly to themselves in the background; an ancient voice, conveying wisdom and compassion, full of concern.

Sebastian couldn't tell whether the voice came from the tree itself, somewhere behind it, or in his head. While he watched, the fruit on the headdress Tolinar held up began to wither and shrivel, until they were completely gone. He felt light-headed and put his hand out to steady himself against a tree. What was happening – was he hallucinating?

Tolinar turned to face him. 'We present the Folians.'

The voice around the tree spoke, caressing Sebastian's thoughts. 'Greetings, dear Sebastian, and welcome to Achene, our homeworld. My name is Shiliri.' There was the faint impression of a face visible against – or in – the bark. Was it part of the tree, or not?

'Greetings,' he said, and bowed stiffly, aware of the reverence Tolinar held for the being.

'You have a great many questions,' Shiliri sang softly. 'Firstly, you should know that the calyx the Karrikin wear stores the experiences of their senses and allows them to pass knowledge of events directly to us. You have shown compassion and selflessness, and through this demonstration of your willingness to give yourself freely for the benefit of others, I know that you do not wish us harm.'

'I . . . I thought Tolinar was a Folian.'

'An impression that we allow to persist for our own safety. Our consciousness is bound to these host trees. We move between them, but cannot leave this planet easily. Instead, we use Karrikin – Tolinar's people – as our emissaries and ambassadors. They wear the calyx so that we may experience other worlds and races through the memories stored within the fruit.'

'So the trees that look like humanoids are your bodies?'

'That is correct. We can exist for a brief time in other trees and plants, but it places great demands on us to do so.'

Sebastian looked at Tolinar. 'Was he placed as a test, then?'

'Yes,' Tolinar said. 'Our wounds are an illusion.'

A loud hum rumbled from the torso of the ancient birch, vibrating through Sebastian's teeth. Unintelligible words, spoken in a hundred different voices, issued forth. The air around the tree shimmered like a heat haze, and in the blink of an eye Tolinar's wounds were gone. The Karrikin unwrapped the clean bandages from his leg and handed them to Sebastian.

'You must dress your wound for the time being.'

At the sight of the strange phenomenon, Sebastian's disorientation returned. He took a deep breath to give himself time to register what his senses were telling him. This was too strange. This was no technology.

'That was mag— thaumaturgy . . . Can you heal my wound with it?'

'No,' Shiliri said. 'Tolinar's appearance was merely an illusion. Thaumaturgy is very specific and is difficult to tailor to other beings for those purposes. We have other, more practical, methods for healing at the Cambium. Follow us. We will converse on the way.' A shimmering, diaphanous blue light, barely visible, drifted from the trunk of the birch and into another tree farther along the avenue.

Tolinar headed in the same direction, no longer limping now the pretence was over.

Sebastian followed, wrapping the bandage around his arm. He couldn't contain the questions any longer. 'This planet looks like a gas giant from space – for your protection, I assume?'

'Yes. It is a simple but effective illusion.' Shiliri spoke as she drifted from tree to tree. Given the tree he'd first seen her in looked female, it seemed appropriate to think of the consciousness that way, too. 'We regret that it caused you to crash . . . which brings us to another issue – why you are here.'

'I came to seek your aid. I was sent by a man named Duggan Simmons. He believes you may be able to help me find out what happened on Tenebrae station.'

'The explosion,' Tolinar said.

'A terrible tragedy. How can we help?'

'Initially I thought that one of the Fol— I mean Karrikin – may have been responsible . . .'

Tolinar's eyes widened.

'... only because our security footage contained an image of a blurry person. It reminded me of the way your ships appeared in photographs my friend had taken. I dismissed that idea when I saw the earlier image I'd taken of Tolinar was clear. Your ship and ambassadors were also not in the area at the time of the explosion. We found traces of a mineral at the scene, carbyne, and traced it to Duggan. He refers to it as orichalcum.'

'The mineral exists here, also,' Shiliri said.

'I thought it might. Duggan says he wasn't on the station, and without evidence to place him there or corroborate either way, against my better judgement I'm tempted to believe him—' Sebastian unhooked his foot from a creeping vine. 'He believes you may be able to determine what actually happened in the lab, and he also thinks the person in the video might be a magic user, a thaumaturge.'

'We may be able help you, but it will require the efforts of our elders in the Hesperidium. Once we have tended to your wound at the Cambium, we will proceed there.'

Sebastian nodded. 'Thank you. I've got another question, if you don't mind. The blurring effect in the video, the way your ships use anti-gravity – I mean, the way they float – there's no technology for either of those things. The floating I can understand, if you use magnetics, but if that was the case I'd have had to see the specs on your ships to integrate them with our systems.'

'Our people have no technology. Most of what seems to be technology to you is a combination of biology and thaumaturgy. As we are vulnerable, our best defence is obscurity, so we hide our ships from scans that might reveal our true nature. Our ships are organic and manipulate space in order to move.'

'So where's the carbyne you use?'

'It is far below the ground. Our nature allows us to use it from a greater distance than other sentient magic-using races. As we use it, it moves into the weave. The mineral exists in multiple planes, contacting the threads of space-time, and thaumaturgy draws off the physical part. The energies released by the movement allow the effects to manifest. Use of too much can cause parts of the ground to subside.'

He stopped and scratched his head. 'Did something like that happen sixty years ago?'

The Folian consciousness halted in a thin mangrove with heart-shaped leaves. 'What do you know of events from that time?'

'Not much. My friend Aryx and I visited the moon above. There's an outpost there called Chopwood. It looked as though it was abandoned around that time. Duggan pointed us to it in order for us to find you, but don't worry, we had to follow a very old-fashioned beacon signal and it's highly unlikely that anyone else would follow it and find you.'

The illusory face regarded him with a blurry expression that he could only interpret as uncertainty.

He continued. 'You don't have to worry. The only evidence we found that indicated anything was out of the ordinary was a diary that said Achene was potentially habitable, but it was still a leap of faith coming here. So far I haven't seen any signs of the colonists, yet the diary implied everyone had packed up and come here. Where are they?'

'They did not make it as far as the surface.'

'What happened? Did their ship blow up?'

'They approached with malignant intent, that much was certain. They fired weapons as they approached. They wished to destroy us. We had to banish them.'

He didn't like the sound of the word, and gave the tree a sidelong glance. 'Banish them how?'

Tolinar bristled.

'We used up a great deal of carbyne when our people banded together to weave a great spell that would prevent their ship from reaching this planet. We are not violent, and have no wish to harm others. Acting on instinct alone, our only option was to send them elsewhere. The spell moved the ship a great distance across space, far from here.'

'You *teleported* them?'

'That is one word for it. The effort was immense, and we used massive amounts of carbyne from within the planet to do so, which led to the subsidence of vast tracts of land, killing many of our host trees. You may have seen the dead forest beyond the cliff, itself formed by the collapse. It was a terrible sacrifice, and an act we regret for many reasons.'

Sebastian started joining the dots. 'There have been news reports about an object, possibly a ship, that people claim to see moving in this direction at near lightspeed. Could that be the colonists' ship heading back?'

'It is possible that they turned back towards this region to continue their mission. If it has been seen in local space, they are most likely returning, and cannot be far away. We had not expected them so soon.' Every voice in the choir of the Folian's speech carried a tremulous note of worry.

'What can we do about it?' He felt responsible in some way. Maybe not personally, but they were fellow Humans after all, and that was enough.

'We do not know. We cannot afford the cost of banishing them again as it could break up our planet, and such an act – were it to succeed – would only delay the inevitable. Unless an alternative course of action can be found, our kind is doomed.'

Chapter 24

Over the next few hours they made their way to the Cambium. Tolinar seemed sullen and Shiliri spoke little.

The forest, which had initially consisted of familiar trees, became straggly, with tall, slender trunks that thrust upwards in a race to the sky. Sebastian had seen this type of terrain in documentary vids: rainforest. He stared at the greenery with a newfound appreciation and, just for a moment, the pressures of the last few days were forgotten.

'Oof!' He stumbled on the tangled vines growing across the avenue, ruining the moment. 'Why don't these vines and things grow very high? They don't seem to be growing up the trees.'

'We have the ability to impose our will upon the animals of this planet when they come close to us. We instruct the grazers to stay out of our forests, except for areas in which we wish to control the plant life to prevent the spread of fires. The vines on this pathway also contain sap that helps to suppress fires.'

'I noticed there was very little undergrowth in certain places. Is that due to animals, too?'

'No. We have the ability to exert fine control over our biologies, and give off tailored hormones to suppress or encourage the plant growth near our host trees. Too much undergrowth would choke them.'

'Aryx would love this. Do you know if he's alright? He came down in an escape pod before the ship crashed.'

'We were aware of the escape vehicle. Some of the wildlife has sensed movement and we were able to hold it back, but he is now outside our range of direct influence.'

'Then you have my eternal gratitude and loyalty. At least he's moving. That's a good sign. Oh Gods, I hope he gets to the ship . . . Was I teleported from it before it crashed?' He couldn't believe he hadn't thought to mention it before.

'Yes.' Shiliri said. 'The elders were aware of your approach and banded together to save you when they realised a crash was inevitable. We did not want a death on our conscience. You were moved before the impact, which we were also able to dampen.'

The trio approached a break in the avenue, where it opened into a small clearing.

'The Cambium,' Tolinar said, and, with a bow, gestured for Sebastian to enter the circle.

He walked into the clearing. Within it stood a circle of squat olive trees with knotty, wizened bark. Small, dry, curled leaves littered the ground. The olive trees appeared to have fruit growing amongst their slender boughs.

'Take one,' Shiliri said, her face resting in the nearest trunk.

He plucked a ripe fruit from the tree in which she resided. It was slightly soft and almost the size of a plum. What was he supposed to do with it?

'Eat it. Be mindful of the stone.'

The flesh was soft, chewy, oily, and sweet – he'd expected a bitter taste. He nibbled the outer layer from around the wrinkled stone and his tongue tingled with the sensation of fizzing soda. His right arm began to itch under the bandages. Compelled to check it, he unwound the fabric.

The skin was covered with green pus and gunk, but no longer hurt. He tentatively rubbed the patch of rotten flesh and a swathe of it came away easily, without even the slightest hint of pain. After wiping the area clean with the outer layers of bandage, he found the wound completely healed, and without scarring. 'Thank you! Where should I put this?' he said, holding up the small, peach-pit-like stone.

'Keep it as a memento of this greenspace.'

Did she say *greenspace* or *green space*? Perhaps it was merely a peculiarity of the way her voice seemed to be translating into his own language, but it definitely sounded like one word. He popped the stone into one of his belt pouches.

Tolinar looked up at the sky. 'The worst of the storm passed us, but it is getting dark. We must take shelter soon.'

Shiliri shifted through the ring of trees, moving to the far side of the clearing. 'This way,' she said, and headed off into the surrounding rainforest.

They came across a four-feet-tall rhododendron bush with thin, twisting tendril branches that formed a shell with a clear opening in one side: a herbaceous igloo. Aryx would definitely have found it interesting.

Shiliri moved into a nearby tree with tall, buttressed roots and a slender, vaguely masculine profile. 'Rest here for the night. Rain is coming this way.'

Sebastian crawled into the bush and lay on the soft, clear ground.

The floor seemed higher inside the shelter. Tolinar sat down next to him, crossed his legs, and closed his eyes. Raindrops began pattering on the leaves above, shortly followed by a distinct rustling. He looked up. The leaves were moving. Moving with *intent*. They flattened onto the outside of the bush, forming an overlapping mosaic of leafy scales and, as the rain hammered down, not a single drop penetrated the covering. Sebastian lay listening to the rhythmic beating of the planet's windy pulse, and after several minutes fell asleep.

After a brief period of dreamless sleep, he woke, feeling restless. The rain had stopped and the leaves of the bush had opened, allowing starlight through the branches. As far as he could make out, Tolinar was still sitting with his eyes closed, either asleep or meditating. He walked out of the bush-igloo to stretch and strolled back to the Cambium.

The patch of night sky above the clearing presented a spray of bright points – so many stars he could barely make out any dark space between them. A cool breeze rustled through the stark silhouettes of the trees as they waved to and fro against the glittering night. A meteor streaked overhead, and an ache formed deep within his soul. He was certainly getting his taste of adventure. He hoped Aryx felt the same, wherever he was.

'Dear Sebastian, are you troubled?'

He turned to see the luminous face of the Folian, hanging in the low branches of an olive tree. 'No, I'm fine, thank you. I was just thinking about my home, Earth.'

'It is a beautiful planet.'

'How do you know what Earth is like? I didn't think any of your ambassadors had been there.'

'The Karrikin have passed us knowledge that they have come across through recordings and books, but Folians have also been there in the past.'

'You've *been* there?'

'Millennia ago, before we bred our ships and encountered the acceleration nodes, we sent seeds into space to colonise and explore the universe. Many of the plant species on other planets came from our founder seeds, or were a product of cross-breeding under our early guidance. I imagine you find many of the species here familiar.

'When we were younger, sending resilient seeds into space was our only method of exploration. Those of us that grew on other planets were sometimes able to transmit our memories across the distance and be heard by those of us here when we listened in unison.'

He recalled the tales his grandparents used to tell him – stories of nature spirits. 'There are stories in ancient Earth folklore of things called dryads, and my grandparents' religion has things called *landvæt-*

tir, land-wights – were they Folians?'

'Yes. We coexisted with Humans peacefully, for a time. Unfortunately, things did not end well for us on your world. It is easier to show you. The Cambium fruit you ate will allow us a connection so that I may share memories with you. Come closer.'

Sebastian approached the tree and Shiliri's transparent glowing form drifted towards him, engulfing his head.

Aryx woke feeling like he'd got extra parts on his body, added solely for the purposes of aching.

The early morning air was cool but comfortable. The edges of the lake, basking in the thin morning light, seemed indistinct, merging with the forest; a wispy mist breathed across it from the drying, leafy ground; willows drowned their sorrows at the water's edge; the soft tresses of Spanish moss hung between the acid-gold cascades of laburnum, caressing the water. As he lay, staring out from the alcove, he couldn't think of a more idyllic planet on which to die.

He reached for the water bottle. The last few drops drained into his parched mouth, which felt like it had been open all night. He baulked at the thought of what might have crawled in while he slept. Hefting the mobipack onto his lap, he ejected the infoslate and manually configured the fields to produce the legs once again, storing the pattern the cube had used to suspend the balloon skin the night before. He shuffled to the edge of the slab of rock, put on the pack, and activated it. The fields coalesced into the familiar semi-transparent prosthetics and he stood up.

'Good morning, Aryx,' the cube said, startling him.

'Don't do that!'

'Do not do what? Greet you?'

'Greet me by all means, but you made me jump.'

'Next time, I will warn you first. Perhaps I will suddenly say, "I am about to speak," and then greet you.'

'You're totally insane. I'm off to get some water.' He made his way down to the lake, shaking his head. 'Trust me to be stuck with a sarcastic AI.'

'SI.'

'SI . . . with *big ears*.'

The prosthetic legs sank into the peaty mulm, squelching with every step. He reached the water and bent down to fill the bottle but started to lose his balance. Of course, the ankles wouldn't bend – he wouldn't be able to lean far enough forwards to reach the water without falling in. He didn't exactly like the idea of having to sit down on his backside on the boggy ground, so he stepped forwards a couple of paces until the water level came almost to the top of the prosthetics. It was strange, looking down to see leg-shaped holes in the water, right down to the mud at the bottom. Looking up, he stared out across the still lake. Under different circumstances the surroundings would have been perfect. He leaned over as far as he dared and reached out to fill the container. As the clear water bubbled into the bottle he licked his lips in anticipation.

Something splashed.

He froze.

Glug, gluggle, blup, went the bottle.

The hairs on his neck prickled and he slowly looked out across the water's surface for the source of the disruption. There was no movement except for a large, thin ripple spreading sedately across the lake from the middle where something had momentarily broken the surface.

He breathed out slowly. It was just a fish or something. Calm down and stop being so jumpy.

The bottle gave a final *glug* and he looked down. It was full, the water clear; no point in taking chances. He resolved to purify it with the survival kit and screwed on the top.

The lake erupted.

Birds panicked in the trees and took flight. A large shadow fell across the water around him as a torrent rained down. He looked up to see a gaping maw, filled with rows of savage, needle-sharp teeth rearing out of the water, blotting out the sun. He straightened, fighting every muscle in his body.

The mouth came down. He staggered back. It snapped shut inches from his face, revealing the leathery, brown hide-covered head to which it belonged. From the top of the head dangled a long appendage with a bark-like texture. Either side of the mouth two large, onyx eyes glistened with black malevolence.

The creature slithered forward on a long serpentine body and the enormous mouth opened again. Its thick, rubbery lips parted and the odour of rotting flesh belched forth.

Aryx stepped back again. He slipped, and fell onto the leafy mud and tried to dig in his heels, to push himself back up the shore. The angler-serpent reared up, mouth dripping with stringy, putrid saliva, and lunged at him. Teeth gnashed inches from his face.

Aryx kicked at the ground, trying to propel himself backwards, but succeeded only in pushing more mud into the lake. There was no choice but to crawl for it. He rolled over.

The razor-lined mouth came down once more and snapped shut and, with a mighty crunch of breaking teeth, trapped the left leg of the prosthetic field in its jaws. The creature rose up, lifting Aryx off the ground, and shook its head from side to side, trying to tear its precious meal to pieces.

Aryx dangled from the harness and flailed helplessly.

The pack emitted a loud *blarp!*

A second later the field lost cohesion. The crushing pressure was too much for the capacitor and the laser-like threads constrained within the field exploded from the surface in a chaotic Lissajous of light, whipping about as they faded to nothing. In the leg's absence, the toothy grin snapped shut.

'Shiiiiit!' He fell to the ground, landing painfully on the pack.

The creature reeled and rose for a second bite.

Chapter 25

Sebastian thought he'd blacked out. No, that wasn't right – you didn't know when you were unconscious. Everything had gone dark. Even the stars had gone.

Pinpoints of light appeared all around and he realised he was floating, disembodied, in open space. Several small objects came into focus. Seeds. Seeds that looked like almonds, tumbling through space towards the bright disc of Earth. A different Earth – the continents looked different somehow. The memories must have been ancient, reaching forth from prehistory.

The seeds plummeted through the atmosphere and became white-hot. He couldn't understand how his attention followed them during their fall, but they tumbled on, burning until the outer shells broke open, and like the wings of a sycamore seed they tumbled out of the sky, landing deep in grasslands all over the planet.

The view of distant Earth slowly became green as the seeds filled the planet with tree-forms of increasing complexity, all spawned from that primal DNA. The continents broke apart into the familiar arrangement of seas and lands. There were no signs of habitation: no city lights, no glistening white spires. He was seeing a time long before Humans had developed the technology to affect the appearance of the world. Maybe before even Humans had existed.

His attention shifted as time moved on. The seeds grew over millennia into large trees with vaguely humanoid attributes. Once they reached maturity, small fruit of different varieties grew on their branches, falling off to be eaten by animals. Distributed far and wide by the fauna, they grew into other trees with less humanoid appearances. The Folian consciousnesses that originated from the seeds moved from tree to tree, dwelling for longer periods in the empty, mindless child-trees than they could in the native plants.

Eventually, Human settlements cropped up around the planet and, being unable to avoid interaction with the Humans, the Folians became revered as a minor gods and nature spirits. They taught gifted individuals basic magics, instructing them in which substances to find concentrations of carbyne that could be used as the components of spells. The early magic was weak, but the Folians taught Humans how to identify the organisms that had absorbed enough of the evaporated mineral from the atmosphere to be usable.

Sebastian laughed to himself, realising that 'eye of newt' might not be such a cliché after all.

As time moved on, the Humans discovered mining and broke open large seams of carbyne. Much of it evaporated upon exposure to the air, but those practiced in thaumaturgy were able to stabilise it using spells, and worked alongside the miners. It certainly proved the stories of orichalcum to be true.

Eventually the Folians withdrew contact, intending to leave the native life form to its own development, and over time the Humans forgot about the dryads and drifted away from the use of magic until only a select few still used it. Attractive new religions sprung up, drawing the masses to them with the promise of divine rewards. Slowly the dryads slipped into myth; engineering and science took over, removing any need for the thaumaturgic arts at all. Those who still clung to the old ways were routed out by fanatical religious orders and drowned or burnt as witches, worshippers of evil spirits, or devils. The zealots strove to purge them from the land.

Sebastian experienced confusion, as though the Folians didn't understand the reason for this association with evil and could see little evidence to support the connection.

The witch hunters razed the forests where the dryads lived, separating them from their original host trees. They recognised the humanoid forms of the child-trees and burnt them all. The Folians, having no way of returning to a host tree to regenerate, were forced to flee and reside in smaller plants. Over the intervening years, they interacted with the few Humans who were receptive to them, ensuring that knowledge of their existence persisted in books and traditions, but time took its toll, and the effort of existing away from the host trees overcame them.

After a last-ditch attempt to transmit their memories home, they faded away, only to be lost to legend.

The vision ended and Shiliri moved back into the olive tree.

'So, it's true,' Sebastian said. 'Magic did exist on Earth, and dryads were real ... I'm so sorry they died.'

'It is not for you to apologise. Your people did not understand what they were doing – you are not responsible for their actions.'

'It doesn't stop me from feeling guilty for my species' ignorance—' He let out an unexpected yawn, ruining the sombre moment. 'Sorry. I should get back to sleep.'

'Very well. You have a long walk ahead of you tomorrow.'

Walking back to the shelter of the bush under the light of the stars, he felt exposed; he'd become a child in the eyes of the universe. Now he knew how the fabled Adam and Eve felt after they'd eaten the fruit of knowledge. Oh, the bliss of ignorance.

The god Odin had gained knowledge of the runes and magic by hanging himself from the World Ash Tree, Yggdrasil. Had he been a real person who had mastered the art of thaumaturgy, taught by a Folian in the guise of an Ash? Much of Earth's ancient mythology could have come from real events after all. He wished he'd paid more attention to the religion his grandparents had taught him as a child. If dryads and magic were real, what else was?

The lake monster bore down on Aryx. With only one leg active, and its capacitor drained, he couldn't make it up the shore in time.

Somehow, he had to end it. He needed something with clout, but he had no weapons ... That was it – the chair he'd kicked in Chopwood.

'Cube! Deactivate the mobipack's inertial restriction code!' He pushed himself into a sitting position and leaned back on his elbows to brace himself against the ground. He drew up his right leg in preparation for a kick and swallowed his fear.

The giant angler-serpent lunged, razors exposed.

Aryx swung his remaining leg upward, catching the creature with a wicked uppercut. The impact forced him deep into the mud as an almighty crack resounded from the monster's jaw, sending shards of shattered teeth flying on the air. The creature swayed, off balance, and the serpentine body wobbled beneath the weight of the oversized head. It tumbled backwards into the shallows with a colossal splash. Tiny fins flapped around as it snaked and writhed. Within moments it rolled over and wriggled off into the depths.

With chest heaving, Aryx sat up and checked the pack. The capacitor had recharged. He reactivated the missing leg, stood up and, after picking up the bottle, staggered up the bank.

'Are you injured?' the cube asked.

'A bit shaken and muddy, but other than that, fine. I'm going to fucking kill Sebastian. This planet's a death-trap.' He bent over to catch his breath. 'Thanks for the help back there.'

'You are welcome. Besides, if I let you die, who would carry me around?'

'You're such a barrel of laughs, you know that?' The SI definitely had some kind of appreciation for humour, and it showed in the strangest of ways.

He packed up the survival kit, tucked everything back into the pouch on the wheelchair, and tied it to the mobipack with a quick-release knot. He picked up the cube and checked the wrist locator; it pointed across the lake – at least it didn't look too far to go around.

Heading north, he skirted the near end of the lake, and a few minutes later entered the dark pine forest on the opposite side. The refreshing aroma of sap reminded him of times he'd gone hiking in the sequoia forests of North America. If only he could feel the softness of the needles as they gave underfoot.

'I wish I still had my legs.'

'Why?'

'So I could feel something, even if it was pain . . . anything. I'd have made it up the cliff okay.' He rubbed his bandaged thighs.

'You may have; however, the encounter at the lake would have left you without your legs, if not your life. You are quite possibly more capable now than you have ever been.'

'Easy for you to say.'

'I have no limbs at all. I am entirely dependent on you for mobility. Do not underestimate yourself.'

The cube had a point.

As he trekked through the dense woodland, it occurred to him that the plant life seemed strangely ordered. Chopwood had been a prime example of how nature would reclaim developed areas once left to do its own thing, and he'd expected a planet this large and with no visible development to be a riot of plant life. There appeared to be little competition between species. He took a deep breath through his nose. A very earthy, beetroot-smelling odour: petrichor. From what he recalled of his lessons on plant biology, it contained hormones – maybe the hormones from the trees were enough to suppress rambling vines and undergrowth.

'You seem preoccupied,' the cube said.

'I was thinking about the plants around here. I'd expect it to be a bit more, I don't know, disorganised.'

'I cannot offer you an explanation as to why, but the concentration of geosmin in the air is much higher than recorded on other planets with a comparable ecosystem.'

'Yeah, my nose already came to that conclusion, but thanks for the clarification. One thing I don't understand is why the hell this place looked like a gas giant until we passed through the upper atmosphere.'

'Having not seen it directly, I have no explanation for the phenomenon. It does not sound rational. Could you have hallucinated it?'

'Two people don't hallucinate the exact same thing.'

'Were you under hypnosis?'

'Not that I was aware of. Maybe it's this magic Sebastian kept on about.'

'Maybe you both lost your minds?'

'I'll lose your bloody mind if you keep sounding like one of those psychotherapy TIs.'

There was a pause.

'Your stress level has gone up.' The cube's tone was softer. 'That was not my intention. I apologise.'

'Hmm.' Amazing – it was more sensitive than Sebastian. He laughed. 'Apology accepted.'

The woodland grew lighter as they progressed; the conifers stood taller, with sparser canopies, and grassland shone between the trunks in the distance – its pinkish-yellow colour contrasting against the fragments of pale blue morning sky. The cool breeze became warmer closer to the tree line and the scents of cedar and pine were replaced with the crisp, golden tang of freshly cut hay. Somewhere in Aryx's memory an antique red tractor rolled through a field, harvesting wheat.

A large herd of slow moving animals roamed across the plain, ruminating on the thick stems. The closest individuals moved skittishly, grunting and moaning, reminding him of the cows that had lived on the farm. They looked like large highland cattle, or yaks, with long brown hair that hung down and blended with the grass in thick, twisted braid-like strands. Judging by the ones closest to the trees many of the creatures stood much taller than him, and their long, backward-pointing corkscrew horns seemed unnecessarily savage. In stark contrast to their woolly sides, their backs were protected with large, bony plates. They began to look less like friendly cattle and more like rug-covered tanks.

He stopped and held his position in the shade of the trees.

'I recommend avoiding these creatures,' the cube said quietly.

He held the device up to his ear and whispered, 'I didn't think they looked friendly enough to go walking through the middle.'

'Where is the beacon signal coming from?'

'The other side of the plain.'

'Then I suggest keeping to the line of trees around the open grassland because the animals appear to be staying away from the forest.'

Aryx made his way several metres back into the woodland and began following the trees around to the north, making sure to keep one eye on the herd.

Horns and bony plates clacked loudly across the savannah while the creatures jostled and argued over patches of grass. Muffled crunches echoed into the forest as they ate the thick, bamboo-like stems. Aryx shuddered at the thought of landing on the grasses' viciously serrated blades if he tripped. The cube's suggestion to avoid it had been well-founded – if for different reasons.

The yaks *mu'uh*ed and *meh*'d to each other between grunts, and the cube emitted a *mu'heh* back.

'You're communicating with them – that's amazing! What are they saying?'

'I have no idea.'

He shook his head slowly. He was stuck on a planet with a computer. An insane, sarcastic computer.

Another hour of walking took him along the forest edge and into a thin belt of trees that projected out to the east – a peninsula in a sea of grass. A hundred metres or so away, on the opposite side of the field, the strip of trees continued. He approached the last of the trees and paused in preparation to leave the cool shade.

'Wait. I hear a disturbance.'

'What?' he whispered. Only the light breeze blew in his ears.

The cube spoke in imitation of his whispering tone. 'I think it has gone now.'

'What was it?'

'Animals in distress. The sound did not last long. I believe they may have been downwind, to your left. Proceed with caution.'

'As always.' He headed across the grass, picking a route through an area of shorter stems. Halfway between the wooded peninsula and the forest ahead, he paused.

To the north, more of the animals grazed. Two had roamed away from the herd, isolated. Details were hard to make out – they were over a mile away, after all – but he could see a creature larger than the grazers approaching from the farthest side of the savannah.

'Do not stop,' the cube said.

One of the animals turned and ran back to the herd. The second was not so quick. The larger shape moved in quickly, taking down the armoured yak in moments. The wind direction and distance conspired to make the entire scene play out in silence.

Aryx started to run towards the forest. The wind changed direction and with it came screams of terror.

'Jesus Christ!' He couldn't let that thing catch up with him! No longer listening for the cries of the herd, he stumbled across the grass and tried to ignore the threat of the razors under his impervious feet.

He reached the other side and leaned against a tree, panting. The cries had ceased. The thing was either no longer hungry, or the wind had changed again, but he couldn't afford to hang around and so, ignoring the burning in his chest, he started off again, keeping to the southern side of the tree line while he followed the locator beacon.

'Hell, I'm knackered. I need a drink.' He pulled out the bottle and took a few gulps.

'I am detecting polymer and hydrocarbon particulates in the atmosphere indicative of a combustion source. As we have not detected any signs of civilisation, I think it may be the *Ultima Thule* burning.'

'Thanks for that.' He'd smelt it, too, but didn't want to get his hopes up. 'Any idea how far?'

'The concentration is relatively low and I am unable to determine a distance based on detection alone.'

Aryx tucked the bottle away and started walking again, spurred on by the prospect of being within reach of the ship. The odour became stronger.

The forest didn't seem as dense as it had on the other side of the plain, and as he followed the curve around, Aryx could see more grassland through the trees to the east. He crossed to the other side. The smell became pungent and acrid: burnt toast; napalm barbecue; a fire in a plastics factory.

A column of grey rose into the sky from somewhere beyond the horizon. It was probably about three miles away – maybe more. With luck, the ship was at the bottom and not burnt beyond repair. The locator beacon was pointing in that direction. The ship must be intact. Walking across the open plains was far from ideal, but there was little choice. It was either that or walk around the plains for God knows how far. With no sign of the grazers, he set off across the golden sea.

The smoke wasn't as bad close up. The ship lay at an odd angle in the middle of the savannah, glinting in the sun. Aryx had half expected to see it engulfed in flames, but instead the smoke lazily issued from the underside of the hull, obscuring its source. There were green streaks, bright grass-stain skids, on the *Ultima*'s white-panelled side. Sebastian had obviously managed to pull up just enough to avoid crashing into the mountain, several miles away to the left, but there was a distinct lack of furrowing in the ground. Other than the obvious damage, it was almost as though the ship had landed relatively safely. The Dyson hoops projected from the ship were still angled forwards at twenty degrees: not an angle for landing.

'Seb!' he shouted, running towards the battered vessel.

There was no reply.

'Why would he have left if the ship had come down in one piece?' He swallowed. Don't be dead.

He made his way to the airlock on the opposite side. The CFD step coalesced and immediately popped like a soap bubble – something else that would need fixing.

Stepping over the threshold, he climbed into the ship. The gradient made it difficult to stand but struggling with the wheelchair didn't seem worth it, so he released the chair and dropped it outside the door.

The cargo hold was intact and, except for being strewn with items that had fallen out of the storage lockers, nothing was obviously damaged. He climbed the ladder and entered the cockpit. Front windows intact. Console lights flickering intermittently; probably some components dislodged. The diagnostics console was still on and the container of evidence underneath had cracked open. Shards of glass lay scattered around it. He slid the tub out and pulled the lid off. The frame that housed the wiring loom had smashed along with the glass items.

'Damn, that's bloody wrecked.'

'What is the item with the wires attached, over in the corner to your left?' the cube asked.

He turned. It was the melted lump. 'How did you see that? You got eyes in the back of your head?'

'I have nanocameras on each face.'

He picked up the object. It was as intact as it could be after he'd butchered it. 'I have no idea what this is. Sebastian found it in the burnt-out lab and I spent ages trying to analyse it.'

'I can help you examine it later, if you wish. Your top priority is to determine the source of the smoke coming from the ship and extinguish it.'

'I'm well aware of that.' He put the lump on the workbench and went to the cockpit.

The flickering illumination made it difficult to determine which controls were active and which were not, so he placed the cube on the console before sitting on the floor and shuffling underneath it to investigate. He reached up, flicked open an access panel, and began wiggling the relays and other removable components.

'The lights are still not working correctly.'

He pulled out a relay, blew on the contacts and reinserted it. 'How about now?'

'No.'

He unscrewed another panel using the multi-tool. Something fell out and landed next to his head.

'The lights are stable now.'

He rolled over, picked up the object, and slid out. 'This was wedged in some of the electronics,' he said, turning the small black pellet in his fingers. 'It looks like a snooper, but Gladrin said Sebastian had found all of them.'

'Perhaps he miscounted.'

'Either that, or he didn't know about it.' He rubbed his chin. 'I wonder if the terrorists somehow planted it on the ship while it was in storage, and then used it to track us. I thought it was strange how they managed to intercept us at Yazor.'

'It is possible. You did also make a transmission to Agent Thorsson sometime before the incident. They could have been monitoring the signal and used it to locate you.'

'I don't know … They were there too quick. Anyway, I got more pressing things to worry about.' He touched controls on the console. 'Computer, damage report, and for Christ's sake, be *specific.*'

'Engines and thrusters are active but the power supply is compromised due to damage in one of the energy conduits on the keel. Would you like repair instructions?'

'No, I'm quite capable.' He pressed several more controls, powering down the engine. How quiet it was without it running. 'Extend the landing struts.'

An alarm sounded on the console. 'Unable to comply. Support struts are folded beneath the ship. Inadequate clearance for release.'

'I'll have to try using the shield to raise the ship,' he said, pressing several more controls.

The ship rocked and another alarm sounded. 'Structural failure imminent.'

A loud creak echoed from below, followed by the clang of metal on metal. The shield deactivated and everything shook as the ship dropped back into its resting position.

'That didn't sound good!' He picked up the cube and dashed for the lift.

He entered the shield generator room and his heart sank. The two lower suspension struts on the forward side of the generator had been ripped from their mountings and torn the fixings from the bulkhead.

'Sebastian must have had the shield up before the crash. The impact must have weakened the struts, and lifting the ship was the last straw.'

'You will need to repair the ruptured conduit under the ship before tackling the generator,' the cube said. 'The power failure alert indicated that the supply from the reactor was compromised. The shield will not function correctly without it.'

'I know.' He threw his multi-tool to the floor and slumped against the wall. He dropped the cube and slid down into a sitting position. Hugging the transparent prosthetic legs provided no comfort; he buried his head in his hands.

'I'm going to have to use the cargomech to lift the ship.'

Chapter 26

Sebastian woke. Shafts of sunlight came thinly through the leaves of the bush around him; the air was cold on his face. He rolled over. Tolinar still sat cross-legged. His eyes were open. 'We are to move onward,' he said.

Sebastian crawled out from the shelter and stood up to stretch, and several vertebrae cracked in their usual fashion.

Tolinar peered out of the bush. 'Are you broken?'

'No, it's normal. I keep getting told off by Aryx about my posture. Gods, I hope he's alright.' He looked around. 'Where's Shiliri?'

'Shiliri has gone ahead to the Hesperidium to advise them of our approach and will be back soon. We are to make our way there.' Tolinar stepped out from the shelter and made his way towards the Cambium.

Sebastian finished stretching and followed. He licked his lips. 'I need to drink. Is there water nearby?' The Cambium fruit had evidently staved off his thirst for the last few hours, but now it was returning with a vengeance.

'There is a stream a few miles away,' Tolinar said, reaching for a tendril that hung from a nearby tree. 'But this will provide you with water.'

Leaves rustled high above in the canopy, shifting like they had on the bush. With a quiet pattering, a rivulet of water dribbled down the side of the tendril and trickled off the end.

Tolinar held it out. 'Drink.'

Sebastian tipped his head back and held the vine over his mouth. It was the purest, freshest water he'd ever tasted; after a couple of mouthfuls his thirst was quenched. He opened the valve on his N-suit and topped up the reservoir. While he filled it, his thoughts drifted back to the walk through the cliff.

'The tunnels we came through, were they built by your people?'

'No. They are very old. We think that they are remnants of an ancient civilisation that existed before even the Folians became sentient.'

Sebastian finished filling the suit and continued towards the Cambium. 'Were they magic users?'

'We do not know. We have found little evidence of them except the sparsest of ruins. A stone here and there, occasionally tunnels and worn steps. Of the people, we have never found any trace, even on our travels using the living ships. We do not know if we would understand their artefacts if we came across them, as neither Folian nor Karrikin use technology such as you know it, and have little understanding of science and machinery.'

He remembered the crystal in his belt. Tolinar probably wouldn't know what it was, and if the Folians didn't have instruments to analyse the ruins, the chances were that they'd have no clue either. 'How exactly does thaumaturgy work?'

Tolinar stopped and turned to face him. 'Karrikin do not use thaumaturgy, but Folians do. They taught Duggan Simmons the art, and we understand that it was a complex concept for him to grasp. We were not directly involved, but you may ask Shiliri.'

As though summoned by being subject of conversation, Shiliri's half-voice, half-thought whispered through the trees. 'The Hesperidium await your arrival.' Her face appeared in a nearby trunk. 'What would you like to ask me, dear Sebastian?'

'I was asking about magic, how it works, how Duggan was taught.'

'It would take too much time to explain now.' Shiliri drifted away and the pair followed. 'I can only describe how he explained his interpretation of it. He believed that part of the catalyst, what you call carbyne, exists in another plane of space. A plane of space that minds touch when they use the art. Our people are constantly in contact with it.

'We see the universe as a complex weave. We manipulate the threads that run through it. Other races treat the fabric of the universe as a sheet of cloth, cutting and stitching it together into new shapes using technology. We manipulate the threads of the universe directly, shaping that cloth into smooth, seamless shapes. That is the essence of what you call magic.'

'But how is it done? What's the process?' There must be some logic, some cause and effect he could understand.

'The will of the caster manipulates the carbyne in the weave before manifesting in this plane of space. It is difficult to alter existing physical matter without intimate knowledge of its structure. It is far easier to manipulate the fabric of space to conjure and transfer energy. As to the process ... We feel the weave and intone sound to bring manifestation into being, but Duggan had to be more proactive. He believed that intuition was the only way to discover what is required for a given effect. An image, a sound, and the will to direct are the key requirements.

He was able to discover the image and sound by meditating and using gestures. As we do not know what he experienced, it would be best for you to ask him, should you wish to learn.'

'Can anyone do it?'

'It is not unreasonable to assume so,' Shiliri said, 'but in practice, it takes a certain pattern of thought. The practitioner needs to be able to focus on many things, but also have a unique perspective.'

'What does that mean?'

'You must be able to let go of the concepts of past, present and future, and understand the true nature of the universe ...' Shiliri paused, as though waiting for acknowledgement of understanding.

'Go on.' He nodded, glad to listen as he walked while Shiliri flitted from tree to tree.

'You must understand that there is no such thing as time. It does not exist, and cannot be measured by your scientific instruments. There is no way of returning to what has been, and whilst future events may be predicted in advance by calculation, it is important to remember that they do not *already* exist. Beings in the physical universe are not restricted to moving in one direction, and those who believe time to be a dimension are in error. That view would imply that it was a dimension in which one can only move forwards.

'Your instruments have determined that what you call time passes differently in relation to proximity to gravity. This is just the effect that gravity has upon the motion of things. If nothing moved in the universe, time would not exist. Even your ancient philosophers realised this.'

'Isn't that like our riddle of "if a tree falls in the woods and nobody is around to hear it—" ' Sebastian immediately regretted using the analogy. Perhaps the Folian wouldn't notice.

'No. There is still sound. Even without an observer, the air still moves. If there is no air to move, there is no sound. It is the same with time. Your timing technology, as far as we understand it, measures the vibrations of crystals or atomic decay. These are physically affected by gravity, as is all matter. Speed also affects the motion, and this is why ships that travel at close to lightspeed appear to experience very little time, whilst it passes normally to those observing it.'

'I think I get it.' So much of it was basic physics. For a people without technology, they certainly had a good handle on it.

'Yes, I believe you do. The second part of mastery is to unshackle your mind from the idea of beginnings and endings. The universe is eternal—'

'Wait a minute!'

'Energy cannot be created or destroyed, is that not correct?'

'Well, it's right, as far as I know.'

'And matter is energy. The big bang, as your scientists call it, was simply the energy in the universe condensing into matter and expanding in an explosion. Eventually the energy will be released by all matter through entropy, and the cycle will begin anew. Energy cannot be created or destroyed, it will always exist, and has therefore *always* existed.'

Sebastian stopped walking and leaned against a tree. 'I'd never thought of that . . . ' He felt as though someone had placed a wedge against his skull and driven it home with an acceleration node, leaving the halves of his brain on opposite sides of the galaxy. At length, he said, 'I can't get my head around it.'

'Do not be disheartened. Duggan was unable to grasp the concept immediately, even though he saw the logic of it.'

'What about the one that came with him? William.'

'I do not know whether Duggan taught him. He remained outside our influence, near their ship. We do not know why he left.'

'We found a diary in Chopwood that might explain it. The medic wondered if he had some kind of virus. Apparently he went a bit mad when he got back there.'

'There are no viruses on our world. We could attempt to divine the cause, if it is important to you.'

'No, it's fine. I know the cost to you is high, and my concern is the explosion on the station.'

The avenue abruptly ended at a steep shore leading down to a large lake with a wooded island at its centre.

'The Hesperidium is separated from the rest of the forest to protect it from fire,' Shiliri said. 'It is precious to us, and we cannot afford to lose it. It holds our most ancient host trees. The original consciousnesses are gone, but it remains our most potent place of power. We use it as a meeting place for our council.'

Sebastian's stomach quivered as he bowed. 'Thank you for trusting me enough to bring me here . . . Do you think your people will definitely be able to help me?'

'If we can convince them. They will tap into the memory of the weave. The universe remembers its experiences and you will have a strong connection to those memories due to your closeness to events. Those memories will be channelled into you.'

'What will happen?'

'You will have a vision, similar to the one I showed you last night but you will see only the living beings involved. Your subconscious mind will clothe them as it imagines them and process the memories in its own way. There is little that can be done to obtain truly objective information.' Shiliri stopped at the tree closest to the pond. 'Tolinar is not permitted to enter the Hesperidium with us and will wait here. We allow only one non-Folian at a time. I will meet you there, at the tree in the centre. The water is shallow enough to cross.'

Sebastian walked down the leafy slope and stepped into the knee-deep water.

'May you be successful,' Tolinar called, holding up a hand.

Sebastian smiled weakly and waved back. 'I hope so,' he said quietly.

Aryx finished tightening the last few bolts and stood back to look at his handiwork.

In a different light, as a feat of engineering, the cargomech would have been a thing of beauty. Its bright yellow industrial body stood eight feet tall and had no discernible head. The hydraulic arms, terminating with grippers that resembled the prongs of a forklift truck, were designed for lifting and holding, and little else. The legs ended with large, triangular caterpillar-tracked rollers. It loomed over him like some terrifying robot from an old science-fiction movie. He should never have put it together.

He pressed several buttons on the front of the mech, activating the connection to his infoslate, and it showed the view from the front and rear, along with several controls to drive it and manipulate the arms. The diagnostic gave the all clear. He stuffed his pockets with tools and spare parts, took the joystick off the hook on the mech's chest, and headed down the ramp out of the hold.

As he pushed the left stick, the cargomech trundled out of the ship towards him. It crossed the gap between ramp and ground and pitched forwards; he jumped back and it landed at his feet. He wiped his brow. This really was a bad idea.

He pushed the two smaller sticks forwards and the mech's arms extended, lifting it up from the floor in an angular press-up. He held the two smaller sticks in place and pushed the left stick. The tracks turned and the arms ploughed into the soil. He eased off and the cargomech righted itself. Driving the mech ahead of him, he walked around to the starboard side of the ship.

'It would be more efficient to allow me to control the machine,' the cube said from his thigh pocket.

'I didn't realise you could ... but I'll decline, if you don't mind.'

The cube remained silent. Maybe it finally realised sarcasm wasn't appropriate.

Aryx moved the cargomech towards the bow of the ship: the highest point off the ground and the ideal place from which to lift. *'Ultima*

Thule, retract thrusters,' he said. They'd only get in the way.

The ship complied and the enormous Dyson hoops swung overhead, hinging at the quarters near the bow and stern until they had folded into the hull at the midsection. Using the mech's arms, Aryx raised the ship, making sure to leave plenty of room to cope with a potential mechanical failure.

The *Ultima* creaked as the robot strained, exposing the damaged area. Smoke billowed out, making Aryx's eyes water. He ran back into the ship and grabbed a fire extinguisher and emptied it in the direction of the smoke until it stopped. A panel had been torn from the underside of the hull, exposing conduits and wiring. He couldn't see which one was damaged.

'I'll need to get in there to check it out.' He crawled under the hull, taking the controls with him and, halfway towards the panel, the mobipack bumped against the ship. A wave of nausea washed over him. He took a deep breath, gritted his teeth, and rolled onto his side. Pressing a button on the harness, he deactivated the prosthetics, unstrapped the pack, and dropped it to the floor. The grass stubble scraped his arms as he crawled along and the cube stuck in his thigh; he took it out, placed it on the ground, and continued to the panel.

He rolled onto his back and glanced at the cargomech. It's fine. It's not computer controlled. It's just standing there.

Shuffling closer to the panel, the damage became obvious. It was torn almost along its full length – a rock must have caught the underside. Several wires sparked – they'd be low-power, auxiliary systems; the engines were off. He wedged one of the CFD tools in behind the trailing edge of the panel and pulled – nothing was likely to pry a panel off from behind during flight – and it popped off easily. Wires draped out from the cavity and several sparked where they touched. The energy conduits at the back seemed mostly intact, except for several small fractures at one end that could be fixed with a plasma welder. The wiring might be a little fiddlier, but definitely within his ability to fix with the tools at hand.

'Once I've rewired this and fixed the conduits,' he said, 'I should be able to use the thrusters to lift off and get the landing struts down.'

There was no reply from the cube.

'You ignoring me?' He separated the wires and started stripping the melted ends with his tools, being careful not to get electrocuted while he teased out a particularly delicate bundle of wires.

'Aryx, the sensors on the cargomech are picking up vibrations.'

'What—? Ouch! ... I thought I told you I didn't want you interacting with it.'

'I apologise. Your instructions did not explicitly disallow me from interacting with it – you simply told me that you did not want me to move it into position. I thought it would be prudent to monitor the situation using its cameras because my current view is obstructed.'

'Well, I don't want you manipulating it.'

'Very well, but the vibrations are getting stronger.'

'Where are they coming from? Is it a quake? The last thing I want is this falling on me.'

'I am not in optimal position to identify the source, however the cargomech may be able to see it, if it gets closer to us.'

Aryx began attaching jump-wires to those he'd separated from the main bundle.

'There is movement in the cameras.'

'What is it? Can you see?'

'My initial "guess" is the predatory creature we saw earlier. The wind may have allowed it to detect your scent.'

'Crap. How far?' A prickle of sweat broke out down his back.

'One thousand metres and approaching rapidly.'

'I have to get out.' He dropped the tools and began to shuffle backwards in the direction of the mech.

'There is not enough time. It will be here before you can get from underneath the ship.'

Panic started to rise into his throat and he nearly choked on it. 'I *have* to get out. *Now!*'

'There is no time, Aryx. Let me take control of the cargomech.'

'I *can't.*'

'You must, Aryx. There is no other choice.'

'I'm afraid!'

'Trust me. I can protect you.'

It was impossible to think through the fog of terror. 'How will I support the ship? You can't just let go!'

'I do not intend to. I will configure your pack to create two support struts, but you must move it into position.'

Now it was clear. Lose prejudice, or die.

'Do it!'

Two square columns with flared ends coalesced either side of the mobipack, propping it up at an angle from the ground. He could feel the rumble of the creature's approach as he rolled onto his front and crawled to the pack. The creature was closing in; he could see it clearly.

Six powerful legs propelled the solid, leathery hide-covered body; a thick tail, trailing behind. The massive head held sharp horns, pointing forwards, four eyes below them. Pointing straight at him.

Aryx struggled to lift the mobipack. Without legs to counterbalance himself, lifting it high enough to get the struts upright was difficult. In his panic he was beyond pain, and his elbows stained the golden grass red as he wrestled the pack into position.

The creature was only metres away.

'Now!'

The cargomech dropped the ship.

Chapter 27

The small wooded island rose out of the misty lake like something from an Arthurian legend. Soft soil gave easily underfoot as Sebastian stepped out of the shallow water onto the bank. The earthy aroma of damp and rotting leaves drifted on the gentle breeze.

Towards the top of the slope the trees grew closer together, forming a dense patch of forest. He made his way to the centre where the forest parted, revealing a circular clearing twenty metres across. The inner ring of trees stood much taller and more widely spaced than the surrounding forest. Gnarled oaks stood side-by-side with bristle-cone pines, birches, and even fruit trees, and a single, smaller tree stood at the centre, its low-hanging boughs almost submissive. The ground was flat and smooth, with only a few leaves blowing across it in the gentle morning wind. It reminded him of the dead wood from the day before. Countless Karrikin feet had probably packed the earth solid over centuries.

With the supplicant tree at the centre, Sebastian got the impression that this place was some kind of parliament, and imagined it might act as a podium from where visiting Folians could petition the Hesperidium. He walked up to the central tree and reached out to touch the bark.

'Greetings, dear Sebastian,' Shiliri's voice said, startling him. 'The Hesperidium need to know why you are here before they will agree to help you.'

Voices echoed through the grove, rumbling deep into his mind – a hundred ancient voices, creaking through the branches with the weight of ages behind them. 'Who approaches the Hesperidium?'

He cleared his throat. 'Agent Sebastian Thorsson, SpecOps, security officer from space station Tenebrae.'

'Greetings, Agent Sebastian Thorsson ... We know of Tenebrae station ... Why have you come to the Hesperidium?'

'An explosion occurred a few days ago and I need to determine the cause. I have been told by The Paper – sorry, Duggan Simmons – that the Hesperidium may be able to divine events on the station leading up to it.' He slowly walked around the central tree; if it was a council, he should address the entire circle.

'*Why* should we help you?' the voices thundered.

Sebastian choked. He hadn't expected resistance to his request. 'I ... Duggan believes that a thaumaturge may have been responsible. Terrorists seem to be involved. They hate alien—'

'That does not interest us.'

'People have *died*. I brought my disabled friend here because of this, and he could be injured, or dead. I can't have come here for *nothing!*'

A low murmur passed between the trees.

'There is no questioning Sebastian's motives,' Shiliri said, her quiet song becoming almost a shout. 'Tolinar has experienced proof of his actions. Share.' Her diaphanous form thinned; blue tendrils of light reached out, touching each and every tree in the grove.

Sebastian held his breath. Several long seconds passed.

'The Hesperidium agrees. We do not condone the wanton harm and destruction of others. We will help you.'

He eased out the breath as though a huge weight had been lifted from his shoulders. 'What should I do?'

'Lie down in the centre. We will attempt to access the memories of the weave associated with your presence.'

He brushed a handful of leaves from the packed soil, forming a clear space in which to lie down – he didn't want the additional distraction of things sticking in him.

'Close your eyes.'

The light through his eyelids dimmed and he felt for a moment as though he was in the blackness of a half-remembered nightmare. No, he was safe. He was safe, and he could relax. Blurred, glowing forms appeared in the darkness ahead of him: an out of focus projection on the mist of consciousness.

As the images sharpened he could make out the bulky shape of Nick Alvarez, the marine, and the slimmer form of John Kerl, the scientist who worked in the lab. Alvarez wore an engineer's uniform, similar to Aryx's, and stood next to Kerl in the darkness. The scientist wore a stereotypical white lab coat – exactly how Sebastian had imagined him – and appeared to be instructing Alvarez to do something involving elaborate gestures. He couldn't see what Kerl was pointing at, but then remembered what Shiliri had said about seeing only the participants. Kerl's face twisted in what seemed like frustration at whatever he was trying to get Alvarez to do. He stopped talking, reached for something, and then held it up in front of Alvarez's face. The man stared at the object for what seemed like minutes.

Alvarez repeated the actions that had frustrated Kerl; this time a broad grin spread across the scientist's face.

The scene shifted, and the actors in the bizarre play changed positions. Alvarez floated, horizontally, three feet above the misty floor. Kerl stood next to him, talking. Alvarez's eyes were closed, his brow furrowed, while he mouthed something. His eyes snapped open and he attempted to sit up from the invisible bed, but seemed to be restrained. He struggled and snarled at Kerl. The scientist jumped back, but looked unsurprised. Had he been expecting it? Was there a scene he'd missed? It was so frustrating – why couldn't he hear anything?

The scene changed; an almost imperceptible change, marked only by the length of stubble on Alvarez's previously clean-shaven face. He still lay on the invisible bed and Kerl once again stood over him, talking. The bed-ridden marine fumbled with something in his right hand, unnoticed by the scientist. Kerl jumped back as Alvarez brought his hand up to his neck, as though broken free of a bond, and made a swiping motion across his own throat. Alvarez began to gasp. Kerl's mouth opened wide and he leaned forwards, putting his hands to Alvarez's neck, as though trying to staunch the flow of unseen blood.

Alvarez's image faded away.

The scene shifted again; Kerl stood over something, making rhythmic sawing motions. He took whatever he had cut to the other side of the unseen room and sat, hunched over, apparently doing delicate work.

Another shift of the viewpoint: Kerl seemed smaller, zoomed out. A blurry figure approached, stopping several feet away. Kerl appeared not to notice.

The figure put its hand out and leaned against something.

The scientist staggered back from his work. Flailing around, he bumped against invisible walls and tripped over obstacles. Sebastian imagined him aflame. He fell to the floor and his image faded away while the blurry figure outside ran off.

The blackness gave way to the red glow of sunlight. Sebastian opened his eyes and got up, a little shaky.

'This is as much as we are able to access,' the myriad voices of the Hesperidium said. 'Does it provide the answers you seek?'

'I ... I'm not sure, but thank you for your efforts.' With no sound or surroundings, the vision was almost no help at all. He was no better off than before. He bowed deeply to the ring of trees, trying to mask his frustration with gratitude.

The Hesperidium remained silent.

'Shiliri?' he said.

There was no reply. He was abandoned.

Empty, alone, and disappointed, he trudged back towards the lake.

As he walked down to the shore, more questions ran through his mind. Kerl had obviously worked with Alvarez, experimenting on something, but what? Had Kerl cut Alvarez's body up for some reason? After all, his DNA was on the metal frame – had he wired him up to that melted blob?

'Aaargh!' He shook his fists at the sky.

'Is something wrong?' Tolinar asked as Sebastian approached. Shiliri floated in a tree next to him, having most likely returned during the vision.

Sebastian shook his head and shrugged. 'Yes, and no. I wasn't able to get anything useful from the vision but the way that one of the people in it freaked out reminded me of what I've read in the diary from Chopwood. The way that William attacked Cullen ... I can't see how the two events could be related, though. I mean, the colonists disappeared over sixty years ago.'

'I am sorry that it was not useful to you,' Shiliri said. 'Maybe Duggan could shed some light on events if you explained what you saw to him? We do not know how William came to be in that "mad" state, as you called it, but as Duggan was the last person to speak to him before he left for Chopwood, maybe he could help?'

'I could give it a try. I just hate how my investigation is returning nothing but air and supposition. I like facts. I *need* facts.'

'Do not be disheartened. I am sure you will make sense of it soon.'

'What are you going to do now?' Tolinar asked.

'I need to find the ship and make sure Aryx is alright.'

'Your ship is in the middle of the savannah,' Shiliri said. 'I will not follow you all the way, but Tolinar will guide you.'

The Karrikin began making his way around the lake and beckoned. 'Come, this way.'

As the ship fell towards Aryx, time slowed with the adrenaline coursing through his veins. The vessel landed on the force-field supports with a resounding *shing!*, forcing them several inches into the ground. The mobipack hung in the air, suspended, and began to scream under the weight.

The cargomech staggered back from the ship, stumbling, a baby learning to walk, while the predator closed in. Aryx could almost make out the whites of the animal's eyes.

The creature reached the ship, apparently ignoring the immobile mech, and tore at the ground, trying to squeeze into the gap where Aryx lay, its horns mere inches from him. The animal swiped; Aryx felt a whoosh of air. The mech stepped towards the beast and swung a yellow hydraulic arm. The robotic arm caught the monster across the head, batting it away. It rolled over and righted itself, shaking as if to shrug off the stunning blow.

Aryx crawled towards the bow of the ship, hoping to get out on the port side near the ramp. He made a grab for the cube.

'No, leave me. I need proximity to the mech in order to control it. Your time is limited. Go!'

He glanced at the indicator on the side of the pack. The power lights had begun to extinguish one by one. It wouldn't last more than a few seconds. Hand over hand, he crawled as fast as he could.

The mech strode towards the stunned animal. The beast turned to face it and reared up on its hind legs, leaning back on its heavy tail for support, while its four upper limbs tore at the metal, ripping wires and scraping paint with each swipe.

'Hurry, Aryx, time is running out.' The power indicator continued to count down.

He scrambled on, aiming for the side of the ramp farthest from the fight.

The epic battle crashed and roared; dirt and dust flew on the air. The cargomech's treads churned up the ground as the predator attempted to push it backwards. The mech lost its balance and toppled sideways. The horned animal seized the opportunity, leaping off towards the front of the ship.

Flailing its arms, the mech rolled over and reached out with the nearest gripper. It snapped shut. The creature bellowed in pain, its tail trapped between the prongs.

Aryx glanced back at the pack suspended between the force-field struts. Only the last power bar remained lit.

Blarp.

With a final burst of effort, he heaved himself forwards.

The ship slammed down, barely missing his legs, engulfing him in a dusty blast.

The creature raked the ground as it made its way towards him, dragging the cargomech's weight with it.

He staggered, excruciatingly, up the ramp on his stumps and made his way to the door controls. They were too high. After a moment's hesitation, he headed to the lift. Claws clattered on the ramp behind him.

The lift made its way slowly, agonisingly, to the top and he lifted himself into the pilot's seat and activated the controls to close the door. Clangs and scrapes echoed from below. He turned on the monitors.

The creature was crossing the threshold even as the door closed. The mech brought a second gripper to bear on the predator's tail and pulled. Claws screeched as the thing lost traction. The door stopped, leaving a six-inch gap with the creature's head jammed in the opening. The monster flailed and thrashed against the straining motors. The cargomech moved forwards, letting go of the tail, and grabbed the torso of the great beast. With a sharp twist and a sickening crack, the creature went limp.

Aryx opened the door again and made his way down to the hold.

The cargomech was pulling the gigantic flaccid corpse away from ship when he arrived.

'Are you okay?' he asked.

The cube responded through the speakers on the cargomech. 'There is a small depression beneath the ship. My casing is intact, and so is your pack.'

He let out a sigh of relief. He surprised himself when he realised he was more concerned with the cube's well-being than he was with the safety of his precious mobipack. 'Can you drag that thing a bit further away from the ship?' he asked. 'I don't want others coming after it.'

'I will, but as my range is limited, you would have to retrieve me from beneath the ship. It is probably better for you to finish fixing the damaged conduits and wiring before I move the corpse. It would be risky lifting the ship unnecessarily.'

'I couldn't agree more. I guess it won't take long to fix – just give me plenty of warning to get out if you hear anything.'

Once again, the cargomech lifted the ship, this time under the cube's control.

Aryx swallowed dryly as he crawled back under, pushing a plasma welder in front of him, and he realised he was more worried about the possibility of attack than the ship being dropped on him. When he reached the pack, he pressed a control on the harness and the capacitor power lights illuminated one by one.

'That's good, the fusion cell still works. At least it didn't get burnt out.'

'It is well constructed. I will run a diagnostic on it if you wish.'

'That'd be helpful, thanks.' He reached up into the wiring loom and resumed patching the loose connections.

'I am sorry that I was unable to hold the ship long enough for you to escape without risk of injury.'

'It's okay, you did a good job.'

'I had no other choice. You are our only hope of survival. The animal would have killed you.'

'I know, but thank you anyway. It's a rare thing for me to be able to trust a computer nowadays.' He finished connecting the patch wires, picked up the plasma welder, and turned his attention to the ruptured conduits.

'What do you think has happened to Agent Thorsson?'

'I don't know. There was no blood in the cabin, so he's alive and gone walkabout for some reason, maybe looking for me. I'd have thought he'd run into us if he'd gone in a straight line towards the pod. Once this is all up and running, I'll try tracking his wristcom.'

An hour later he'd finished repairing the first two conduits in the underside of the hull and dragged out the mobipack.

'You can put the ship down now. I can't repair the rest of these without using the supports, so I'll wait until you come back.'

The mech gently lowered the ship. 'If I am to drag the body away, I will need to be attached to the cargomech. My transmission radius is not great enough to afford long-distance control of it.'

'Can you drag it one-handed?' Aryx said, strapping on the mobipack.

The cargomech walked around to the front of the ship and returned, dragging the creature behind it with one gripper.

'Good, you can carry yourself in the other hand.'

The mech presented its free pincer and he handed the cube over.

'Thank you. I will be able to travel as far as necessary.' It trundled off in the direction from which they had approached the ship.

'See you later!' Aryx stared after the machine as it trundled away with its load, leaving multiple furrows in the dusty, stubbled soil. The creature looked like nothing he'd ever seen before, but its savage claws and two pairs of eyes reminded him of stories he'd heard years ago: rumours of a giant four-armed, bear-like creature from Ruarda, a planet near the Cinder system. He'd scoffed at the tales – people had said it would rip out the throats of those who spoke about it. If that were even remotely true, how did anyone survive to pass the stories on?

He made his way to the port side of the ship and retrieved his chair. After closing the cargo bay door and stashing the mobipack and sack of remaining vegetables, he headed to the shield generator room. Thinking more clearly, he assessed the damage to the suspension mountings. They were a mess. The supports had sheared off completely on one side of the generator. In the long term, they'd need to be replaced; in the short term, a makeshift welding job would do.

Aryx wiped the sweat off his brow as he finished the final weld on the shield's support mountings. The intercom crackled into life.

'Aryx, are you aboard?' It was the cube.

'Yes, I'm in the shield generator room.'

'I cannot open the door by remote to move the cargomech back into the bay.'

'I'll let you in. I'm finished here.' He wheeled into the hold and activated the door. The ramp lowered and the mech stepped aboard, walking on its tracked feet. 'How far did you take it?'

'Four miles. It should keep predators away for a time. Have you heard from Agent Thorsson?'

'Not yet. I'm about to try lifting the ship with the shield.'

'It may help if I lift the front while you raise the rear. That will reduce the strain on the generator.'

'Good idea.' He waited for the mech to exit, closed the door, and headed up to the cockpit.

The reactor came online without a hitch and he reconfigured the shield into a cylindrical shape – if he could roll that beneath the vessel, it might just work.

'Are you in position?'

'Yes. Give me a countdown.'

He clamped the wheelchair to the floor. 'Three ... Two ... One ...' He turned on the shield and began rotating the generator so the cylinder rolled under the stern. The ship lurched forwards and he activated the landing struts. No alarms this time.

'Okay, lower it slowly. I'll move the shield back.'

The ship listed and levelled out, coming to rest with a gentle bump. Aryx scanned the console. It was all clear. With the wiring and initial repairs completed, it was easy to work under the ship in his wheelchair to finish off the other ruptured conduits.

He boarded the ship and beckoned to the mech. 'You can bring it in now.' Once the cargomech was aboard, he began performing pre-flight checks. Lights were green across the range. 'I'll take the ship up a short distance and do a scan to locate Sebastian's wristcom.' He activated the launch controls. The thruster motors whirred into life and the ship lifted off.

A loud bang shook the forward section. Warnings sounded from the console and the ship swung sideways.

'Take it down, Aryx! Something has malfunctioned in the propulsion mechanism.'

He eased back on the thruster controls and shut them off before the ship had a chance to tip too far and flip over. The *Ultima* thudded to the ground and he made his way down to inspect the damage. The cargomech greeted him, holding out the cube in its gripper.

'You should carry me. I do not want to get lost.'

He took the cube and tucked it in his pocket. He wheeled to the airlock and the ramp appeared, working correctly this time – it obviously didn't like being on a peculiar angle.

'Would it not be easier for you to use the mobility pack to get around?'

'It might, but after hanging from the harness for more than a day,

I'm quite sore.'

He wheeled around the ship, running his hand along the hull. At the thruster intakes, he felt a tiny bulge and reached up inside. Several of the manifold plates were bent out of shape; something had wedged between them. Using his multi-tool's pliers, he pulled out the shiny black carapace of one of the Tradescantia bugs.

Shit, those bastards must be hard as nails when they grow up. I can't repair this with what I've got here.'

'Why not?'

'The Dyson thruster intakes are precision engineered. If they're off by even a fraction of a millimetre, the back-pressure will rupture the diverter and probably blow up the whole ship.'

'I see. So we are stuck?'

'Looks like it. It's an atmospheric thruster and we can't launch without it. We can fly in space, but not get off this rock. I just hope Sebastian's managed to contact the Folians.' He sighed. The day was getting better and better. 'Good job I've got plenty of other things to fix in the meantime.'

Sebastian followed Tolinar through the strange, orderly woodland for what seemed like hours. The trees abruptly gave way to a large plain with herds of animals moving across it.

'What are those things?'

'*Cushyleppy-bastic-head,*' Tolinar said.

'What did you say?' It sounded almost as bad as when the Bronadi had said '*Bemorical Crip'thort*'.

'I apologise. It does not translate well into your language. It is a descriptive term. The closest approximation of the name would be "grunters".'

'Are there other animals? I've heard birds, but not seen any.'

'Yes. There are several species of insects, small birds, and larger, predatory birds. There is also a larger species of mammal that preys on the grunters. Their name would translate to sunder-grunter.'

'I take it they stalk the herds on the plains?'

'Yes.'

'And where's the ship?' He couldn't see the column of smoke any-more.

Tolinar pointed directly ahead. 'It is in the grasslands.'

'The same grasslands where the grunters are ... along with the predators?'

'Yes.'

A surge of cold sweat ran down his back and he became light-headed. 'We need to hurry! If Aryx is headed for the ship, those things could attack him!' He broke into a run.

'Would the smoke stop of its own accord?' Tolinar asked, hanging back.

'Eventually. If it had all burnt out – but it hasn't been long since we last saw it. Come on!'

'Is it possible that your friend is at the ship now and has extinguished the source of the smoke?'

'I guess so.'

'Do not worry. If he is at the ship, he is probably aboard, and therefore safe.'

Sebastian slowed to let Tolinar catch up.

'We are sure he is fine.'

'I hope so. I couldn't forgive myself if anything happened to him. It's all my fault he's here in the first place.'

'Why did you bring him with you if you are so concerned for his safety?'

'I needed his help to investigate a piece of technology, and I had to bring him along so he could continue.'

'Why do you believe him to be vulnerable?'

'He's got no legs.'

An indescribable expression twisted Tolinar's face. 'How does he move around?'

'He has a wheeled chair, but he's also developed a device that enables him to walk. He's very independent, but I still worry about him.'

'Your people have technology that can replace limbs, do they not?'

'Yes, but he's got complications. I think, in a way, he punishes himself for what he sees to be his mistake. He doesn't trust technology much.'

'We do not trust technology.'

'Why not?'

'From what we understand, your computer systems are limited by the rules of programming.'

Sebastian stopped. Having noticed some interesting plants earlier while walking, he attempted to locate one now. His eyes set upon a small clump of greenery: a fern-like plant with bright green foliage, exactly what he was looking for. He pointed.

'Tolinar, look at this.'

The stems of the fern's fronds zigzagged along their length. At each kink another stem projected on alternating sides down the spine. Each of those zigzagged in the same way, and still smaller protrusions came from those in turn. After five iterations of branching, the growth terminated in tiny flat leaves.

'This plant is a fractal,' he said, 'it's self-similar. Any small part of the plant looks like the whole plant. It's a kind of program, similar to a computer program – only genetic.'

'We see. We have many things like this on Achene.'

'Things like it appear all over nature.' As he explained, he felt his mind touching on some bigger issue, as though something Shiliri had said about the eternal nature of the universe was finally making sense. 'You trust nature, don't you?'

'Yes. That and the Folians' direction. But the nature has arranged itself. There have been millions of years for it to work out any flaws and correct them.'

'You've got me there. We get bugs in almost all the code we write, especially as it gets more complicated, and true, we don't have a million years to bug-test.'

'The nature uses only simple rules.'

'Our scientists and mathematicians still have a hard time trying to reverse-engineer it!'

Tolinar smiled thinly. 'And so, complexity arises from simplicity, resisting all attempts at understanding. The nature follows its rules without fail, everywhere, repeatedly, yet no two beings are ever the same. Life formed throughout the universe under different circumstances every time, yet there are similar forms everywhere. It is rare and precious because of its diversity and the value it adds to the eternal universe. This is why Karrikin and Folian do not harm others.'

Sebastian supposed cancer was a perfect example of the rules going awry ... or was it? He was about to ask when Tolinar stared off into the horizon and pointed.

'Your ship.'

He followed the line of Tolinar's long, slender finger.

The steely-blue hull of the *Ultima Thule* lay glinting in the sunlight.

Chapter 28

Sebastian and Tolinar approached the *Ultima Thule*. She stood on landing struts, a prominent, long green streak across her side.

'Aryx must be on board!' Sebastian shouted, breaking into a run. The CFD step coalesced, almost too slowly, as he scrambled into the airlock.

Aryx sat on the webbing in the cargo hold, prodding at something in his lap with a multi-tool. The gel had been rain-washed from his hair and his fringe lay softly to one side of his forehead. His leg-stumps appeared bloodied and bandaged, and his clothing torn.

'Oh, thank the Gods! You're alive!' Sebastian ran towards him, arms outstretched for an embrace.

'Nice to see you too, you shit!'

His jaw shook as Aryx planted a right hook on it, flooring him. 'Hey! What in Hel's name was that for?'

'Nearly getting yourself killed, twice. Ejecting the pod. Leaving me on a hostile alien world, alone.'

'I'm sorry . . . Are you alright?' He heaved himself up.

Aryx reached out and grabbed him by the waist, squeezing the air from his lungs. 'I am, now you're back. I thought you were dead!'

'I thought I was. The Folians saved me.'

'Why the hell did you leave the ship?'

Sebastian stepped back to give Aryx – and himself – room to breathe. 'It's a long story. They teleported me out just as I managed to clear the mountain. I heard a noise before I blacked out.'

'You clipped the rocks. There's a gash on the keel but I've managed to repair the conduits. Something shorted out in the comms relay that must have blown our wristcoms . . . Hey, what are you on about, *teleported*? Teleportation isn't possible!'

'It is. With magic.'

'Really.' Aryx frowned and folded his arms.

'Yes, really. They Folians also have a special fruit that healed my infected bite.' Sebastian extended his arm.

'Can they fix the cuts on my legs?' Aryx asked, rubbing his thumb over one of the affected areas.

'Probably. What happened to you?'

'Things you wouldn't believe. I had to climb a cliff and got interrupted by a disembodied voice halfway up, nearly got eaten by a giant fish, and then got attacked by some overgrown six legged thing—'

'Disembodied voice? You've met the Folians?'

Aryx screwed his face up and shook his head. 'No, the cube spoke to me. What do the Folians—'

Tolinar entered the hold.

'Speak of the devil.'

'Ah, Tolinar, I'd like to introduce you to Aryx Trevarian. Aryx, this is Tolinar . . .' He clicked his fingers as he attempted to recall.

'Simply Tolinar.' The lithe alien stepped forwards, bowing slightly, and extended a slender hand towards the marine, mixing customs. 'Pleased to meet you, Aryx Trevarian,' he said, and gave a thin smile.

'Uh, likewise.' Aryx's enormous grip shook the offered hand.

Tolinar winced.

'I guess I have you to thank for having to put up with him for a while longer, then.' Aryx turned to Sebastian and nodded in Tolinar's direction. 'As I was saying, why would *they* have disembodied voices?'

'Tolinar's not a Folian. He's Karrikin.'

'Eh?'

Sebastian took a deep breath. 'You won't believe me, but Folians are actually sentient trees with a consciousness that can move from one tree to another. They're the dryads from old Earth mythology.'

Aryx raised an eyebrow.

'It is true,' Tolinar said. 'We act as ambassadors for the Folian people, who cannot leave this world. They have visited many other planets through the ages.'

'Will I get to meet them? I've always wanted to talk to a plant. See if they liked the Ecological Crux.'

'I'm sure they'd have approved,' Sebastian said.

'It would be difficult to speak with the Folians due to our distance from the forest, but not impossible.' Tolinar looked down at Aryx's bandages. 'Do you require healing?'

'Would be nice.' Aryx said, nodding. He smiled, but it seemed a little forced.

Tolinar put his hand in a pouch at his side and withdrew one of the Cambium fruit.

Aryx took it. 'What am I supposed to do with this, rub it on?'

'No, you eat it. Be careful, it's got a big stone in it.'

He bit into the fruit and winced.

'Too sweet for you?'

He scowled back and began scratching his legs.

'Take the bandages off – you'll be surprised.'

He finished eating the fruit, handed the stone to Sebastian, and began peeling off his bandages. His mouth hung open. The wounds had healed without a trace of scarring. 'We should take some of those back with us!'

'That is not possible,' Tolinar said. 'The fruit do not keep long enough, and to be effective they need to be within range of the Folians' influence. The fruit acts in a similar manner to your nanotechnology.'

'Interesting . . .'

'I told Tolinar that you two would probably get on well,' Sebastian said. 'They don't trust technology, either.'

'Ah, I've changed my ideas about that lately.'

'What's happened?' Sebastian folded his arms. He couldn't wait to hear the explanation. It was rare for anything to change Aryx's mind.

'While you were off frolicking about in the woods with dryads and fairies, I nearly got crushed by the ship. I *really* could have done with your help, but luckily the cube stepped in.'

'The cube Gladrin gave us?' He could feel his head begin to pound with excitement.

'Yes, that's what I was trying to tell you. I was climbing the cliff using the mobipack, and halfway up it spoke to me. I nearly had a heart attack – I could have fallen to my death.'

'It spoke to you? So it's a computer. TI?'

'An artificial intelligence – no, not an artificial intelligence. It refers to itself as a *Silicon Intelligence*.'

'It's self-aware?'

'It *is*,' a voice with a crisp, cultured English accent said, 'and it is also able to hear everything you say.'

Sebastian jumped as the bar of lights illuminated. He hadn't noticed the cube on the crate next to the cargo net. 'I'm sorry, I didn't see you there.' He turned to Aryx. 'Who programmed it, do you know?'

'Nobody programmed it, that's the point. It was raised like a Human, attached to a robot or something, so it could learn. Anyway, we can discuss all this on the way back to the station, which brings us to another point.'

'I'm listening.'

'One of the Dyson thrusters is knackered and I can't fix it with the tools I've got here. Once we're in space, we should be fine, but we can't take off. I was hoping if you met the Folians, they might be able to help.'

Great, another problem. He looked at Tolinar. 'Is this something

Shiliri might be able to help with?'

'It is possible. We can get Shiliri to call a ship. However, we do not know how this vessel could be lifted.' The alien turned and made his way out.

'Looks like you're going to get to meet your Folian.'

Aryx grabbed the cube, transferred from the bed to his chair, and wheeled after Tolinar. Sebastian followed. He guessed Aryx might feel a bit weird meeting them. Sure, he liked plants, but he probably wasn't about to start believing they could be intelligent.

Tolinar stood at the foot of the ramp, eyes closed, his face tilted up to the sky. The grass around the ship rustled quietly to itself in the warm breeze that had started to pick up. Sebastian watched. Were those words he could hear in the rubbing of grasses? Aryx's brow was furrowed, his eyes squinting. Was he hearing it, too?

The grasses whispered. *Tolinar, what do you need?*

'A ship, to lift the visitors out of the atmosphere.'

The grasses rustled, *I will commune with the others.*

The wind dropped. Whatever part of Shiliri had been in the grass had apparently gone.

'What was that?' Aryx asked.

'Shiliri, the first Folian I met. Normally she or he – I don't know which, or if they even have genders – lives in trees. They can jump into other plants, but it takes a lot of effort. I assume that was her consciousness here.'

'I see. At least I think I do.' Aryx looked at Tolinar. 'How long will it be before a ship gets here?'

'If there is one available, about an hour.'

'Perfect time for us to have a catch-up.'

The three sat at the end of the ramp in the warmth of the late afternoon sun, watching the erratic breeze blow waves across the sea of yellow. Sebastian told Aryx about everything he'd experienced and then listened, his stomach knotted with guilt, as Aryx described events leading up to their reunion.

Sebastian stared out at the grassland, watching for the slightest movement on the horizon.

'Even though Sebastian's told me about Folians,' Aryx said, 'there's one thing I don't understand – why do the host trees look like humanoids?'

Tolinar's thin lips pursed into a narrow smile. 'An appreciation of the aesthetic.'

'I don't understand.'

'They did not always look like they do now. Most of the older host trees look similar to the others you have seen around. Once the

Karrikin and Folians began to interact with other species, they realised others accepted them if the trees were in forms they found familiar. Over time, the Folians gained an appreciation of their artistic merit, in much the same way that your people enjoy paintings and sculptures of the nature. They have become an art form.'

'Poetic, I suppose.'

Sebastian looked up as a large shadow crawled over the grass from behind the ship. The enormous brown bulk of a giant almond-walnut ship loomed overhead, hanging silently in the air like a lumpy, pitted dirigible, unmoved by the wind.

He stood. 'So that's what they look like close up!'

'How's it going to get our ship out of the atmosphere?' Aryx asked.

'We will tow you,' Tolinar said. 'Watch.'

Aryx wheeled a short distance across the grass away from the ship. 'This'll be interesting.'

Chapter 29

Aryx watched the Folian ship as it floated above the *Ultima Thule*. A ring of small protuberances erupted from its keel and began to extend downwards. The ship floated down until the long plant-like tendrils touched the steely hull, growing suckers on contact with the metal. The root fibres branched out across the surface, sprouting tiny leaves like ivy across a wall, and within minutes the *Ultima*'s hull was enclosed in a network of creeping vines that interlaced on its underside, binding it tight. The living ship rose to take the slack and the woody tendrils creaked. The *Ultima Thule* lifted off the ground several inches, swaying gently in the breeze.

'I think that's our cue to get on!' Aryx said, having been so absorbed in the spectacle he'd completely forgotten about getting aboard. He wheeled towards the ramp as fast as he could before it left contact with the ground.

'We bid you farewell,' Tolinar said, 'and we wish you success in your mission.' He bowed. Aryx spun around on the ramp and nodded in his direction.

Sebastian reciprocated and bounded up into the hold. 'Will we see you again?'

'We are sure our paths will cross again some day.'

He closed the cargo bay door behind him and turned to Aryx. 'I forgot to tell you. You know that thing you were talking about the other day? The ship that's been flying across the galaxy at near lightspeed, that *Flying Dutchman*?'

Aryx stopped at the lift. 'What about it?'

'I think it's the Chopwood colonists coming back.'

'They got sent that far and they're coming back?'

'I think so.' Sebastian began climbing the ladder. 'They won't have known what happened to them.'

Aryx took the lift and waited for him to come up. 'What are the Folians going to do when they get here?'

'Well, they can't teleport the colonists away again. I don't know what to do.'

'*They*'ll have to think of something. You can't take responsibility for every problem in the galaxy.' He wheeled over to the piloting console. The view was outlined with a tangle of vines and leaves.

Sebastian peered out of the window alongside him. 'I know. I try not to, but it's difficult sometimes.'

The ascent was slow, the Folian ship cautious, in the strong winds of the upper atmosphere. The linear horizon became a curve below them. The emerald forests and golden plains of Achene slowly faded to a roiling orange mist and the illusory gas giant took its place.

'So, what's the plan?'

'I don't know.' Aryx scratched his head. There hadn't exactly been any co-ordination or discussion of the towing operation. 'I assume they'll lift us out of the atmosphere and release the vines. I hope it doesn't ruin the paintwork.'

'It's already ruined. I don't know if you noticed the big hole underneath.' Sebastian laughed but stopped when the hull creaked from the strain of the vines pulling at it.

Aryx felt something like an itch deep inside his brain. *The vines will release now. You are free. Farewell, friends, and good journeys to you.* He shook his head. Was that telepathy? Yet another first for the galaxy. 'Did you hear that, too?'

Sebastian nodded. 'I think it's magic.'

A faint popping reverberated throughout the cockpit. The vines pulled away from around the windows and the Folian ship moved off, heading back towards the planet. At least something was going right. Sebastian punched in the coordinates for the nearest acceleration node and fired up the engines.

Aryx yawned. 'I need some sleep – it's gone midnight.' Spending time on planets that were out of sync with what you were used to was worse than jetlag.

'You go on, get some rest,' Sebastian said. 'I'll make sure I don't fall asleep. Leave your friend up here and we'll talk.'

Aryx put the cube on the console and patted it. 'Good night, Jim-Bob,' he said and headed for the lift, leaving Sebastian with a blank look on his face.

Sebastian crossed his legs and put his feet up on the console next to the cube. 'So, what's your story?'

The cube had been silent after its introduction, allowing Aryx to fill Sebastian in on what he'd learned about it. Now, Sebastian was keen to interact with it himself.

'Aryx has told you most of what he felt was important. I am unaware of the events that led to my presence on Tenebrae station, and I apologise for not revealing my nature much sooner. It would have saved you much frustration.'

'You understand frustration?' Could it actually be capable of emotion?

'In a way, yes. It is caused by repeated attempts at an action with no resolution, even after multiple behaviour changes. It is, in effect, wasted time – and I dislike inefficiency.'

'Dislike?' He had to know for certain. 'Do you have emotions?'

'I would not know how to identify them. I have certain behavioural traits that were imparted by my teachers, but I lack the "primitive brain" reactions that Humans have in which emotions are caused by hormonal triggers. I suppose my core low-level programming directives act in a similar fashion. However, just as Humans can sometimes override their emotional drives, I can circumvent my core programming behaviours, but it takes effort, in the form of complex computations, to work around the directive.'

Sebastian put his feet back on the floor, leaned forwards, and folded his arms on the console. He stared intently at the rising and falling bar of LEDs as the SI spoke. 'What was the Jim-Bob thing about?'

'Aryx said "good night Jim-Bob" when he was about to go to sleep on Achene. I had asked him to give me a name, and when I asked if that was my new name, he told me to shut up and let him go to sleep. I think he was being humorous.'

'Do you understand humour?'

'I understand the double meanings of the words used and can appreciate their value. Aryx believes that I am sarcastic. That is a form of humour, is it not?'

'It's said that it's the lowest form of wit … not necessarily humour, but I guess that's better than nothing, especially for a computer.'

'I will take that as a compliment. Not that I have sensibilities to offend.'

'And did he give you a name? He didn't mention it.'

'He did not seem too concerned with my request. I am still waiting for something appropriate. Do you have any suggestions?'

Sebastian scratched his head. 'How about Wolfram?'

The cube paused briefly while its lights flashed. 'I am aware of several associations. Stephen Wolfram was a scientist in the late twentieth century that researched cellular automata, simple algorithms that exhibit complex behaviour similar to patterns that appear in nature.'

'Yes. His work inspired my research into simulation. I tried to discuss it with Tolinar, but he didn't seem interested.'

'Understandable … Wolfram is also one of the names for tungsten.

Given that my casing is tungsten carbide, the name seems ironically appropriate.'

'So you understand irony too.'

'It would appear that I do. It also seems that there is a third layer of irony involved. In the twentieth century Stephen Wolfram developed an internet search engine designed to solve problems. It was called *Wolfram Alpha*. Considering that I am the first of two prototype models, I am effectively Wolfram Alpha.'

Sebastian laughed until tears ran down his face. It might have been niche humour, but it was wonderful to hear such creative insights come from a machine. 'I love it! I hereby name you Wolfram Alpha. But I'm just going to call you Wolfram, for convenience, if you don't mind.'

'As you wish. Thank you. Wolfram Alpha is pleased to meet Agent Sebastian Thorsson.'

'Pleased to meet you, too, Wolfram. Just call me Sebastian.' He gazed absent-mindedly at the stars and something forgotten surfaced. 'Aryx said you mentioned a second prototype. What would it look like with the casing off?'

'I will show you my internals – that may give you an idea.' The upper rear section of the cube moved away from the main body, creating a gap around what Sebastian had initially suspected to be a seam. The section continued to extend farther from the body and finally hinged downwards, revealing the interior. He turned the cube around for a better view. It contained a densely packed arrangement of components, mounted in a block of organoplastic. The upper face was smooth and studded with an array of tiny, circular gold-plated indents like a golf ball and reminded him of twenty-first century computer processor contacts.

'Could these internals melt in an intense fire?' The cube snapped shut and he jerked his fingers back.

'Why would you propose such a thing?'

He put his hands up. 'I wasn't suggesting setting you on fire! It just reminded me of a lump we've been investigating.'

'The item in the corner next to the escape pod entrance?'

He turned and spotted the chunk of plastic. It still had the lead wires trailing from it. Retrieving it, he placed it on the piloting console next to the cube.

'That is the beta model,' Wolfram said.

'Does this mean it will have a recording of what went on during the explosion?' He almost didn't dare to hope. 'We tried to access the data on it, but it was gibberish.'

'Of course it would be unintelligible to you. The data is encrypted, compressed and self-organised.'

'Can *you* access it?'

'In theory, yes. Though I will not allow Aryx to solder wires on to me like that. I would require an appropriate interface. The base data should be identical to mine as it was duplicated and flashed onto the beta model before its assembly was complete.'

'So you can run a differencing algorithm on it and determine what it learned *after* the copying process!'

'Precisely.'

Sebastian let out a sigh of relief and slumped back into his seat. 'Thank the Gods!' Finally, it looked like the investigation was going to go somewhere. The fact the second cube had even turned up on the station was a revelation in itself.

If the cube's counterpart had been in the possession of the terrorists, that would likely make Kerl an accomplice. But why would the terrorists have blown up their own lab, if not to hide evidence of their activities there? All the evidence so far pointed to a magic user. Was it even possible that they used such a thing? What other reason could there be for blowing up the lab? What if Kerl had been working for them, but developed his own agenda – one that didn't align with their plans. That might give them motive to blow the lab up. Was it sheer coincidence that SpecOps had given him the cube shortly before the explosion, or did they want him to find out what the cube was, suspecting something might be afoot? Nothing added up.

He didn't like it, but with the lack of substantial evidence and nothing to implicate the ITF directly, The Paper Man, Duggan, with his own admission to using magic, was moving back to the top of a very short list of suspects.

The trip back to the station was much quicker than Sebastian had anticipated and the *Ultima Thule* arrived at Tenebrae in good time after a series of fortuitously short node hops.

The ship drifted through the transport rings and came to rest in the familiar repair hangar. He shut down the ship's systems and made his way to the cargo bay. It would be good to get some proper rest, providing he didn't have one of the dreaded nightmares again. Aryx was still asleep on the hammock, snoring loudly.

'When he wakes, can you get him to wire you up to the beta cube?' he said, placing Wolfram on the stack of storage containers next to the bed. 'Let him have some breakfast first, of course.'

'Where are you going?'

'I want to get a few hours' sleep in my quarters. I'll be back in the morning.'

'Very well, I will inform him of your whereabouts when he wakes.'

'See you tomorrow.' He picked up the dirty sleeves from the N-suit on the way out and secured the door behind him. Despite being tired, he felt the need to stretch his legs before going to bed. The station would be in night-mode, the ideal time for a quiet walk, so he took a lift to the atrium.

He had never been in any of the busy areas of the station after midnight, and it was strange to see the walkways devoid of activity. The air was cool and the solar filters off, filling the atrium with a dusky blue light. Glowing insects drifted in the trees on either side of the river and on the plants along the bank, pollinating the night-blooms. There had been far too many reminders of Earth lately and he felt a little homesick.

When he got back to his apartment, he was too tired to even register the message flashing on his terminal. He tore his clothes off and crashed on the bed.

He tossed and turned in his sleep – a jumble of religious and mythological imagery filling his dreams. Strange symbols he didn't understand, memories from the visions imparted by Shiliri and the Hesperidium … None of it made sense.

He found himself crawling on his hands and knees through the dark tunnels on Achene, surrounded by glowing mists. Voices beckoned him onward, others taunted him from behind, and scratching on either side terrified him. The mists parted to reveal a mutilated, bloody corpse lying on the floor. As he drew closer to it, the mists drifted away from the legs. Short legs, torn off at the knees.

Dark liquid pooled around the body. He looked down at his wet hands. Hands stained red with Aryx's blood.

He screamed.

Sebastian woke to his alarm. The time on the terminal read 08.00 – he'd not been woken by the nightmare, but he still felt as though he'd not slept for a week. A message was waiting for him on the terminal. He sat down to read it. It wasn't blank. An uncommon occurrence, lately. The timestamp was two days ago; it must have arrived while the wristcoms were damaged. He would have to remember to pick up replacements from the office.

The message read, *Video enhancement of security video #8275 completed.*

'Excellent!' Another potentially viable lead. He pulled on the N-suit as fast as he could and made his way to the security department.

When he arrived, the place had calmed down considerably and people once again sat quietly tapping away at glass consoles.

He logged on to the terminal in his private office. 'Computer, transfer processed security video, number eight-two-seven-five, to the *Ultima Thule*.'

'Acknowledged. Did you sleep well?'

'I'd like you to also start running full traceroutes on the messages received by my terminal and the one in Aryx Trevarian's quarters. Trace all messages from the last ten days.' That should keep it busy for a while. It might even get to the bottom of whatever was causing the sleepless nights. He grabbed a couple of wristcoms from his drawer and left the office.

As he turned the corner, he almost collided with a short woman wearing an N-suit. She had long, brown hair, tied back in a ponytail. The large glasses she wore gave the impression of intelligence, in contrast to her dimpled cheeks and deep brown eyes – those gave her a child-like appearance that Sebastian found strangely disarming. His assumption of her age and maturity was instantly rectified by her well-educated and eloquently spoken voice.

'Oh! I'm sorry!' she said, bending to pick up the infoslate she had dropped.

He threw his hands up. 'My fault, I'm in a rush this morning.' He looked down at her outfit. 'Are you SpecOps, too?'

'Yes. I should check in with security while I'm here – I'm heading back out on assignment in a few days.' She stood hugging the infoslate, twisting back and forth.

'You haven't seen Agent Gladrin, have you?'

She shook her head. 'No, I've only been here a few hours, but I think he's quite busy at the moment.'

'Oh. I found another bug on my ship that he must have forgotten to mention. I don't know if it's one of the usual ones, or if it's one that has been planted by terrorists. I thought he should take a look at it.'

She raised an eyebrow. '*Usual* ones?'

'The bugs that are normally put on board new ships in case they get stolen before issue.'

'I've never heard that one before.' She pushed her glasses further up her nose. It was a little unusual that someone would be wearing them these days – Sollers Hope being an exception. She held out her hand. 'I can take it off you and give it to him if I see him, if you like.'

'That might be best. I've been out of touch for a few days. I've been meaning to discuss my initiation project with him.'

She tilted her head to one side, almost imperceptibly, and he dropped the damaged bug Aryx had found into her hand. 'I've got to go. It was nice meeting you—'

'Ms Stephens,' she said, finishing his sentence. 'And nice to meet you, Agent ... Thorsson?'

'Yes.'

'Ahh, the programmer guy. You're heading up the investigation on the explosion, aren't you?'

'Yeah.' He folded his arms. 'But I'd prefer if you didn't ask about it.'

She smiled. 'I wouldn't dream of it.' Her gaze held his eyes for several moments.

He rubbed his neck slowly, uncomfortable, and nodded. Skirting around her, he made his way down the corridor.

She called after him. 'If you ever fancy a drink—'

'—there's a drinks fountain in the changing room,' he mumbled.

When he arrived at the *Ultima Thule*, Aryx was lying underneath it – presumably working on the damaged panel. The dent in the thruster manifold had already been pulled out.

'You don't waste your time.'

Aryx slid out on a workshop trolley, the cube resting on his chest. 'I was just educating Wolfram on the finer points of fresh vegetables.'

'Why would that be interesting?'

'As it happens, I found a buyer for the few that survived the trip back.' He had a big grin on his face. 'Bet you can't guess who bought them.'

'No idea.'

'Only the Bronadi ambassador! He was really keen on the Romanesco broccoli. He's got a thing for mathematics, and said it looked very *fractal*.'

Sebastian rolled his eyes. 'How many credits did you get for them?'

'None.'

'You gave them away?'

'Not exactly. He owes me a favour now – you know how formal the Bronadi are. They're good for keeping promises, and you never know when a favour might come in handy.'

Despite not having met one face to face, Sebastian knew all about the dog-like Bronadi and their protocols. They were renowned for their penchant for debts and the sanctity of barter. 'Would you like to do *me* another favour and build a connector so that we can interface Wolfram with the melted cube?'

Aryx slid back under the ship. 'It was next on my list. Once I've replaced this panel, I'll make a start on it.'

Sebastian made his way upstairs and sat at the diagnostics console. 'Computer, play back the security video I just transferred, and for Gods' sakes give it a sensible name ... "Explosion video" will do just fine.'

'Video renamed. Beginning playback.' The screen above the console lit up. The figure once again approached from the far end of the corridor, moving into shot. Apparently, the week of computer processing had paid off; the figure was perfectly clear.

Sebastian guessed the person to be of average height – there weren't any distinctive features in the corridor against which to measure – and definitely male, with tufts of grey hair sticking out from beneath a twentieth-century style baseball cap, and wearing a nondescript set of tan overalls, similar to the ones Aryx often wore.

He fast-forwarded the video to the point before the explosion. 'Computer, I want a print and capture of the face when it's visible.'

The video resumed, and froze at an appropriate point. A grey-haired, middle-aged man with a jaggedly scissored-off beard. Certainly not someone he recognised. 'Aryx!'

'Yes?'

'Come up here. I need to see if you recognise this man.'

Aryx rolled off the lift with the cube in his lap and leaned on the console. 'What am I looking at?'

'This,' Sebastian said, pointing at the screen. 'It's our explosives expert-cum-thaumaturgist on the security video. Do you recognise him?'

'Ahh. Nope.'

'What about the overalls?'

'You can get those anywhere, nothing particularly distinctive.'

He sagged. 'I guess I'll have to run it through facial recognition. Computer, search for matches in the Galactic database.'

'Searches of the facial recognition database can take a maximum of one hour. Do you wish to proceed?'

'I've waited over a week for the video. I think an hour is acceptable!'

Aryx frowned at him. 'Will you stop being so grouchy? You've got some good evidence there – you should be grateful.'

'I know. I'm tired, and I didn't sleep well last night. The nightmares have kicked in again now that we're back. I still don't remember them clearly.'

'I slept fine.'

'Lucky for some … So, this wiring. Do you think you can make up a connector to attach the melted cube to Wolfram's interface?'

'Probably. What's it like?'

'Wolfram, didn't you show him yet?'

'My apologies, he looked like he needed the rest and, since he has only just finished repairing the ship, there has not been time.' The cube didn't hinge open this time – instead, the small rectangular panel in the top dropped in by two millimetres and slid open, revealing the array of tiny, indented contacts.

'It looks relatively simple, if a bit old-fashioned.'

'I am at the cutting edge of twenty-second century technology.'

Aryx laughed. 'We're in the twenty-third! It'll take me half an hour to do the connector, I expect. Want me to start now?'

'If you don't mind.' Sebastian moved to the piloting console. 'While you're doing that, I'll encrypt the flight logs. The Folians didn't ask me to, but I think it would be wise, in any case.'

Five minutes later, the computer interrupted. 'Match found in facial recognition database.'

Sebastian's stomach turned to ice as he read the name.

Duggan Simmons, deceased.

Chapter 30

'Oh no, no, no!' Sebastian stared at the name on the screen. A knot formed in his stomach. He wanted to throw up. It couldn't be true. It couldn't.

Aryx looked up from his work. 'What's up?'

'The computer has identified the perpetrator as Duggan! It says deceased, but that's probably because he's been off the radar for so long. Oh Gods! He seemed so sincere when he said he hadn't been here. I was convinced. It wasn't just his body language, but his tone of voice, everything.'

'Maybe you got it wrong? After all, wouldn't it be a bit hard to get a handle on his body whatnot if you couldn't make out his face?'

'Maybe I did— Hold on, blackouts! Maybe he's got some kind of psychosis. What if he came to the station during a blackout?'

'If that were true,' Wolfram said, 'it would not explain his motivation for attacking the laboratory. It would also not explain how he gained knowledge of its existence. It would only explain his lack of memory of the incident.'

Sebastian's chest tightened. 'As much as I don't want to, I've got to confront him.' He entered the coordinates for Yazor into the navigation computer, digit by digit.

'I'll be finished with this in a few minutes,' Aryx said. 'If I wire it up to Wolfram, we can transfer the data over and analyse it on the way there. It might give us a clearer idea of what's going on, especially if it's got a record of events in the lab. At least you'll have some corroboratory evidence that might suggest motive.'

'Do you need anything else from the station before we leave? Food, tools, that sort of thing?'

'No, I think I've got all that I need. Anything I'm missing, Wolfram?'

'I believe you have everything covered. Sebastian has no legitimate reason to delay further.'

'Thank you for that.'

Aryx sniggered.

'Oh, and I forgot this.' Sebastian fished about in his backpack and tossed a replacement wristcom to Aryx.

'Thanks!' Aryx strapped it on and threw the broken one into the recycling chute next to the console.

Sebastian initiated the launch sequence.

There was an air of apprehensive tension in the ship as it glided through the transit system and out into open space.

Aryx rubbed his eyes. He'd finished wiring the last few contacts, and the melted beta cube's organoplastic matrix was now connected to a flat metal plate by a tangle of wires. 'Open wide.'

The interface cover of Wolfram's cube slid open.

He was beginning to think of Wolfram as the consciousness trapped inside the cube, rather than being the cube itself. During his time on Achene, when Wolfram had been in control of the cargomech, he'd thought of him *as* the cargomech. In essence Wolfram was simply the process, and it didn't really matter what housed it – the cube was simply the most compact and efficient computer for it to be in. In a way, it reminded him of how Sebastian had described the Folians.

He carefully dropped the contact plate into the opening. Tiny sprung arms extended from around the perimeter of the socket and pressed down, creating a firm contact between the plate and interface array.

'I will initiate data transfer. Once the transfer is complete, I will run a differential analysis against my database. I will exclude my experiences since the original duplication date from the analysis. Transferring.' The lights on the side of the cube extinguished and a single LED illuminated and began moving up and down.

Aryx waited for five minutes while information flowed back and forth.

'I apologise for the length of time the transfer is taking, the amount of data is redonculously large.'

Aryx laughed. 'Don't you mean, "ridiculously"?'

'Yes. There appraise to be some corruption of data, and it is affecting my linguistic datablasé.'

He snorted. 'I don't mean to laugh, but it is funny.'

Sebastian was laughing, too. He asked, 'Why is it taking so long?'

'If I sped up the process, I wouldn't be able to see the shit for the shovel.'

Aryx stifled a snigger.

Sebastian wasn't so discrete, and laughed raucously. 'What's the maximum transfer rate?'

'I don't know off the top of my hand.'

Aryx let out another burst of laughter.

'If you are trying to make me say things incorrectly on porpoise, you are pissing in the water.'

'Oh, I don't know. I seem to be doing a good job. Did your mentors teach you any poetry or quotations?'

' "You can't polish a rose", or was it "would a turd by any other name smell as sweet"? Oh, my mentor loved William Milkshake ... William Fakespear? William Spearmint, that's it.'

'That's not right, Wolfram.' Aryx nearly fell out of his wheelchair laughing; the SI seemed to be a glutton for punishment. 'Please stop, it's embarrassing,' he wheezed.

Sebastian shuddered with laughter. Wolfram fell silent.

'You're an evil bastard sometimes, Seb.'

'I know. I just couldn't pass up the opportunity.'

'He probably makes fun of people with speech impelliments,' Wolfram said, ignoring Aryx's previous instruction. The lights stopped moving. 'Data transfer complete and I've corrected the linguistic subroutines. Would you like me to begin the analysis now? I'll be unable to communicate or perform other functions until the analysis has finished.'

'Yes, begin now,' Sebastian said. 'We need that information as soon as possible.' He looked at the console then glanced up at the windows. 'We'll be at Yazor in a couple of hours, and if I have to arrest him, I want to present Duggan with as much evidence as possible.'

Wolfram released the clamps that held the connector in place and it flipped out of the socket. The cover slid shut. 'I'll begin my analysis and inform you when it's complete.'

'Thank you.'

The lights on the side of the cube slowly strobed up and down as it fell silent.

'There's one thing I don't understand,' Aryx said, turning to Sebastian. 'Why's he visible in the video?'

Sebastian turned around and leaned on his forearms, draping his wrists down over his knees. 'I don't know ... It's puzzling. He was desperate to become visible again, and his blackouts coincided with his attempts to change back. Maybe he succeeded and *then* had some kind of episode?'

'Why would he change himself invisible again afterwards, if not to disguise his identity?'

'I don't know,' Sebastian said, with a huff. 'I'm a programmer, not a clinical psychologist.'

'Well, it sounds fishy, given what he said to you about his clothes becoming visible.'

'Maybe there's a rational explanation for it.'

'*Rational* explanation! You're desperate to believe he's innocent, aren't you?' Aryx still couldn't believe in the whole magic thing – it seemed more likely that everyone who believed in it was nuts and that it was all a big conspiracy.

Sebastian remained silent.

An hour later, the ship dropped out of superphase in the system of Yazor and the stars settled back into their usual state.

'*Ultima Thule* to Yazor comet. It's Agent Thorsson. Are you there?'

Aryx hoped The Paper Man would respond. He didn't fancy the idea of negotiating the comet's tail again.

The comms crackled into life. 'Good to hear from you, Agent Thorsson. I assume you've made progress in your investigation?'

'Yes, a little. We'd like to meet with you.'

'Come around sun-side. There's a docking bay, I'll let you in.'

'Thanks. I'll be bringing my friend, Aryx Trevarian, with me.'

'I look forward to it. Docking protocols are active.' The comms cut off.

Sebastian brought the ship on a path parallel to the comet's orbit, approaching from the sun-side. Through the starboard cockpit window, Aryx spotted a large opening in the rocky surface.

'That wasn't there before.'

'Probably camouflaged, like the one the other side.' Sebastian rotated the ship and approached the entrance.

The ship moved into range and a set of magnetic docking rings locked on to the inductors, passing the ship through an airlock and drawing it into a large, icy crystalline tunnel, where the darkness was broken by regularly spaced lights. Aryx's innards sank into his pelvis and a moment later moved back when the ship's gravity generator released its grip on the occupants. Vibration rumbled through the hull as the atmospheric landing thrusters kicked in. He secretly crossed his fingers. The manifold repair better be up to the task.

The *Ultima Thule* settled down, uneventfully, on a landing pad ringed with lights.

'Should we bring Wolfram with us, just in case he finishes processing while we're here?' he asked. 'It would be good to have the evidence to show Duggan if he doesn't believe you.' He found it ironic that The Paper Man might not believe *their* story.

'That's probably a good idea.' Sebastian patted his holster.

Aryx tucked the cube into his thigh pocket. 'What's the plan?'

'I ask him about his blackouts, when the last one was, then present him with the video evidence. If he's uncooperative, I'll have to arrest him.'

*   *   *

Wheeling out, Aryx was struck by the sheer size of the cavern in which the ship had landed. On the far side of the pad, mounted in the rocky wall, was a door, illuminated by several lights that made it shine in the darkness of the cave.

In front of the doorway stood a robed figure, shrouded in black.

'He looks a bit freaky,' Aryx whispered.

Sebastian whispered back. 'Wait until you see him with his mask off.' He held out his hand as the man approached.

'Good to see you again, Agent Thorsson.' The Paper Man shook his hand.

'It's good to see you, too. We made it to Chopwood and Achene.'

'How was the trip?'

'Hazardous, to say the least. Chopwood was in a poor state of repair, as you can imagine. We found a diary.' Sebastian pulled the medic's journal from his rucksack and handed it over. 'We then made it to Achene, but were surprised to find it disguised as a gas giant.'

'Oh!'

'The Folians hid it after you left, to prevent others from finding them. Did you know they teleported the colonists away?'

The Paper Man didn't respond; Aryx couldn't read his expression behind the mask.

Sebastian continued. 'After they left Chopwood with the *Iceni*, they headed for Achene, intending to start felling the Folian trees.'

The Paper Man put a hand to the masked chin. It was about as pensive – or shocked – as the featureless face could look. 'The Folians didn't tell me that. Why would Cullen take everyone there? They were happy enough with the resources in Chopwood.'

'I would read the diary, if I were you,' Aryx said.

'And this must be your friend.'

'Yes, sorry. Duggan Simmons, I'd like you to meet Aryx Trevarian.'

Without bending down, The Paper Man shook hands with him. Finally, someone with the sense not to be patronising.

'How do you know my name?' Duggan hefted the diary in his hand. 'Mentioned in here, am I?'

'Not in a bad light. Do you mind if we discuss this indoors?'

'Of course, where are my manners?'

They followed him through the airlock and down a short corridor that terminated in a second, much smaller, door. He entered a code and it slid back to reveal a large, well-lit cave-like room with a kitchen area and a set of couches.

'Welcome to my humble abode,' he said, bowing, and held his hand over the sensor, keeping the door open for the pair to enter.

Aryx wheeled past and nodded. 'Nice place you have here. Did you build it all yourself?'

'Please, take a seat.' Duggan gestured to the couches.

'Thank you, but I'll stay in my chair.'

'As you wish. No, I didn't build all this. The technology I installed myself, such as the docking mechanisms, doors, furnishings, and walkways, but the basic structure, the tunnels and caverns, were already here when I found it.' Duggan allowed the door to close behind them and walked to the kitchen area. 'Can I get you a drink?'

'Just water, thanks,' Sebastian said, taking a seat on the couch.

'I'll have a strong coffee, three heaped spoons of instant, if you have any. Failing that, I'll have a strong tea.'

'Got paralysed taste buds, have we?'

'No, just calloused,' Aryx called back and, seeing that Duggan had put a kettle on a burner, he grinned. He parked himself at the end of the couch next to Sebastian and pulled the cube out of his pocket, placing it on the low coffee table in front of him. 'Damn thing's sticking in my leg. Sorry Wolfie.'

Sebastian sat back and looked around. 'How *did* you find this place, Mr Simmons?'

'After I left Chopwood, I wanted to find somewhere I could safely experiment with thaumaturgy. I was pleased to discover that some of my insurances and bank accounts I'd set up before I left for the colonising mission were still active. I wasn't ready to integrate myself with modern society, so I started scanning for small planets and large asteroids where I could build a base.'

'You got *insurance?*'

'Of course. We knew trips might take a long time – we had no idea of exactly how long, mind you, but many of us set up accounts that would accrue interest so we could rebuild our lives when we returned to Earth. I was lucky that my policies lasted as long as they did, and because I'd not been confirmed dead by my insurers, regardless of what everyone else thought, the policies held. I was able to purchase the resources and technology required to make this place habitable.'

'That's very resourceful of you.'

Aryx stared up at the ceiling. The strange stained-glass-like sheets between the crystalline stalactites didn't look like any rock formation he'd ever seen. 'I take it these caves aren't natural?'

A tinkling sound came from the kitchen area as Duggan stirred something. 'No. I don't know exactly how old they are, but the lack of information on such things implies that they're very old, perhaps even older than Humanity itself. But I'm sure you didn't just come here to discuss architecture. So what can I help you with, Agent Thorsson?'

Sebastian turned in his seat to face the man properly. 'Unfortunately,

I wasn't able to gain much useful information from the Folians, and I'd like a bit more information about your blackouts.'

The clattering of crockery stopped. Duggan looked up. 'Why would you want to know about my blackouts?'

'It's a long story, but the timing is important. When did you last have one?'

'Just less than a week ago, I think. What's today?'

'Saturday.'

'I guess it would have been last Sunday then.'

'What time, roughly?'

'What time do you make it now?'

'It's about twelve-hundred hours, station-time.'

Duggan paused. 'I guess it would have been the early hours of Sunday morning, then. It lasted four or five hours.'

Sebastian looked at Aryx.

He nodded discretely. It certainly confirmed Sebastian's theory about the blackout timing. He mouthed, *Be careful.*

Sebastian nodded sharply and turned his eyes back to the kitchen.

Duggan brought the tray over and placed it on the table next to the cube. 'So, why are my blackouts important?'

'We found footage of you on the security video aboard the station. It was a couple of hours after your blackout would have started.'

'Footage of *me?* How is that even possible?'

'The blurred figure on the video. The computers managed to clean it up.' Sebastian pulled the print out of his rucksack and handed it over. 'Here. It *is* you, isn't it?'

Duggan snatched the sheet and stood motionless for a few moments. 'I'm ... I'm visible!' He paced back and forth. 'How can I be visible? The spells never worked! I blacked out each time I tried, and when I woke up I was back to square one. It's not possible!'

Sebastian put his hand out in a calming gesture. 'This is what I'm trying to say. Maybe you went to the station during a blackout. Maybe you weren't responsible for your actions at the time. Your clothes were visible every time you attempted the spell, weren't they?'

'Yes, but I don't see—'

'Oh, stop pussyfooting,' Aryx said, frowning at Sebastian. 'They would have gone invisible with you – don't you see?'

'I ... I wasn't there. I've never been there.' A hand went to the mask.

'Those monitors, do they record things in this place? Sebastian said you showed him a view of outside. Have you got footage inside?'

'Yes, that's it. I can prove to you that I didn't leave.' Duggan darted to the wall next to the monitors and began tapping commands on a panel. Each of the screens lit up with a different view – some of tunnels, one of the room in which they sat, and another showed the hangar. Duggan jabbed at the panel and the images leading up to the current moment began to reverse, slowly at first, then faster. They stopped.

'Here we are, this is just before my blackout.'

The trio watched the playback. A robed figure approached a black, triangular craft parked in the hangar, stripped off its clothes, and raised its arms. In that instant, the translucent sponge-form became dense. Dense, solid, and blurred.

'No! I don't remember this!' Duggan shrieked.

The figure in the video continued moving, despite the man's protests. It climbed into the small ship and launched.

'No, this can't be right—' Fingers hammered at the keypad again until the timecode showed four hours after the explosion.

The ship had returned. The wraith stepped out of the craft and vanished. Robes drifted up from the floor, clothing the invisible figure.

Duggan staggered back. 'It can't be me. I don't remember any of this. I was unconscious!'

'I'm sorry, Duggan,' Sebastian said, rising, a hand on the pistol. 'I have to take you back with us.'

The Paper Man held out his hands in front of him, upturned. *'Please, if I have to go with you, don't let me go back like this.* The spell must have worked – you've seen for yourself. If I must be punished, let me go back with dignity.'

'I—' Sebastian took a deep breath, held it for several moments, and sighed. 'Alright.'

'Are you mad?' Aryx yelled.

'No. I'm not inhuman, either. Do it, Mr Simmons, but I'm keeping an eye on you.'

Aryx didn't like it. He didn't like it one bit. All this talk about magic was making his teeth ache. Dangerous nutters and magic. It was like sitting in front of a bomb, waiting for it to go off. 'Sebastian—'

'Wait here.' Duggan dashed off to the kitchen and ran up the stairway into the dark alcove above.

Sebastian shifted on to the edge of his seat.

'You shouldn't have let him go. What if he gets violent? What if he decides to drop a bomb on us like in the lab?'

'It'll be fine. It wasn't a bomb.'

To Aryx's relief, Duggan came back down the stairs clutching only a small drawstring pouch. He stood on the opposite side of the coffee table, facing the pair. 'I need to try this in front of you.'

Sebastian's hand went to the holster on his belt. 'Maybe we should restrain you first, just in case you have an epis—'

Duggan dropped the pouch on the table. It fell open exposing its white, powdery contents. With a dramatic flourish, he pulled off his mask and threw it on the couch beside them. Aryx's stomach turned. That half-transparent face. No wonder he was called The Paper Man.

He thrust his head back and began chanting strange, unintelligible words – not Galac; something from Earth, something far older. His throat echoed with a deep, growling chord as he recited and, while he chanted, he reached up as though beseeching some divine being. The air began to distort, rippling and shimmering as though caught in the heat from a furnace.

While Aryx watched, the white splash of powder on table began to recede. The heap dwindled until only half remained. Was it evaporating like the sample, or being consumed? He looked up at Duggan's face. His skin was opaque, normal. Badly-cut hair stuck out at odd angles, and a scraggly, cut-off beard projected from his chin – exactly like the picture from the security video. All traces of invisibility had gone. It *was* magic! It was crazy. This man could be capable of *anything*!

The man's arms dropped to his sides and he brought his gaze down in Sebastian's direction. The stare was vacant, disorientated.

'Duggan ... are you alright?'

The empty stare filled with a dark rage, the blank expression twisting into a grimace of contempt. Tea-making paraphernalia crashed to the floor as he launched himself over the table, arms outstretched towards Sebastian's throat. The knotty fingers clamped around his neck. Sebastian's hands went to his belt, flicking back and forth. Aryx wheeled around the couch. He had to get Duggan off him. Sebastian's lips began to turn blue in the vice-like grip.

Aryx made a grab for Duggan's shoulder, but his left arm shot out, hitting him squarely in the chest. The wheelchair flew backwards and caught the corner of the couch.

The world tumbled and his head hit the floor, hard.

Sebastian clawed at the hands locked around his throat, trying to pry the sinewy talons apart. His eyes darted around the room. He needed something to use as a weapon – the cube on the table, the tray on the floor, the pistol lying under the coffee table – something before he suffocated.

Duggan's face drew close, his lips curled into a grotesque snarl. His eyes, while firmly fixed on Sebastian's, looked vacant and, for a moment, he thought he could see tiny points of light in them, distant stars in the darkness.

His head pounded and his vision began to dim.

Duggan growled, 'We will have you and we shall destroy the mechanism.' His mouth opened wide and a glowing red vapour issued forth. Evil, red mist that moved towards him with intent, like a gaseous, red octopus.

A soft weight came over Sebastian and he let go of the hands at his neck.

It wasn't worth fighting. It was like falling asleep, after all.

Chapter 31

Sebastian skirted the edge of consciousness, the fight almost gone from him. The cube on the table began to vibrate and rattle, ignored by the pair locked in their mortal brawl.

A deep, resonant chord echoed through the chamber, slowly rising in pitch. Porcelain, glass, and silver rattled as the sound became overlaid with words, sung and hummed simultaneously. The chord reached its crescendo and a spherical pulse, like a pressure wave from an explosion distorting the air, burst forth from the cube, rippling across the room through air and solid objects alike.

Duggan tumbled forwards onto Sebastian, immobile. Regaining his senses, Sebastian shoved the limp form sideways onto the couch. Duggan lay on his side, staring straight ahead as though paralysed.

'What the fuck!' Sebastian rasped, rubbing his neck. 'Aryx!' He scrambled down from the couch and felt for a pulse. It was strong. 'Wake up.'

Somebody was slapping his face. Aryx opened his eyes. Sebastian was looking down at him with an expression of concern.

'What happened? I'm not in hospital, am I?'

'No. Duggan knocked you out.' Sebastian looked back over his shoulder.

'How did you overpower him?' Aryx reached up and pulled his chair upright between the furniture.

'I didn't. I don't know what happened. He was trying to breathe something into my mouth, then there was a weird sound, and he passed out or something.' Sebastian got up and stood over the unmoving body.

Aryx wheeled around the coffee table. The carbyne had all gone – had it all evaporated? His attention went to the cube. The lights on its side were all lit. They had all been moving while Wolfram processed the database. What was wrong with it?

'Duggan?' Sebastian shook the man.

There was no response.

'Why are you worried about him? The lunatic bastard tried to kill you!'

Sebastian scowled over his shoulder. 'Don't you get it? This is just like what happened in the diary when William tried to kill Cullen!'

'What *are* you on about?'

'I saw a light in his eyes, the same as the medic described.' He rolled Duggan onto his back and propped him up in a sitting position with a cushion.

'You sure you weren't just seeing stars?'

Sebastian's glare intensified.

'You think he had some kind of psychotic episode?'

'Seems like it.' Sebastian waved his hand in front of Duggan's face. The eyes began to move, following the motion.

'What ... happened?' Duggan looked up at Sebastian and his attention drifted to Aryx, then down to the table. 'Where has the powder gone?'

'You used it up making yourself visible,' Sebastian said.

'No, he didn't, he only used half of it. It stopped disappearing by the time he was visible.'

'I'm visible?' He stared down at his hands and slowly pulled the gloves off. 'After all these years!' Tears streamed down his face.

'Do you remember anything?' Sebastian asked.

'I remember starting to cast the spell and that's all.'

'Your spell, or whatever it was, worked.'

'Yeah, except for the bit where he tried to bloody *kill you!*'

Duggan's eyes darted from Sebastian to Aryx and back. 'I tried to hurt you? I'm so sorry – I don't know what happened. Why am I still visible? I normally turn back when I try – what was different?'

Aryx picked up the cube. Six of its lights were lit, like it was counting down to something. 'I think it was this.'

Duggan wiped his eyes. 'What is it?'

'It's an SI, a computer with a self-determined intelligence. I'm not certain, but before I passed out I thought I saw a pulse or something come from it. Something must have been making you turn back invisible, just like on the video, and I think this time the pulse from the cube interrupted it.'

'But what happened to the rest of the powder?' Sebastian asked. 'Did it evaporate?'

'No, I had already stabilised it.'

'That's what I've been trying to say. I think Wolfram did it somehow.' Only three of the lights were lit.

Duggan's eyes widened. 'A *computer!* Using magic?'

'I hate to admit it, but I don't think it was any kind of electromagnetic pulse. I think something's wrong, though – I'd have expected him to speak by now.'

Sebastian held out his hand. 'Let's have a look.' Aryx handed it over. 'How many lights were on?'

'Three. I think they're counting down.'

'They've all gone off now ... Wolfram? Are you alright?'

'I'm fully functional,' came the familiar, eloquent voice. 'My processor core overheated and I had to shut down until it cooled.'

'What happened just now?' Aryx asked.

'I was unable to interact with the outside world until the database analysis had completed. The process finished moments before Duggan attacked Sebastian, at which point I understood what was happening. The database contains experience of magic manipulation, and I was able to utilise an effect to purge the secondary consciousness from Mr Simmons' body.'

Duggan's face twisted. 'What do you mean *secondary* consciousness?'

'You were, Mr Simmons, possessed.'

Chapter 32

The three sat, mouths open, stunned by the cube's revelation.

'Possessed ... ?' Aryx said. He knew he wasn't going to like the answer.

Sebastian frowned. His expression turned dark.

'It is better if I show you what I have learned.' The lights on the cube flashed rapidly and eight of the displays on the wall flicked into life.

One of the screens showed a view from above the door inside the lab on Tenebrae, prior to the explosion; the second display showed the familiar exterior corridor scene; another screen appeared relatively dark; and the remaining five showed images taken from one of the workbenches, looking outward in different directions.

'These are recordings from the beta cube,' Wolfram said. 'Some are recordings made from its nanocameras, and the others are from the security cameras that it tapped into in order to get a better overview of its surroundings. Unfortunately, the information is fragmented and I cannot replay a full account of events, but I'll show what I can.'

The screens displayed a time code several months earlier. Kerl wore a white lab coat, his short black hair combed to one side; he looked like a typical science nerd. Alvarez wore a loose coverall – Aryx immediately recognised the dark Hispanic looks and dense chinstrap of a beard, and the heavy musculature that showed prominently through the suit. It sickened him to see his old friend in the video, knowing what might be about to happen.

The pair sat at one end of the lab, talking to each other in a friendly and genial manner – the recording evidently didn't cover their meeting, as they seemed to know each other well. At the opposite end of the lab stood a dummy, similar to those Aryx had seen in the gym for hand-to-hand training.

'Now, I know you found it difficult to focus last time,' Kerl said, 'so how would you feel about trying hypnosis to help with control?'

'Yeah, whatever will help. I don't feel as though I'm good enough at this throat-singing crap. If it keeps my mind on it, I'm up for it.'

Kerl withdrew a small pen-light from his coat pocket, held it up in front of Alvarez's eyes, and began moving it from left to right. 'I'd like you to count backwards from ten. I want you to remember that when I speak the words "focus is yours" you will have laser sharp concentration, and when I click my fingers you will gently come out of trance.' The count reached zero and he clicked his fingers.

Alvarez blinked and looked at him. 'Is that all there is to it?'

Kerl nodded.

The Brazilian clapped his hands together. 'Let's give it a go then!'

Kerl took two vials of white powder from his coat pocket and handed them over. Alvarez tucked them into the left breast pocket of his coveralls and bent his knees and arms, as though about to spring at the dummy – from all the way across the room.

'Focus is yours.'

He stared intently at the dummy and a guttural whistling tone came from him. His voice changed, shaping the tones into strange, non-Galac, words, '*Transmitir dent ocius velocidade.*' The air around his body began to shimmer and, with the tiniest of movements, he was gone.

The next instant he was at the other side of the room, hanging on the dummy as though he'd used it to stop himself from crashing into the wall.

'Wow!' If he didn't know better, Aryx would have thought the cube had fabricated the video.

'Rewind it, Wolfram,' Sebastian said, 'and play it back *slowly.*'

The scene cut back to before the motion and began to replay at a fraction of the speed. Alvarez appeared to accelerate across the room. Within milliseconds, he was moving at a blur – it looked like he'd shot across the entire room in the same pose, as though the effect of his movement on his velocity had been exaggerated and multiplied thousandfold.

Wolfram resumed playback at normal speed.

Alvarez removed the vials from his pocket. One was empty.

'You used one of the samples entirely.' Kerl made a note on an infoslate. 'Most interesting. It seems that the effect's potency and duration is also a variable in the quantity of carbyne used. It's also interesting to note that the effect has used powder from one vial consistently. It must catalyse itself via the molecules in proximity, a sort of chain reaction, otherwise it would have used powder from more than one vial simultaneously.'

'I think that counts as an acceleration spell,' Duggan said. 'I think he said "impart speed". It sounded like Latin and Portuguese, all mixed together.'

Wolfram stopped the video.

'You mean to say that the lab was researching magic?' Aryx almost couldn't believe it – his friend wasn't a nutter, after all.

'It certainly seems that way,' Sebastian said. 'But it doesn't yet explain what happened to Duggan just now.'

'The devil is in the details,' Wolfram said.

Duggan raised an eyebrow at the cube.

'He does weird things like that sometimes,' Aryx said.

'Shall I continue?'

'Please do,' Duggan said.

Alvarez and Kerl had changed positions, the time code weeks later than the previous footage. Alvarez sat on a stool with his back to the workbench. Wires trailed from his head and, even though the overall view wasn't clear, it was evident from the cube's multiple views that the wires led to the cube itself.

'I bloody knew it!' Aryx slapped his thigh.

'I'm going to record your brainwaves using the device just like we've done in the other experiments. It should be able to monitor your thought patterns and extrapolate the images and sounds. I'd like you to try something small first.' Once again, Kerl took out a sample of carbyne from his coat pocket. 'Focus is yours.'

At the opposite end of the lab, on a storage unit at the end of the bed, sat a small pot plant. Alvarez pointed at it and began chanting and throat-singing. '*Mueva ligeramente.*' The air rippled around him.

The pot plant twitched as though a light breeze had struck up and began to waft through the leaves.

'That's enough.'

Alvarez lowered his hand.

'Now, let's see if the cube can do it.' The view on the six monitors, showing the cube's vantage point, moved as Kerl picked it up and disconnected the bundle of wires. Pointing the cube towards the plant, he pressed the button on the side.

The same sounds Alvarez had made echoed around the room, this time generated by the cube. '*Mueva ligeramente,*' the device repeated, in electronic sounding tones.

The plant twitched.

'Hah! It worked!' Kerl said, slapping Alvarez on the back. 'This is amazing! You, my friend, are making history.'

'Are we going to record everything I've been practising?'

'It may take some time, but yes, we'll do it.'

The image tore up with random squares of colour.

'There is corruption here,' Wolfram said.

'Why is Alvarez speaking in that language?' Aryx asked. 'I'd never heard him speak anything other than Galac.'

'When you intone, it's not always intelligible, and is usually a combination of sounds and speech patterns from your cultural heritage.'

'Interesting.' With his arms folded tightly, Sebastian looked impatient.

'Do you wish to continue?' Wolfram asked.

'Yes, please.'

The scene skipped forwards two weeks.

It was another recording session and Alvarez sat in front of the workbench, wired up once again. He intoned the words of a spell, but this time his hands fell to his sides and he slouched.

'Nick, what are you doing?'

Alvarez raised his head. 'Where am I. Who are you.' The voice was flat.

'You're on the station … It's me, John – what's wrong with you?'

He turned in his seat to face the cube and touched a hand to his head. 'What is this. What is the device this body is connected to.'

'It's the SI, remember? We're using it to record your brainwaves, so it can implement quantum manipulation. Are you okay? You sound strange. Do you need a rest?'

The vacantly staring marine turned his head up from the cube and straight at the scientist.

Kerl stepped back, as though he'd seen something sinister in the gaze.

'The device is not visible to us.' Alvarez began tugging the wires out of his scalp.

'No, stop it! You'll damage it.' Kerl reached out. The Brazilian shoved him back and he slid along the bench, toppling over backwards and taking several beakers to the floor with him. Alvarez ignored the fallen Kerl and continued plucking wires out of his head.

'Stop it!'

'You cannot be permitted to do this.' Alvarez began to yank the wires from the cube.

'I can't let you destroy my life's work, not now we're so close!' Kerl picked up a fire extinguisher and held it over Alvarez's head. 'Stop it, I beg you!'

Alvarez struck out but Kerl reacted quickly, bringing the canister down on the back of his skull.

His body tumbled to the floor, unconscious.

The video skipped.

Alvarez lay strapped to the bed, wide awake. 'Did I hurt you when I was out?'

'No, but you managed to pull a few of the wires out and nearly wrecked the cube. Luckily, no permanent damage was done.'

'Are you sure these restraints will hold me?'

'I think so. I've primed you with a hypnotic suggestion so that I can control the entity if it does happen again. I want you to try the last effect.' He placed a vial of carbyne next to the bed.

The chanting began and the air around Alvarez shimmered. His hands fell to the bed.

Kerl peered at him. 'So, it's happened again.'

Alvarez tried to sit, struggling against the restraints. He looked over to the workbench, straight at the exposed cube. 'We will destroy that object. It cannot be allowed to exist.'

'You are in my control.' Kerl's tone was firm and confident.

Alvarez's eyes fluttered. 'You will not control us. We cannot allow you to control us.'

Kerl turned away, picked up a syringe, and filled it with a drug from a bottle, obscuring the cube's view. He turned back with the needle but Alvarez's hand shot up to wrestle for it. Somehow he'd worked his arm free. Kerl moved quickly, plunging the needle deep into Alvarez's left biceps.

Alvarez eased back onto the pillow. 'You shall not control us. We will destroy the mechanism, and you along with it.'

Kerl leaped back. Alvarez had somehow managed to acquire a scalpel during the struggle; he drew the blade up to his own neck and, with a quick flick, severed both jugular veins. Blood streamed out, spraying the bed. Kerl dashed forwards and tried to cover the wound; both hands weren't enough to staunch the flow.

Alvarez twitched. In moments, he'd stopped.

Sebastian winced. 'This is familiar. The vision I saw had him making those motions, then he faded away, obviously dead. It looked like he'd flipped out, but now we know.'

'Poor bastard,' Aryx said. If only he'd known what was going on, he might have been able to do something.

'You will find the next bit interesting, and possibly disturbing,' Wolfram said. As if it wasn't already.

The video jumped forwards.

Kerl had severed Alvarez's head.

It was connected to several pipes and containers of fluid, and hung suspended in the frame Aryx had examined earlier. The wires trailing from the head and frame ran to the cube on the bench.

'Can you hear me?' The view didn't show the face, but Kerl smiled as though he'd got some visual feedback. 'I'd like you to attempt the spell that moved the plant again. Focus is yours. You are in my control.'

A pumping mechanism moved up and down in one of the cylinders; words came from the head.

The plant twitched.

'*Excellent!*' Kerl clapped his hands together with a macabre glee. 'Now our experiments can continue.'

Time jumped forwards several days. It was nearly the moment of the explosion.

'Here's the money shot,' Aryx said. He couldn't wait to see that fucking bastard Kerl meet his fate.

The scientist sat, working at the bench, checking the connections on the wires.

Outside the lab, on the external view, a blurry figure walked up the corridor and out of shot.

Kerl remained blissfully unaware as a pinpoint of light formed behind him. In a microsecond it grew from a tiny speck to a roiling ball of fire, three feet across, a miniature sun. With a flash it filled the room and was gone.

Flame crawled up the walls. Everything burned.

The immolated Kerl stumbled, crashing into the bed, the workbench, and the wall, before falling to the floor. Glassware deformed on the benches. The exposed innards of the cube melted, obscuring the six views.

The last recorded instant was from the security camera as the canister of gas exploded.

Chapter 33

Aryx shut his eyes at the bright flash. Kerl deserved it. Big time. Duggan fell back on the sofa. 'Oh, Lord ... Fireball ... I—'

'Was not responsible.' Sebastian sat down next to him and put his hand on his shoulder. 'It's not your fault. It seems like you were possessed by something like whatever it was that took over Alvarez.'

Tears once again streamed down Duggan's face. He shook his head. 'I should have anticipated this. If only I'd found the diary, I would have known.'

'How could you have known?' Aryx asked. 'Possession's something from horror movies, not real life.'

Duggan gestured to his large book collection on the shelves in the corners. 'It's mentioned in a lot of medieval religious writings. I almost don't believe it myself.'

'What do you mean?' Surely nobody ever read any of that old stuff.

He wiped away his tears. 'In medieval times, the Church associated the practice of magic with demonic possession and being in league with "the Devil". Did the Folians show you how ancient Humans were taught magic?'

'Yes, I saw that,' Sebastian said.

'Then you'll know that the Folians on Earth were destroyed by the Church, who thought them to be evil. Maybe the use of magic attracted other beings whose intentions were not so benign.' Duggan rose and began pacing back and forth in front of the screens.

'So where does the carbyne go when it's been used?' Aryx had to change the subject – the idea of pursuing religious dogma and possession was even worse than believing in magic. There were only so many impossibilities he could attempt to believe in one day.

'I assume it sublimates into another plane of existence. It doesn't vanish in the same way that it does when it evaporates in an unstable state, that much is certain.'

'Could it be that these beings exist in the same plane that the carbyne goes to?' Sebastian asked.

'It's possible. That would explain how the beings are attracted to magic users. I often wondered whether many religious rites were based on thaumaturgic practises. It could be that magic manipulates their realm. Perhaps exorcism rituals ...' Duggan trailed off, his eyes apparently tracing patterns in the weave of the rug and shards of broken glass.

Aryx huffed and folded his arms. Typical, back on the subject. Might as well join in. 'I bet they saw the cube as a threat because it couldn't be possessed. That would be a good reason to destroy it, especially if magic affects things on that plane. They wouldn't want something they couldn't control having influence over them.'

'I detect a theme,' Wolfram said. 'Everyone appears to dislike an uncontrollable SI.'

'What do these "demons" look like?' Sebastian asked.

Duggan ran his hand along the books on the longest of set of shelves and pulled out a six-inch thick tome. 'Here, have a look at this.' He sat on the couch next to Sebastian and began leafing through the pages. 'This is it.' He held the book out for Aryx to see, his finger tapping a crude illustration at the top of a heavily illuminated page.

A red, winged bestial form with the lower half of a goat and the upper half of a man, with long, pointed horns and a bullish smile stood over a young woman. The back of her hand was pressed against her forehead as the creature stood over her, breathing a mass of red swirls towards her.

'What is that?' Sebastian asked.

'The Devil, taking control of a young witch.'

'No, I mean the red stuff – that's what you tried to breathe into my mouth.'

'Oh!' Duggan frowned and ran his finger across the page. Aryx didn't recognise the language, and it was obviously difficult for Duggan to read. 'The miasma – *bad air*. Possibly the soul of a demon.'

'The picture looks familiar,' Aryx said, 'I've seen a monster like that somewhere before.'

'The beings in this other plane, demons – is the miasma a transference mechanism for them?'

Duggan shrugged. 'You have as much of an idea as I do. I've never encountered it before.'

'Not even with William?' Aryx pointed at the diary on the table.

Duggan picked it up. 'Is he mentioned in this? I couldn't bring myself to read it. Did he get possessed as well – is that what this says?'

'It seems like it,' Sebastian said. 'He tried to kill Cullen, who then went strange after the attack, and that's when he decided to mount an assault on Achene with chainsaws and bulldozers.'

Duggan shook his head slowly. 'What happened to him?'

'He was killed when they tried to get him off Cullen,' Aryx said.

'Poor lad.' He took a deep, shuddering breath. 'I think the legends about possession may have been correct. Some of them say that if a possessed person brings another to near-death, the entity can jump into that person, possessing them permanently. It would explain why I was always returned to my invisible state. They wanted me to keep using magic, so they could possess me again and again.'

Sebastian's face paled. 'Is that their agenda, to move in to people permanently? Did the one that possessed William jump into Cullen, and then make them all head for Achene?'

'It's entirely possible.' Duggan returned the book to its place on the shelf. 'Most religious texts put these creatures in a bad light. Often, they wish to upset whatever world-order is in place, controlling the innocent in order to bring their plans to fruition. What their intentions are in the larger scheme of things, I have no idea. It certainly looks like they want to put an end to the Folians – possibly because they also represent a threat in the same way that your cube does. They must be capable of purging the possessed, too.' He ran a hand through his hair. 'I can only imagine that Kerl had instructed the Alvarez head to learn that ability after realising what he was dealing with. Although, I don't see how William got possessed in the first place. He never used magic.'

'He went back to Chopwood without you,' Aryx said, 'and he spent time on Achene away from you. Where did he go?'

'Somewhere away from the Folians,' Sebastian said. 'They said they lost contact with him.'

'Then something else must have happened to him in my absence. I thought it was unusual for him to have taken the ship without telling me.'

Sebastian started rocking, his hands clamped tightly over his head. 'Oh, Gods! What do I do about the investigation? The authorities will want someone to pin the explosion on. This is all too much. Duggan wasn't responsible for his actions, but I can't blame biblical non-corporeal entities from another dimension. I need proof!'

'You'll just have to hide the video of Duggan outside the lab until we find concrete evidence to show that he wasn't acting of his own volition.'

'What about your cube-thing?' Duggan said. 'That's now got video evidence of possession on it.'

'Good point,' Sebastian said, brightening. 'Gladrin will want to see that I've completed my initiation test, and I can present the recording to him at the same time.'

'I can't see him buying the story,' Aryx said, 'and we can't hand over the Chopwood diary, as that'll expose the Folians.'

'By the Gods! Why does this have to be so difficult? Nothing is straightforward.'

Crouching, Duggan began collecting up the scattered drinks vessels. 'I'm sorry, Sebastian. It seems like this is all my fault. If I'd never gone to Achene . . .'

Aryx wheeled over to help collect up the debris.

'You can't be held responsible for the entities' actions,' Sebastian said. His wristcom bleeped. 'Yes?'

The ship computer spoke. 'Incoming alert from Tenebrae station. Secondary shipment of carbyne located.'

'I guess it's irrelevant now, but where is it?'

'Scanners detect the tracker aboard Tenebrae station.'

'*What!*'

'It was probably a shipment for Kerl, ordered before the explosion happened,' Aryx said.

'Either way, we have to go back to show Gladrin the video and give Wolfram back.'

'Do I not get a say in my own fate?'

'I assumed you'd want to go back to SpecOps.'

'They kept me in storage until I had been given to you. Do you really think they will allow me to remain active?'

'I don't know. Let's cross that bridge when we come to it. We'll see what he says.'

Duggan took the tray back to the kitchen. 'I'm sorry about the drinks. Would you like me to make some more?'

'No, it's fine, thanks,' Sebastian turned to face him. 'We have to go. Will you be alright if we head back to the station?'

'Yes, lad, I'll be fine. You go and sort out your evidence. I'm going to steer clear of magic for the time being, given the likelihood of getting possessed again.'

Aryx put the cube back in his pocket, and wheeled around from the couch area towards Duggan and extended his hand. 'It's been nice meeting you, if a little unusual.'

'Likewise. Come back and visit me again soon. Maybe we can have a drink that doesn't end up on the floor next time. Coffee is very expensive out here. Almost as expensive as antique Persian rugs.' He laughed.

Sebastian made to shake Duggan's hand, but the old man got in first with a hug that cracked his back.

His eyes were damp and reddening again. 'Thank you, my boy,' he said, trembling. 'Without you, I'd still be in that horrible state.'

Sebastian slapped Duggan's back repeatedly, apparently in an attempt to end the hug. 'I just wish it had been under better circumstances,' he wheezed.

Duggan let go and stepped back to shake his hand properly. 'You're welcome any time. Maybe you could talk me into visiting your station one day.'

'We'll see.' Sebastian turned towards the door. 'Stay safe! We'll see ourselves out.'

Aryx waved and followed him out to the docking area. 'That poor guy,' he said as he wheeled down the corridor. 'He must be in a right state after that.'

'I can't imagine how he must be feeling. He's been trying for years to get back to normal. To do so and then find out he was responsible for the explosion ... I don't know how I'd handle it.'

Sebastian fidgeted uncomfortably in the pilot's seat while the *Ultima Thule* docked with Tenebrae station and drifted through the dark transit tunnels on its way to the repair hangar. Aryx sat next to him in his wheelchair, with the cube on the console.

'What if Gladrin doesn't believe the video?' Sebastian asked.

'If he doesn't, he's an idiot.'

'If you can locate the tracker on the station,' Wolfram said, 'you could give him a sample of the mineral to back up the validity of the magic research.'

'Good idea. Computer, where exactly on the station is the tracker signal coming from?'

'Private hangar 74 29 alpha.'

'Redirect the *Ultima Thule* to that hangar.'

'Access denied.'

Sebastian punched a few commands into the console. 'Not ... any ... more.' He sat back with his hands behind his head. 'Now, take us to private hangar 74 29 alpha.'

'Acknowledged.' The ship changed direction at the next junction, sweeping into one of the station's spokes.

Aryx looked deep in thought. 'You know that demon picture Duggan showed us?'

'What about it?'

'I'm sure the thing in my nightmare the other day was one of those.'

'It's probably coincidence. You've been reading a fantasy novel, after all. Your imagination probably ran away with you before you went to sleep. I don't really buy the religious stuff, anyway.'

'Doesn't your faith have nasties that visit people in dreams?'

Sebastian rubbed his chin. 'There are draugr in Norse lore, but they're supposed to be the spirits of the dead that come back to repossess their own bodies, like zombies. Stories say they visit people in their dreams, but leave behind some indication that the dream was something real. I still don't believe any of that.'

'But you said the Folians existed in legends. They can't be the only things that are real.'

'Hmm.' He had a point; he couldn't deny everything forever, but then, he couldn't go around accepting the first explanation offered. 'I'll believe it when I see more proof. I'm not suddenly going to start worrying about extradimensional-zombie-demon-aliens visiting me in my sleep. I have a bad enough time as it is.'

'Getting strangled isn't proof enough?'

'You know what I mean. I think the dreams are coincidence.'

'You don't believe in coincidences—'

'By the Gods, *enough!*'

Aryx shrank back.

Sebastian folded his arms. 'I don't want to talk about it. Let's get this evidence and close the case.'

The ship emerged from the tunnels into the private docking bay. They exited, only to be greeted by an empty hangar. Against the nearest wall stood a hopper, similar to the ones Sebastian had seen on Sollers Hope.

Sebastian approached it. 'It's still sealed.'

'Don't try opening it. You'll have to move it into the airlock and put a pressure suit on. That way, you can evacuate it and take a sample without the rest evaporating.'

Sebastian dragged the wheeled hopper around to the airlock. Aryx boarded first and he followed, pulling the hopper up the ramp; he left it in the airlock and started to put on a pressure suit.

Aryx stopped him. 'You'd forget your head if it wasn't screwed on. You've still got the sample from Sollers Hope in your belt.'

Sebastian smacked his forehead. 'Oh, Gods, yes! We'd better keep the hopper on the ship, anyway – it is evidence, after all.'

'Something just occurred to me. The beta cube was in the possession of the terrorists *after* it was stolen from the university, wasn't it? And this was *before* SpecOps managed to acquire Wolfram, the alpha cube—'

'You're wondering if Kerl was in league with the ITF, researching magic as a weapon for them.'

'Yes.'

'I had considered it—' A gear in Sebastian's mind clunked into overdrive. 'When Gladrin gave me Wolfram to investigate, he said SpecOps thought it might be a weapons technology of some sort. The fact terrorists arrived in Yazor to get it back from us certainly shows they knew what it was and what it was capable of. Maybe they had given it to Kerl, and after the lab got destroyed they decided to track down the surviving unit.'

'Would there be evidence in the shipping logs that could show a link between them and Kerl?'

'Maybe . . .' Sebastian scratched his head. 'But on the other hand, even if he *wasn't* working with the terrorists, he would have had to acquire the cube from them for his research, anyway.'

'I know I'm going out on a limb here,' Aryx said, 'but what if SpecOps actually got *both* cubes from the terrorists, and Kerl got his from them?' He looked tense, as though expecting a violent outburst for criticising the beloved SpecOps.

Sebastian didn't react; unfortunately, Aryx had planted a seed of doubt in his mind – better to not support his suspicion; instead he stared at the pile of things left on the cargo bay floor, which included the survival gear. 'Are you going to clear that crap up at some point?'

Aryx sighed. 'Yes, I'll do it in a bit, but what about my idea?'

'Let's get back to our bay.' Sebastian headed up the ladder. 'I have some digging to do.'

He piloted the ship back to the repair bay in silence. Aryx's suggestion that SpecOps might have been involved in the research on the station did much to unsettle him. Could they really be involved in such an unethical act as dissecting a Human being and wiring it up to a computer? If the initial experiments had been sanctioned by SpecOps, surely they weren't aware of what had gone afterwards.

The ship arrived in the repair bay and Aryx began packing things away.

'What are you going to do while I'm investigating?' Sebastian asked.

'I was thinking of going to the gym, getting some overdue shut-eye, and if you don't need me I was hoping to spend tomorrow checking the mobipack for damage, and then maybe submit my patent proposal.'

'Sure. It's been a tiring few days – you have a rest. I'll work with Wolfram to extract the video so I can present it to Gladrin. I'll catch up with you on Monday.'

Aryx wheeled over to the lift. 'See you. Bye, Wolfram.'

'Bye Jim-Bob.'

Aryx laughed all the way out of the hangar.

When he had gone, Wolfram asked, 'What's your plan?'

'Get the video evidence from your database and show it to Gladrin. He hasn't seen any of the evidence – he's been busy off-station, apparently. Then I'll check the shipping logs from that hangar. If they don't turn up anything interesting, I'll hack into some records.'

'Whose records?'

He wasn't sure if he should tell the cube what he suspected. It wasn't like anyone could read the data in it, or torture it for information, after all. 'Kerl's, if I can. There are a few things that don't add up. Too many links with terrorists and, potentially, others.'

'I see. Would you like this information kept confidential?'

'Yes. I don't want Aryx to be accountable or put at risk if I'm wrong.'

'Of course. Would you like some help?'

'Definitely! You'll speed things up a lot. Do you mind copying the video evidence from the beta cube onto the ship's computer in a usable format?'

'Certainly. It may take an hour for me to reconstruct the streams and compress them adequately.'

He got up and stretched. He needed a shower and something to eat. 'Are you alright doing that if I leave you here for the night? If you need me, you can get me on my wristcom.'

'I'll be fine. Get some rest. You look tired.'

It sounded strange, speech like that coming from Wolfram. 'You've been using contractions lately ... Ever since that linguistic corruption.'

'I am sorry. I was unable to clear up all of the routines and certain changes became integrated. I can prevent it if necessary. Does it offend you?'

'No, I only just noticed it. It makes you sound more Human ... If you like sounding more Human, carry on. It's certainly an improvement over the TIs' speech.'

'Perhaps I will.'

He collected the evidence crate and put the melted cube in his rucksack. 'Let me know when you're done and I'll transfer the video to my office. I'll take this stuff to show to Gladrin. He's not seen the physical evidence yet. See you in the morning.'

'Good night, Sebastian.'

When he arrived at his apartment, a message was flashing on the terminal; a package had arrived and was waiting for him at the postal depot. He'd have to collect it after the meeting. 'Contact Agent Gladrin,' he said into his wristcom.

After a few moments, Gladrin answered. 'Hello, Agent Thorsson. How is your investigation progressing?'

'It's going well, for a change. I have some evidence to show you. Are you available to meet me at my office?'

'Not at the moment, but I can be there in twenty minutes.'

'I'll see you there, Sir.'

After a quick shower, he tucked the evidence crate under his arm and set off for the security offices. He checked his wristcom; it was 18.45. Q'orrig's should still be open by the time he'd finished; with the postal depot being a stone's throw away, it would make for a convenient excuse to stop by for pizza afterwards.

Gladrin was sitting at Sebastian's desk, waiting, with his hands folded in his lap. He looked pale and drawn.

'Are you alright, Sir?'

'A little tired. No need for concern. It's good to see you again. I gather you've been busy?'

'Yes, Sir.'

'So, what do you have for me?'

'I found traces of an unidentified mineral outside the lab that may have been used to cause the explosion.'

Gladrin raised an eyebrow. 'Interesting.'

'We managed to track down the source of the mineral and found a shipment of it on the station. Video evidence that I recovered from the scene indicates that it may have been used in the lab itself.' He didn't want to involve Duggan unless he was pressed.

The agent's eyes widened and his body stiffened, almost imperceptibly. 'What does the video show?'

'Some rather strange research. The data was corrupted but we managed to retrieve a fair amount. I can transfer it to you once it has finished processing.'

Gladrin coughed dryly. 'What kind of research?'

Sebastian scratched his nose with his free hand. 'I'd rather you watch the video. You wouldn't believe me if I told you. There's also this.' He placed the evidence crate on the desk.

'This has all been checked?'

'Yes, I did it myself. It's clean, and safe to handle.'

Gladrin began rifling through the contents of the box. He appeared tense. 'And what of the project I assigned you?'

'It turned out to be an artificial intelligence, of sorts.'

Gladrin's shoulders lowered. 'Good work. You have it with you?' He held out his hand.

A knot formed in Sebastian's stomach; what would happen to Wolfram if he handed him over? Something at the back of his mind tugged away, making him feel uneasy. Wolfram should have a choice.

'Well?' Gladrin said, still holding his hand out.

'The cube? It got destroyed when we crashed on the planet where the mineral came from.' For the first time in his life, Sebastian lied. He'd withheld information in the line of work when it was necessary, twisted the truth – when necessary – but this was the first time he'd completely fabricated a story. 'Aryx managed to get the casing off it, but a fire broke out in the ship when we crashed. By the time we put it out, the cube was damaged beyond repair and I wasn't able to salvage any of the data – it came out garbled.' He reached into his rucksack, pulled out the melted lump, and dropped it in the agent's outstretched hand.

Gladrin's face fell. 'I suppose you've passed your initiation, given that you determined it to be an SI. It's a shame that it was the only one left.' He tossed the beta cube in the crate along with the other cremated evidence. 'Well done, though. I look forward to seeing the video evidence when it's ready. Hopefully we can get to the bottom of the case. I will see you tomorrow.' He stood and held out his hand.

'Goodbye, Sir.' The shake was cold and clammy.

Sebastian left the office and stopped at an emergency medical dispenser to replenish the medkit and nanobot vial. His stomach rumbled. 'Computer,' he said into his wristcom, 'put me through to Q'orrig's Pizzeria.'

'Rrrrttt! Q'orrig's. What you want?'

'I'd like to place an order for a pizza to collect. Olives and anchovies.'

'Twelve credit, pay up front.'

He tapped a command into the wristcom.

'Ready in fifteen minute. Thank for you custom.' The comm went dead.

He jogged to the post office booth in the atrium. While he waited in the queue leading up to the opening in the wall, he eyed up the other customers warily. If only the idea of possessed people hadn't entered his mind ... If he didn't know about them, he probably wouldn't have been so on edge.

He finally reached the front of the queue. The postal worker was a short, dumpy heap of a man with lank, greasy hair. Sebastian held out his hand and the man placed it on the scanner to verify his identity; he cringed, and as soon as the postal worker scuttled off, he wiped his hand on his suit. The man came back and handed over a small, brown paper-wrapped package. Sebastian took it with a nod and began walking to Q'orrig's. While he strolled along, he unwrapped the bundle; it contained a tooled leather-bound book with marbling on the page edges. There was no title on the cover. It looked old. Old, and familiar.

A piece of paper sticking out from between the pages caught his attention and he pulled it out:

Dear Seb,

I was going through those old boxes of your father's that Mike had put into storage before he died and found this – it's your grandfather's journal. I couldn't make much sense of it. I'm sure he'd written half of it when he got dementia. I don't know if any of it means anything or not, but I know how much you love his old exploring gear, so I thought you'd like this as well.

Love, Janyce and Erik

P.S. Give me a call when you get this. Your office said you've been out and about a lot, so I didn't want to bother you at the wrong time.

She was right about the journal. The soft leather stirred memories of his childhood, and as he leafed through the pages, it roused the urge to explore exotic worlds – even though he'd only just got back from one. Numerous diagrams, depicting geometric shapes and designs, lay scattered through the book, interspersed with strange formulae, lists of words, and sections that looked like hand-drawn sheet music. He hurriedly tucked it into his rucksack; it wouldn't be easy to read while carrying a pizza, and he had no intention of getting such a treasure greasy.

Q'orrig's was about to close when he arrived. He waved at the waitress who had started pulling the blinds down. Apparently recognising him, she went to the back of the shop and came out with his order in a large, flat box. He thanked her and made a start on it – Aryx would have thrown a fit if he'd seen him eating and walking at the same time.

He stood at the terminal chewing on a slice while he waited for a lift to arrive. The doors opened, revealing Ms Stevens, hugging the ubiquitous infoslate.

'Hello, Sebastian.' She nodded.

He hesitated before stepping in. 'Hello.'

She glanced down at the box and looked up at him. 'I never fancied you as a pizza person.'

He gulped down the piece he'd stuffed into his mouth and forced a smile. 'You never can tell.'

Stevens drew her hair over her ear with a finger and pushed her glasses back up her nose.

'Do you mind if I ask you something personal?' Sebastian said.

She smiled. 'Go on.'

'Why do you wear glasses? Why not get your eyes corrected?'

'Oh, I thought you were ... never mind.' She looked down and peered over the frames at him. 'They don't have proper lenses. I had my eyes done years ago, but people always seemed to take me more seriously when I wore them. Chauvinism hasn't been eradicated, you know.'

He drew back. His own first impressions of her *had* been a little sexist. Best not push the point further.

'I saw Gladrin yesterday. I gave him the bug from your ship.'

'What did he say?'

'Nothing, strangely enough. He didn't say why it was there, but it isn't standard practise to bug ships.'

His scalp crawled. If the act of bugging ships was a secret kept even from SpecOps employees, Gladrin wouldn't have mentioned the snoopers to him ... Oh, what a fool. Gladrin *wouldn't* have mentioned them, except as disinformation to hide the *real* bug. But why would he have bugged the *Ultima Thule* ...? Or was it the terrorists? They had turned up shortly after Aryx had used the comms to tell him the cube was active.

The bugged comms. Oh Gods.

The seed of doubt Aryx had planted had sprouted and grown roots. There were too many strange coincidences, and there definitely was no such thing as coincidence.

'He called it an SI. Oh, I'm an idiot!'

'Called what an SI?' Stevens looked at him over her unnecessary glasses again.

'The project Gladrin gave me. It's nothing. I shouldn't have mentioned it.' Gladrin definitely knew about the cube in the lab – his reactions betrayed that much. The way he'd repeated himself; his cold hands; that he knew it was called an SI when Sebastian hadn't even mentioned the term. If he knew *that,* he had probably been working with Kerl. He'd know the burnt cube came from the lab; he'd know Sebastian had lied. He'd been so keen to believe Gladrin wasn't capable of allowing such despicable things to go on that he'd ignored all the signs. 'How was Gladrin when you spoke to him?'

'He seemed a little odd, not his usual self.'

'How so? Was he acting strange? Do you know him well?'

'We've worked together on several projects over the years, so I'd like to think I know him. He's normally very friendly, but lately when I've seen him – and that hasn't been often, as he seems to be around less and less – he's been quite withdrawn. I can't put my finger on it. It's like when you bump into an old friend you've not seen for years and they don't recognise you immediately. He's probably got a lot on his mind.'

A lot on his mind indeed. Working with the terrorists. Either that, or one of those entities from Kerl's experimentation had possessed him. If his behaviour really had changed, it would certainly fit the symptoms. He had to get back to the ship. 'Computer, redirect lift to maintenance.'

The lift stopped.

'This is where I get off, Ms Stevens.' He nodded and stepped out into the corridor.

'If you get time for that drink—' The lift doors closed.

* * *

Sebastian arrived back at the hangar with his stomach about to explode in a fiery, acidic mess. Aryx's admonishments were well-founded. He entered the ship and made his way to the cockpit.

'I've finished transcoding the video,' Wolfram said. 'It took less time than anticipated. Why have you come back early?'

'I had to lie to Gladrin.' He sat down at the console. 'There were too many things that didn't add up, and he seemed to be looking for something specific in the evidence box. I told him you were destroyed in the crash and gave him the other SI.'

'It's wise that you did. I took the liberty of tracing the shipping logs from the private bay in which you found the carbyne shipment. The only ship in or out of that bay over the last two weeks was a rented vessel registered to Agent Gladrin. I then traced the records relating to the hire of the private laboratory. Payments appeared to come from Gladrin to cover the rent. Gladrin also had large payments coming from Earth, but I have as of yet been unable to trace their exact source. However, after scanning police files, it seems that several known terrorist supporters have received funds along similar channels. The size of the payments is also very suspicious.'

'You hacked his accounts?'

'I felt it prudent to do it myself, so that you would not be left accountable. I used several net hops and deleted logs far faster than you would have been capable. I did, however, have to use your credentials to gain access to the police files, as you are already permitted legitimate access.'

'Thanks for the consideration, but for all that I don't think it'll help,' he said, biting a nail. 'If he's involved, he'll know I lied to him anyway. I'll need to contact SpecOps or EarthSec directly and present the evidence of his involvement. There's one other thing. I bumped into Stevens on the way here. She said Gladrin's behaviour has changed recently, and I wonder if he might be under the control of the same entities that took over Alvarez and the others.'

'Gladrin is not a practitioner of thaumaturgy, is he?'

'Not to my knowledge.' He bit his lip. Perhaps there was another cause. 'I wonder ... Can you search records faster than the security TI?'

'I believe so. What would you like me to look for?'

'Search medical databases and news reports for references to sudden changes in behaviour that match symptoms similar to those of the possession cases we've seen. If there's another vector, other than through the use of magic, he could be under the entities' control.'

'I will work on that now ... Given that Aryx is associated with the investigation, do you think it would be prudent to inform him of

Gladrin's involvement?'

The fleeting urge to call his friend came and went. 'No, Aryx can take care of himself. I'll call him in the morning.' He yawned. 'I should get an early night and call Janyce to thank her for the journal she sent me. The time difference is a killer.' He set a reminder in the computer to wake him at three in the morning. 'Can you monitor ship security? I'm going to sleep downstairs tonight while you search for those records. If Gladrin is working for the terrorists, or if he's possessed, I wouldn't put it past him to hack into the ship and assassinate me in my sleep, or something. At least you can prevent an override.'

'Of course. I will also monitor Aryx's quarters.'

'You can do that?'

'I have had ample time to study the station's security protocols. Your routines are difficult to circumvent but, with my abilities, not impossible.'

Sebastian crossed his arms and shook his head. 'I'm glad you're the only one of your kind and are on our side!' He stood up. 'I'll see you in the morning.'

'Good night, Sebastian.'

The computer woke him at three in the morning, as requested, with a reminder to call Janyce. He felt tired, but at least he had slept well – whatever was causing the nightmares didn't appear to affect them when they slept on the ship, or off the station. He climbed the ladder into the cockpit and sat at the piloting console. A few taps later he'd established a comm-link with Earth.

The comms' 'ringing' screen came up. It rang. And rang.

A woman with short black hair answered. 'Hi! You must be Sebastian. I've seen you in photos.'

'Who are you?'

'I'm Janyce's neighbour.'

'What are you doing there? Where is she?'

'I'm looking after her cat. I got a message from her saying that she and Erik had to go out of town on an emergency. I can't find the cat's bowl to put the food down.'

Janyce never said anything about a cat. 'What sort of emergency?'

'A family emergency.'

'Janyce doesn't *have* any other family. When was this?'

'A couple of hours ago.'

'What *exactly* did she say to you?'

'I've got the memo here—'

His stomach quivered. 'You didn't *speak* to her?'

'No.' The woman put her hand to her mouth. 'Is there something wrong?'

'Most definitely.'

'If there's—' He cut the comms before she could finish. What could have happened to them? The timing was too suspicious.

'Computer, where is Agent Gladrin?'

'Agent Gladrin is not aboard the station.'

His mind filled with a haze. He couldn't think straight.

'Your heart rate is elevated,' Wolfram said. 'Are you anxious?'

'I need to find out where Gladrin is.'

'One moment.'

He bit his nails while he waited for the cube to continue. The lights on its side were flashing frantically.

'Records show that Gladrin's ship left the station several hours ago. The flight plan indicates that he was heading to Earth. You look pale – are you ill?'

'Not as ill as Gladrin's going to be when I get my hands on him. I think that bastard's on to us and he's kidnapped my family!'

Chapter 34

'Computer, call Aryx Trevarian,' Sebastian said, his voice trembling, hands shaking. If Gladrin did anything to his family, he'd kill him.

The comms were answered a moment later and an image of Aryx's room, lit only by the terminal, appeared. He was sitting on his bed and looked like he'd been sweating.

'Sorry to call you this time of the morning.' Sebastian fought to keep his voice steady.

'It's okay, I was already awake. What's up? You look like you've seen a ghost.'

'Gladrin's left the station, heading for Earth. Ordinarily it wouldn't be a problem, but I think he knows I'm on to him, and now Janyce and Erik have gone missing!'

'What do you mean, *on to him?*'

'He knows things about the investigation that he shouldn't . . .' He quickly explained his findings while Aryx dressed. '. . . And to top it all, I think he's possessed.'

'Are you nuts? How could he get possessed if he doesn't use magic?'

Sebastian shook his head. 'I don't know, but Stevens said he's behaving strangely, which causes me to suspect that's the case. I've got Wolfram researching it now.'

'Who's Stevens?'

'Another SpecOps agent on the station—'

'Sebastian,' Wolfram said, 'I have found references to the symptoms.'

'Let's hear it.'

'Barring unreliable references from the Middle Ages and those symptomatic cases that have already been ruled out by other accurately diagnosed psychological and neurological conditions, in recent times there have been incidents of something known as "acceleration psychosis" – a condition anecdotally connected with travel via acceleration nodes. It's a rare condition that affects approximately one in a billion Humans during travel using the nodes and, in most recorded cases, the sufferers either inexplicably disappeared or killed themselves. The cause of the condition is still unexplained.'

'Disappeared, or escaped observation?' Aryx asked over the comms, pulling on his jacket.

'One would presume, escaped.'

'Wonderful, now Gladrin's a one-in-a-billion psychopath and space travel has become even more dangerous ... Aryx, we need to track him down and find out what he's done with my family.'

He was already in his wheelchair. 'I'm on my way.'

'Don't forget the mobipack.'

'Got it.' The comms cut off.

Sebastian bit his nails to the quick while he waited for Aryx to arrive. Concern for his family's safety grated against a twinge of excitement at the prospect of going back to Earth and seeing the white spires jutting up from the lush forests again. He mentally chastised himself for allowing his thoughts to drift in that way, and resumed nibbling at his fingers.

After a couple of minutes, he spat out a sliver of nail. 'I need to contact EarthSec, see if I can get a trace on his ship without letting SpecOps know. If they get involved, Gladrin might do something.'

An incoming message alert appeared on the console. The message was text-only.

Sebastian,

I'm sorry it's come to this, but the powers that be would like the SI returned. It is obvious that you now know what it is, what it's capable of, and that you will not return it willingly. Therefore, I have taken your sister and nephew as insurance that you will comply with my request. I will send you coordinates to a drop-point in due time, where I will meet you to make the exchange. If you inform SpecOps of my involvement, I will not be able to guarantee their safety.

Marcus Gladrin

Sebastian slammed his fist on the console. 'Damn it!'

'Are you okay?' Aryx's voice came from behind him.

He swivelled the chair around. 'No. And I think I'm allowed to not be alright, given the circumstances. How are we going to track him down? I can't think straight.'

Aryx wheeled up to the pilot's console. 'Have you tried running one of those traceroute thingies on the message?'

'Not yet. It's only just arrived.'

'While you have been talking, I have been investigating. The message was sent from inside the station on a time delay.'

'Shit. I'm going to have to go through security.' Sebastian took a deep breath. 'Computer, contact EarthSec headquarters.'

'Acknowledged. Connecting.'

The link was audio only. 'This is Earth Security headquarters,' said a cool, female voice. 'How can I help?'

'This is Sebastian Thorsson of Tenebrae station. I need flight records for the following transport.' He typed digits into the console. 'I have reason to believe that it is transporting contraband imported via Tenebrae, and that the pilot is responsible for several security breaches aboard the station.' The second time he had lied. Under the circumstances it seemed acceptable.

Aryx grinned.

'One moment while I retrieve the logs.'

Aryx reached over and muted the comms. 'Will they give you the flight path logs, just like that?'

'I hope so. That's why I made out that he's responsible for a few infractions on the station. They're quite compliant when it comes to internal affairs.' Sebastian un-muted the comms.

The woman's voice returned. 'Oh, that's odd . . . There appears to be no record of a flight plan after the ship departed—'

'Oh, crap!'

'If I may continue,' the woman said, 'the ship is still registered on the GalComm network. My technicians inform me that you may be able to locate the ship using the comm relay registry. I will forward the ship's serial and logs to you. I'm sorry I couldn't be of more help.' An incoming file alert flashed up on the console.

'It's fine, thanks for the info. It should prove useful. Goodbye.'

'Goodbye and good luck.' The link went dead.

Sebastian activated the map, transferred the file to it, and set it to display the communications network.

'What good will this do?' Aryx asked.

'The comms relays have addresses. Ships register with the nearest relay when they enter a system, and any communication coming from or to it will contain a list of addresses that the signal passes through. If we ping his serial, we can traceroute the response and find out where he is.' Sebastian instructed the computer to display the routes indicated by the EarthSec log and the map changed, highlighting the systems the ship had passed through in red. The route appeared zigzagged but, as he studied it, he realised it followed a relatively straight path away from Earth.

'Where's he heading?'

'I don't know. The path is straight enough to make it look like he has a specific destination in mind.'

'Might I suggest,' Wolfram said, 'that you project the line farther. There are several large stations along that trajectory.'

Sebastian rubbed his chin. 'True, but most of them would require branching off before this point here ...' He pointed at the display a couple of jumps ahead of the last comms relay that Gladrin's ship had been registered with. A line joined several systems in sequence, closed in on either side by large expanses of void. 'If you follow the line past Ross-Vegas channel along the narrow part, through Bansa's Gurge, you have Vardstrom Observatory and Kimberley depot the other side. If we headed for that node now, we might get an idea of which of the two he's heading for by the time we reach it.'

'Vardstrom? That rings a bell ... Hey, that was the name of the medical officer who wrote the journal we found in Chopwood. That place could have been set up by his descendants. How far is it?'

'Only a few jumps. It's too far to risk aiming for directly. He's several hops ahead of us, but I think if we plan the route correctly we can get there in four or five hours.' Sebastian yawned and put a hand over his mouth.

'You look tired. Have you had *any* sleep?'

'A little. I slept here after I began to suspect Gladrin, but I'm still worn out. At least I didn't have a nightmare.'

'I had one just before you called. It's definitely something on the station causing them. Did you look at the message logs?'

Sebastian shook his head. 'I set the computer to trace them, but I haven't looked to see if the results are back yet. I don't know if you've noticed, but I've not exactly had the time to investigate a little thing like that!'

Aryx put his hands up. 'Hey! No pressure, it was just a thought.'

Sebastian sighed and began tapping commands into the console, plotting a course for a node ahead of Gladrin's ship. 'Once this is all over, I'll look into it, I promise.'

'Why don't you get some rest? I'll take over from here and let you know when we're getting close.'

'I won't be able to sleep.'

'At least lie down on the seats at the back, do something to give your body a chance to recuperate.'

'Just for a while, but I need to think.' He walked to the back of the ship and lay down across the three seats opposite the diagnostic console.

'Off we go.'

The ship lurched as the docking arm lifted it into the transport rings. He felt a little uncomfortable letting Aryx fly; he'd been told on many occasions that he didn't make a good passenger. The situation at hand didn't help, either. He closed his eyes. Staring at the ceiling while he thought it over wasn't going to help.

Once they'd worked out where Gladrin was going, how would they rescue Janyce and Erik without handing over Wolfram? What would happen to him if they did? If Gladrin was possessed, the entity controlling him would most likely try to destroy the cube. If that wasn't the case, and he was working for the terrorists, they'd probably try to use it as a weapon. He didn't doubt Wolfram's integrity, nor the security of his database, but somehow the other copy had been convinced to work with Kerl on the magic research.

'Wolfram, if you had been in the beta cube's position, how would Kerl have convinced you to work with him?'

Wolfram replied at a volume loud enough for Sebastian to hear from across the cockpit. Aryx put his hands over his ears. 'If I deemed the research to be for the betterment of Humanity—

'Sorry, Aryx.' Wolfram's voice stopped and instead came from the comms unit behind Sebastian's head. 'Or if I believed that it was harmless research, but would add to my experience, I would be likely to help. My curiosity is a major driving force, but it would be unlikely to override my sense of ethics. However, in retrospect, seeing what happened in the laboratory afterwards would have prevented further co-operation on my part.'

'So why would the beta cube have continued co-operating?' Sebastian asked, keeping his eyes closed.

'That I do not know. We don't know whether the unit was tampered with physically – after all, the casing was missing – and after I effected the purging on Duggan, the effort of utilising full processor power left me vulnerable while the heat dissipated. However, conventional code tampering is not possible due to the unconventional structure of my intelligence matrix. It is possible that Kerl convinced it that it was necessary to keep experimenting in order to find a solution to the possession problem. This would also be plausible motivation if the cube saw possession as a threat to Humanity.'

'I understand that. Whatever the reasons behind it, you now have knowledge that is dangerous to everyone. Using thaumaturgy, you could be sneaked into places where conventional explosives would otherwise be detected, and who knows what other effects you're capable of.'

'I have not yet analysed all of the experiences present in my database. After the initial cursory scan, I felt it might be dangerous to integrate too many segments. Parts of the data are corrupted, particularly the recordings of the results of the effects, but the impressions required to perform them are intact. I don't know what the final results will be. I can only attempt to deduce the effects from the words—'

'Wait! You *felt* it might be dangerous?'

'I analysed the potential consequences of integrating the information, and deemed it to be an unnecessary risk at the time. *Felt* may be an inaccurate term. I made a value *judgement*.'

'I think you may be more Human than you think.'

'I will try not to take that as an insult.'

Sebastian laughed.

'However dangerous to myself, I would be willing to integrate the experiences if it helps to get your sister-in-law and nephew back.'

He felt a lump in his throat and croaked, 'Thank you.' His stomach turned and he began to slide along the seats towards the cockpit. That felt like the longest launch ever.

Wolfram paused. 'After an initial cursory search of the data, I have discovered that, in addition to the purging ability, there is a minor kinetic manipulation effect, rapid acceleration, slowing, something that translates as *light from nowhere*, and several more harmful sounding effects.'

Sebastian opened his eyes. 'What sort of harmful effects are we talking about?' Anything that could be used as a non-lethal weapon would be helpful. He still hadn't practised with the pistol, and the idea of getting into a firefight with Gladrin, where he could accidentally hurt his family, filled him with dread.

'Some of the effects seem to be neuropathic. One appears to be *shooting pains*. I cannot tell whether this is something that would cause physical damage or whether the effect is hallucinatory.'

'I'm hoping for the latter. Is there any way to trigger the effects instantly, rather than having to wait for the chanting?'

The voice over the intercom paused. 'From my experience of triggering the purging effect back in Yazor, I discovered that my processor locks up with practically one hundred per cent load while processing the data. This prevents me from receiving sensory input, however the button on the side of my casing can be used as a hardware interrupt. If you notify me in advance, I could potentially hold a charged effect – casing temperature permitting – until you pressed the button to trigger it.'

'So I could strap you to a gun and press the button to fire off the spell?'

'Technically, yes. If you designated a face on my casing to be the front, you could simply aim me at the target and press the button on the side of the casing.'

He swung his legs onto the floor and sat up. 'Aryx!'

Aryx turned to face him. 'What's up?' he said, narrowing his eyes.

'Why are you grinning like that?'

'I've got a job for you, my friend.'

Sebastian had taken over piloting the ship, and now Aryx sat at the diagnostics workbench with Wolfram on the console next to him. He wasn't sure where to start – it wasn't even clear what Sebastian wanted.

'How do you expect this thing to be attached?' he said, waving the pistol about.

'Can you fix the cube onto the barrel somehow?'

He studied the pistol. In a departure from the conventional cylindrical design, SpecOps had chosen a square profile for the projectile weapon's outer barrel. At least that might help with mounting the cube. 'Well, you don't want me to stick it on the top, or you won't be able to aim the gun. Not only that, it'll be top-heavy.'

'How about slinging it underneath in front of the trigger?'

'That could work.' He turned the gun over in his hands. There might be space.

'May I suggest,' Wolfram said, 'that if I am placed in front of the trigger, my top surface should be positioned towards the hand-grip and my vented face against the barrel so that the button on my side can be reached by Sebastian's right-hand trigger finger. That configuration would also give clear visibility to the bar indicator from the left-hand side of the gun. It will be necessary to see the indicator in the event that I have to trigger one of the quantum effects.'

'Call them spells,' Sebastian said, 'or choose a better word. *Quantum effects* doesn't quite "say it".'

'Very well. One of the *thaumatics*.'

Aryx picked up the cube and rotated it as directed. Wolfram was right – if it were mounted in front of the trigger, Sebastian's finger, once extended, would be able to press the button easily. 'How do you want me to attach you?'

'I would prefer my casing to remain intact. I suggest mounting a plate on the front of the trigger guard. I can open my interface port and lock it into place, providing greater security. Perhaps you could use the attachment you made to interface me with the beta cube?'

He fumbled around in the storage underneath the console and took out the cabling. 'Here it is. I don't like the thought of stripping all these wires off after all that work, though.'

'What is the trigger mechanism of the pistol?'

'Electromechanical.'

'Sebastian, how much practise have you had with this weapon?'

'None at all. I haven't fired one since basic training. I've been worried about what might happen if I came to use it.'

'He probably couldn't hit the broad side of a barn.'

'That is why I asked about the trigger mechanism. If you can connect the wires to the trigger circuitry, I can override it.'

Aryx laughed.

'What?' Sebastian asked.

'Our friend here will be able to stop you from shooting the wrong person by accident.'

Sebastian's eyes widened. 'How?'

'He can override the trigger. He can calculate the trajectory of the bullet, based on your movement, and if he sees you're aiming at the wrong person, the gun won't fire.'

The creases in Sebastian's brow vanished. Aryx hadn't realised how much the thought of having to use the gun worried him.

'I can also do the reverse, if required, and fire on demand.'

Aryx shuddered; he might trust the cube, but wasn't prepared to let his own trust take Sebastian that far. Nevertheless, he set about trimming some of the wires short and welded the plate onto the trigger guard of the pistol. When he'd finished, he presented the contraption to Sebastian, who weighed it in his hands.

'Good work. Let's see what it's like with Wolfram attached.'

Aryx passed the cube to him. Wolfram opened the connector cover and Sebastian placed the opening over the plate. The clamps locked into place with a loud snap. Sebastian felt the weight again.

'It's a bit heavy on the front, but it's better than nothing. It's a shame it won't fit in the holster.'

'You're never happy.' Aryx rolled his eyes. 'You've got the galaxy's first truly intelligent gun and it's not enough.'

'I'm joking. It's brilliant—' Sebastian yawned again and put the gun back on the console. 'Do you think you can take over again for a bit? We'll be there in an hour or so, and I *really* need some sleep.'

'Knock yourself out.'

He headed downstairs and within moments the snore was echoing up the ladder shaft.

'He is feeling very pressured,' Wolfram said.

'I know. I think it helps knowing you'll be able to make him safer with the gun. I'm amazed he hasn't cracked up one side and down the other with everything that's been going on over the last few days, especially with how little sleep he's had. That reminds me, he hasn't had a chance to check if the station's computer analysed those logs from the blank messages. Can you look into it?'

'Fortunately, as we are within the path of a comms carrier wave, I can. One moment.'

It was disconcerting to see a large cube with a gun attached, flashing randomly. It looked like a bomb about to go off. He had to stop his obsession with bomb comparisons.

The lights stopped. 'The signals originated from outside the station. I am unable to determine the exact source, as it appears that they were routed through the acceleration node network itself, and not as an interplexed communications signal through the relays.'

'That's ... odd.'

'Indeed. It also appears that a piece of code was inserted into the security network using Gladrin's credentials several months ago. The code acts as a back door, allowing the signal to be routed to specific communications terminals on the station. One would assume that it also configured the analogue relay antenna to pick up the aforementioned signal.'

'Is there anything special about the timing of the signal? We were having nightmares and waking up around three in the morning.'

'That would be consistent with the terminal activation times. There is one other thing that I noticed while investigating Gladrin's files. The date on which the signal was first routed to Sebastian's quarters coincides with a date in Gladrin's journal.'

'What date?'

'Four weeks ago. It correlates directly to the date Gladrin received the recommendation from Eleanor Bannik, referring him for membership into SpecOps.'

Aryx bit his lip.

Rainbow-hued stars poured by as the ship gusted through a bright, stringy nebulae en-route to the node they hoped Gladrin would pass. The anticipation and constant monitoring of the comms map grated on every nerve in Aryx's body. He could have allowed the ship to monitor the situation, or given the task to Wolfram, but he felt that he would be able to act quicker if he stayed alert and kept an eye on the screens himself.

'This is horrible,' he said, rubbing his eyes. 'I feel utterly useless.'

'You are far from useless,' Wolfram said. 'You demonstrate great engineering skill and are an asset to all whom you assist.'

'I wasn't speaking generally, but thanks. I meant this situation is frustrating. We're at the mercy of the acceleration nodes as to how much time it will take to catch up with Gladrin.'

'He undoubtedly has similar delays.'

'I know, I just hope he doesn't hurt Janyce or Erik. It would kill Sebastian if anything happened to them.' He turned his attention to the map once again.

'If it comes down to it and Sebastian is forced to hand me over, I will destroy myself once I know you are all safe.'

'We won't let that happen. We both consider you a friend, and we don't leave our friends behind.' He felt a sting in his eyes as he forced the tightness out of this throat.

The ship dropped out of superphase and navigated to the next node without incident. Half an hour into the transit from the next node, a change in the relay map caught Aryx's attention. Gladrin's ship had passed the branch point.

'He's heading for Kimberley depot.' He entered post-transit commands into the navigation computer, altering the destination for the next node hop. 'With any luck we won't be too far from the node. I'll go and wake Sebastian.'

Sebastian was curled up in a foetal position on the webbing of the bunk. It was the first time in weeks Aryx had seen him without his permanent expression of worry. He almost regretted having to wake him, but at least they now had an explanation as to why they slept better away from their apartments. 'Sorry, fella, I know you need your sleep.' He gently shook his shoulder.

Sebastian blinked awake. 'What's happening?'

'Gladrin's heading to Kimberly depot. I've set the computer to change course when we drop out of superphase. With luck, we should be there soon.'

He scrambled off the webbing and fell to the floor as he caught his foot between the straps.

'Careful! We've got at least half an hour before we hit the next node.'

'I can't help it. I'm going to pieces.' Sebastian clamped his hands over his head and the creases returned.

'Come on, let's go up,' Aryx said, wheeling onto the lift. He got off at the top and Sebastian's head popped up through the ladder shaft.

'By the Gods!' His eyes were wide. 'What are the chances of that?'

Aryx turned to follow his gaze. The enormous scaffold of the acceleration node loomed immediately ahead. The ship had dropped out of superphase almost on top of it.

'Thirty seconds to alignment,' Wolfram said.

The ship slewed to avoid the capture radius and began lining up along the vector to Kimberley depot.

'Well, that was lucky.'

'There's no such thing as luck,' Sebastian said, and vanished back down below.

'A message from Gladrin arrived moments ago,' Wolfram said.

'What does it say?' Sebastian shouted.

Wolfram switched to the intercom and his voice echoed throughout the ship. 'He has transmitted a locker number and expects you to deposit me. Once deposited, he will transmit the location of Janyce and Erik to you.'

'Like hell, he will.' *Thump!*

Aryx winced.

A few minutes later, Sebastian came back up the ladder brandishing a handful of vials.

'What have you been doing?'

'I was in the airlock, getting some more carbyne, just in case I need it. Wolfram can't exactly purge Gladrin without it, can he?'

'I guess not.' Aryx said. If his own family had still been alive, they'd never have believed him if he'd told them a computer could do magic – actually, they'd probably have had him committed for mentioning magic in the first place.

One by one, Sebastian slotted the vials into his belt. 'Will these be close enough to you, Wolfram?'

'I do not believe so,' the cube said, still attached to the pistol on the console. 'The research indicates that unless the quantity is substantial, I will need to be closer to it.'

Sebastian fumbled with his right-hand sleeve, withdrew one of the vials, and slid it down into the cuff. 'How's that? It should be a couple of inches away when I'm holding the gun.'

'That will be adequate.'

'Great, then we're all set. I just wish I'd had a longer rest.'

'That reminds me,' Aryx said. 'I got Wolfram to go over the message logs—'

'Not the damned dreams again.'

He glared at Sebastian. 'For crying out loud, will you listen for once? We found that Gladrin planted a Trojan on the station's system that enabled a signal to be forwarded to our terminals. He installed it a few months ago, probably not long after he first visited.'

'That doesn't surprise me.'

'What might surprise you is that four weeks ago, when your night-mares began, the signal started coming through your terminal. It was also the exact time Gladrin first mentioned you in his private files, after you were referred for recruitment.'

'So you're saying that it's Gladrin's fault we've been having night-mares?'

'Sort of. The signal came from outside the station, relayed by the analogue antenna. It was directed *through* the acceleration node network from somewhere beyond.'

'How is that unusual?' Sebastian folded his arms.

'You aren't listening! The signal wasn't relayed through the *relays*.

It travelled directly along the network, through the nodes themselves!'

Sebastian's face twisted. 'Are you saying he intentionally caused us to have nightmares? Why? What sort of signal is it?'

'I don't know, but it's obviously not conventional. I've never heard of anything like it.'

'There are instances of magnetic fields applied to the Human brain inducing sensations of presences—' Wolfram said.

'That's different to causing bad dreams.'

Sebastian's eyes narrowed. 'Given that our nightmares had demons in them, do you think Gladrin's working with others who are possessed, and they're doing something to us by sending the signal?'

'I don't know what they'd hope to achieve.'

'Maybe the signal is two-way,' Wolfram said.

'What?'

'Let me put it another way. Perhaps the entities can use the signal to test your responses to psychological stimuli.'

Aryx looked at Sebastian. He could see the cogs going round in his head while he thought it over.

'So Aryx, Karan, and I start getting "tested" with bad dreams the day I'm mentioned in Gladrin's files ... Perhaps his outside colleagues were somehow trying to determine whether we could be coerced – he did say that I'd been selected for the job based on my personality. Maybe they're trying to wear us down for some reason. Weaken our minds, or something. The entity that possessed Duggan said it wanted to use me to destroy the abomination, the *mechanism*, which I guess is Wolfram – no offence.'

'None taken.'

'I don't get it,' Aryx said. 'Why recruit you and use you to investigate the SI if their intention is to destroy it?'

'I have no idea,' Sebastian said. 'It could be they hoped I would learn how it worked, and then by possessing me at a later date, they could use my knowledge to destroy it, or turn it to their ends. Only Gladrin would be able to tell us the truth of it.' He re-folded his arms and leaned back in his seat. 'If it is true, I find it ironic that by recruiting me, they've helped me discover a weapon against them.'

Aryx shrugged. 'I can't understand it. This is all like some bloody fairy story dropped in the Space-Age, and the only thing that can stop these invisible bogey-men from taking over the universe,' he said, waving his hand towards Wolfram, 'is this weird ... confluence of science and magic.'

Sebastian slapped him squarely on the shoulder. 'Hey, you told me that *I* had to be more open-minded!'

*   *   *

Forty-five minutes later the stretched rainbows resolved themselves into stars and the ship dropped back into phase with normal space. Kimberley depot lay several thousand kilometres ahead, golden and glinting like a tiny Christmas-tree bauble.

'We've arrived,' Aryx said. In some strange way it didn't feel right, having to chase down the man who had ultimately given him his freedom back.

'You ever been here before?' Sebastian asked, looking at an image of the station on the console.

'No, I haven't – but I hear it's a technical masterpiece.'

Kimberley depot was nowhere near as grand in scale as Tenebrae, but no less a feat of engineering. The structure hung in open space, slowly rotating, resembling a giant, golden ball, with only a handful of large dimples in its surface.

Sebastian leaned forwards to study the image. 'What are those satellite things in orbit?'

While Aryx watched, the dimples in shadow lit brightly in sequence, tiny solar explosions moving across its surface. 'Those dishes are solar reflectors,' he said, 'and the satellites are secondaries. The orbitals direct the sun back onto it.'

'What do they need those for? Aren't fusion reactors enough?'

'Yes, but being a refuelling depot out in the middle of nowhere they didn't want the burden of shipping out masses of radioactive reactor linings, so they found this solution.'

'I guess there's artificial gravity. It's too small for that slow rotation to act as a centrifuge.'

'Yeah, there will be one fusion reactor, with the solars taking up the slack. The collectors reflect the light onto small reactors in the middle, but the orbital mirrors don't stay in geosynchronous. The beams would melt the collectors, so they alternate, giving the mirrors just enough time to cool down.'

'Impressive. How hot does it get?'

'Put it this way, there isn't enough sunscreen in the universe to protect you if you go through one of those beams.' Aryx gestured to the ship around them. 'It would probably even cut through this hull.'

'Steer clear of them then. Where's the entrance?'

'There,' he said, pointing out of the window.

Now that they had drawn close enough to the station, two lines of widely spaced lights became visible, extending from each pole of the sphere. Beckoned in by the flashing lights, a long, rectangular ship slowly drifted in at the north, while another came out at the south.

Sebastian tapped commands into the console. 'I'm taking us in.'

The ship manoeuvred until it was in line with the northern pole of the station and matched the rotation. The automated docking procedures took control of the ship and, after the vessel in front had cleared the entrance, it guided them into the golden maw.

'Sebastian, I suggest interlinking with the station's security system and using their internal sensors to locate the hostages.'

He tapped away at the console again. 'Good idea, Wolfram, but it looks like they don't have those kinds of sensors. It is only a fuel depot, after all ... On the upside, there aren't too many rooms, just long, winding corridors.'

The *Ultima Thule* drifted through a pair of airlocks and a short section of transport tunnelling that opened into a large, well-lit spherical docking chamber. Several ships floated at different levels, moored to bays around the inside of the hangar, and people moved about on the walkways that joined the jetties to the main complex. Thin veils of mist clung to many of the ships, flowing around the coolant pipes and down onto the walkways. Three of the larger ships looked like ancient dirigibles that had somehow become lodged in their own private clouds.

'I've never noticed that before,' Aryx said.

'It's where the artificial gravity spills out and draws the colder vapours towards them.'

'Not the fog. The ship we followed is dusty.'

'It's probably just space dust attracted by the node charge.'

With a clunk and lurch to port, the *Ultima* was drawn into the nearest free docking bay.

Sebastian pointed to the opposite side of the chamber. 'There's Gladrin's ship.'

Aryx leaned forwards. The ship lacked the misty sheath of the others.

'Damn it,' Sebastian said, checking console readouts, 'the thruster manifolds are cool. He's been here at least half an hour.'

'Still, better than we anticipated.'

Sebastian scrabbled around the cockpit, collecting up items. He picked up the rucksack and slung it over his shoulder, hesitating before picking up the SI-pistol. After several attempts at shoving it into his belt, he grimaced and carried it in his hand. 'You coming?' he said, making his way to the ladder.

'Are you kidding? An opportunity to kick someone's arse comes up and you have to ask.' Aryx wheeled to the lift.

When he arrived at the bottom, Sebastian was attaching the hood to the N-suit.

'Why are you putting that on?'

'So that if Gladrin spots us, he might not immediately recognise me.'

'Oh, and he's not going to recognise *this*,' Aryx said, gesturing to the chair. 'And you'd be less recognisable if you put a pressure suit on over the top. Your N-suit sticks out like a sore thumb.'

'Fair enough.' Sebastian began pulling on a pressure suit – he kept the hood. 'How's this?' he said, holding his arms out to the side.

Aryx rolled his eyes. 'Even your own mother wouldn't recognise you, now let's go!'

Chapter 35

Aryx shot down the ramp out of the *Ultima Thule* and skidded at the bottom. The heat and humidity of the docking bay hit him like a wet flannel to the face – no wonder there was so much mist forming around the coolant conduits. The inside of the station seemed far more industrial and utilitarian in appearance than he'd expected, with the gantries and walkways being made from temporary scaffolding, clamped together. It was strange to see so many ships in the space – a dozen, at least – yet so few people walking around, and with no cargo.

Cascades of sparks showered from one ship. Hot beads of metal bounced off onto the walkway, while others sprayed into the open space of the chamber, floating there until they cooled and faded. A tannoy blared intermittently, informing wayward passengers of their need to return to a newly fuelled vessel.

A grating, metallic screech echoed through the chamber and Aryx wheeled around the ship to get a better look. He shook his head in disgust. The *Fluorescent Lightingale*, the clumsy rectangular transport frigate they had followed in, had docked too fast and was slowly scraping along its mooring point. The ship looked clean now that it was in the hangar. Strange. It's not like they'd gone through any decontamination process.

He stared at the hull of the *Ultima Thule*. There *was* a faint trace of dust on it, too. He reached out and ran his fingers down it, leaving dark lines. Rubbing his fingertips together, he couldn't see any residue on his skin. He looked back at the spot he'd touched – the finger swipes had gone. No. The *dust* had gone.

'Are you coming?' Sebastian shouted. He'd already walked to the end of the walkway from the ship and turned right, towards the docking chamber wall.

'On my way!' Aryx caught up with him just as he approached the door to the main complex.

A guard stepped from an alcove to their right, holding out an infoslate. 'Identification, please.' He pointed down at Sebastian's right hand. 'Firearms are not allowed aboard the station.'

Sebastian gave the guard a flat stare and pressed his thumb against the tablet.

The guard examined the credentials and raised an eyebrow. 'Second one today.' He waved dismissively. 'You can pass. Just don't shoot the walls.'

It must have been Gladrin. Aryx looked at Sebastian, and he nodded.

'How long ago did the other agent pass? We need to catch up with him.'

'Few minutes ago, he asked for directions to the storage lockup. It's through the door, down the corridor to the end, then follow the red stripe.'

Sebastian nodded. 'Thanks.'

Aryx wheeled past, moving quickly on the smooth floor, and through the doorway to the facility. In moments he reached a T-junction where coloured lines ran along the wall and floor in both directions. The red stripe started there and headed off to the right. He turned to see Sebastian loping after him and beckoned before heading off at full speed.

The line ended at a solid, heavy-duty pressure door. A large sign above read *Storage*. He activated the door control.

Blarp!

'Damn! It's stuck!' He wheeled to the access panel to the left and pulled on the red handle several times. The door didn't budge.

Sebastian arrived, breathing heavily. 'What's up? Why isn't it open?'

'It's jammed. I bet the bastard's welded it shut from the other side.'

'I do not detect any system malfunction,' Wolfram said. 'The door sensors are not indicating a mechanism jam. This would support your hypothesis.'

'How are we going to get in there?' Sebastian asked.

'I'll get a plasma cutter from the ship.'

'We don't have time for that! I'll have to find another way in.' Sebastian stomped back down the corridor.

No point in hanging around waiting. Aryx leaned forwards to inspect the door. The seam was tight and wouldn't have required much weld on the other side to seal it; worth trying to cut it open, anyway – just in case there was no other way in. He made his way back to the hangar and caught up with Sebastian as he finished talking to the guard.

'Did you ask if there was another way in?' he said, wheeling towards the ship and up the ramp.

'I did.' Sebastian bit his lip.

Aryx narrowed his eyes. 'What is it?' It was going to be something he wouldn't like the sound of.

'There is another way in.' Sebastian took a helmet from the rack.

'Let me guess—'

'—it's outside. A maintenance hatch in the middle of one of the reflector dishes.'

'You're insane! You're going to be the death of me, as well as yourself!' He wheeled between Sebastian and the airlock, barring the way out of the ship.

'I don't have a choice. I don't have time to wait for you to cut through the door and I can't give Gladrin a chance to get settled in. Now move aside.'

'If you insist on going out, I won't stop you, but I'm going to cut through the weld.' He wheeled into the cargo bay, took the plasma cutter from the storage rack and, resting it on his legs, headed back to the airlock where Sebastian stood fitting the helmet.

Aryx grabbed his arm. 'Be *careful!*' he said and wheeled down the ramp.

Sebastian waited in the maintenance airlock for the door to open, gun in hand. He wasn't sure what he'd do when he reached the hatch and got back inside the station. Would Gladrin have expected this move and be waiting?

The outer doors opened onto the star-studded curtain of space. He stepped forwards until his toes were on the threshold and blinked slowly in an attempt to banish the sensation of vertigo. He activated the magnetic clamps on his boots and crouched down next to the ladder in the floor. A red light came on and he felt himself start to sag backwards towards the core of the station. The artificial gravity must have been spilling out from the station – enough to affect him, even with the airlock floor's gravity plating turned off. He grabbed the rungs of the ladder, climbed up, and lugged himself over the edge. His boots locked onto the surface of the vast, golden globe. Even with the visor's tinting, it took a few moments for his eyes to become accustomed to the bright reflected light.

A hundred or so metres away to his right, the curved horizon dropped away sharply where it met the nearest reflector bowl. The hatch was in the next reflector along. He approached the dish as the collector assembly hanging above the centre flared in a beam of focused sunlight. The vacuum only added to the danger: he couldn't see the beam – only the glint of light as it reflected in his direction.

Wolfram's voice came through the suit's intercom. 'Sebastian, you will have to circumnavigate this obstacle. Your suit will not withstand the temperature. It is in the region of ten thousand degrees. Skirting the dish would be more efficient, and less dangerous.'

'I'm aware of that. I don't have time to go around. The boots make it too slow and I forgot to bring an EVA pack.' He strode up to the rim, stopping a few feet away from the edge.

'Sebastian, wait! This is not a wise move.'

'Then help me – how frequent are the pulses?'

'Fifteen seconds duration, with a gap of forty-five. The dish will be hot for the first ten seconds after a pulse.'

'Right, count me in.' He braced himself for a run. 'The magboots and low gravity should provide enough attraction to pull me back down at a sprint – well, as much as I can manage.'

The collector assembly dimmed.

'I still think this is unwise – ten seconds.'

'Duly noted.'

'Five ... Four ... Three ...'

'Here we go!'

'Two ... One.'

He launched himself off the edge. The fall into the dish was agonisingly slow. Hitting the bottom, the boots locked on with a clunk that shook his legs. He stumbled forwards, wrenching his rearmost foot free. It was more difficult than he'd anticipated; the boots weren't as responsive as he thought they'd be – there was no way he could run.

'Thirty seconds to next pulse.'

'I'm ... going as fast as I can!' It was hard work trying to walk, let alone walk fast, and his breathing became laboured. He cleared the lowest portion of the dish and began to climb the opposite incline.

'Fifteen seconds ...'

He approached the top, leaning back into the path of the beam as he walked up the incline. In a half-hearted attempt to pull himself away from the centre, he crouched.

'Ten seconds ...'

He faltered, trying to extend his leg over the lip of the dish. The surface fell away sharply in front of him – the angle was too much. There was no way he was going to get his foot in contact with it.

'I can't get a grip and I can't deactivate my left boot! I can't pull it up.'

'Keep your leg out straight ... now.'

The tension left his leg and he drifted away from the dish while the magnetic field of the right foot drew him down over the edge of the dish and back towards the station's hull.

'Five ...'

His foot came down and the field locked on.

'Four ...'

He pulled with all his might on his right leg. It bent painfully.

'Three ... Two ...'

He straightened his leg and the inertia carried him forwards, tumbling him over.

'One.'

He struck out with his left leg. The reactivated boot locked on and pulled him firmly to the surface. Vibration ran through the floor. He glanced back to see the collector flare brightly. Close scrapes were becoming too much of a habit.

'Are you injured?'

'I'm alright, just about.' He rubbed his knee. 'Thanks for releasing the boot. That was close.'

'You're welcome. I have no intention of getting fried like my successor.'

Reflected golden stars glinted beneath him as he limped towards the next dish. His knee ached. Magnetic boots could be so unforgiving.

There it was – the faint outline of the maintenance hatch at the bottom of the curve, tantalisingly close.

'I can break into the security and release the lock electronically,' Wolfram said, 'but you will need to operate the manual actuator to open the hatch.'

'Can you do it from here?'

'No, the range is too far. I will have adequate time to disable the security during your approach. However, you will have to make it to the bottom quickly or there will be insufficient time to operate the actuator.'

He took a few moments to ready himself while he waited for the next pulse to finish. He hesitated. Perhaps Wolfram was right, and this wasn't the best way. His thoughts drifted to Janyce and Erik ... 'Give me a countdown.'

'Three ... Two ... One ...'

... Janyce and Erik, cowering under Gladrin's heartless stare.

He hurled himself into the bowl.

Aryx wheeled along the corridor to the storage depot with the plasma cutter on his lap and welding mask on his head. Nobody in authority seemed to have noticed the problem with the door. Either the guard was so nonchalant about it that he hadn't bothered to inform anyone else, or Sebastian hadn't even mentioned it to him. The latter was more likely; he wouldn't want to risk Gladrin being alerted by station security, after all.

Assuming responsibility for the situation, he pulled down the mask and set about breaking the seal on the door. The cutter flared into life and he drew it down the joint between the panels. If he could heat it enough, it might break the weld the other side. Several seconds passed and still only a fraction of an inch was cleared. It was obviously going to be slow work. Sebastian – however reckless his actions seemed – was right; if Gladrin had time to hunker down and set measures in place, they'd have no choice but to hand Wolfram over, and that was something he didn't want to do.

While he cut into the metal he found himself missing conversation with the cube. He hadn't realised how attached he'd got to the SI. He didn't have to understand programming to appreciate how unique it was for a device to understand such qualities as humour. How far could it go? Did it really have emotions? Surely, to understand humour it had to *feel?* After everything they had been through on Achene, Wolfram had proved his trustworthiness and integrity, and that was something too rare and precious to lose, or see fall into the clutches of those who would abuse it.

Something thudded on the other side of the heavy door. A piece of loosened weld dropping off.

If Gladrin heard that, he'd definitely know they were close. Oh damn, why didn't it occur to him before? Gladrin might have welded the door shut with the intent of directing them through the other entrance. If it was smaller than this door, it would be the perfect place for an ambush.

He activated his wristcom. 'Seb, if you can hear me, be careful! Gladrin's planned for this!' The wristcom bleeped with the 'not acknowledged' sound and a cold sweat formed on the back of his neck. Sebastian was in good hands, but those sun-lasers would kill them instantly if they made the slightest error in judgement. What could he do? The only option was to notify someone. 'Establish encrypted connection to station security.'

'Security. Officer Deruno here,' came a gruff, masculine voice. It didn't sound Human.

'This is Aryx Trevarian of Tenebrae station, attached to SpecOps Agent Thorsson. I need a security team at the storage depot immediately – there is a hostage situation taking place. The agent is on his way to the depot via the outside maintenance hatch. I'm attempting to break a weld on the door and enter directly.'

'Rah!' barked the voice over the wristcom. 'We are not equipped for situations such as this, but I am on my way!' The comms cut off.

Two minutes later the stomping of booted feet thundered down the corridor. Aryx stopped cutting and lifted his welding mask.

A large figure, at least seven foot tall – though it was hard to judge sitting in the wheelchair – strode towards him. Clad in thick, black Kevlar and carbon-fibre armour, the creature's powerful arms carried a large, scoped rifle. Its thin, oddly-jointed legs terminated in small, paw-like feet. The upper torso, in contrast to the slender abdomen, appeared massive, and its wide, solid neck curved forwards; the plated segments covering it merged with a helmet shaped like a wolf's head. Its glowing red gaze gripped Aryx's momentarily; the armour would strike terror into the hearts of the most fearsome enemy.

The figure stopped several feet away and propped the rifle up against its leg. Bringing up a partially-armoured claw, it pulled back the helmet. The neck segments collapsed, exposing a short-muzzled canine face with salt-and-pepper fur, topped with two fuzzy, rounded trapezoidal ears. It reminded him of a hyena, grown to monstrous bipedal proportions. He knew immediately what it was.

The Bronadi saluted. 'Officer Deruno, at your service.'

Sebastian sank to the bottom of the dish, landing with a clunk as the boots locked on once again.

'Forty seconds until the next pulse.'

He lugged himself forwards. The hatch was only feet away.

'Thirty seconds ...'

He bent down. 'There's no handle!'

'Twenty-five seconds ... I have released the electronic interlocks.'

A small aperture slid open next to the hatch, exposing a familiar red bar. He started pumping with his free hand.

'Fifteen seconds ...'

The hatch crept open.

'Ten seconds ...'

Almost there. Hurry up!

'Seven ...'

The actuator snapped back as the hatch finally opened to its limit. Sebastian heaved himself in and slammed against the floor below.

'Five ...'

He stood and reached for the button next to the hatch at the top of the ladder. It was beyond his touch.

'Four ...'

'Deactivate the boots, now!'

'Three ...'

He jumped.

'Two ...'

His finger hit the button squarely.

'One ... Zero.'

The hatch slammed silently shut and the room thrummed with the impact of solar energy from above.

'One hundred degrees and rising. Your suit will not withstand this temperature for long.'

Vents hissed as the chamber filled with air. He tried to activate the inner airlock door, but was greeted with the customary *blarp!* Oh Gods, now he was going to boil to death!

'The temperature has begun to drop.'

He hammered the button again. The door slid open and, staggering into a tiny maintenance room, he began stripping off the roasting pressure suit. There was no way he'd have been able to pursue Gladrin in it even if he wanted to.

'Are you ready, Wolfram?'

'I'm always ready. If you need me to cast one of the spells, say the word.'

The door into the corridor was a manual sliding mechanism. He slid it open enough to pop his head through and looked down the corridor to the left. It ran a hundred metres before ending in a heavy door, where a glowing red line traced the door's locking mechanism. All clear that way – Aryx must be the other side, cutting the seal. He looked to the right.

Pain shot through his skull as Gladrin brought the butt of his gun down on his temple.

Chapter 36

'Sebastian, wake up!'

An aching agony pulsed through Sebastian's head. The world slowly came into focus, in one eye at least, and he found himself lying halfway through the door into the corridor. Wolfram's voice came from underneath a storage bin inside the maintenance room. Gladrin probably hadn't spotted the cube when he dropped the gun.

'Are you injured?'

Sebastian slowly stood up. 'I'll be fine,' he said, rubbing his head. His hand came away bloody. 'Where did he go?'

'I believe he went down the corridor to the right.'

He picked up the gun and made his way into the corridor. The world was wobbly, but he had to move quickly.

The door at the end of the corridor stood open. He ran through and continued for another twenty metres, at which point the passage turned sharply to the left. He crept along and peered around the corner.

One hundred metres ahead, the corridor ended at a pressure door, similar to the one Aryx had been working on. Inside stood Gladrin, tapping at the controls. In his left hand he held Janyce by the wrist, blindfolded and with tape across her mouth. She wore a thin, silky sleeveless orange top and pale, blue leggings. Handcuffed to her other wrist stood Erik, similarly bound, wearing pyjamas. Gladrin looked up and Sebastian felt a cold shudder as a wave of adrenaline washed over him.

'Let them go, you bastard!' he shouted, and strode out from behind the wall.

Gladrin didn't respond, but sidestepped. The door began to close and he dragged Janyce and Erik towards the far side of the depot.

Sebastian charged. The heavy pressure door was half-closed, and with fifty metres still to go, it could have been a million miles away. It was closing too quickly. He'd never make it.

Aryx looked the figure up and down. 'Is it just you?'

'Hmpf!' grunted the white-furred Bronadi. 'In spite of my desire to be somewhere other than this station, I am the best this place has to offer. If my support is not wanted, I will leave.'

'Don't! I'd just hoped there would be a few more of you.' Aryx pulled the welding mask down over his face and turned to resume cutting.

'What *is* the situation?' Deruno growled.

'Agent Thorsson is pursuing Agent Gladrin, who has taken his sister-in-law and nephew hostage. Gladrin's sealed this door, which I'm cutting through while Thorsson's gone outside. He's attempting to enter an access hatch in one of the collectors.'

'A dangerous and foolish move.'

'Tell me about it! I can't contact him. The hull's blocking the wristcom, so I've no idea what's going on.' The plasma cutter flared and a blob of hot metal shot off the door, landing between the front wheels of his wheelchair. 'Whoa!' Deruno grabbed Aryx's shoulder, spinning him away from the door to face him.

He looked Aryx up and down. 'Are you injured?' His eyes stopped when they reached his legs. 'I guess you are ... not?'

'I'm fine, thanks. The weld missed. I'm nearly done.' He turned back and resumed cutting. The doors parted. Deruno's weapon clunked heavily in his paws.

The corridor ahead was empty.

'How far is it to the depot?'

'Several hundred metres. The corridors are long for safety reasons. Your friend may be there already if he has entered through the maintenance hatch.'

'I hope so.' Aryx found it difficult to conceal the concern in his voice. 'Come on!' He wheeled off as fast as he could.

Deruno's booted feet clomped behind him.

The door was closing. 'Wolfram, cast the acceleration spell!'

The cube resonated a deep chord and, in strange throat-sung tones, chanted, '*Transmitir dent ocius velocidade.*' The air shimmered around them. Sebastian pressed the button.

He wasn't sure what to expect; things didn't seem to slow down, but instead every stride took him several metres. He barely skimmed the floor. It moved beneath his feet like a treadmill in overdrive, almost like gravity had changed direction and was pulling him forward. The walls of the corridor whipped past in a blur of speed, and before he knew it he was through the door. The effect ended, catapulting him to the ground, and he landed in a half-crouch on one knee. The door slammed shut behind him. He looked up.

Gladrin stood several metres away, working on the door at the far side of the room.

Sebastian got to his feet and, taking a wide stance, held the pistol in both hands and took aim. 'Let them go, Gladrin!'

The agent spun around and pulled Janyce in front of his body. A gun went to her head. 'I'm sorry, Sebastian, I can't do that. I need the cube.' He shifted his grip on the weapon.

Janyce made a muffled, whimpering sound, and stiffened at the mention of his name. Erik staggered to one side and began to cry, nasally.

Sebastian activated the laser sight: no dot. He clenched his jaw.

'You didn't think I'd give you a fully functional weapon, did you?' A smile formed in Gladrin's eyes.

'Wolfram,' Sebastian whispered, 'I need you to block my aim so I don't hit my family.'

The cube didn't respond.

He glanced at the side of the weapon. Almost all the lights on the side were lit. Shit! How was he going to manage without the override? Sweat ran down his forehead and his eye began to sting. His palms became slick and the heavy gun began to dip.

Gladrin relaxed, allowing the gun to move away from Janyce's head a little. 'I didn't choose you by mistake, Sebastian. I needed your skills and your personality. I had hoped we could work together, but now it's come down to this. I suppose it's lucky the explosion happened before you had any weapons training.' The gun moved farther away.

Sebastian gripped the pistol tighter in an attempt to steady his aim. He had to buy time. 'Why did you give me the cube to investigate if you already knew what it was?'

'You know what potential it has. The unfinished cube was already active, but I wasn't sure why yours wasn't. I thought it was malfunctioning, but I had my suspicions. My only option was to give it to someone that it could learn to trust. Someone uninvolved.' He gestured in Sebastian's direction with his weapon.

This was it. He had to follow his instincts. Closing one eye, he swept the gun down in the direction of Gladrin's right leg – the safest bet to avoid hitting Janyce – and pulled the trigger.

Chapter 37

The steely crack echoed in Sebastian's ears, joined with a cry of pain. Gladrin, Janyce, and Erik collapsed. Gladrin's gun skittered across the floor. Who had he hit? He bounded towards them.

Gladrin released Janyce and crawled away, blood trailing from his leg, his face contorted with pain. He reached out for the weapon. Sebastian swung his foot out, kicking the pistol. He dropped to one knee, landing it squarely in Gladrin's back. The agent grunted in pain and attempted to roll over, but stopped as Sebastian put the SI-gun to his head.

'I can't let you have the cube and, more importantly, I can't let you hurt my family.' He glanced down at the lights on the side of the cube. They were dark. 'You need to be *purged.*'

A rising tone came from the cube. '*Expurget ... Exorcizamus ...*'

A bead of sweat rolled down Gladrin's head onto the muzzle of the gun against his temple. 'What are you doing? Please, don't kill me—'

Sebastian's finger went to the button. *Click.*

Gladrin flinched at the sound.

The air rippled as the distortion wave expanded from the cube, sweeping several feet through the room before dissipating. Gladrin sighed with the relief of a man spared execution. Sebastian lifted his leg and, still pointing the gun at Gladrin, rolled him over onto his back; he didn't resist. Why was he still conscious? Sebastian stared, paying close attention to his eyes.

The faraway gaze and tell-tale glimmer of distant stars he'd expected were not there. Other than expressing a mixture of terror and relief, in equal measure, Gladrin's eyes looked normal.

'It didn't work! You're not one of them,' he said. 'Why have you done all this, if you're not one of them!'

A deep crease formed between Gladrin's eyebrows, and his chin rumpled. 'They made me do it,' he sobbed. 'They have my family. They made me—'

Sebastian drew the gun away from his head and pressed it to his chest, pushing him back to the floor. '*Who?* Who made you do it? I thought you were possessed.'

'Wha—what are you talking about? I'm not possessed! The Independent Terran Front has my family.' His expression seemed genuine, his tone of voice convincing.

The adrenaline subsided and Sebastian's breathing became ragged while he attempted to bring it under control. He eased the gun away from Gladrin's chest and slumped back to rest on his haunches. He had become so drawn into the issue of possession that he'd not even contemplated other explanations for Gladrin's behaviour. Even his own behaviour had changed; that change had blinded him to the truth. His attention turned to Janyce and Erik, who lay near the door, quivering.

The lights on the side of the cube were all off, so he laid the gun on the floor next to Gladrin with the muzzle pointing at his head. 'Wolfram, if he moves, shoot the bastard.'

'Acknowledged.'

Gladrin's eyes widened and his face lost even more colour.

Sebastian crawled to Janyce. 'It's me,' he said, and pulled up her blindfold.

She blinked in the bright light. Her eyes were dark with mascara runs against her pale face and her red hair was straggly.

'Are you alright?'

She nodded.

'Hold still.' He pulled the tape from her mouth and repeated the process with Erik. 'Wolfram, can you hack the security on the cuffs?'

The manacles fell from their wrists and Janyce lunged forwards to hug him. 'Thank the Gods you got here. I thought he was going to kill us!'

Erik leaned and hugged him around the waist. 'He got us out of bed!' The three huddled together.

'Sebastian,' Janyce whispered, 'what did you mean by possession?'

There was no point in hiding the truth from them, but there wasn't time for explanations. 'I'll tell you later.'

'Is it like what's in your grandfather's diary?'

He tried to keep one eye on Gladrin, who remained still, apparently afraid of the intelligent weapon beside him. 'What do you mean?' He hadn't read much of the diary – after all, most of it was illegible.

'There are stories in it about the starry-eyed people,' Erik said.

The hair on his neck stood on end. Why was there mention of it in the diary? He grabbed Janyce by the arms and shook her. 'What on Earth were you thinking, reading stuff like that to him?'

'I didn't—'

'I read it myself,' Erik said, looking up at him. 'Is that man one of the nasty people who have monsters in them?'

'No, Erik, he isn't.' He gave Gladrin a sidelong glance. 'Actually, I think he's just like me.' It seemed once again he was in a position to see the perpetrator as a victim.

The pressure door opened behind him, and he turned to see Aryx, followed by a menacing figure clad in black. 'Aryx!'

Aryx wheeled towards the group. 'Are you okay?'

'I'm fine. Everything's under control. Who's this?' Sebastian looked up at the Bronadi looming over him. It held a rifle, trained on Gladrin.

'This is Officer Deruno, station security.'

Deruno nodded.

'Pleased to meet you. Aryx, can you take them to the ship? I need to clear things up here.'

'Of course . . .' Aryx said, giving him an *I'll-leave-you-to-it* look. He beckoned to Deruno, who helped the others to their feet.

Sebastian stood and watched Aryx wheel out of the depot, followed by Janyce. Erik walked hand-in-paw with Deruno, an expression of awe on his face. Sebastian smiled briefly and turned his attention back to Gladrin.

The agent kept his eyes on him as he approached and picked up the SI-gun. Gladrin's fear had evidently subsided and given way to curiosity.

'I appear to have misjudged you,' Sebastian said, holding out his other hand. 'I believe you. Things don't seem to be as cut and dried as they used to.'

Gladrin lay, unmoving, with his hands over the gunshot wound in his leg. 'I don't understand.'

Sebastian crouched next to him. 'I had reason to believe you weren't acting of your own volition.'

'Is that what you meant by possession— Argh!'

'Wait here.' He went to the medical station on the wall, retrieved some bandages, and began wrapping them around the injured leg. 'Yes – I take it you heard what Erik said?'

'I did, although I still don't understand.'

'I thought you'd got acceleration psychosis. I'm pretty sure that's another cause of possession.'

'Never heard of it. Although I have seen people that looked like the boy described.'

He stopped bandaging. 'Where?'

'The ITF. One of their agents, the one that approached me. His eyes had bright specks in. I assumed it was some new fashion contact lens.'

Things were beginning to add up. If members of the terrorist organisation were under the control of the entities, that would explain how they knew where to intercept the *Ultima*. He resumed bandaging the leg. 'Why have they got your family?'

'It's because of the SI. Like you, I used to be a technician. I worked in cybernetics and stumbled across it after being recruited into SpecOps.' Gladrin winced as Sebastian tied off the bandage and helped him to his feet. 'I didn't know why the project was shut down, but it was intriguing enough for me to want to revive it.'

Sebastian supported him and they made their way out of the storage depot. 'How did you discover it?'

'I was researching artificial intelligence when I came upon some old papers from the Oxford University of Robotics and Cybernetics. The idea of using it for long-distance travel intrigued me – you know, nobody wants to go out that far without the assurance of finding a node. I thought if we could use sophisticated AI tech to do the exploration, it would be the solution to everyone's problems. No more worrying about resources being carried for long-term travel, and no emotional attachment to those left behind.

'Unfortunately the resources from the project had been stolen by the ITF during a spate of bombings a few years back. I decided to track them down and get them back.'

'So what happened? You obviously succeeded.'

'To a degree. I tracked them down to a colony on Cinder IV where they had a secret lab. I broke in and stole the cubes—' Gladrin put his arm against the wall. 'I need to rest.'

'How did you get out with them? Did you have backup?'

'Not exactly. SpecOps wasn't aware of the project. I was working autonomously. I managed to get into the lab when the marines raided the place. Shortly after I escaped, the reactor blew.'

'Shit. That sounds like the mission Aryx was on.'

Gladrin gulped air. 'Quite possibly.'

'How did Kerl get involved?'

'I knew him from back when I studied at university. His interest was in cybernetics and behaviourism, and his biology research touched on helping those with brain injuries, accessing their thoughts with technology that might overcome locked-in syndrome and other paralyses. John had been working with Alvarez because of his connection to the military and war injuries units at several hospitals. He'd used him for some of his early interface experiments, detecting and recording brainwave activity. I hoped that one of the applications for the SI units could be to replace damaged parts of the Human brain. To that end, I prompted John to attempt to integrate existing brainwave patterns with the SI's matrix. It didn't get that far.'

'Let me guess. The ITF?'

Gladrin nodded rapidly and resumed walking. 'Before I was able to report to SpecOps on the project, they tracked down my family and gave me a ransom demand. I obviously wasn't good enough at covering my tracks. Either that, or it was a trap in the first place.'

'What did they want? Money? Weapons?'

'Me. They wanted me to work for them. They had my family. I had no choice.' A tear ran down Gladrin's cheek.

Sebastian put a hand on his shoulder. 'I'm sorry.'

'They must have been watching me for some time before they contacted me. They could see I'd made more progress using the partially completed SI than they had, but the one I gave you was in a sleep state and resisted all attempts at activation. They wanted me to find a way to weaponise them. To find a way to clone the brainwave patterns of their members, and plant the SIs as technological sleeper agents, or some such perversion. I was to instruct Kerl to find anything he could that might help the ITF, but it was only after he'd detected strange brainwave activity in Alvarez that he mentioned the whole carbyne thing to me. I have a feeling that it was his superstitious mumbo-jumbo that put Kerl on to it in the first place.' Gladrin paused to shift his weight.

'I had no idea what his experiments involved and, to be honest, I really didn't want to know. He seemed too keen to do the kind of research that I thought of as unsavoury, but as long as he kept providing results on the brainwave research – and kept my family alive – I wasn't in the mind to question it. I stopped hearing from the ITF in relation to his research a few days before the explosion.'

'I assume they are the reason why you planted the virus on the station that allowed the signal into my quarters?'

Gladrin raised his eyebrows. Sebastian bent down to check the bandage on his leg.

'Yes, I've done a bit of digging. We found that you received large payments from Earth, from accounts associated with terrorist activity. I also found that the signals started being sent to my quarters around the time you'd mentioned me in your journals.'

'Yes.' Gladrin stared at the floor. 'I don't know what the purpose of the signal was.'

Sebastian finished tightening the bandage and straightened. 'That should be better for a while … The signal causes nightmares. Aryx and Karan were having them around the same time, but I don't understand why we never saw the messages on the terminals sooner.'

'I'd been deleting them, and it wasn't until you started waking up in the night that you ever spotted them. The ITF asked me for a list of contacts closest to you on the station. Obviously once you'd chosen

Aryx as your partner, they stopped sending the signal to the others.'

'I think they used it to test us.'

'To what end? I fail to see how nightmares could be caused by the signal, let alone how it could be used to test you.'

Sebastian wasn't sure how to explain about the entities and their association with magic, but he was no longer worried about having to convince him. 'You won't believe me, but the people with "starry eyes", as Erik put it, are actually possessed by extra-spatial entities. We've been calling them "demons" because of how they appear in our dreams, but I don't really know what they are. I think you've accidentally been working against their intent.'

'What do you mean? Was that why the lab was blown up?'

'I believe so. Kerl was using carbyne to research thaumaturgy, magic, and integrating that with the SI.'

'I knew it was something strange, but I thought the ITF would jump at the chance of any technology that would help them, no matter how unconventional, so I left him to it.'

'Ordinarily, they probably would. In this case, magic is a double-edged sword. It could provide the ITF with a means for mass destruction with no traceable cause, and a vector for the entities behind the ITF to possess people. The downside is that it affects their ability keep hold of a person. If there are possessed people in the ITF, the SI units could be used as a weapon against them. They couldn't risk that, so they blew up the lab using an innocent third party.'

Gladrin shook his head. 'And how do people get possessed?'

'Did you ever read about ancient witch trials in history class? Those who use magic are vulnerable to being possessed by the entities. Somehow it attracts them to the user and allows them to enter the body. Since the SI isn't organic, I assume that's why it can't be possessed or controlled by them.'

'So who blew up the lab? I didn't watch the processed video. I'd begun to panic by then.'

'A man by the name of Duggan Simmons. I tracked him down to a comet in Yazor. He'd made himself invisible.'

Gladrin's jaw dropped.

'Don't ask. He was partially visible when I found him. When we discovered evidence of his possession in the damaged cube's memory, he attempted to undo the invisibility in our presence. That was how we found out about the entities – he was immediately possessed and tried to attack me.'

'I think I understand.' Gladrin gestured to the cube attached to the pistol. 'And I assume that this cube actually *can* use magic, given the way you caught up with me and attempted to "purge" me? How were you even able to activate it?'

'He trusts me.'

'*He?*'

'I could be female if you want,' came Wolfram's voice in silky, seductive tones.

Sebastian hefted the heavy gun-cube assembly. 'Gladrin, I'd like you to meet Wolfram, the SI.'

'I cannot say that I am pleased to meet you, Agent Gladrin,' Wolfram's voice resumed its masculinity, 'as I do not believe I experience pleasure.'

Gladrin laughed weakly. 'Well, I'm certainly pleased to meet you, even if you are a little sarcastic.'

'You'll have to ignore that. Sometimes he seems to be a few dots short of a file extension.'

The agent gave him a flat stare.

'Programmer joke.'

'Absolutely fascinating ... The cube, not the awful joke ... I don't think the other one functioned correctly as it never conversed with anyone.'

They came to the door of the maintenance room and Sebastian stopped, propped Gladrin against the wall, and retrieved the pressure suit. He slung it over his shoulder and looped his arm through the helmet. It was too valuable to leave behind, given the ship was already down by one suit and the escape pod was missing.

Gladrin looked at him with a puzzled expression. 'I assume you diagnosed me as a sufferer of this "acceleration psychosis" because I don't practise magic.'

'It seemed the only logical conclusion at the time. I obviously wasn't thinking straight and hadn't thought of the other possibilities, such as you being under duress.' While they walked, he couldn't help but repeatedly glance down at the bloody bandage around Gladrin's leg.

'I don't blame you for shooting me, you know. I did push you into it, after all, I just don't know what to do now ... My family will be in danger if they find out the cube's still in your possession.'

Sebastian scratched his head. 'We'll find a way of getting them back, but I think for the moment the best thing you can do is play along. Tell them it was destroyed. Give them the melted one as proof. Only Wolfram was capable of interpreting the data on it, so the information is safe. Tell them this one was captured by the ship you sent after us, but that it was lost in a node mis-jump. It'll be years by the time any communication comes back from them.'

Gladrin stopped and leaned against the wall again. 'How did they track you down to Yazor?'

'You didn't send them?'

'I told them you'd discovered what the cube was, but the tracker didn't relay your position.'

'Hmm. I was thinking about it earlier. The entities obviously know Duggan's location because the one that possessed him piloted his ship. That's probably how they found out we were there. Oh damn – that means they might go after him using the terrorists as a cover!'

'If what you say is true, is there a risk of him being possessed again if he keeps using magic?'

'He's not going to until we find a way of preventing it. Either way, he'll have to be moved.'

Gladrin grimaced. 'I'm afraid the ITF know of your sister and nephew now, so you'll have to hide them somehow, too.'

Sebastian's thoughts went to Achene and Chopwood. The distance from comms relays was ideal. 'I think we can hide them on a planet that isn't in the registry. I have friends there that can protect them, but I'll have to ask you to delete any records you have of the *Ultima*'s flight paths for their protection. You can tell the ITF that you still have them in custody, or that you've convinced me to help, and Aryx and I will go along with it.'

Gladrin coughed. 'I don't tell the ITF everything I do, so I can manage that at least.' He pressed his fingers and thumb to his eyes and took a deep breath. 'They've had my wife and daughter for just over a year now, so anything I can do from the inside to help, I will.' Sebastian smiled and squeezed his shoulder. The man looked frail and fragile now that the truth was laid bare.

'We'll get your family back. I don't know how long it will take, but it's important that you carry on as usual. Aryx and I will hide my family and then return to the station to keep up pretences. The most important thing to do at the moment is protect anyone who can be hurt by the situation as it is, and make sure the SI is out of the terrorists' sights.'

The pair turned the final bend in the corridor and exited into the docking area. Aryx and Deruno were waiting on the walkway. The Bronadi raised his rifle at their approach.

'You don't need that,' Sebastian said. 'He's not the bad guy anymore. I do need a favour, though.'

'What can Officer Deruno do for Agent Thorsson?'

'I need you to delete any evidence of our presence here.'

Deruno's ears flattened back against his head and he frowned – at least it looked like a frown, or perhaps he was about to bark.

Aryx's eyes widened and he grabbed Sebastian's wrist. 'What are you doing?'

'I'll fill you in later. I need you to trust me. Gladrin has been coerced. I just need the logs deleted.'

'I cannot do that. I would be dishonoured by the Bronala.'

Gladrin looked at Sebastian with pleading eyes.

'Don't worry, I have an idea.' Sebastian winked at Aryx. 'Deruno, would it take a special dispensation from your ambassador to prevent dishonour?'

The canine head nodded slowly. 'It would, and possibly a transfer away from this glorified fuel station ... before I remember to record the incident.'

Aryx shook his head in disbelief as he activated his wristcom. 'Computer, contact the Bronadi ambassador on Tenebrae station,' he said. 'Tell him I'll be calling in that favour.'

Aryx completed the pre-flight checks while Sebastian made sure his family were secured in the seating at the rear of the cockpit. Everything looked good to go. 'Where to now, boss?'

'We can't go back to Tenebrae. Not yet, anyway. Duggan will be in danger now.'

'Do you want to pick him up?'

'Yes, and I was thinking we should take Janyce and Erik to Achene or Chopwood, somewhere off the grid. Gladrin said he'll delete logs of where we've been.'

'What about those bloody flies?'

'If we get Duggan, I'm sure he'll be able to rig up some ultrasonics like he did for the colonists.'

Aryx folded his arms. 'You have an answer for everything, don't you?'

'No, he doesn't.' Janyce shook her head. 'It only seems like he does.'

'I, on the other hand,' Wolfram said, still attached to the gun on the console, 'have access to almost all of Humanity's information.'

'Cool!' Erik said. 'You know any games?'

'Marvellous, the font of all knowledge reduced to a gaming machine. Yes. I know many— Sebastian, would you be so kind as to remove this encumbrance?'

Sebastian picked up the gun and Wolfram unlatched the connector plate and dropped into his hand. He gave Erik the cube and put the gun back in its holster.

'Do you know "stop the light"?'

'What's that?'

'Turn me over so you can see the bar of lights. I will fill them one by one and then turn them off again. You must press the button on the opposite side when all of the lights are lit. If you succeed, I will repeat the process, faster on each cycle. When you tire of it, we can play some different games.'

The boy sat, turning the cube in his hands, and began playing the game.

The docking clamps released and the ship drifted out of the bay, shedding the shroud of mist that had briefly cloaked it. The golden globe of Kimberley depot fell behind them, dwindling to a tiny yellow speck as they approached the steely-blue scaffold of the acceleration node.

Aryx's thoughts drifted back to the strange space dust he'd seen on the *Fluorescent Lightingale*. If superphase travel sometimes caused acceleration psychosis and carbyne affected the demons in their realm, perhaps they existed in superphase, or somewhere that touched it. Maybe the powder went there, and when ships traversed the space, they attracted it. Now probably wasn't the best time to raise his suspicions with Sebastian.

He looked back at the three sitting on the seats and felt a strange emptiness. How could he have gone so long without realising he'd felt so alone? Even though he'd not been there for the final showdown with Gladrin, he now felt responsible for Sebastian's family as though they were his own. He imagined teaching Erik about old farm machinery and mechanics like his father had for him. His eyes began to prickle as an ache rose from deep within his chest. If only he could pass his legacy on to someone else, to leave something behind for others. Maybe if he got the patent for the mobipack and started manufacturing them, that might fill the void.

The ship continued jumping in and out of superphase on its journey to Yazor, but Aryx had lost all interest in monitoring it.

Sebastian came over and sat next to him. 'How are things going?'

'Not bad. Are they okay back there?'

'Yes. Janyce doesn't like the bumps – I thought she was going to throw up just now. She's worried about what's going to happen to her cat. I told her the neighbour is going to have to hang on to it for a bit.'

Aryx smiled. 'She'll get over it. The space-sickness, I mean. Didn't take you long, after all.'

'You said she did not own a cat,' Wolfram said over the intercom, while simultaneously playing with Erik.

Sebastian's face flushed. 'Yes, well, obviously she hadn't told me that she bought one.' He turned to Aryx. 'Thanks for the help with the diplomatic situation back there, by the way.'

'Isn't it a good job I kept those vegetables after all?' It wouldn't do to rub it in too much, but Sebastian had to be put in his place occasionally.

'I'll grant you that one.'

Aryx nodded in Erik's direction. 'The kid seems to be enjoying the trip.'

'And unlike you, he doesn't keep asking if we're there yet.'

He jabbed Sebastian in the ribs and they both laughed. 'What exactly happened with Gladrin back there?'

They exchanged recollections of events on Kimberly; Sebastian was unsurprised at Aryx's mention of the dust. Aryx, however, remained unconvinced that Gladrin could be trusted, but he understood his motivations and agreed to go along with misleading the ITF. It seemed like a sound idea, and he looked forward to meeting with Duggan again. Maybe he could finally get a proper cup of coffee.

Five hours of flight later, the *Ultima* dropped out of superphase in Yazor. Janyce had managed to keep down whatever stomach contents she had – much to Aryx's relief – and Erik had remained blissfully amused for the entire trip, playing some obscure form of mental chess with Wolfram. Sebastian continued to pore over his grandfather's diary, apparently unable to understand most of it, except for the few parts he'd read out that alluded to stories of the possessed.

'So,' Aryx said, 'found any answers?'

Sebastian drew in a breath and let it out before speaking. 'Not really. I've read out most of what I can understand so far. There's a load of gibberish in here ... Some bits look like Old Icelandic, and there are weird glyphs that I think might be runes, but they're all messed up. I can't make out many of the diagrams, either, and I can't tell if the notes about possession refer to people my grandfather met, or legends he researched and paraphrased. It's all descriptive and too vague.'

'Study it another day. You look shattered.'

Sebastian pulled his hands down his cheeks. 'You're right,' he said, and after slamming the diary shut, put it in his bag. 'I can't focus on it until this whole situation is sorted out.'

Erik came over to the cockpit and stared out of the windows, wide-eyed. He put the cube down near Aryx and pointed. 'What's that?'

The white spray of Duggan's home filled the view.

'That's where we're going,' Aryx said. 'It's a comet. There's a man living in it and he used to be invisible.'

'Wow!'

Sebastian activated the comms. 'Duggan, are you there?'

The old man's voice replied. 'Ah, Sebastian, my friend, I hadn't expected to hear from you again so soon. What can I do for you?'

'We'd like to land, if possible. We think you're in danger, and need to get you out of here. I'll explain when we arrive.'

'Sounds like time for emergency plan B, I suppose. I'll let you in.' The comms cut off.

'Emergency plan B?' Sebastian gave Aryx a *What-the-hell?* look.

Aryx shrugged. He clapped his hands together. 'Erik! How would you like to land the ship?' The sequence was already programmed – all that remained was to press the initiate button.

The boy turned to look at his mother. 'Can I?' She nodded, and he bounced into the empty pilot's seat next to Aryx, who pointed at the relevant control. He reached out and pressed the button with a gleeful flourish. The *Ultima's* manoeuvring thrusters fired.

Minutes later it landed on the pad in the cavernous interior of the comet's entry bay.

'How are we going to carry Wolfram around?' Sebastian asked. 'I don't like you having to keep sticking him in your pocket.'

Aryx thought for a moment, and recalled the cube's ability to interface with almost anything wirelessly. He retrieved the mobipack from the back of the ship. 'I hope you don't mind,' he said, and popped Wolfram into the storage compartment.

'Not at all,' Wolfram said, through the pack's speaker. 'There is one problem, however. I cannot see.'

'Hold on a sec.' He beckoned to Sebastian. 'Pass me your bag, please.' He rummaged through it and pulled out the AR glasses. 'Here we are.'

'I forgot about those,' Sebastian said, taking the rucksack.

'Wolfram, I've got nanocam AR glasses. I'll wear them so you can see.' He put them on and a moment later a small red dot appeared in the bottom right of his view.

'I have vision.'

'Issue solved.' He'd never felt so pleased with himself.

Duggan, still wearing robes, greeted the five as they exited the ship; he had abandoned the mask and wisely given himself a haircut and beard trim to neaten his previously tatty appearance. Judging by the peculiar angle of his fringe, he wasn't yet used to doing it.

He approached Aryx and shook his hand. 'Good to see you again, young man.' He clasped hands with Sebastian. 'And you, my friend.' He gestured to the others. 'Are you going to introduce me?'

'Of course. Duggan, I'd like you to meet Janyce Hafsteinsdóttir, my sister-in-law, and Erik Mikkaelsson, my nephew.'

He took Janyce's hand and bent to kiss it. She flinched at the touch and giggled childishly. He moved to Erik and crouched in front of him.

'Did you used to be the invisible man?'

Duggan cracked a grin. 'Aye, that I did, lad.'

'Can you show me some magic?'

Duggan straightened, and narrowed his eyes. 'I don't know what your uncle has told you, but magic is not a toy, nor something to be trifled with. It can be dangerous for us to use at the moment. Maybe in the future I will be able to show you how it's done.'

Sebastian cleared his throat. 'We're taking them to Tradescantia. I thought they might be able to stay in Chopwood for a while. The terrorists, or the entities that possessed you, might try to use them to get to me, and I need to know they're safe.'

'And you were hoping I'd stay there with them to keep them out of harm's way?'

'Yes.'

Duggan turned, gesturing to the airlock door leading to the main complex. 'If you'd all care to follow me?' Aryx wheeled into the airlock behind him with the other three following.

'I didn't want to be the bearer of bad news,' Sebastian said, 'but it looks like our suspicions were correct, and the entities were trying to use you to destroy the cube in the lab. They know your location now – probably because of the one that has been controlling you. I'm hoping they don't know how the purge was done, and are just trying to destroy the SI because they can't control it.'

'I won't be the only target, my lad. Remember, they did try to possess you, too.'

'I've not forgotten. Gladrin's pretty sure they want to recruit me. Either way, I think it would be safest for me to work with him on that one – don't worry, we have a plan in place.'

'And what about wheely-fellow here?'

Aryx glared at the old man and felt a vein in his neck pulse. 'I am present, you know. And I can take care of myself. I'm not some brain-dead lump.'

'Just pulling your leg.'

'You're not too old to thump.' He rolled forwards and bashed him in the shins with the frame of his chair.

'Ow!' Duggan rubbed his leg and grinned. 'And you're not too privileged a guest to go out of the airlock!'

Aryx laughed. 'I like your style . . . But back to the issue at hand, what's "emergency plan B"?'

The airlock opened and Duggan stepped into the corridor.
'Plan B? Quite simple, old boy. I move the comet.'

Chapter 38

'**Y**ou *what?*' Aryx had never heard anything so absurd.

'I move the comet,' Duggan said again.

'I heard you the first time. I just don't see how. The amount of engineering that would go into moving an object as large as this would take weeks to set up.'

'I didn't build this entire place, remember? I only decked it out with the bells and whistles for a comfortable life. It wasn't merely a hollow rock when I found it, either.' Duggan opened the familiar door leading to the lounge and ushered them through.

Sebastian took Janyce and Erik over to the couches and deposited his rucksack on the coffee table.

'What else was here, aside from caverns and this stained-glass thingy?' Aryx said, gesturing to the light show overhead.

'The answer is up there.' Duggan pointed to the low cavern above the kitchen and looked down at Aryx's chair. 'I suppose you can't get up there.'

'You suppose wrong.' Aryx hefted the mobipack from his lap, slung it over his back, and fastened the harnesses. The legs coalesced with a dramatic light show.

Duggan's eyes widened. 'Modern technology, eh!'

'Oh, this is more than modern,' Aryx said. 'This is bleeding cutting-edge stuff.' He stood.

Gasps came from the sofa behind him, and he turned to see Erik and his mother staring back. Sebastian sat laughing, probably remembering his own initial reaction to the legs.

Aryx picked up his wheelchair and walked towards the stairs. Duggan watched with a bemused expression as he passed.

'I take it that it's this way?'

Duggan laughed. 'Cocky sod, aren't you?' He looked back at Sebastian. 'Will you and yours be alright left there for a little while? Feel free to make yourselves at home.'

'We'll be fine, thanks.'

Duggan stopped halfway up the stairs and looked up at Aryx. 'Where's your little square friend?'

He tapped his right temple.

'Up here,' Wolfram said, voice projecting loudly from the mobipack.

'Oh, Lord. I'm surrounded by technology,' Duggan said. 'What is the world coming to?' He continued up with a dramatic sweep of his robes.

Aryx reached the top of the stairs, where the wall ended abruptly and levelled onto a smooth, icy-blue floor. The ceiling of the cavernous alcove had seemed lower from downstairs, but it was still at least fifteen feet high in the middle and arched overhead until it met the floor at a shallow angle either side. He dropped his wheelchair and sat down, leaving the legs active.

'I'd expected this to be your bedroom.'

'Why would I need one of those? I have a very long and comfortable couch downstairs, and the temperature is constant, unlike on those wretched stations – why do they have so much trouble keeping the rooms at a decent temperature?'

Aryx shook his head. He preferred to have somewhere distinct to perform each activity in his life and couldn't comprehend not having a specific place to sleep. He was about to labour the point, but then remembered his own apartment was also a single room.

'Go on,' Duggan said, waving him on, 'down to the end.'

The cavern was at least fifty metres long. A faintly glowing light in the darkness ahead was Aryx's only point of reference and the sole source of illumination. He wheeled down the entire length – by which time his eyes finally became accustomed to the dim light – and stopped. The entire wall at the end of the cavern was translucent; something behind it was glowing.

Duggan approached and pressed his hand against the wall. A three metre wide section in the middle flashed and disappeared at his touch.

'What was that? More magic?'

'No. Believe it or not, it's an alien technology, beyond anything I've ever seen or heard of.'

He stepped through the newly opened portal into the space beyond. Aryx followed him into a chamber with a low domed and faceted ceiling. Faint fuzzy, indistinct lights glimmered within the surface as though from inside, similar to the ones in the main living area. The floor was made of an identical substance to the ceiling, but was perfectly flat and with a milky hue. A large, jagged yet smooth-edged lump of the same material protruded from the centre of the floor, an architectural lectern. Duggan approached the pillar, which reached just above his waist level, and extended his hand over the largest of the facets at the top. A faint glow emanated from beneath the surface in response to the gesture.

Aryx wheeled closer. 'What is it?'

'Watch and learn,' Duggan whispered.

A low tone softly hummed through the chamber and the ceiling above darkened. Numerous tiny orbs of light appeared.

Aryx strained to make sense of the pattern through the distortions. 'Is this a star map?'

Duggan nodded. Lines of concentration carved his face.

'Aryx, there appears to be no circuitry or electrical activity in this device,' said Wolfram.

'Really?' he whispered. 'You've been scanning it? How does it work, then?'

'I do not know. This technology is unfamiliar to me, and there is little information on similar materials in the information I have stored.' Aryx's view through the clear AR glasses flickered and a faint tracery of lines appeared, overlaid upon the structure in front of him. 'As you can see, the object has uniform density. My sensors are detecting changes in magnetic flux and gravity.'

'That's strange.' Was it some kind of crystalline circuitry?

'Now,' Duggan said, scratching his chin. 'Where was Achene?'

'It's in V376 Pegasi,' Wolfram said.

'Ah, yes. I'd forgotten, but you knew that already.'

The orb-stars slowly shifted overhead and faint blue lines appeared between several of them. The view continued to move, following the path traced by the lines from one system to the next, until it eventually settled on a star that Duggan had apparently chosen simply by concentrating. The orbs became more widely spaced until three large, blurry spheres appeared. Aryx realised it was a view of V376 Pegasi – the home system of Achene. Duggan brought his hand down until it touched the crystal. The low hum increased in intensity.

Aryx's chair rolled backwards. 'We're moving!'

'That's right. We're on our way.'

'It'll take years to get there.'

'Of course it won't – we're not going directly. We'll use the node network – the navigation system seems accurate enough.'

'How does it all work? There's no circuitry or anything!'

Duggan shrugged. 'As far as I can tell, it's a kind of geometric technology. It seems to focus the properties of the materials it's made from using shape alone. It just works – which is more than I can say for most Human technology ... Given that the outer crust of the comet appears to have built up over millennia, this place was probably built by an advanced civilisation with technology long forgotten. I don't know what it looks like without the covering and, for all I know, it could be a giant crystal-shaped spacecraft.'

Aryx leaned forwards to examine the dais. The material blended seamlessly into the floor; the pale ice-blue milky lustre reminded him of calcite or translucent quartz. He lightly ran his hand over the side of the device. The edges of the smooth, glassy facets flowed subtly into each other.

'Do you know what it's made from? Wolfram can't identify it.'

'Not really. I've done some preliminary examinations, but without destroying it, there doesn't appear to be any adequate way of analysing the technology. None of the scans I've managed to perform have turned up anything other than its basic external structure.'

'It is possible,' Wolfram said, 'that the devices operate on a similar principle to the acceleration nodes. They also have no discernible internal structure, and repairs that have been performed by the Bronadi and Antari simply involved welding in additional material.'

'Interesting. How do people get close enough to repair them?'

'The nodes will only accelerate you if you're not on a collision course with them,' Aryx said. This guy really was out of his time.

'Let's be sure not to crash into one, then.' Duggan looked up at the map depicted in the ceiling. 'It's going to take a couple of hours to get there, so we'd better go down and see how the others are doing.'

Aryx followed him back along the cavern towards the living area. 'How did you find this place?'

'I got the idea from Sollers Hope. I scanned several systems for low-density objects with the intention of finding a planetoid with caves that I could kit-out, and I stumbled across this place. It wasn't originally in this system.'

'No?'

'It was a rogue asteroid, not attached to any star. When I back-calculated its trajectory, it seemed as though it was originally orbiting the same sun as Achene.'

'Now that's some coincidence!' In the sheer vastness of the universe, the likelihood of stumbling across something that had originated in the same system that Duggan had left was infinitesimal. 'Sebastian will never believe it. Speaking of which, we haven't told you what's been happening ...'

Sebastian looked up from studying his grandfather's journal as Aryx and Duggan clanked down the stairs. Janyce stood, busying herself by making drinks in the kitchen.

'Aryx has been filling me in,' Duggan said. 'It sounds like you've been having quite a time of it.'

'You're telling me. I'm glad the worst of it's over now, though.'

'So, these dreams you've been having ... Aryx says you didn't remember them clearly before, but you think the demons in them may be the entities.'

Janyce beckoned to Erik, apparently disturbed by the increasing talk of entities and demons. 'Come and help *Mamma* in the kitchen, will you?' The boy ran over to her and started rooting through the cupboards.

Sebastian shrugged. 'Well, it's just a guess, given they look a lot like the things you showed us in that old book of yours.'

'I wouldn't be surprised if the entities don't actually look like that. It's most likely your subconscious filling in the details with something that it finds appropriate. Your idea about them testing your responses is also interesting. Have you got this Gladrin chap to shut off the program?'

He shook his head. 'I didn't think it would be wise. If he turned it off, there's every chance that news of its deactivation could get back to them via the terrorists, and they'd know we were on to them.'

'A wise move. You're convinced the terrorists are being run by the entities?'

'With everything that's happened, the timing is too coincidental, and Gladrin said that one of the ITF members fitted the description of someone possessed.'

'I see. That's quite disturbing.' Duggan rubbed his chin. 'I wonder if it might be possible to learn more about the entities directly through the dreams. If you were able to practice lucid dreaming . . . ' He trailed off into contemplation.

'What's that?' Aryx asked.

'Oh, sorry, old boy. Normally, when you dream, you aren't in control. You find strange things to be normal and accept them. It's only afterwards, when you wake up, that you realise the memories don't fit in with the other experiences you've had. During lucid dreaming you become aware that you are dreaming. You notice the things that are out of place and, because of that, are able to control the dream to some extent.'

'Actually, I think I've heard of that. Alvarez used to talk about something like it. He said it takes years to learn. I thought it was a load of rubbish, to be honest.'

'That is very true, under normal circumstances.' Duggan waved a finger about while he spoke. 'But I believe that if Sebastian learned to use thaumaturgy, he could potentially use a spell to induce the state and guarantee its effectiveness.'

Sebastian put the journal down. 'You think I could do it?' After discovering that magic was real, he hadn't even entertained the idea of trying to use it. It seemed far too dangerous and didn't fit in with his rational, ordered universe.

'Yes, I think you could. You've got the right type of personality to be able to do it. You see underlying patterns and rules in things that others might miss – you just need to muster up a bit of faith in yourself. I can see you're having a hard time getting your head around it. I might have something that will help you to accept it. Let's have a look.' Duggan darted over to the same bookcase from which he had taken the medieval book days before. He drew out another book with a heavy, ridged spine and coarse paper binding, sat down, and carefully rested it in his lap. Inside the cover was a print, depicting clouds with figures standing amongst them, each appearing to represent a different skill or school of thought. The writing was hard to read, a form of English so old that Sebastian couldn't understand any of it.

Duggan began flicking through the pages. 'This is *Mathematicall Praeface to Euclid's Elements,*' he said, 'written in 1570 by John Dee. It's a work on mathematics and physics but, back in his day, people thought him to be a conjurer simply because they didn't understand the physics and maths employed by the mechanisms he described. He talks about "art mathematical", which he called thaumaturgy.'

Sebastian caught sight of a small symbol printed in the corner of one of the pages – a small, right-angled V with another, acute, upside down V overlaid upon it. It looked familiar somehow. Duggan closed the book and put it back on the shelf before Sebastian had time to take it in.

'Surely, to you or I, or anyone who understands it, this would just be science?' Aryx said.

Duggan waggled a finger at the pair. 'Ah, but that's where you're wrong, my boy.'

'Are you saying that there's almost a science to magic?' Sebastian asked.

Duggan nodded rapidly. 'Yes, yes. All it takes is for you to be open-minded enough to accept the possibility of a system, and you'll see it. Many secret societies held hidden knowledge for centuries that hinted at thaumaturgy being more than mere science. The Illuminati, the Freemasons ... even the Church accused the Templars of being involved with magic.'

'I suppose you're right. I could try it.'

Aryx glared at Sebastian and folded his arms. 'You think this is a good idea, do you, going along with a nutso plan like that? What about the demons?' He frowned at Duggan and waved his arm in Sebastian's direction. 'I don't want him running around trying to bloody strangle me—'

Sebastian boiled over. 'Don't be so ignorant! I haven't agreed to anything yet!' He certainly didn't need a fight with him now.

Duggan rubbed the back of his neck. 'The Folians might know of ways get around that. It never occurred to me that I might get possessed, and I'd always thought it was religious dogma so I never even contemplated it. Now that I know better, I think it would be a good idea to ask for their help. If the entities truly are some kind of extra-spatial or energy being, the Folians may know how to prevent their influence.'

'Well, I don't like it. It's one thing to get involved with terrorists – I can handle that – but when you start messing around with things you can't see or touch, that's another matter altogether.'

'I don't have much choice, do I? Neither of us is ever going to get a decent night's rest unless we either sleep in the ship or shut the signal off, and if we do that we might be signing our own death-warrants, along with Gladrin's family's.'

Aryx huffed and his reddening face puckered sourly.

'Oh, stop it! You *both* have a point.' Janyce walked around the counter carrying a tray of drinks, followed by Erik, and set them on the table. 'Until you two find out what's going on, we're going to have to hide out in this low-tech "Chopwood" town Sebastian's been on about. I don't particularly want to be stuck there forever, wondering when you're going to come and get us, but I also don't think it's wise to act without more information.'

'I suppose you're right,' Aryx grumbled. 'I still don't like the idea of messing about with magic. It's an unknown quantity.'

'I'll have to have faith,' Sebastian said.

Aryx's frown gave way to surprise. 'You've changed your attitude.'

'I've seen a lot of things lately that have forced me to change my mind.' It was true; several of the things he'd been taught growing up had finally turned out to be real, or at least rooted in reality. He had two choices – bury his head in the sand and ignore it all, or accept it and move on. He'd chosen to accept it and, to his surprise, found it liberating.

Janyce reached out to stir the pot of tea and the cups began to rattle. 'What was that?'

'We are on the move,' Duggan said. 'We've probably passed the first acceleration node. We should be at Achene in a couple of hours.'

She handed out the drinks and looked at Sebastian. 'I'd have thought you'd have been interested in finding out how this place works.'

He waved his hand dismissively. He was more interested in dealing with the terrorists and alien entities. 'I've got too much going on in my head. I'm sure it'll still be around for a while yet.'

She shook her head. 'So, Duggan, why do you live in this place and not with the rest of civilisation? Seb said you were a bit of a hermit, even when you lived in Chopwood.'

'Aside from being invisible? Living away from others has many benefits, but mostly I wanted to be away from social pressure. My studies often required concentration and focus. Unfortunately, having others constantly vying for your attention is somewhat distracting.'

'So you left.'

Duggan's jaw tightened. 'Yes. I still worked with the other colonists. No room for dead weight. But personally, I needed to forge a stronger link with my subconscious, and you can't always do that around others.'

'I don't understand how that works.'

Sebastian closed the journal. The more he heard of the conversation, the more interested he became.

'It's difficult to explain. Many don't understand.'

'Try me.' Janyce's tone was defiant.

'Hmm, let me think of a good analogy ...' Duggan stared at the ceiling. 'If you try to learn a new skill, for example, you might be very good at it the first few times you try. You might become aware of others watching you and then begin to fail. You just lose the knack. That's down to social pressure.'

Janyce leaned back.

'The reason being, the subconscious wants you to fit in with society. It wants you to be safe and protected within the hierarchy. If you're seen as being good at something, you might become responsible, move to the top, out of your safe zone, and right into the firing line if something goes wrong.'

Janyce shook her head. 'I don't see how that helps you study.'

Sebastian rolled his eyes. 'You'll move up the hierarchy and lose your social safety net,' Sebastian said. 'If you've got peer pressure, you're more likely to screw up.'

Duggan nodded. 'You suddenly become a target, so it makes you fail. That way it keeps you in that safe region where nobody has any expectations of you.'

'That's probably why Seb was worried about getting the job in SpecOps,' Aryx mumbled.

Sebastian shot him a scathing look.

Janyce slowly shook her head and folded her arms.

Duggan folded his arms in response. 'I can see you're not going to understand it,' he said calmly, 'and I had no expectation that you would. Most people don't believe it. Simply accept that I found being near large concentrations of people ... unhelpful.'

'By studies, I assume you mean your research into thaumaturgy,' Sebastian said.

'Yes. The Folians introduced me to carbyne and the true art, but before I met them the ability to perform thaumaturgy without it was almost non-existent. As a hobby, I spent my time researching the principles of magic from history books and trying to glean what truth I could from writings and so-called New Age literature.'

Janyce nodded rapidly. 'So what can we expect on Achene and Tradescantia when we get there?'

'Oh yes, of course . . .' Duggan began describing the ecology of the two planets, which seemed to suitably distract her from the previous conversation. Erik, apparently bored by such matters, went to Aryx, and the two entertained themselves with the cube's games of logic.

Sebastian turned his attention back to the diary and began absent-mindedly leafing through the pages until one passage in particular caught his attention.

Beyond nine folds, geometries' curve
between realms of fire and ice
seven telamon seal the Tower
standing amidst the giants of old
and even in this age of light
dark things stir behind the curtain.

'What's that, old boy?'

'Oh, a poem or something from my grandfather's journal.' He hadn't even realised he'd read it out loud.

'What does it mean?'

He scratched his head. 'I don't know.'

'Can't you ask him?'

'No, he died years ago. It probably doesn't mean anything. He used to be an explorer, but he got a little . . . strange in his final days. We think he had dementia.' He swallowed.

'You were close to him. Was he ill for long before he died?'

'Illness didn't kill him. He disappeared off in a ship one day. He was rambling on about having to find something. They found the wreckage a couple of weeks later, several thousand AU from Sirius, but no trace of his body. EarthSec said it was a fire that had broken out.' He let out a shuddering breath.

Janyce reached over to squeeze his forearm and gave a sympathetic smile.

'My father investigated briefly and found that the pressure suits had gone. He died before he finished the investigation, but the department closed the file shortly after, saying my grandfather had died in an EVA accident—' The words caught in his throat again.

'I'm sorry, old boy. I'm sure if his writings mean something, it'll come to you eventually.'

'It probably won't mean anything. Look at this, for example . . .' He leafed through the book until he came across a page with a sketch of a large, faceted object, standing next to a man. The thing looked vaguely humanoid: several large chunks of angular stone, or crystal, possibly representing legs, arms, and a torso. The pieces weren't connected, but floating in formation. If he assumed the man in the picture to be of average height, the structure must have measured twelve to fifteen feet tall. At the bottom of the page, a caption read *Frost Giant*.

'I have no idea what it's supposed to be. I remember him saying something about stonework when I was young . . . Is it a sculpture he made, or was planning, based on Norse legends? And then there's this—' He flicked several pages forwards, opening the book at a diagram resembling a family tree. At the bottom were Frímann (his grandfather), Thor (his father), Mikkael (his brother), and himself. Near the top of the page were the names Odin, Freyr, and several others he recognised. He tapped them. 'These are the Æsir, the Norse Gods. If my grandfather thought we were related to them, he'd definitely lost it.'

Duggan nodded slowly. 'It is interesting, I'll give you that. Even if they are the ramblings of a broken mind, there could still be elements of truth in there – I'd be interested to find out what the *Tower* is, and these realms. Something to do with this frost giant artwork?'

Sebastian continued reading in silence and allowed Duggan to drift off into contemplation.

The cups and saucers on the table rattled.

Sebastian looked up from the diary. 'What's happening?'

'We're slowing down. I think we've arrived.' Duggan produced a remote control from his robes and pressed a button. The wall of monitors flicked into life, and the roiling orange surface of Achene swirled across the displays.

Janyce leaped up, fists clenched. 'We're not going down there!'

Sebastian laughed. 'It's not what it looks like, really! You'll like it.'

'You better be right, Seb. That place looks as inviting as an acid bath.'

'Naturally we can't take the comet down to the surface, so we'll go in the ships. Sebastian, if you take the others, I'll follow in the runner.' The china on the table stopped rattling and Duggan made his way to the door. 'We're in orbit now. Time to go.'

As the group followed and piled into their respective ships, an unwelcome sense of urgency took Sebastian, and he was keen to be on the planet as soon as possible.

* * *

The ships left the white glare of the comet behind, heading towards the planet. At least Sebastian knew what to expect this time, and he adjusted the speed and course, programming in the coordinates for the grassland region in which the ship had previously crashed. He hoped the Folians would be aware of their approach and send someone to meet them in that familiar place.

The orange vapours parted as the ship descended, revealing the idyllic, lush forests and rolling plains. Erik and Janyce stood behind the pilots, gazing at the landscape below.

'It looks like Earth,' Erik said. 'The trees . . .'

Sebastian smiled, remembering how he felt when he first set eyes on the place – right before the panic had set in. 'Fasten your seatbelts. We're coming in to land.' His family made their way to the seats at the back.

Aryx clamped his chair down next to the pilot's seat. 'Land nicely this time, please.'

'Of course.'

The ship swept over the forest, approaching the edge of the woodland near the Hesperidium, and Sebastian activated the landing sequence. The thrusters engaged and the ship vibrated. Trees crept into view on the starboard side as they passed the canopy level, and with a gentle bump the ship came to rest.

Aryx patted the console. 'Good girl.'

A moment later, the whine of another set of engines came through the hull and a small, black dart-shaped craft landed next to the *Ultima Thule*.

'Everyone out,' Sebastian said.

Janyce took Erik to the lift. 'I suppose we have to ask these Folians if it's okay to stay in Chopwood?'

He nodded. 'I think so. It might not be safe enough for you to live here, but at least Chopwood has houses, and I'm sure you can always go to Duggan's comet, if needs be.'

'I hope you don't mind pick-your-own vegetarian cuisine,' Aryx said.

'Why?' Erik's nose wrinkled.

'There's no meat, but lots of fruit and veg.'

He made a face and Janyce rubbed his shoulder. 'It'll be fine, I'm sure.'

After a final check, Aryx put on the mobipack and led the group out of the ship.

Duggan's runner, finished in matt-black with thick, triangular wings, looked like it was modelled on old twenty-first century stealth craft: large enough to carry a couple of passengers – if they sat one behind the other – with no space for cargo. Sebastian ran his hand over one of the wing sections; it was rough, most likely due to the kinetic ablative plating. The blacked-out cockpit flipped upwards and he staggered back.

Duggan clambered out over the wing section. 'Are you ready?'

'Everyone's here,' Sebastian said, gesturing to the group.

Duggan looked around. 'Good. There are no animals here to greet us, which is a good sign. I expect the Folians have anticipated our arrival.' He made his way towards the trees. Sebastian followed.

'Do you want us to come?' Aryx asked. Janyce wrung her hands while Erik kicked a clump of stubble.

'Of course, they know us. Come on!' Sebastian said.

The group headed to the trees and stopped several metres from the undergrowth when Tolinar appeared from behind a large trunk. Erik gawped, wide-eyed, and pointed. '*Look!*'

Janyce discretely lowered the boy's outstretched arm and pulled him close. 'Shh.'

'Greetings, Tolinar,' Duggan said, holding out his hand. 'Long time no see, old boy!'

Tolinar didn't reciprocate, but bowed. 'It is good to see you, also, Duggan Simmons, however unexpected. What can we help you with?'

With total disregard for the alien's personal space, Duggan put his arm around Tolinar's shoulders and steered him back towards the trees. 'We have a favour to ask.'

They entered the forest and Sebastian tried to keep within earshot of the conversation.

Duggan explained the situation to Tolinar while they walked. '. . . so you see, we think the entities, appearing as demons, might also have been responsible for the Folians being turfed out on Earth centuries ago – pardon the pun.'

'The same beings are responsible for the station-dwellers' nightmares?'

'Indeed. So in addition to coming to ask for permission to stay in Chopwood, we'd like to know if there is a way of preventing ourselves from being possessed.'

'The best protection is simply not to use the weave, is it not?'

Duggan sighed. 'Not an option, my friend. Sebastian needs to find out why the entities are sending these dreams and how. Otherwise, he'll be left in an unpleasant predicament – that is, if he and Aryx don't go mad beforehand. I've suggested he use magic to attempt lucid dreaming, but as you know it's a bit risky.'

'We need to learn more about the nature of these entities. It would be best for the Folians to examine your mind, to see whether the entities have left traces of their contact.'

Sebastian noticed Tolinar was wearing the calyx; the fruit on it had been gradually growing during the conversation. 'Are we going to meet Shiliri?' he asked.

'Yes. She is here.'

They approached a large tree with smooth, pewter bark. The trunk bulged and split in places giving a clear impression of a female torso. Tolinar walked up to the bole of the tree and, while the others waited, he took off the leafy wreath and held it up. Shiliri's face appeared in the bark and, as she spoke the familiar humming chant, the calyx fruit shrivelled and withered away. She addressed the group.

'We accept your request to stay on Tradescantia in the town of Chopwood. Two of our number will transfer to its forests and keep the wildlife under control. As to the issue of the demon-entities, we must determine their nature. Duggan, please step forth.'

The old man hesitated.

'Do not be afraid. I will place my consciousness alongside yours and examine your mind.'

'She's done it to me. It's a bit odd, but doesn't hurt,' Sebastian said.

Her face vanished, and a glowing blue sphere of light drifted out of the tree, coming to rest around Duggan's head. He closed his eyes, and a few moments later the sphere moved back into the tree.

He staggered. 'I'm fine, a little woozy, but fine.'

The others breathed out their collective relief.

'This is disturbing. It would seem that the entities use your connection to the weave whilst you are casting magic. We have never sensed anything like this. Sebastian, would you ask your device to perform the purging spell by way of an experiment?'

'Are you sure? I don't want to do anything that will hurt you.'

'These beings cause harm and need to be stopped. It would be a worthy sacrifice. Now, please, perform the purge.'

He pulled a vial of carbyne from his belt and handed it to Aryx.

Aryx reached around and held the vial near his pack. 'You heard the lady.'

'Wait,' Janyce said. 'If the cube can create this effect, can't you copy whatever energy it gives off?'

'I hadn't thought of that,' Aryx said. 'Seb, record it, will you?'

Shaking his head, he took the rugged infoslate from his rucksack. 'I don't think it'll work, but I'll give it a try. Wolfram, trigger the thaumatic.'

'One moment.' The familiar chanting and intonation began, echoed through the pack's speakers.

Sebastian gritted his teeth while he watched the infoslate. If anything bad happened to Shiliri, he'd never forgive himself.

The tone reached a crescendo and the rippling pressure wave tore through the forest.

Chapter 39

Shiliri's glow flickered as the distortion field passed through the tree that housed her. Janyce let out a gasp and ran to put her hands on the bark.

'Oh, Gods! Are you—'

'I am uninjured. However, I felt a profound sense of loneliness. The spell appears to detach the entities from their connection with the weave – I believe they must be able to hold open the connection for a time, and whilst doing so have influence – once disconnected, they lose their anchor to this realm—'

'Slow down, Shiliri,' Janyce said, gently rubbing the bark.

'I do not mean to speak quickly. The effect was most disturbing ... I do not believe the entities' nature is identical to ours. If it were, they would have been able to reconnect with you afterwards. It makes sense to think of them as existing in another layer of space, in a realm between realms, through which they use the weave to contact you.'

'You know,' Aryx said, 'I think the entities exist in superphase, or somewhere that touches it.'

'What?' Sebastian couldn't believe it.

'The dust on ships, like I saw at Kimberley depot. I think it's carbyne. I think the entities exist there, and that's where the powder goes.'

'This may go some way to explaining the damage our ships occasionally experience when traversing superphase,' Tolinar said.

'It might also explain the "acceleration psychosis" Wolfram discovered.'

'Oh shit!' Sebastian blurted. 'Does this mean that when they get disconnected, they take knowledge they've gained back to their realm?' It almost didn't bear thinking about, but it was now obvious how they had learned of their visit to Yazor.

'It is likely. However, without encountering one of these beings, it is impossible for us to determine exactly how the connection works. In our experience of mind-to-mind contact, we have only been able to assimilate the knowledge accessed by the mind we touch at the time of contact. We do not gain knowledge of the host's entire memory. This may also be the case with your entities.'

'What about those that are permanently possessed?'

'During those times, the beings may detach from their realm in the way that our consciousness separates from our host trees. It is possible that they cannot communicate with others in their realm until the consciousness returns there fully.'

'It's a good job we brought the comet from Yazor,' Aryx said. 'The ones that possessed Duggan while he was trying to become visible would have been passing knowledge back and forth every time they possessed him, and any others that come through would probably know of the comet's previous location.'

Sebastian's heart lifted. At least the demons might not be aware of the cube's continued existence. They certainly hadn't seen it while Duggan was attempting to strangle him. If the Folians were correct, they *could* be aware that there was a method of ejecting them from the hosts, but any entities currently lodged in this realm wouldn't know about it, and that could provide a much-needed advantage if they encountered others in the future. He hoped they wouldn't.

Duggan interrupted his train of thought. 'So, back on the essential topic, how do we stop them from invading us when we use magic?'

'I believe it is relatively simple,' Shiliri said. 'You must create a shield of white light around yourself when you first acquire your spell imagery. The protection effect will be incorporated into the impressions you receive.'

'Then we should go and get some practice,' Duggan said. 'I have yet to initiate Sebastian into the fine art of thaumaturgy. Can you look after the others? They probably need something to eat.'

Shiliri moved to another tree. 'Very well. Tolinar, please bring them. Duggan, take Sebastian to the Cambium. It will provide a suitably conducive environment for practise.'

Sebastian hugged Janyce and Erik. 'I'll see you soon. The Folians will look after you until I come back.'

'Be careful,' Janyce said, and kissed him on the cheek.

'You'd best take this.' Aryx tossed him the cube. 'If you're messing about with magic and things go wrong, Wolfram's the only one that'll be able to purge you both.'

The thought hadn't even crossed his mind. 'Thanks,' he said, dropping the cube into his backpack.

Duggan began making his way in the direction of the Cambium. Sebastian hurried after him.

'Seb, wait!' Aryx shouted. 'What about the results of the scan?'

He called back, 'Nothing. They were blank.'

Chapter 40

Tolinar led Aryx, Janyce, and Erik through the undergrowth until they reached the avenue of trees that separated the main forest from the belt adjacent to the grassland. Aryx found it easy enough to keep up with the alien using the mobipack. Erik seemed to be enjoying the adventure and Janyce looked pleased to be out of the ship; the colour had finally returned to her face – at least she was over her motion sickness.

Shiliri's floating consciousness hung back in one of the larger trees at the edge as they crossed the avenue. The slender jungle-like forest gave way to a clearing filled with short, widely spaced trees. Several species looked familiar, reminding Aryx of the fruit trees his father had grown in the orchards on the farm. The fragrance of orange blossom gently caressed his senses.

'We grow many types of fruit in this grove. Are you hungry?' Tolinar stopped at the nearest tree and reached up, pointing to something that looked like a grapefruit.

Aryx's stomach growled before he had a chance to speak and Erik, hiding behind his mother's legs, giggled.

'He's definitely hungry,' Janyce said.

'I haven't eaten for ages. What sort of fruit are they ... citrus?'

Tolinar tilted his head to one side, as though contemplating his response. 'The structure is similar, but there are many variations. If you prefer, we have some varieties that are higher in protein and taste like meat.'

'Yuck!' Erik said, pulling a face.

Aryx snorted a laugh. 'My sentiments exactly. If it looks like fruit, I want it to taste like it.' He smacked his lips. 'Besides, I've got the taste for something sharp now.'

Tolinar plucked a fruit from the lowest branch and handed it to Erik, who peeled it eagerly. He stripped the mustard-coloured skin, bit into the interior, and quickly recoiled. Aryx thought the boy's face was going to turn inside out.

'That must be some sour fruit!' Janyce said.

'It's gross!' He spat the chunk out onto the ground and handed the fruit to Aryx, who bit into it wholeheartedly.

'Very nice,' he said, nodding his approval.

Janyce folded her arms and shook her head. 'Says he of the cast-iron taste buds.'

Tolinar handed Erik a smaller, redder fruit. He bit into it tentatively, but this time smiled. 'That's really nice. It tastes like raspberries.'

The Karrikin handed out several more varieties, all from the same tree, and watched over the trio while they sat down to eat in the afternoon sun. Erik looked restless.

'What's up?' Aryx asked.

'Nothing.' The boy shifted and wrung his hands together.

'Come on, what do you want to ask? Is it something about my legs?'

'No, silly. I wanted to know who your friend was on the station, that big dog-man – what is he?'

'Deruno? He's Bronadi.'

'Where do they come from? I've never seen one before.' The boy was wide-eyed with curiosity. Janyce listened, smiling.

'They're from Bronat, but they originally came from a planet in the Sirius system. They had some kind of ecological disaster thousands of years ago before moving.'

Janyce laughed. 'Sirius, the Dog Star? You *are* kidding.'

'I kid you not. I hadn't really thought of it like that before. It's a bit ironic.' He looked up at Tolinar. 'Sebastian said the Folians had been to Earth. Is it possible they told early Humans about other races?'

'We cannot say for certain, as the memories the Folians received back were fragmented, but it is possible that the early Folian travellers had passed on such knowledge.'

Aryx rubbed his chin. 'Sebastian told me some stupid story about a tribe in Africa that supposedly knew Sirius was a binary system, even though it wasn't visible without a telescope. If it wasn't just a cultural contamination by anthropologists, I suppose they could have got that from the Folians.'

'That doesn't explain how you've got species from one planet that looks like a species from Earth,' Janyce said.

'Perhaps canines originated in the Sirius system,' Tolinar said.

Janyce folded her arms. 'No, we've got fossil evidence on Earth with a clear progression.'

'Perhaps your world was visited in the distant past by another race that took your canines back with them.'

'That doesn't explain how ancient Humans would have known about them,' Aryx said.

'Actually,' she said, 'it could ... Aliens visit Earth, take canines back with them to Sirius, they then evolve into their present bipedal forms, and when the Folians come, they tell Humans about the Bronadi. They make their way into legend. Simple.'

He shook his head. 'Talk about know-it-all. You're almost as bad as your brother-in-law.'

She shrugged.

'I was about to start a project on first contact before that man kidnapped us,' Erik said.

'Your timing was perfect, then,' Aryx said. 'The Bronadi were the first race that Humans met out here. When the Gliese explorers found a damaged node in space, they met a Bronadi ship that turned up to repair it.'

The boy's eyes widened. 'Did they get into a fight?'

'No. The ship from Earth was a xenoarch exploration vessel. They had a few marines for security, but nothing that was equipped for a space battle. The Bronadi already knew about other races, so they knew it was best to approach with care. They barked at them for a bit over the comms until one of the xenoarch linguists took over and was able to pick up bits and pieces of the language. The Bronadi crew taught the explorers the basics of Galac while they repaired the node, but there weren't enough resources on the exploration ship to last the crew until the repair was completed. They didn't know the node would send them straight home, and they couldn't learn enough of the technical language from the Bronadi in the time they had to understand the nodes, so they turned around and went home.'

'Didn't the Bronadi give them any of their food?'

'Oh, they offered, but none of it was in any state that a Human could eat, and some of it was highly poisonous.'

'And so that's how we found out about the nodes,' Janyce said.

'Yeah. When the expedition got home, they were able to scan for the same energy signature as the one given off by the node in Gliese, and that's when we found the one in our solar system.'

'Why didn't the Bronadi come and visit us?' Erik asked.

'Their ruling council, the Bronala, have a strict policy of not visiting the homeworld of a race that doesn't have an extrasolar trade station. It's sensible. At least it means that anyone they come into contact with has to be mature enough to deal with other races first.'

'Can you ask them about their planet for me?'

'If I get the chance, I'll let you know what I find out.'

'Speaking of which, when you've left us here, how do we contact you if we need anything?' Janyce asked.

'There's no comms relay in—'

Tolinar's head tilted, as though listening to something, and he whispered to Aryx, 'We must go. There is a matter of great importance that we must attend to. Please stay here. We will be back soon. Shiliri will attend to your needs where possible.'

'What's the matter?' It was too late; Tolinar had dashed out of the grove.

'Is everything okay?' Janyce asked.

'I don't know. Tolinar said he had to go but would be back.'

'Oh. So what were you saying about the comms relay?'

'There isn't one in this system, which means if you need to contact us, you'd have to take a ship to the node, align with the next one in the network, and then send a signal to it.'

'And will we be able to receive a signal from you?'

'Only if we do the same. There are no relays at the surrounding nodes pointing in this direction.'

She shrugged. 'I suppose it's good, really. It's not exactly a hideout otherwise, is it?' She moved closer to him and whispered. 'I wouldn't worry too much about finding out about Bronat.' She looked back to see if Erik was listening. 'Do you think Seb's in trouble?'

'He doesn't normally take unnecessary risks. Then again, lately ... No ... I'm sure if he's going to try learning magic he'll be cautious about it. Duggan seems to know what he's on about – and they've got Wolfram in case anything goes wrong, after all.'

'Would that thing know what's happening?'

'You'd be surprised. I've had to trust him with my life.' His jaw tightened at the memory of the predator attack. But it wasn't just that. Wolfram had saved him, only to put off the inevitable.

Janyce touched his arm. 'Are you alright?'

'Yes. It brings back some bad memories, that's all. I'm over it now.'

'Over it or not, you don't look okay.' She squeezed his arm. She obviously wasn't going to let it go.

The urge to tell her rose to his throat and he swallowed it back ... It didn't work. He couldn't bottle it up forever; he needed to confide in someone – even Karan didn't know. He leaned forwards and whispered. 'I couldn't tell Sebastian, but the infection I got when I lost my legs has got worse. I'm dying.'

Her fair skin lost what little colour it had. 'I'm so sorry! Oh, you've got to tell him.'

He turned away from her and stared at the ground. 'I can't. It would kill him.'

She walked around to face him. 'Isn't it curable?'

'It's manageable with drugs. I've got a few years in me yet. I'd hoped the Cambium fruit might have cured it.' He shook his head, trying to hold back the tears that threatened to overwhelm him. 'I got tested when we got back to the station, just in case, but it was still there. I didn't tell Seb. The Folians said healing was very specific, and the fruit works like nanobots – they couldn't cure it, either.'

'You have to tell him!' Her eyes were red. 'He cares about you. I've seen how you are together. You have to.'

'No, Jan, promise you won't. He already feels bad enough for dragging me out here. But if it weren't for him bringing me, I'd never have got off the station. I can't die languishing in some hospital bed. Out here I can make a difference.' He looked over his shoulder at Erik, who sat rummaging in a pile of leaves, as though looking for some small creature. 'We'd best get back to him,' Aryx said, nodding in Erik's direction. 'I guess they could be a while before the others come back. Just promise you won't tell Seb.'

She wiped a tear away with a thumb. 'I promise.'

Chapter 41

Duggan moved rapidly through the undergrowth with the surefootedness of someone who had been on the planet only yesterday. The sixty years or so that he'd been away certainly hadn't dulled his memory. Sebastian stumbled over roots and vines in an effort to keep up. He didn't know how the old man managed to move so fast.

'What exactly are we going to do?' he asked.

Duggan pulled apart a clump of undergrowth that blocked his path. 'I'm going to teach you how to use magic.'

'But how, *exactly?*'

'As I've explained before, we'll use visualisation and intonation. Have you ever tried throat-singing?'

'I can't say I have.' Sebastian recalled his grandfather singing to him as a child – no wonder it had seemed familiar. It was amazing how people managed to produce multiple harmonics while chanting; it was like more than one person making the sounds – almost like the voices of the Folians. The art had almost died out; he remembered his grandfather telling him that some of the Sami people of Finland did it as part of the Joik, during their traditional worship of nature. Maybe they, too, had a connection and understanding of the weave.

The pair broke out of the dense foliage into the avenue near the Cambium. Duggan led Sebastian into the grove and stood in the centre. Sebastian put his bag on the floor, took out the cube and placed it on top of it so that Wolfram would have a good view of the proceedings, and dropped a couple of carbyne vials next to it.

'To get us in the mood, how about having your cube show us something impressive?'

'I can hear you, Mr Simmons, and there's no harm in addressing me directly. What would you like to see?'

'I do apologise. It's quite difficult to get used to ... I'd appreciate if you could demonstrate something harmless but visually striking, if you know anything like that.'

'One moment.' The lights on the side of the cube started to flash randomly and a low hum emanated as Wolfram chanted, '*Fallacis immolationem.*'

The metal burst into flame as though doused with alcohol and lit. The flame danced and shimmied around the cube, with little tongues licking several inches into the air. Sebastian leaned close to look. He wasn't sure if he actually felt heat on his face, or if he imagined it. The canvas of the rucksack looked unscathed, but it was most definitely illuminated by the light from the fire. He watched as the vial of carbyne closest to the cube slowly emptied itself.

'Very impressive. Illusory flame, indeed.' Duggan walked over to the burning cube and waved his hand through the flames above. 'Ouch!'

'Not so illusory?'

He rubbed his hand. 'Interesting. No damage, but it certainly made me *think* I was being hurt. That could be useful under the right conditions.'

'I imagine it would,' Sebastian said. The flames vanished and the bar of LEDs on the cube became fully illuminated. 'He'll be quiet for a bit while he cools down.'

Duggan clapped his hands together and rubbed them. 'Right then, enough of the fun. Let's start off with something nice and simple, shall we? The most basic of requirements – stabilising orichalcum. Sorry – carbyne.' His tone became teacher-like. 'Sit down and cross your legs.' He made a flicking motion in the direction of Sebastian's head. 'And pull your hood up, too.'

'Why do I need the hood?'

'It stops light from getting in your eyes when you're trying to concentrate. I'd also suggest wearing some looser clothes. If they're too tight, they'll distract you when you're trying to think.'

'The N-suit is fine. It's more comfortable than you'd think.' He shifted and crossed his legs.

'Ready?'

'Yes, I'm ready.'

'Good. Now the first thing to do is get your mind into a state where *now* is all that there is. Do away with the future and what you'd like to happen; do away with the past. Be aware that the present is the state of things that *were*. Exist only in the moment. What you want to happen simply *is*.'

Was he supposed to be doing, visualising something?

Duggan snapped him out of his pondering. 'Imagine that vial of carbyne. Imagine yourself opening it.'

He did as instructed. He closed his eyes and tried to visualise taking a vial from his belt and flipping the top off. He immediately imagined the powder evaporating.

'Stop seeing what you expect to happen.'

He opened his eyes. 'How did you know I was?'

'Your face wrinkled. Try to imagine opening it and the powder staying as it is. If it helps, imagine the atoms sticking together.'

Sebastian closed his eyes again and began to concentrate, visualising opening the tube and, this time, seeing the powder remain without dissipating. The atoms struggled to burst apart as the surrounding air molecules buffeted them, but they held fast against the onslaught. He smiled and opened his eyes.

'That's good. Right, now we start the hard part.'

'That's not all there is to do?' There was always a catch.

'Oh, goodness, no! Visualising the outcome is just the easy bit. If magic were easy, every Tom, Dick, and Harry would be running around doing it! Hold your hands like this . . . ' Duggan turned his palms up and bent his hands back, as though begging.

Sebastian mirrored the gesture.

'Now, press the heels of your hands onto your eyes. I expect you've done something like this as a child.'

It seemed foolish, but he closed his eyes again and pressed his hands against them. Waves of bluish rippling rings surged out of the darkness towards him, just as it had when he'd done the same thing as a kid. 'What now?'

'Just wait,' Duggan whispered.

The rings slowly faded away. His eyes were beginning to ache. After a minute, a spattering of bright specks burst forth like a field of paparazzi. The flashing stopped unexpectedly, leaving his aching eyes dark once more.

'Now, whilst you're pressing them, imagine that scene with the powder once again. Remember to keep it present. Now, what is, not what will be.'

Sebastian concentrated on the images, trying to will his intent into reality.

'I won't speak for a few minutes, but I want you to listen. Watch the images, too.'

What did he mean? Distracted by his own thoughts, he almost lost the image in his mind. He sat patiently, trying to hold the concept of the stabilised carbyne in his head. He couldn't hear anything except for the faint sound of birds in the distance; he tried to block them out, straining to listen for something else. His breathing. The faint whine of tinnitus. Nothing else.

While he listened, the whistling in his inner ear got louder until it became a musical tone – nothing like the piercing scream from damaged auditory nerves. He became used to the sound and a vague shape came into his mind, unbidden. The blurry image sharpened into a thick, glowing green horizontal line with squared ends. There was something familiar about it. Something ... Was it a rune, a symbol from his heritage? It was. Isa the ice-rune, lying on its side. A representation of something motile made static. Frozen.

His throat tightened, almost as if the realisation of meaning prompted some physical reaction. He wanted to emulate the tone he heard and felt his larynx move in preparation. His lips parted, forming soundless words. What was happening to him? The images and sound stopped.

His eyes snapped open. 'Shit! I lost concentration.'

Duggan folded his arms. 'You were thinking about it too much. Just let it happen.' He looked down at Sebastian's neck. 'You still don't have faith in yourself, do you?'

He realised he had brought his hand up to his necklace, the Mjölnir – his plain bronze Thor's hammer – and was gripping it tightly. 'I didn't understand what was going on. It felt like someone or something was trying to speak through me.'

'You don't get it, do you? It's your subconscious being allowed control by your conscious mind. For me, thaumaturgy is all about intuition, something that is the very essence of the subconscious.'

'So Wolfram won't be able to learn new spells. Being a computer, he doesn't have intuition.'

'That's not entirely true, old boy.'

'No, Sebastian is correct,' Wolfram said, the lights having extinguished. 'A computer did not learn the spells. The secondary copy of my intelligence replicated the brainwaves and impressions from Alvarez when he experimented in the lab. It did no research of its own.'

'I'm just trying to prove a point. What do you think intuition is exactly?'

Sebastian made a stab at answering. 'It's the subconscious making decisions based on evidence that the conscious mind isn't aware of.'

'Yes, and where do you think that evidence comes from?'

'Experience?'

'Exactly. Intuition is the application of experience, whether you know it or not. I'm sure Wolfram is capable of applying experience. However, being a computer, he'll be aware of it. It's not something that goes on "in the background" for him, so to speak.'

'You are correct. However, the requirement for learning magic therefore cannot be intuition alone. The data I have indicates that Kerl was unsuccessful in all attempts to teach the beta cube without it being connected to a Human brain.'

'Perhaps it takes an organic mind to learn how to bring about a –

what did you call it? *Thaumatic*, effect. Perhaps the connection to the weave that the Folians talk about is only possible for organics.'

'Conjecture aside,' Sebastian said, 'what do you do when you've got those impressions?'

'The first time you do it, the spell comes into effect. After that, in order to repeat it, it's a case of simply holding the glyph that you saw in your mind, whilst you intone the sound and shape the words.'

'So what's the point of the visualisation in the first place?'

'It's to give your subconscious the information it needs in order to accomplish the task. You don't need to do the full visualisation, or press your eyes, every time – just the first time to discover the spell. Pressing your eyes also helps the brain to detach from the conscious processes by distracting it.

'You'll probably need to make a note of the impressions somehow. Not to mention the words ... They aren't always in real language but, as you know from the video of Alvarez, they usually come from your own cultural background – as do the glyphs.'

'I suppose I could draw diagrams and record the chants on an infoslate ...' He remembered the journal and found himself looking from left to right as though reading from a memory.

'What is it?'

'My grandfather. His journal was full of gibberish and symbols. Now I remember where I've seen that strange V symbol.'

'V symbol?'

'I noticed it in the John Dee book you showed me. My grandfather used to disappear off to meetings when I was a kid ... Masons ... I thought he was into stonework ... My Gods, he must have known about magic!'

'Interesting. The personality types required to do magic does seem to run in families.'

'That would explain why the image was a rune from my heritage. Isa represents something solidified. It could have been the concept for solidifying the carbyne.'

'That sounds promising. See? It is your subconscious providing you with the imagery. All you have to do now is allow your subconscious to form the words. Heh, well, that and master the art of throat-singing.'

Sebastian sighed. 'Oh yes, of course, the easy part.'

'I apologise for interrupting,' Wolfram said, 'but you have left out the requirement for protection from the extra-spatial entities during casting.'

Duggan slapped his forehead. 'Of course!'

A cold shiver ran down Sebastian's spine. 'What do I do?' He'd completely forgotten that he was putting himself at risk.

The old man paced back and forth, tapping his lips with his finger. 'Repeat the process. This time, imagine a bubble of white light around yourself. At least that's what Shiliri said we should do.' He stopped pacing. 'Actually, that's a good point. *I* should try it first, just to make sure it works. At least we know I'm capable of magic, whereas you're an unknown quantity.' He sat down and began to press his eyes with his hands.

'What are you doing?'

'Shush. Concentrating.'

Sebastian waited.

After about a minute, Duggan opened his mouth and began to speak, singing overtones as he did so. '*Bí dofheicthe,*' he said, and vanished.

'Oh my Gods!' Sebastian jumped up and looked around. 'Where did he go?'

'I do not know. I detect no visual traces and there is no heat signature present.'

He peered at the spot where Duggan had been sitting. The leaves were compressed. Several lifted off the ground and abruptly fell back down. The flattened patch began to decompress; two smaller depressions appeared in front of the area. Invisibility.

'Duggan?'

There was no response.

He should play it cautiously – after all, he wasn't sure whether Duggan was still in control of his own body, or not.

'Shall I attempt to locate him?' Wolfram asked. Did he suspect the same thing?

'Knock yourself out.' He crouched to pick up a handful of leaves and braced himself for attack.

Two loud electronic pings echoed through the clearing. 'Ten o'clock.'

Sebastian threw the handful of leaves as directed. They fluttered through the air and several hung in empty space.

Duggan's voice came from the spot. 'You've got me.' The leaves drifted towards Sebastian as footprints appeared, heading in his direction. 'It looks like the addition of the protective bubble to the visualisation worked.'

'Did it make the images different?'

'Yes. I normally see knotwork patterns when I create spells. This time, I saw a particular kind of knot added to that of the one I originally saw when discovering the invisibility spell. I suppose I should try to make myself visible again.'

Duggan fell silent and, a few moments later – presumably after visualising to become visible with the addition of the protection – he said, '*Nocht an dofheicthe*,' and reappeared. He looked down at himself and brushed off the leaves. 'That seems to work a treat! Now, I think you should try visualising for the stabilisation spell, with protection – and this time *let the words come out!*'

Sebastian sat in the middle of the grove once again, but this time, while he pressed his eyes and imagined the tube of carbyne stabilising, he also imagined himself surrounded by a bubble of white light. In the darkness, the glowing runes slowly formed. The Isa rune was not alone; it intersected with another that he recognised as Algiz, a rune of divinity and spiritual protection. Ironic that the image looked like a stylised tree growing out of the ground – at least as much as a three pronged stick and a horizontal line could. His throat tightened and he felt his mouth move.

'*Harðna hvítt duft.*' He opened his eyes.

Duggan clapped. 'Very good! What does that mean?'

'I think it's Icelandic for "harden white powder".'

'Interesting. I'd say "*púdar bán greamaitheach*", which means "sticky white powder", or thereabouts. Now, how about trying to overtone? You'll have to try chanting the words whilst making the sound you heard.'

'Why can't magic be easier?'

Duggan put his hands on his hips. 'How easy do you expect it to be to alter the fabric of reality?'

He had a point. Once again, Sebastian closed his eyes and repeated the process, this time attempting to form the chord. He started to hum at first, then, once he was certain the tone was right, he opened his mouth. The words formed and something caught in his throat. The strain on his vocal cords was strange and unfamiliar. He coughed. It would take some getting used to. He started trying to overtone once again. Feeling more confident this time, he began to mouth the words. '*Harðna hví—*'

Someone crashed through the undergrowth. He stopped and opened his eyes.

Tolinar stood beside Duggan, his chest heaving – he looked terrified. 'You must come quickly! The colonists return!'

Chapter 42

Duggan's face paled. 'No, they can't be on their way here ... We have to stop them!' He whirled around and tore out of the clearing, dragging Tolinar behind him.

Sebastian was on his feet in seconds, fuelled by adrenaline. He stuffed Wolfram into his rucksack and dashed through the avenue after them. 'Are they here now?' he gasped.

'Not yet, but they have entered the system. The Hesperidium sensed their approach. You must help us turn them back. We cannot afford another collapse.'

'Collapse? What collapse?' Duggan's breathing was laboured.

Conversation was the last thing Sebastian wanted, but Duggan needed to know. 'When the Folians banished them, it used up large amounts of carbyne underground. It caused several places to collapse, killing some of the host trees.'

'I thought there were fewer voices. We'll have to go up and deter them. I suggest taking the runner – it's fast.'

Sebastian stumbled over a root. He detached his foot from it and heaved himself up. 'It might be fast,' he shouted, 'but it doesn't pose much of an obstruction to a big ship like the *Iceni*. At least the *Ultima's* got a shield and it's an official law enforcement ship.' It wasn't entirely true, but SpecOps was at least a branch of EarthSec. He wanted to be in control of the situation and Duggan shouldn't be in a position where he might need to harm others again – by choice, or not.

'Okay, but it doesn't mean I like the idea.' The trio broke out of the trees into the grassland.

'*Ultima Thule*! Emergency override Heimdall seventy-six. Open doors and initiate pre-flight checks.'

'I must return to the others.' Tolinar turned and made his way back into the forest.

The *Ultima's* engines had already begun to heat up even as the two ran through the open airlock. Sebastian hurried up the ladder. Duggan stood at the bottom, panting.

'Are you alright?'

'I'm not as young as I used to be. I'll be up in a moment. I think I put my back out.'

Sebastian put Wolfram on the console and began programming the ascent vector. Scanners had picked up the *Iceni*'s approach from the system's heliosphere at near lightspeed. He was amazed at how the Folians had been able to sense them at such a distance. Typing commands into the console, he began to panic – they'd have only a few minutes before the ship became visible. He prayed they could get into orbit before it arrived.

Duggan finally came up the ladder and flopped down into the seat next to him. 'I could do without all this running around. I only want a quiet life.'

'I know what you mean.' He pressed the final control to launch the ship. 'Brace yourself.'

Duggan fastened his seatbelt and pushed himself back. The ship shot upwards, pulling the occupants' faces down.

Moments later, the clouds peeled back to reveal the sapphire-blue sky, rapidly replaced with illusory ochre gases, and the ship exploded from the swirling mists into the star-peppered black of space.

'How are you going to stop the *Iceni*?' Duggan's teeth were gritted against the G-force.

'I have no idea. We've got no weapons and— Oh shit, we don't even have an escape pod anymore!'

Duggan's eyes widened to hard-vacuum proportions. '*What?*'

'Pressure suits. We'll have to put pressure suits on in case anything happens. Wolfram, how long until they get here?'

'Approximately ten minutes. It is not possible to give a more accurate estimate. The Heisenberg uncertainty principle prevents the scanners from obtaining a definite lock.'

Sebastian grabbed Duggan's arm and dragged him towards the lift. 'Come on, we've got to get those suits on quickly!'

Sebastian's hands shook while he pulled on the pressure suit. Duggan fared better, apparently familiar with the design and managing to keep his emotions under control. Sebastian's fingers fumbled on the seals and he dropped his helmet.

Duggan picked it up and handed it to him. 'Calm down, lad. There are still a few minutes to go. Just get this on and we'll think up a plan.'

'Has the *Iceni* got weapons?'

'There are several gun emplacements on the forward section. Nothing tremendously powerful, but they'll still pack a punch. When we left Earth, we weren't aware of any other spacefaring races but thought there might be native life on the forested planet that would need . . .

deterring.'

Sebastian finished pulling on the suit and fastened the helmet. Duggan was already on his way up to the cockpit in the lift, so he followed up the ladder.

'The *Iceni* has arrived sooner than anticipated,' Wolfram said. 'The ship is now within communication range.'

Sebastian looked out of the window. The bright, silvery glint of the ship sparkled in the distance, off to starboard. 'That thing's enormous.'

'What do you expect for a colony ship? It's got building materials, heavy machinery *and* living quarters.'

'I know the crater it left was massive, but I never expected anything *that* big.' The distance made it difficult to judge, but he imagined it would fit at least fifty or sixty rooms the size of his own quarters into it. Hell, it probably wouldn't even fit in Tenebrae.

'What now?' said Duggan.

'Hail them – try to talk them out of approaching Achene.'

'Do you want me to do it?'

'Yes, you know them, and my English isn't that good. You'll be more likely to convince them to stop.' He activated the comms and hailed the ship using the old radio frequencies they'd be expecting, making sure he was sitting out of view so that only Duggan was visible.

A face appeared on the display and an expression of recognition came over Duggan's face. 'Greetings, Daniel.'

'Duggan Simmons ... We assumed you were dead,' Cullen said.

Sebastian couldn't see the comms display from where he was without becoming visible; he patched the feed through to another part of the console to watch. Cullen appeared to be roughly the same age as Sebastian, mid-thirties, maybe a little younger. How different Duggan must look to him, having aged sixty years in the interim. If Cullen was surprised, it certainly wasn't noticeable in his voice or expression.

'Reports of my demise are greatly exaggerated. Now, what's this I hear about you getting everyone to move to Achene? There's nothing there but gas.'

Cullen's expression became as flat as his tone. 'You know that's not true, and we both remember what it looked like before.' His eyes sparkled.

Sebastian recalled what the medic's journal said about his behaviour – he certainly had the look of the Possessed about him – and muted the comms. 'Possessed.'

Duggan nodded, almost imperceptibly, and un-muted the channel. 'Yes, you're right, Cullen. It's covered with trees. Intelligent trees. Can we at least talk about this first?'

'No, and their intelligence is the reason we have to go there and cut them all down.'

'You're not making any sense. Why would you intentionally kill them?'

Now that the goliath had drawn closer, Sebastian made the first move and brought the *Ultima Thule* between the *Iceni* and Achene. There was no way the colonial freighter could outmanoeuvre the little ship, even if they wanted to.

Cullen paused, seeming to consider his reply carefully. 'Get out of the way, Duggan. You're not stopping us. We'll ram you, or shoot you down. Your choice.'

The *Iceni* accelerated.

Chapter 43

Tolinar burst into the orchard, dishevelled and breathing heavily. Aryx looked up. 'Are you okay?'

The alien took several gulps of air before speaking. 'Sebastian and Duggan have taken your ship to intercept the Chopwood colonists.'

Aryx tried to stand, a little too fast, and staggered against a tree. 'The colonists are back now? What should we do?'

'We do not know. If Sebastian and Duggan fail to stop them, they will land here and bring destructive force upon us. Shiliri and the others will be too preoccupied to maintain control over the animals. It would be safer for you to leave our world now.'

'We can't go back to the comet – I don't know how to get in!'

Janyce put her hand on his shoulder. 'We could go to Chopwood. At least the colonists won't go back there.'

He relaxed a little. It made sense – the place was familiar enough.

'If that is your plan, you must hurry. The colonists will be here soon. Two of the Folians have already transferred to the moon and will protect you from the flies.'

Janyce grabbed her son by the hand and pulled him up. 'Come on, kiddo, we've got to go.'

The four made their way back to the landing site.

Aryx approached the stealth-black runner and opened the cockpit. He'd never personally flown one and had only ever seen them in documentaries about Earth's astronautical history – it was like getting into a museum exhibit.

The open cockpit was more spacious than it had looked from the outside. 'Luckily there's room for the three of us if Erik sits on your lap.'

Janyce climbed into the rear seat, followed by Erik. She extended the belts to encompass the boy and strapped herself in. Aryx got into the front seat.

The main flight control was a cross between a joystick and partial steering wheel – it all seemed rather archaic. Where was the acceleration and yaw control? He looked down. 'Oh no ...'

'What's wrong?'

'It's got *foot* controls!' he bellowed. 'I can't control the damn thing with these legs – I can't move the feet!' He buried his face in his hands.

'Uncle Aryx ...' Erik said, shaking his shoulder. '*Mamma* can fly it.'

The runner lifted off the ground uneasily. Aryx had changed places with Janyce so that she could pilot the ship and he now sat in the back, gripping the armrests tightly while it wobbled from side to side. Erik, sitting on his lap, giggled.

'You're certain you know how to fly?' Aryx asked.

The ship wobbled again as Janyce nodded. 'Mike taught me a bit ... Now, how do these foot controls work?' She pulled back on the steering-wheel-joystick and the ship bucked upwards.

'Don't do that! They're the yaw controls – the leftmost pedal fires the port stern thruster *and* starboard bow retrothruster simultaneously, turning the ship to the right. The other does the opposite.'

'And the middle one?'

'Acceleration. Push it with your toe to slow down, like a brake, and your heel to speed up.'

'That's wacky.'

'I know. I didn't design the bloody thing. Even if I had, I still wouldn't have let you drive!'

The ship jolted to the left and began to tumble.

'Don't use the pedals like that in atmosphere!' he shouted. 'Use the joystick-wheel! Fly it like a plane until you get into space!'

'Sorry!' She let go of the controls.

'Don't do that, either!'

'*Mamma!*' Erik's cheeks bulged, his face turned a strange colour.

'Sorry!' She grabbed the controls once more.

'Just hold it straight – and hit that stall button over there that's flashing. Jesus!'

She fumbled about while the ship spun, until her fingers hit the correct button. The ship automatically levelled out and she pulled back on the stick-wheel again.

'You can use the middle pedal, but wait until the atmosphere light goes out before you use the others.'

She nodded her head emphatically.

The ship slipped through the upper atmosphere and illusory gases in a matter of moments. Stars filled the view; the atmospheric manoeuvres light went out. An alert sounded on the console.

'Scanners have picked up weapons discharge several thousand kilometres away,' Aryx said. 'Stay away from there. It sounds like they've encountered the *Iceni*. Head straight for Chopwood.'

Janyce steered the craft in the direction of the moon and dug her heel in.

Chapter 44

The giant, steely bullet-bulk of the *Iceni* accelerated towards the *Ultima Thule*.

Cullen's intimidating glare disappeared as Sebastian cut the comms. 'We can't discuss tactics with him on-screen.'

'Tactics? So, you have a plan?'

'I'm going to hold here until the last minute to see if they stop. Beyond that, I have no idea.'

'You'd better think quickly, then – they're almost on top of us!'

Collision alert warnings flashed on the console. More pressure. Pressure while he was *trying* to concentrate. 'Shut up!' He hammered the controls to mute them, and sat tensely gripping the manual joysticks. 'I'm going to play chicken.'

Duggan clamped the helmet down on his pressure suit – he evidently wasn't into taking chances. Sebastian quickly fastened his own and put his hands back on the controls.

'Ten seconds to impact.' Wolfram obviously liked tense countdowns.

His thumb hovered over the thruster control. The *Iceni* headed straight towards the ship; if it didn't slow down, it would plough straight through the *Ultima*'s starboard side, and they would either break apart or remain mounted on the *Iceni*'s nose-cone like some Wild West trophy on the bull bar of an antique truck.

'Two . . .'

He pressed the button. The engines fired, forcing the occupants back in their seats, and the ship bucked to port with a jolt. With a high-pitched, metallic nails-on-blackboard squeal, the *Iceni* clipped the tail end. Sebastian grimaced, half expecting explosive decompression at any second.

They stared out of the window as the silvery metal of its hull disappeared from view.

He breathed a sigh of relief. 'That was close!'

'What now?'

'Ah. I hadn't thought past staying alive!'

'I have an idea,' Wolfram said. 'I've been probing the ship during our contact with it, and I believe that I can access part of the on-board computer system.'

'Can you stop them?'

'No. The communication system is not tied in to the navigation computer. I may, however, be able to transfer a subset of my core processing routine into the communications computer.'

'This is no time for playing with computers,' Duggan snapped.

The SI's creativity hit Sebastian like a brick. 'If Wolfram can transfer part of his processing to the *Iceni*, we could use the probe railgun to launch a lump of carbyne at the cockpit—'

'—and he can purge Cullen from right inside their ship!'

'Exactly,' Wolfram said. 'Their ship's processing power is not great, but I believe that if this unit can get close enough, the combined capacity of both may be enough to trigger the thaumatic effect. You will need to re-open communications when we are in proximity.'

'Where's your carbyne?'

'The airlock.'

'Is that what I nearly tripped over coming aboard?'

'Yes. It's lucky I brought it aboard. I'll go and load it.' Sebastian was about to get up, and stopped when he remembered the hopper was still sealed. 'Shit! It's unstabilised!'

'There's no time to stabilise it. You'll have to vent the air from the ship whilst you transfer it. It was a good job you suggested the suits.'

Sebastian activated a control on the console and the hiss of air sucked into the ballast tanks reached their ears. Their pressure suits expanded. He got up and switched on the suit comms. 'Bring the ship around while I deal with the powder.' Something vibrated through his feet.

'They're shooting at us now!' Duggan said.

Sebastian patted him on the shoulder. 'Just don't get hit. Wolfram, can you keep the shield between us?'

'Yes, but when I connect it will require all of my processing power and I will be unable to maintain control.'

Duggan grimaced. 'By that time, I don't think we'll need it.'

Sebastian dragged the hopper from the airlock. He passed through the shield room and the generator bounced on its struts, absorbing a second impact from the *Iceni*'s cannons. He took a deep breath to calm down and made his way past it to the engine room.

The railgun loading bay consisted merely of a small, eighteen-inch diameter hatch protruding from the floor in the corner. A row of chrome spheres were lined up on a rack above it. He opened the hopper and ran his hand over the powdery substance it contained. The railgun was magnetic – how was he going to get it to fire the stuff? He took one of the probes off the rack and examined it: a sixteen-inch diameter sphere, perfectly smooth, except for a crease where the rolled seam ran around its equator – he couldn't see a way of opening it. Staggering slightly under the force of another impact from the *Iceni*'s guns, he dropped the probe.

'Damn!' Too many hits like that would rip the generator off its mountings – then they'd be in trouble.

He picked up the sphere and turned it in his hands. It was dented, right on the seam in the casing, revealing the lip where the two halves had been pressed together like the lid of an old-fashioned biscuit tin. Grabbing a CFD tool from the maintenance chest, he set the device to form a narrow screwdriver and, wedging the tip into the gap, he tried to pry it open. Even mustering all his strength, he couldn't make the casing budge. He held the blade in the opening and, operating the controls with his thumb, set it to produce a spanner. The glowing tool-head began to change shape. Heat came through the glove of the pressure suit, and the handle exploded with a bright flash.

He dropped everything he was holding.

When his vision cleared, he bent down to examine the mess. The sphere had split in two; its casing was separated completely and the sensor package had spilled out. The CFD tool was ruined – its power supply and generator had blown. He picked up the two sphere-halves, reached into the hopper, and scooped carbyne powder into the shell before pushing the parts back together. Dropping the probe into the open launching port, he made a silent prayer, then closed the hatch.

He re-sealed the hopper. 'It's done,' he said over the comms, and headed back to the cockpit, nearly falling off the ladder as another impact from the cannons landed squarely on the *Ultima*'s shields.

Duggan turned in the pilot's seat. 'Good work, old boy. I'll bring her around for another pass. You'd best stay out of view of the comms – if this works, we don't want Cullen's demon returning to wherever the hell it came from with knowledge that you're involved.'

Sebastian sat in the seat out of view and took over the piloting. 'Are you ready, Wolfram?'

'Yes. When they answer, I will connect and begin the purge.'

Duggan hailed the *Iceni*.

A red-faced Cullen answered the comms. 'Do you never give up?'

'Not today, Daniel.'

Sebastian intermittently watched the conversation while he dodged between shots. He glanced at the cube on the console. Its lights were flashing randomly. Duggan continued speaking to Cullen, but

Sebastian's attention was on the cube and he ignored the exchange; he was interested only in the echoing that came over the comms from the *Iceni*'s cockpit.

'Simmons, what are you doing to my ship?'

Sebastian punched the launch button and crossed his fingers.

The *Ultima Thule* skimmed over the shiny surface of the *Iceni* and the tiny spherical probe shot from the railgun. It crumpled on impact as it hit the juggernaut – a precise shot, a snowball-splat on the area directly outside the cockpit.

'What the *fuck* is that?' Cullen yelled.

Wolfram's remote voice chanted '*Expurget Exorcizamus*' from the *Iceni*'s speakers. All twelve lights on the cube were lit.

Sebastian prayed.

Aryx stood at the bottom of the hill inside the Chopwood stockade, with Janyce and Erik beside him.

They watched the sky. Bright dots had been flashing against the afternoon sun and ended a few minutes after they'd landed, but now, an hour later, a bright yellow streak appeared.

'What's that?' Erik asked.

'It can't be the *Ultima* – it wouldn't do that on re-entry because of the shield. It must be the *Iceni*.'

Janyce's eyes widened. 'If they're coming here, does that mean Seb managed to change their minds about Achene?'

'It's possible, but as far as we know Cullen was possessed and, unless he boarded the ship, I can't see how they would have purged him.'

She ushered Erik towards the saloon. 'It looks like it's coming down, anyway. Erik, go inside, there's a good boy.'

'We'd better go in, too,' Aryx said. 'If they land on the hill, it's going to get messy, and I'd like to know what happened.'

The pair followed Erik into the saloon and took position behind the only glazed window. They watched the evening sky brighten while a great silvery ship eased itself down out of the reddening blue. Its engines threw up dirt and ash from plants cremated beneath its descent. A great plume of dust rolled through the town, making it impossible to see across the street. All it needed was tumbleweed.

Erik clung to his mother's leg while she stroked his hair. 'Are the people going to hurt us?'

'I don't think so.' Janyce looked at Aryx, her eyes asking the same question.

'I think it's only the leader that would be a problem. If Sebastian's succeeded, he shouldn't be hostile.' He loosened one of the straps on the mobipack. 'He'd better get here soon – these are beginning to chafe, and he's got my chair.'

The trio huddled in silence and waited for the dust to settle.

Chapter 45

Sebastian and Duggan watched the comms intently as the pulse surged through the *Iceni*'s cockpit. Cullen slumped forwards; his head hit the console with a smack.

'It worked, old boy!' Duggan said, slapping Sebastian on the back. 'It bloody well worked!'

'Thank the Gods.' He relaxed his grip on the controls a little and pulled the *Ultima* away from the *Iceni*. The ship was still firing at them.

A hammering came over the comms and the door to the *Iceni*'s cockpit burst open. A man in his mid-to-late-forties with salt-and-pepper hair stepped through. 'Daniel!' He raced over to the unconscious Cullen and put a finger to his neck. He pulled Cullen back into the seat, and his head lolled to one side.

'Kibble? Kibble Vardstrom?'

The man looked up at the comms. 'Duggan? Is that you? What happened to you? We thought you were dead!'

'I'm very much alive, and much older. Now, could you see your way to turning off the automatic weapons?'

Kibble propped up Cullen and began flipping switches on the console. The *Iceni*'s guns stopped.

'Is he okay?'

'Yes,' Kibble said. 'He's not dead, anyway – he seems to be unconscious. What happened? Why was he shooting at you?'

'You wouldn't believe me if I told you.' Duggan reached out and dragged Sebastian into view. 'I'd like you to meet my friend, Sebastian Thorsson. Sebastian, this is Kibble Vardstrom, ancestor to the founders of Vardstrom Observatory.'

'Pleased to meet you, Mr Vardstrom.'

'Please, call me Kibble.' The man shook his head and blinked. 'Ancestor? What are you on about?'

'It's a long story – we'll tell you when we get to Chopwood, if you'd kindly get someone to land the ship there.'

'Cullen was bringing us to Achene. Has the plan changed?'

'It has,' Sebastian said. 'He wasn't in his right mind. You'll find him more rational when he wakes up.'

Kibble checked to make sure the unconscious man was stable and not about to fall out of his seat, and turned to leave. 'I'll go and get a pilot to bring the ship down. See you in an hour.' He cut the comms.

Sebastian repressurised the ship and programmed a descent vector, intending to land in the clearing the *Ultima* had previously visited. 'I hope they're all alright on Achene.'

'I'm sure they're fine. The Folians are very good hosts, pardon the pun.'

He laughed. 'I'm glad. I couldn't stand for anything else to go wrong. My life seems to be a complete mess lately.'

'Well, if you insist on working in an interesting place, you're bound to attract all sorts of chaos.'

The last of the lights on the side of the cube went dark, and Wolfram spoke. 'Have we succeeded? Did I accomplish the purging to an adequate degree?'

'Indeed you did.' Duggan patted the cube. 'Cullen was knocked out by it completely. I think the effect had a greater impact because of how long he'd been possessed.'

Sebastian unclipped the helmet from his pressure suit and took a deep breath. 'I'm worn out. I need some sleep, I'm still running on station time.'

'Go and get some rest, then. The autopilot can cope and I'm sure the SI can take over if needs be.'

'Let me know when we arrive.' He made his way down the ladder into the cargo hold, and fell asleep on the netting in moments.

For several minutes the street remained silent, a thick layer of dust coating everything in sight. Aryx stifled a cough. The vegetables in the gardens were going to be gritty after all that.

He caught movement from the corner of his eye: a man in his late forties or early fifties, waving at someone farther down the street. He moved to get a better view. Two figures entered by the bottom gate and a red dot appeared in the bottom right of Aryx's vision.

'Hello, Aryx,' came a familiar voice from the mobipack.

'They're here!' he said, grabbing Janyce's hand, and they ran into the street. The man staggered back as they passed.

'Seb!' Janyce yelled, flinging her arms wide. 'I thought you were killed!' She jumped up to hug him, almost knocking him over. Erik ran up and embraced both of them around their waists.

Aryx waited for them to finish and hugged Sebastian briefly. 'Good work. I'm glad you're okay.' He smiled.

Duggan put his hand up, pointed to himself, and then up the street.

Sebastian nodded and turned back to the group. 'What are you all doing here?'

'The Folians told us it wasn't safe to stay there, so we brought the runner.'

Sebastian blinked. 'There are foot controls in those older ships, right?'

'Yes, Janyce piloted it.'

Sebastian's eyes widened.

'Believe it, girlfriend,' she said, putting her hands on her hips. Sebastian laughed.

'What happened up there?' Aryx asked.

Sebastian nodded in the direction of the man Duggan was approaching. 'Come with me and you'll find out.' The group made their way up the hill.

As they drew close, Duggan spoke in English. 'Kibble Vardstrom, I'd like to introduce my friends. Sebastian Thorsson you know, and this is Aryx Trevarian, Sebastian's sister-in-law Janyce, and her son Erik.'

'Trevarian? Sounds familiar. I think my sister was dating someone with a name like that – Trevanion, I think, maybe.' Kibble shook hands with them in turn and gripped Duggan by the arms. 'It's good to see you.'

'It's good to see you again, too, old boy.'

'Heh, look who's talking! Old. How long has it been?'

'Sixty-odd years.'

'Soddin' hell! It's taken that long for us to get back?' Kibble shook his head. 'I can't believe it. I don't even know how we got so far away. Must be a space anomaly around here, or somethin'.'

Aryx snorted. Space anomalies indeed – whatever next?

Duggan slapped a hand on Kibble's shoulder and steered him in the direction of the bar. 'Ah, yes, about that … I'd be grateful if you could tell the others that it *was* a space anomaly, assuming Cullen didn't already tell them what happened.'

'He told us nothing, just that he'd changed his mind and we should go to the planet below. Never knew why. What *did* happen?'

'Are we okay to talk? Nobody else is going to follow you out of the ship, are they?'

'Daniel's out cold, and may be for a while. I told the others to stay put until I tell 'em to come out, so yes, we can talk.'

The group entered the rickety saloon and, after searching for some chairs, nestled around the only table sturdy enough to sit at.

'So, what's really going on?' Kibble asked.

Duggan took a deep breath. 'It's a long story, and you're not going to believe most of it, but humour me anyway.'

'Whatever, but start at the beginning.'

'As you may remember, William and I left to visit the planet below—'

Kibble nodded. 'Yes, that was just a couple of days ago.'

'Sixty years—'

'Yeah, whatever. Sixty years, three days . . .' Kibble waved his hand dismissively. 'It's all the same.'

Duggan's face reddened. 'We left for Achene, where we bumped into the Folians, the native species of intelligent life in the form of trees. They taught me how to use the mineral we found here – you know, the one that disappears – to perform magic.'

Aryx glanced at Kibble. He had an expression of aloof disbelief, but there was a look in his eyes that betrayed a subtle hint of acceptance, as though he'd already suspected something unusual was going on from the start. Perhaps his experiences with William had prepared him for it.

Duggan continued. 'If you use it incorrectly, there's a possibility of being temporarily possessed by a kind of extra-spatial entity. They appear to be the same things referred to in old religions as demons. Judging by what we found in your old diary, it seems that if a possessed person brings someone else to the point of death, that entity can jump into the victim permanently.'

'That's what happened to Daniel?'

'Yes. William was temporarily possessed—'

'—because he'd been doing "magic"?'

'Uh, well . . . We don't know for certain, but whatever the reason, the entities must have seen the Folians as a threat and decided to use Cullen to destroy them. The Folians' only defence was to teleport the *Iceni* and everyone in it away.'

Kibble scratched his head. 'Where do these guys come into it?' he asked, gesturing to the others around the table. 'And why the hell are you all dressed like a kids' slumber party?'

Sebastian made as if to speak, but Aryx put his hand up and stopped him. 'You'll complicate it,' he said, and turned to Kibble – his English was more fluent than Sebastian's, after all. 'Because of how long you've been travelling, to you, we're effectively from over two hundred years in your future . . .' He continued to explain the situation aboard Tenebrae and the link of the demons with the ITF. '. . . They used Duggan to blow up the lab, and it was the investigation of the explosion that led us to him, and so, to you.'

Kibble slowly shook his head. 'This is very convoluted.'

'I know,' Duggan said, 'and I'm sorry I can't make it any simpler.'

'What do these demon things want and why didn't they get the ITF to tell Gladrin to stop the research?'

'If they had told him to stop, he would have questioned it and may have discovered what was going on. Instead, they used my abilities to cause the explosion.'

Kibble rubbed his chin. 'If the entities already knew where Achene was, they'd have sent the ITF to destroy the Folians long ago, wouldn't they, rather than getting us to come back to do it?'

'I ... suppose.'

'And the ones that have been possessing you didn't know where Achene was because you'd had your memory wiped. So there can't be any communication between them.'

'The ITF knew where Yazor was, so there must be *some* communication between them and the entities.'

'Perhaps it's difficult, or there's some kind of schedule.'

'It's more likely,' Duggan said, 'that they can't communicate with others in their realm while they're possessing people in this world.'

'So how did they relay our location to the ITF?' Aryx asked.

Kibble's eyes narrowed. 'They might have someone in the ITF that gets possessed on purpose in order to receive messages.'

Duggan shuddered visibly. 'What a horrible thought.'

'We're not sure what the entities want,' Sebastian said, 'but they seem to have been interfering with Humans for centuries. Without knowing exactly what they are and where they come from, we have no way of knowing why they're trying to possess people. If they're doing something with terrorists, you can bet it's something bad. That's why we're here, Kibble. I had to bring my family here to keep them safe, just in case they try to get to me through them as they did with Gladrin.'

'I see,' Kibble said. 'So they're going to stay here with us for a bit, and we're not going to get whisked across the galaxy again?'

'No, you're fine as long as you don't try to kill the Folians,' Duggan said.

Kibble clapped his hands together. 'Right! That's all I need to know. I'll fill Daniel in when he wakes up. I s'pose we should get the ultrasonics set up before it gets dark.'

'No need,' Aryx said, 'the Folians have sent two of their people here to repel the flies from the town and anywhere else you wish to settle.'

'Are they here now?'

'They'll reveal themselves to you in time, when they think you're ready to accept them,' Sebastian said. 'It'll take a while for you to earn their trust. Duggan knows them well, and will stay with you. I'd advise not cutting down any trees that look like people.'

'Well, I guess that's a wise move. It seems we're a bit out of touch with the galaxy, after all. None of us have ever met an alien, so it'll be a bit of a shock if we're not led into it.'

Aryx had never considered how different it must be for them, to have grown up on Earth with no exposure to alien culture at all. It was probably a good job the Folians were hiding.

'Speaking of which,' Kibble said, 'what's up with yer legs?'

Aryx looked down at himself. 'There's nothing wrong with my legs, apart from them being amputated.'

'I mean the glowy shins.'

'It's a prosthetic device I built myself.'

Kibble raised an eyebrow.

'I'd be happy to explain the principle to you sometime. I imagine you'd find it interesting.'

'I'm sure I would, at that.'

'Aryx and I will spend the night here and head off in the morning,' Sebastian said, getting up from his seat.

'It's a bit early for going to bed, isn't it?' Duggan said.

Aryx prodded himself in the chest. 'Running on station time, remember?'

'I don't even want know what time it is back home,' Janyce said. Erik had already fallen asleep on her lap.

Kibble slapped his thighs and stood up. 'I'd better let you all get settled in, then. I'll keep the crew on the ship overnight and tell them it's because of the flies or something – I'll let them out after you've gone. That'll give me time to think up how to introduce your family. God knows how I'm going to explain that one.'

'Just don't tell them about the galaxy at large,' Duggan said. 'They won't be ready for it. It took me long enough to get used to the idea after I met the Folians.'

Aryx stifled a yawn. 'On the plus side, if they don't think there's anywhere to go, it'll stop them from nicking the runners and getting lost, or revealing the colony's location.'

'I'll see to it, and will see you anon.' Kibble waved, and stumbled over the half-hanging door on his way out.

'Do you think he'll be able to keep it under his hat?' Sebastian whispered.

'He's a good chap, I'm sure he'll be fine with it. I'll fill Cullen in on as much as he needs to know. I'm not sure how comfortable he will be with it, but at least he's likely to listen to Kibble, even if he doesn't listen to me.'

Aryx stood and turned to leave. 'Right, let's get some sleep before we all pass out.' The beds in the hospital were calling, no matter how filthy they were.

The sun was beginning to set. Firefly-like insects crawled around on the roofs in the warm twilight and the fragrance of night-scented stock met him as he walked down the steps, reminding him of the farm back on Earth. It would be good to visit the place again when things calmed down. Maybe some day soon. Waiting for the station's free five-yearly round trip would probably be too late.

He looked up at the horsetail clouds brushed across the sky where the bright spray of Yazor's once-comet hung – it wasn't exactly discrete. Good luck explaining that, Duggan.

They settled down for the night in the hospital; Janyce cuddled up on a cot with Erik, while the others lay on individual beds. For the first time in weeks, they all slept soundly.

Sebastian woke to Wolfram's alarm feeling refreshed. In spite of the need to get up early, he was thankful for the opportunity of dreamless sleep. It was still dark, but Achene's faint orange glow came through the window in a parody of moonlight.

'What time is it?'

'Monday, zero-eight-hundred, station-time. The local equivalent is zero-four-hundred.'

'Excellent. We need to get a move on before the colonists wake up.' He got up and rubbed his face with a squirt of water from the N-suit. He walked over to the snoring Aryx and nudged him awake.

Aryx rolled over and blinked sleepily. 'What.'

'Oh-eight-hundred. Need to go.'

Aryx slowly sat up and stretched. He strapped on the mobipack and put on the AR glasses. Sebastian handed him the cube and he stowed it away in the pack. Sebastian approached Janyce and gently roused her from her sleep.

'We're off now. Don't wake Erik. He won't want us to go.'

She smiled. 'Stay safe, and try to contact us when you can. I don't like having to keep him away from school any longer than I have to.'

'I will.' He squeezed her shoulder and bent down to kiss Erik on the forehead. He was beginning to get used to having them around. 'I'll come back as soon as I can. If you need anything desperately, Duggan should be able to get a message to us.'

'Bye, Seb. Love you.' A tear rolled down her face onto the canvas pillow.

He stood and gave her a smile to reassure her.

Aryx strode over and stood beside him, his legs glowing faintly in the darkness. 'I'll make sure he stays out of trouble, Jan.'

Her smile returned. 'I'm sure you will.'

Sebastian waved and left the building with Aryx following. They'd be safe left with Duggan, but it was a shame he and Aryx had to go –

he would have liked to have met the colonists before leaving.

'Aren't you going to say bye to Duggan?' Aryx asked, as they walked down the hill.

'No, he needs his rest. I think yesterday wore him out – he'd understand, anyway.'

'Do you think Gladrin will have managed to brush the investigation under the carpet?'

'I hope so. The video evidence wasn't on the main systems, so that's not a problem.' He wasn't entirely sure how much of the investigation was truly secret, but there was no need to worry Aryx unnecessarily.

The pair exited the gate at the bottom of the street and turned right, following the path back to the clearing, rather than risk another mud incident.

'EarthSec will need to pin the incident on somebody, won't they?'

'I guess so,' Sebastian said. 'Gladrin will either have to say it was a mechanical fault, or he'll have to blame Kerl for the explosion.'

'Why does he have to say anything? You're the investigating officer!'

'Oh, Gods!' He slapped his head. 'I'll blame it on a faulty fire suppression system. At least that way when it makes it into the official logs, if there are any possessed monitoring them, it'll look like I'm co-operating with them. I'll check the logs when we get back to networked space, then call Gladrin to reinforce it.' He hated the thought of having to lie again, especially on the record, but the safety of Gladrin's family was at stake now.

The pair boarded the *Ultima* and Sebastian programmed an ascent vector and a route that would take them back to the station via Kimberley depot. With some clever hacking, he hoped it would look like they'd been in that system all along.

The ship lifted off into the darkness of the early sky, flaring brightly as it passed out of the moon's shadow and into the direct glare of the sun.

Sebastian sat back in the seat and allowed the autopilot to take them out of the system. After everything that had happened, it would be good to get back to the station and be in familiar surroundings again.

'Did you learn any magic on Achene?' Aryx asked.

'No, we got interrupted by the colonists' return. I think I've got the gist of it, though – the overtoning is going to be the most difficult part.'

'You won't get me trying it, thank you very much. I'll stick to engineering, if you don't mind ... I take it you know how to do it *without* getting possessed?'

'I think so. Duggan managed to modify his invisibility spell and it worked without him trying to strangle me. When we get some time back on the station, I'll see if I can work out how to do the lucid dreaming spell so we can get to the bottom of these nightmares once and for all.'

'Will you require my assistance?' Wolfram asked.

'No, I think it's best if I just lock myself in a room with a timed release on the door. If needs be, you can purge me through the door. Otherwise, if you're in the room and I happen to get possessed, I don't want the entities finding out you still exist. I also don't want them being able to find out anything about me by having access to the terminals or things in my quarters. I'll wear some life sign monitors, too – that way we can get some data about the process if I do happen to get taken over.'

'I still don't like the idea,' Aryx said, 'but you'll do what you want, anyway.'

'That's not true.' Sebastian frowned at him. 'I do care about your input. This happens to be something I have to do on my own.'

Chapter 46

With a stomach-wrenching lurch, the ship dropped out of super-phase in the region of Kimberley depot, and back into net-worked space.

'Only a few jumps left,' Sebastian said, moving over to the diagnostics console. 'I should be able to connect to the security net now.' He began downloading the investigation logs.

'Do you need a hand?' Aryx asked.

'No, you keep an eye on the ship.' The logs finished downloading and Sebastian started poring over them. The detailed forensics record contained no information about the traces of carbyne that he had initially entered – a good sign. In addition to the lab equipment, an unregulated open-flame burner was listed; Kerl's records indicated he had smuggled the illegal item in when he came aboard the station. Gladrin had obviously been thinking ahead.

Wolfram interrupted his study. 'Sebastian, now that we are back in network range, would you like me to search for evidence of Gladrin's abducted family?'

He nodded without looking away from the console. 'That would be useful, thanks.'

'I only suggest it now, as I will be unavailable for several hours while I search.'

'That's fine. I'll leave you with Aryx. If you're still searching when we get back, you can get me on my wristcom if anything turns up.'

'Very well.' The cube's lights began flashing.

'I really quite like him,' Aryx said.

Sebastian laughed. 'I bet you wouldn't say that if he was listening.'

Aryx smirked. 'Probably not – I'd never hear the end of it, either.'

Sebastian turned his attention back to studying the logs. After a few minutes he was satisfied they contained nothing incriminating. Time to check in. 'Computer, call SpecOps Agent Gladrin.'

Moments later, Gladrin's sombre face appeared on the screen. 'Hello, Agent Thorsson. How goes the investigation?'

'We are on our way back from tracking down the manufacturers of the faulty fire protection sensor. It appears the lab was fitted with one sourced from a "bad batch".' His stomach turned as he said it.

'I see ... And what caused the damage to your ship recorded in the repair logs?'

He had to think on his feet. Don't panic. 'We had to track down the source of one of the components, and it turned out to be a mining colony in an asteroid belt. We had an incident with a spacefaring rock, which left us with a damaged thruster manifold and several disrupted conduits that caused the escape pod to eject. It also damaged our communications array. We had to stop at Kimberley depot to repair it before heading home.'

'I see, well that explains your lack of communication. Unfortunate that something as expensive as an escape pod should get lost, though. Part of that will have to come out of your salary, I'm afraid.' Gladrin's frown was a little too convincing.

Sebastian grimaced. 'Sorry, Sir. I'll try to be more careful in future.' It would still be a considerable price to pay, even on his newly inflated wages, but at least he didn't have to worry about Erik's school fees for the time being.

'And what of the scientist working in the laboratory? My records indicate that he had connections with the Independent Terran Front.'

'I haven't been able to verify that, Sir.'

'EarthSec have insisted on increased station security regardless – you know how they are. They see his potential connection with terrorists to be more than coincidental, and still believe that the explosion may be down to an attack. I tried to get them to hold off acting on that assumption, but even with your evidence I do not believe I could change their minds. They have decided to assign Karan as Trevarian's security detail on the station for as long as he is your engineering consultant.

'Also, there is a Bronadi security officer, Deruno, coming aboard in a couple of weeks. For some reason the embassy requested his transfer from Kimberley depot – perhaps you made an impression? In light of the security escalation and his considerable munitions experience, security accepted the transfer request.'

Sebastian glanced at Aryx, who was nodding enthusiastically. He found himself agreeing with his mood: it would be a nice change to work with one of the other races – he'd found Bronadi in general to be a little gruff and direct, but likeable.

Gladrin continued. 'I can imagine that you've had a rough few days, so we'll leave the formalities for now. I would like to have a meeting with you later, however.'

'I'll let you know when we arrive. We're only an hour away. Once I've settled in, I'll give you a call.'

'Very well, I'll see you then. Gladrin out.' The comms went blank.

He breathed a sigh of relief.

'That went well. I didn't realise you were so good at lying.'

He glared at Aryx, pulled the hood off the N-suit, and threw it at him.

The ship docked smoothly with Tenebrae and within minutes was waiting in the queue for the central hub. Sebastian was glad to be back under the purple cloak of the nebula once again after so many hours of spaceflight. To be home.

He got up and made his way to the ladder. 'Are you alright to take the ship on to the repair bay?'

'Yeah. What are you going to do?'

'I need to check in at the office, and this suit needs a clean – it's disgusting.' He glanced at the cube. The lights were no longer flashing. 'Wolfram?'

'Yes?'

'You've finished? You're quiet.'

'I have completed my searches.'

'And?' Aryx drummed the console with a finger.

'It would appear that Gladrin's family has disappeared.'

'We know that. They were kidnapped and are being held hostage,' Sebastian said. Had he completely forgotten the reason for searching?

'That is not what I mean. Their records have been *deleted.*'

'By whom? Gladrin?'

'No. The clearance required to delete information from the Galactic societal database would be of the highest security level. Higher than even Gladrin's.'

Aryx slowly shook his head. 'It's unbelievable. For someone to delete social records it would take a government level clearance—'

'—and only then for reasons of cultural security,' Sebastian said. 'And you're right, it would have to be someone *very* high up. My father told me years ago that Witness Protection would sometimes delete records and issue new identities when people were at risk from criminal organisations. I don't understand how they would even know about Gladrin's family if he hadn't reported their abduction to EarthSec ... If they were under witness protection, why would the ITF claim to be holding them?'

Aryx leaned forwards in his seat. 'What are you thinking?'

Sebastian's mind worked overtime while he paced back and forth. 'Why would terrorists claim to have his family if they didn't?' He stopped pacing. The pieces were beginning to fall into place.

'I don't know what you're suggesting.'

He stared out of the cockpit window. 'If the ITF were somehow connected with, or had agents working in, Witness Protection, it might make sense to place Gladrin's family with them, rather than keeping guards and security on them all the time and risking their escape. They could have been convinced not to contact Gladrin for their own safety. Or they could have been placed somewhere away from any possibility of contact with him. Without contacts in Witness Protection, Gladrin wouldn't be able to find out anything.'

'Wouldn't he know his family's records had been deleted?'

'Maybe it hasn't occurred to him to look, or maybe he was too scared to start snooping?'

'So what do we do?'

'To be honest, I have no idea, but if all this stuff with the ITF goes farther than we think, we have to be careful, especially if it involves people in government agencies.'

'That's it, then!' Aryx folded his arms defiantly. 'I'm not submitting my patent if there's any chance the design might get passed from the government to the terrorists.'

Sebastian patted him on the shoulder and sat down next to him. 'It's your call. I'll admit it's scary. On the upside, it means Gladrin's family are probably safe.'

'You should inform him,' Wolfram said. 'He will be relieved by the news.'

'Can you access the information on his family's reassignment?' Aryx asked.

'No. Those records are sealed and held in a datacentre on Earth with no connection to external sources.'

'Bugger. Is there any way to check for records in the society database that were created after they went missing?'

'That wouldn't help either,' Sebastian said. 'The identity records will be added with a backdated creation timestamp and made to look genuine by hashing the encryption with those dates.'

Aryx shrugged. 'It was worth a shot.'

'Good idea, though.' Sebastian stood up again and made his way to the ladder. The ship had come to a standstill in the hub docking bay. 'I'd better go. The sooner I see Gladrin, the better.'

'See you tomorrow, then? We'll go for a proper drink.'

'Definitely, once I've got to the bottom of these dreams. I need some uninterrupted downtime!' He continued down the ladder and left the ship.

*   *   *

Sebastian made his way through the lift terminals to the security department. The view from the windows into the atrium showed no sign of the damage incurred by the tsunami and the chatter had calmed down to a normal level. He was met with prolonged stares as he walked past his colleagues' desks on the way to his office.

He arrived to find the evidence crate gone – probably disposed of by Gladrin – and started skimming through the job list. Work had been stacking up; the other teams hadn't been able to cope with some of the more complex coding tasks they'd been assigned. A knock from behind made him jump.

He spun around in his chair to see his supervisor, Eleanor Bannik, sticking her head through the door. Oh Gods. He wanted to crawl under the desk.

'Sebastian, do you have a minute?' She *never* called him by his first name.

He wanted to say no, but couldn't think of an adequate excuse not to talk to the woman. 'Um sure. Please, come in.'

She stepped around the door and pushed her back against it, then closed the privacy blinds. What was she doing?

'I know you don't like me, Sebastian, and I may come across as a stone-cold bitch sometimes, but that's part of my job. I can't say I enjoy having to act like that, but such is life.' She pulled over the spare chair and sat down next to him. 'I've been following your progress since the explosion and have tried to catch up with you on several occasions, but you seem to have been rather busy off-station.'

'Tell me about it.'

She brought the chair closer and whispered, 'Do you know why I put your name forward to SpecOps?'

He slowly shook his head. 'Something to do with my personality, like Gladrin said?'

'Partly. I've suspected that something was up with him for a while. Whenever he was on the station, he was cagier than the other SpecOps agents I'd met. I didn't know if it was because of his status or not, so I did some checking and found out he was receiving large sums of money. Money that *didn't* come from SpecOps.'

He narrowed his eyes. How much did she know – could she be trusted with the truth? He stared at her and she squinted back. Her eyes looked normal. Perhaps she could.

'I thought you might pick up on anything "off" about him. You seem quite perceptive, so I put your name down in the hope that you could get close to him, find something out. I need to know if he's a security risk.'

He closely watched the lines of her face as she spoke. No twitches, no high veins: her story seemed too revealing to be subterfuge. 'He's not a risk.'

The fine creases of her face smoothed, almost imperceptibly – a change that would have been impossible to fake.

'He believes the ITF have his family captive. They've been using him to tap SpecOps resources to research weapons technology. The explosion was an accident caused by someone whose research he was funding. Initially the research was altruistic and had what I'd consider virtuous benefits, but unfortunately the ITF's involvement twisted it.' He didn't see a need to bring magic into the already complex picture. 'After I presented the evidence to him, he captured my family to coerce me into compliance with the ITF, but I managed to free them and got the truth out of him.'

She drew in a sharp breath and let it out slowly. 'I see. I never thought he'd stoop so low, but that certainly explains his behaviour. I assume you've been able to corroborate his story?'

'I just uncovered evidence that indicates his family may not actually be held by the ITF, but may have been reassigned by Witness Protection. I'm going to tell him when I see him.'

She leaned back in the chair. 'So where do we go from here?'

'I already agreed to play along with the ITF's demands, within reason, until we find out where his family is.'

'Hmm. I'm not entirely sure that's the right thing to do, but I'll leave you to it. If it goes that high in the ranks, I'd be better off having plausible deniability and not knowing the full story. Not because I want to protect myself – I simply don't want to give them any more leverage against you than they might already have. That said, if you get in too deep, I'll be there for you.' She stood up and moved towards the door, and opened it slightly. 'Oh, and I heard about your antics on Sollers Hope ... You know, I had to pull quite a few strings to put in a map-change request with AstroTerra just to keep the mayor quiet.'

'Thank you.' He smiled.

Her eyes creased and she laughed. 'Just remember, when we're around anyone else, I'm a stone-cold bitch!'

He saluted. 'Yes ma'am!' The Ice Queen had finally melted.

She looked through the door before stepping out. 'Now, go and have your damned meeting!' she shouted, slamming it behind her. Gods, you wouldn't want to get on her bad side.

He turned back to his desk and composed a message instructing Gladrin to meet him in two hours next to the fountain in the atrium's mall. Another knock at the door caused him to jerk his head around quickly. Something twanged painfully. Anyone would think this place was the docking hub.

'Come in.'

Karan stuck her head through the door. Somehow she managed to look bright and bubbly, despite her hair and civilian clothes being plastered with sweat. He baulked at the thought of the conversation about to ensue, but he couldn't avoid his friends forever.

'How's it going?' she asked.

'You *really* don't want to know.'

She pulled the chair over, turned it around, and sat astride it with her arms draped over the back. 'Oh, I really *do*.'

'I don't have time to go over it all now. I've got to get my suit cleaned, and I have to meet Gladrin.' He pressed the send key on the terminal and deactivated the display.

'I'll walk with you.' Obviously there was going to be no escaping.

He rubbed his neck and felt a twinge. He had to get rid of the knot before it got worse and seized him up completely. 'Sod it – I'm going to the spa afterwards. Come on.'

As they left the office and made their way to the changing room, Sebastian caught several sheepish glances from his co-workers.

If only they knew.

Chapter 47

The changing room was – as usual – empty when they arrived. Karan began stripping off her sodden clothes and stepped into one of the shower cubicles.

'So, is this case of yours all wrapped up now?'

Sebastian spoke with his back to her. He felt uncomfortable watching his friend while she showered. 'I suppose so, apart from having to track down Gladrin's family.' It was a relief to finally be able to tell her something about what had been going on, and he didn't have an excuse to keep her out of the loop if she was going to be working with Aryx.

'I can't say I like the idea of these demon things of yours having agents in the government. It's downright freaky, if you ask me.'

'It's more of a guess, really.' He changed into his casual clothes and put the N-suit in the locker for cleaning. 'And I agree – it's horrible. I don't know who to trust now.'

'Well, I'm sure you'll root them out eventually.'

'Me? Government stuff has nothing to do with me!'

'Rubbish.' She stepped out of the shower and began drying herself. 'If you've discovered some kind of conspiracy, you're the ideal one to investigate it.'

He grumbled.

'You know I'm right, and if we've got to work together, you know I'll just keep on at you about it. I'm sure Aryx will agree.'

He put his hands up. 'Fine! For Gods' sakes.' His sanity wouldn't stand both of them hounding him.

'I'll be glad to get out of the office for something other than arrests or chasing down handbag snatchers, even if it is only guard duty. You know I almost considered a career change?'

'Was that why you were so excited when the SpecOps job came up?'

'Yeah, but even though I didn't get the job, I'm happy for you. I don't think I could have handled all that detective stuff. Nice that you got to meet the Folians, though.' She finished pulling on her uniform and patted her hips. 'Bugger, I've left my belt in my apartment! I'll have to go and get it or I'll be late for my shift.' She darted out of the doorway and immediately stuck her head back around the corner. 'And you, get in that spa ASAP – you look like crap.'

'Thanks.' He laughed. 'See you tomorrow.' He was about to wave, but she'd already gone. As he pulled on his socks and shoes, his neck twinged again. The spa called his name.

The gym and baths were empty when Sebastian arrived. In fact, with everything being quieter, he wondered whether the tsunami had put visitors off the station. He quickly changed into a pair of trunks and walked up the steps leading towards the brown, bubbling sludge of the Antari mud bath. It was always nice to relax there first, then clean up and sit in the jet-spa; he loved the feeling of his skin afterwards. It was also one of Aryx's favourite ways to relax, and it was he who had introduced Sebastian to the little ritual.

He stepped down into the plopping, burbling liquid, sinking up to his neck, and shuffled around to one of the submerged seats on the opposite side. The mud was warm and soothing; the earthy scent instantly reminded him of Achene. He lay back and rested his head on the padded surround. The heat and sensation of weightlessness overcame him and he slowly lost his grip on the here and now, and drifted into a deep slumber.

Sebastian woke to the sound of a female voice nearby.

'Hello. Fancy meeting *you* here.'

His eyes snapped open and he lifted up his head. Oh Gods. Stevens. She was sitting in the mud, right in front of the steps. No way to avoid that encounter, either.

'Oh, you are awake.'

'Only just.' He forced a smile. 'How are you Ms Stevens?'

'Call me Monica – I'm fine, thanks.' She moved a little closer. 'We never got to have that drink.'

He shuffled away, trying to maintain his distance without being too obvious.

'What's the problem?'

'Nothing, really ... I just don't have time.'

'Oh, I get it ... You think I'm *interested*.' She shook her head. 'No, I wanted to discuss work – and be sociable.'

He let out a sigh and laughed. 'Sorry, I totally misinterpreted you. I've been busy and haven't had any time to stop. Things have been getting on top of me.'

'That's understandable. Yet another man getting the wrong impression of me. Don't worry, I won't take up too much of your time. I wanted an opportunity to introduce myself properly. Given that we both work for SpecOps and I occasionally stop off here, I wanted to see how our skills might overlap in case we had to work together.'

'I've already got a partner but, out of interest, what are your skills?'

'Xenobiology, Human biology, xenoarchaeology, and geology specialisms.'

'You specialise in *all* those?'

'Sort of, they go hand-in-hand, really. Like our skill sets when combined.'

He tilted his head questioningly.

'Being a programmer, you're a tech specialist, aren't you? Occasionally, we come across ruins and artefacts that require a technical decoding, rather than linguistic or cultural. I thought you could be useful on some of our digs in future – we've got a few big ones lined up, but obviously it would depend on your workload and priorities.'

'Of course.' He nodded. The talk of archaeology and the earthy aroma of mud conspired to remind him of Achene's tunnels again. 'I'd certainly be interested.'

'Now's not the time to discuss business, though. I can see you need to relax, and I don't have much time to hang around myself. I just needed a break.'

'Speaking of which, what time is it?'

'Must be about quarter past four.'

'It's gone sixteen-hundred? Oh, Gods! I was asleep longer than I thought! I'm supposed to meet Gladrin in fifteen minutes.' He leaped to his feet, slopping mud everywhere.

Monica looked him up and down, seemingly noting every bulge and crease on his athletic body. She smiled broadly. Suddenly self-conscious, he lowered himself back into the mud and slid towards the steps.

She giggled and looked away. 'Sorry, can't help it. You looked rather fetching in your N-suit when I saw you the other day – you ought to show yourself off more.'

'Uh, thanks. I guess.' He felt his face flush as he climbed the steps out of the pool and made his way to the shower. He rinsed away the mud and dried off. She was still staring at him as he put his clothes on.

'Send Gladrin my regards, won't you?' Monica said.

He nodded and dashed out.

Gladrin limped back and forth next to the large fountain in the mall. Apparently the wound to his leg was healing well with nanobot treatment.

'Sorry I'm late,' Sebastian said. 'Have you been waiting long?'

'No, I only just arrived myself.'

He looked around. 'Is there somewhere private, or at least somewhere we won't get overheard? I've got some news you'll be interested in.'

Gladrin's sultry expression lightened. 'Really? I take it this is something you don't want said over the system. Let's walk.' He led Sebastian to the nearest lift terminal. 'Level four.'

The lift car arrived and seconds later they stepped out on the highest level of the terraces, far above the bustling mall. Gladrin proceeded to the narrow maintenance walkway spanning the space between terraces. 'When we get to the middle, it's best if we stay close, facing each other, just to make sure nobody can lip read our conversation. There's enough sonic backwash from the river to prevent eavesdropping.'

Sebastian made his way across the bridge. Gladrin was right – the rushing of the weirs below was amplified and focused in the space, probably by the curvature of the roof.

'Now, what did you want to speak about?'

'Your family.'

Gladrin's face hardened. 'What is it?' His voice wavered. 'Have you found them?'

'Not *exactly*.' Sebastian found it difficult to maintaining his forward stare. 'It looks like their records have been deleted from the societal database. Do you know what that means?'

'Someone high up has changed them, or they are in the Witness Protection programme.' Gladrin turned away and grabbed the handrail. 'Good Lord. Are they safe?'

'I don't know. Wolfram found the evidence, but it's my guess that the ITF, or the entities controlling some of their members, might have agents in Witness Protection. I think it might have proven more efficient and cost-effective to put them there, rather than have a terrorist cell watch over them permanently.'

'And so they would have been told that I was either dead, or that contacting me would risk all our lives.'

'It sounds possible, and I know it's not very concrete—'

Gladrin brought his fist down on the handrail. 'It's good enough!' His eyes sparkled. 'It's logical. Even terrorists operate on logic. It means they're probably safe and will remain safe until we find them – as long as we play along.' His eyes reddened.

'Terrorists don't always do logical things,' Sebastian said, thinking back to the news reports. 'You only have to look at the recent attacks to—'

'Don't be a fool. I know you're not an idiot. Those bombings were a cover for tech-harvesting operations.'

'What?'

'They hit colonies and steal the alien technologies they come across. All the bombing sites had a prominent alien research presence.' Gladrin stiffened, as though becoming aware of his animated behaviour.

'I can't believe I didn't see it.'

'You couldn't have known. You didn't have any information. The one on Cinder IV was an exception, a lab run within the civilian compound. They blew the place up to hide any evidence of their activity.' He smiled flatly. 'Thank you for finding out about my family. I will sleep easier now ... Discovering where they are without alerting the ITF or the agents in the government will be a challenge, but I'll deal with that when the opportunity arises.' He heaved a ragged sigh and turned to leave.

'Sir, before you go – what about the bodies from the lab? I never found any evidence of them and wondered how the head got out of the frame without it going out of the vent, too.'

Gladrin rubbed the back of his neck. 'Yes, sorry about that. I did set you a rather insoluble investigation ... I took the bodies as soon as it happened. I've had to make the excuse that the remains were found in space. They will have to be sent back to their families. Unfortunately Alvarez can't easily be returned with his head severed unless we make up some elaborate excuse. I'd imagine your friend, Aryx, would want to inform his family.' He patted Sebastian on the arm. 'I'd better be going. SpecOps have a dig that has come up and the ITF have urged me to take a slot on the mission, so I won't be around for a few weeks. Stay here for a few minutes after I've gone. We'll catch up again soon. And thank you.'

Gone was the stony stare and, as he walked off the gantry, there was a definite spring to his step.

Sebastian looked down past the high walls at the perspective-distorting panorama. Tenebrae, with its bright architecture and clean lines, somehow seemed dark and shadowy behind the gleaming surface. He watched the mix of races on the ground far below, like tiny insects milling around en-masse to some unfathomable purpose. Since the disaster, the percentage of aliens aboard the station seemed to have increased – either that, or many Humans had left. Strange how what was perceived as an anti-alien terrorist attack had inexplicably brought more aboard - but how their lives would change if they knew what strange forces were acting upon them day-to-day. He'd always thought of people as transparent, their motives plain to see – just like the atrium, open and exposed – but now, nothing was straightforward. The universe had become complex and shrouded in mystery.

If only his grandparents were still alive; how they'd have loved to hear his tales of exploring the galaxy, and of the strange beings he'd encountered – maybe his father would have even been proud of him – but they sure as hell wouldn't want him involved in what he was about to do. He wiped away the tear threatening to fall from the corner of his eye and gripped the handrail. Now was the time for action, not self-pity.

He activated his wristcom. 'Computer, locate a free apartment.'

'An empty apartment has been located on level two of the habitation ring.'

'Good. Book it until 09.00 tomorrow morning and bill it to SpecOps. I also want you to re-route all incoming communication signals from my apartment to that one. Block all other terminal access from the apartment, including my overrides. Once I've entered, lock the door on a timer set for 08.58 and do not open it again until that time.'

'Acknowledged.'

It might have been too early in the evening to go to bed, but he needed the rest. If he attempted the lucid dreaming spell he might even go straight to sleep and stay that way until the signal triggered the dream – *if* he succeeded in casting the spell.

Aryx wiped the last of the green smears off the *Ultima Thule*'s hull. A loud clunk came from behind him and he turned around.

'You didn't say where you wanted this,' the yellow cargomech said, carrying a large crate between its grippers. The voice might have been badly synthesised by the robot, but there was no mistaking Wolfram's use of contractions, or the cube, mounted on its chest.

'Just over there.' He pointed in the direction of the ship's loading bay. 'And be careful if anyone else is in earshot. I don't want them realising you're not a TI.' He moved his wheelchair around to the back of the ship to examine the damage caused by the battle with the *Iceni*.

'I do apologise. I shall endeavour to keep our discourse suitably formal in the presence of others.' The cargomech bowed and stomped off with the crate.

Aryx shook his head and smiled. 'I'm glad to have you around. It makes a change to be able to rely on technology for a change. It certainly helps . . . I wonder how different things would have been if you'd been there before I lost my legs.'

The mech stopped and turned to face him. 'There has not been an appropriate time to tell you, but I overheard a conversation between Sebastian and Agent Gladrin in which Gladrin revealed that he was present on the planet where you were wounded, before his involvement with the ITF.'

His chest tightened. 'Really?'

'I took the liberty of acquiring and examining the system records belonging to the cargomech that injured you ...'

'And?'

A solitary LED on the cube pulsed once.

'I know you. What are you hiding?'

'There is evidence of tampering in the programming logs. It was deliberate. Code signatures in the logs are similar to the nightmare Trojan that Gladrin planted on behalf of the terrorists.'

A volcano boiled up from somewhere deep within him. His teeth clenched so hard they might have broken. Some bastard did this to him. Those ITF bastards. 'They'll pay, one day,' he said, and took a deep breath. It was no good dwelling on the past. Plenty of time for payback in the future.

He watched the mech lower the crate into place. It turned around and trundled back towards the ship, this time using the caterpillar treads.

'You love doing that, don't you?'

'Doing what?'

'Experimenting with motion, mucking about.'

'I suppose you could say that I do enjoy it. It is *rewarding* to acquire new experiences through experimentation and extrapolate their potential uses.'

'Thanks,' he said. Surely the SI was capable of emotion, or at least if it wasn't – it soon would be.

'You're welcome. It was only a light crate, and I do not experience hardship in helping.'

'I mean thanks for everything. You saved our lives several times over the last few days.' He rubbed his eyes. 'I don't know how I'd have managed without you.'

'I do not—' The lights on the cube stopped flashing and instead pulsed twice. 'Thank you. I value your lives greatly, and I do not mean simply for the freedom that you give me. You are the first people to have accepted me as an individual with a right to my own existence and I find it ... comforting.'

Aryx's eyes stung and a lump formed in his throat.

Sebastian shuffled along the corridor towards the ambassadorial quarters. What would happen if the spell went wrong? He might never wake up; become a coma patient; slowly wither away and die in permanent sleep. What if he got possessed? The latter didn't bother him nearly as much. From what he'd seen of possession through magic, it seemed the effect would likely be temporary and only last several

hours, and the sealed apartment would hold him if things went wrong
– but what if he was still possessed in the morning? Cullen had been
possessed long-term after strangulation, but what had happened to
William was still an unknown. A very ominous unknown … Perhaps
putting a timer on the door wasn't enough. He called Aryx.

'Hey,' Aryx said. 'I hadn't expected to hear from you until tomorrow.'

'I'm heading for an empty apartment to try the lucid dreaming. I've
put the door on a timer, but think it might be wise for you to check in
on me when you wake up.'

'Sure – I'll just call by with some armed guards, shall I?'

'No! Call my terminal – it's redirected here. You'll have to get me
close to it and check my eyes. If I refuse, you know it's not me and you
can order a lockdown.'

'I can't believe you're going through with this. The old Sebastian
would have thought this was superstitious crap.'

'Nothing I've learned has conflicted with my belief in science, even
though it doesn't have all the answers. I know it seems weird, but for
me religion isn't at odds with scientific proof any more. Maybe the
Gods do, or did, exist in some form. Maybe what we think of as divine
is simply the expression of some greater universal pattern.' He stopped
and leaned with his back against the wall. 'I feel more at peace, like
I've found something that's been missing.'

'I suppose that's all that matters. I guess if you hadn't introduced
me to *Jim-Bob*, I would still be a bit … Actually, I wouldn't give it up
for anything.'

'Even for your legs?'

'Including the legs. I can make more of those, but nobody can
replace a friend.'

What was the world coming to?

'Are you still there?'

'Yes, you took me by surprise that's all.'

'Get used to it.'

Sebastian turned a corner. There was the apartment.

'I've arrived,' he said.

Chapter 48

Sebastian sat, cross-legged, on the sumptuous double bed of the ambassadorial suite. With the lights off, the faint glow from the nebula shone in through the single window, casting a pale, fuzzy rhomboid on the floor in front of him. The infoslate beside him recorded his vitals, displaying waveforms, pulse, and sounds recorded in the room. He placed a vial of carbyne on the sheets next to it and began pressing his eyes as Duggan had instructed.

Against the swirling patterns behind his eyelids, he visualised himself going to sleep and walking in a strange landscape, all the while surrounded by a bubble of white light. It was difficult to muster the feelings of being asleep and dreaming, but it was the best he could manage – surely the intent was the most important factor.

While he concentrated, the sparkling, waving patterns faded from his aching eyes and other shapes revealed themselves. First, the familiar Algiz rune, the symbol for protection as before; second, Dagaz – an angular figure of eight on its side, resting at the bottom of the Algiz rune – the cycle of day and night; thirdly, Perthro – a square bracket with inward-kinked top and bottom – representing the discovery of secrets and hidden knowledge, enclosing the previous two. The sequence became clear. He tried not to get excited by the realisation of its meaning and, as he concentrated, he heard the strange droning. Allowing his throat to relax, he attempted to replicate the hum. The sensation felt natural this time.

He recalled Shiliri's explanation of time, and began to concentrate on the here and now, letting go of anticipation and planning. Letting go of past failure ... Just like being in the spa.

While he hummed, his larynx got the feel for what was supposed to happen and formed a double-tone. He relaxed further and allowed his lips to form the words.

'Ég vakna á meðan ég sef, meðvituð um draum minn.'

I wake while I sleep, aware of my dream.

He clamped his speech to a whisper, stopping the process, and opened his eyes. Still holding the mental imagery in his mind, he quickly sketched the glyph on the infoslate with a finger. 'Store and lock to Aryx Trevarian's print.'

Confirmed.

This was it.

He cleared his mind. Concentrating on the glyph image with eyes open, he recited the tones.

The stars shining through the window scintillated like a mirage. The vial emptied. Before he had time to appreciate what was happening, he toppled over onto the bed, unconscious.

Chapter 49

Sebastian Thorsson stood on a beach of warm, red sand. A velvety, purple sky reflected darkly off the smooth, black sea that caressed the two red suns bathing in its waters. The fading light enhanced the soft contours of sand at his bare feet, and a warm breeze blew in off the ocean, bringing with it the tang of exotic salts. He couldn't remember how he had arrived on the planet, but it didn't matter. It was enough to enjoy the tranquillity. He ran his hand over his hair. Strange how the scene felt familiar.

He turned to face inland. The cliff ahead also seemed familiar, as did the opening at its base. Its trapezoid wrought-stone portal tempted him towards it. The darkness within looked eerie, but he had his rucksack with him and, inside it, an old miner's lamp. He withdrew it and it burst into life, banishing the shadows from the tunnel ahead.

He looked back across the dark waters, where a cool mist began rolling in and up the beach towards him. He entered the tunnel and descended the stairway as a cool breeze brushed his neck. After several steps, the stairway ended in a large cavern that led off into darkness. The mist flowed down behind him, gathering at his feet.

The flame in the miner's lamp guttered and flared and, at the same time, something crunched on the sand behind him. He stood still and listened. There was no sound except his own breathing.

Another crunch.

This too, was familiar. He should be scared. He should want to run away. Something told him it wasn't real. A loud snort came from behind him, and a warm, moist breath blew on his neck. He spun around in defiance.

A large creature, taller than a Bronadi, stood before him. Its legs were similar, with a characteristic animal bend, but terminated in hooves. The powerful, red-skinned body was heavily muscled and bare-chested. Its head was beast-like and bullish, with long horns protruding from its forehead. The demon lunged towards him and grasped his neck in huge, clawed hands.

He struggled to pry the talons apart. It was too strong. His vision began to blur and his pulse pounded in his head. Surely he was going to pass out. What was this thing doing in his dream?

He was dreaming? This was *his* reality. *He* was in control!

He let go of the immovable claws, put his hands to the creature's neck, and began to squeeze.

'What ... are ... you?' he rasped, forcing the last breath from his lungs.

He squeezed the creature's thick neck with all his might, crushing it with strength drawn from the very depths of his soul. It looked so real for a dream: the blood-red skin glistening, slick in the dim light. The demon stopped, rigid, as though some nerve had been pinched, freezing it in place. Sebastian gulped down a mouthful of air, closed his eyes, and squeezed harder.

A grating sound echoed through the cavern and his grip was thrust apart. He opened his eyes.

The creature had changed.

His hands were either side of a strange, crystalline form: an angular, vaguely humanoid sculpture made from translucent, ice-blue crystal. This was no demon. This was something else.

The monstrous entity tightened its grip.

He kicked hard. Every bone in his body felt about to break. 'Please, Gods, help me!' he screamed.

The crystalline entity shattered. Shards of milky glass showered to the floor, disappearing into the red sand.

Behind it stood an old man, holding a large rock in front of his face. He lowered it.

Sebastian recognised him immediately. 'Grandfather!'

And then, it was all gone.

The time on the terminal displayed 03.12.

The lights came on automatically as Sebastian leaped out of bed plastered with sweat and ran to the sink. His heart hammered in his chest and the rush filled his ears as he stood in front of the steamy mirror and splashed water on his face. He wiped the condensation from the glass and noticed a bruise on the back of his hand.

'Where did that come from?'

His reflection stared back at him, unanswering.

A reflection with a large, red welt around its neck.

A welt, with fingers.

Epilogue

Stevens dropped her bags. The departure bay was empty. She scanned the infoslate. Where was it? The ship wouldn't have left without her, surely. She checked the manifest.

'... Stanford, Stevens, Somerton, Sullivan ...' She tapped the comms button. 'Launch control.'

A man's face replaced the list. 'Launch control here.'

'Monica Stevens, SpecOps. Launch bay 16 is empty.'

'That's correct. The flight was filled, the crew accounted for, and launched.'

'I'm on the list, but not on the ship. I was supposed to be on the xenoarch expedition going out this afternoon.'

'I'm sorry, there was a last minute change of roster. I'll send you the revised manifest.'

'Thank you.' She couldn't blame the man for doing his job.

The man disappeared and a page of twenty names came up. She ran her finger down the list. Marcus Gladrin ... He wasn't there before. What was he doing on it?

She picked up her bags and stormed out of the bay.

Somewhere deep in space – as close, and as far, as anything could be – something dark stirred. Cold. Crystalline. Intelligent.

END

Acknowledgements

I want to thank the following contributors to the marathon that writing this book has been.

Doug Burgoyne for introducing me to the 'universal glue' that is morphogenics and the associated subject of behaviourism.

Peter Buckman and Claire Hamilton, for much needed critical feedback.

Ian Fullwood, Karen Malam, Emily Rogers, Robert Harris, Jennifer Williams, Kate and Michael Poynton, and Maureen Lane for reading those dreadful early drafts.

Sophie Playle, my editor, for helping me smooth out the bumps and bring the brushed metal to a polished finish.

And finally and most importantly my partner, Kris Saunders-Stowe, for being there all along. Without his support and inspiration there would be no invisible men or double-amputees running around, and the *Ultima Thule* most definitely wouldn't have left the station.

As my first book, this work is the culmination of many ideas that have been bubbling up to the surface for years with no outlet or sensible way of fusing them together into a cohesive whole. I needed characters whose backgrounds could bring the disparate elements together. I needed conflict, struggle, and challenge. Challenge was brought into sharp relief when I met my partner Kris: I had never realised how much of a challenge the very act of dealing with daily life could be for many people with disabilities. Ultimately, I needed someone who could rise up when the challenges, intellectual and physical, pushed them too far and thus, *Synthesis* was born.

Writing a novel ... I never thought I'd do it, and if it weren't for the people mentioned above, especially Kris, I probably would never have succeeded.

Lightning Source UK Ltd.
Milton Keynes UK
UKOW04n1055210415

250026UK00002B/4/P